SCOTLAND THE STRANGE

Weird Tales from Storied Lands

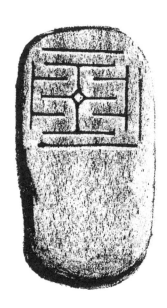

SCOTLAND THE STRANGE

Weird Tales from Storied Lands

Edited by

JOHNNY MAINS

THE BRITISH LIBRARY

This collection first published in 2023 by
The British Library
96 Euston Road
London NW1 2DB

Selection, introduction and notes © 2023 Johnny Mains
Volume copyright © 2023 The British Library Board

Cataloguing in Publication Data
A catalogue record for this publication is available from the British Library

ISBN 978 0 7123 5454 7

The frontispiece illustration and illustrations throughout the book are by members of The Spalding Club, sourced from *Sculptured Stones of Scotland*, volumes 1 (1856) and 2 (1867), edited by John Stuart.

Cover design by Mauricio Villamayor with illustration by Mag Ruhig. Original interior ornaments by Mag Ruhig.
Text design and typesetting by Tetragon, London
Printed by Bell & Bain Ltd, Glasgow, Scotland

MIX
Paper | Supporting
responsible forestry
FSC
www.fsc.org
FSC® C007785

CONTENTS

INTRODUCTION

Storys to rede ar delitabill,
Suppos that thai be nocht bot fabill

THE BRUS

JOHN BARBOUR (1376)

By the 1820s the Industrial Revolution was in full swing in Scotland and, as expected, this saw a dramatic increase in her population. At the beginning of the 18th century there were around a million people living there. By the beginning of the 19th century there were more than 1.5 million. Yet, in this world of steam and foundries, of education and expansion, the other world of Scotland—one of fairies and darkness, fury and witches, bloodshed and nightmares, drew breath simultaneously. In fiction, the supernatural exploded within the publishing houses and magazines and spread like spilled ink on blotting paper; a revolution against modernisation. Those stories, those words, which had been passed from clan to clan, family to family, were dripping through to a world as hungry for tales from the gloaming as they were tales of this strange new world they were entering.

Scots were at the forefront of the critical conversation when it came to the short story. James Hogg (someone well versed in the oral tradition, having been born and brought up working the land) expanded tales told in the old ways into novellas using more literary techniques. Hogg's *The Hunt of Eildon*, published in 1818 in *The Brownie of Bodsbeck and Other Tales*, sees an author really trying to battle with form and structure. *Eildon*, which appears in this volume, is a rudimentary, important work. Allan

Cunningham's *Traditional Tales of the English and Scottish Peasantry* (1822) is another volume that's long been forgotten, but still plays a vital role in these early explorations. Two important, formative, and what we might consider "modern" (or maybe "literary") short stories written in English were by a Scotsman. "The Two Drovers" and "The Highland Widow" appeared in Sir Walter Scott's *Chronicles of the Canongate* (1827/1828). Without Hogg, Scott, and to a lesser extent Cunningham and John Mackay Wilson's visions of nationalism and folklore driving those early tales, we would have no Irving, Hawthorne, Melville and Poe—which means no invention of the short story in America, no philosophical and structural examination into what a short story actually is. Yes, the short story would have continued—it was flourishing in France and Russia—but English-language entries would have come much later and we would have lost, potentially, many of the tales we now call classics.

This volume contains examples of the Scottish weird—not, I hasten to add, a fixed term or a school of writing, but tales written under that church of the supernatural, a boiling pot of weird and cruel, ghastly and grim. As well as works from James Hogg and notable Scottish authors such as Robert Louis Stevenson and John Buchan, I feel privileged to include tales by Catherine Sinclair, Elizabeth W. Grierson and, especially, by Neil M. Gunn, a name whose work appeared many times on the shelves of second-hand bookstores I've been foraging. He's an author born in 1891 and who died only a few years before I was born, writing of the old Scotland of his parent's time, but with a new eye and a new approach. He is a favourite and cherished author.

Scotland the Strange is a deeply personal book for me to edit. Born in the Scottish Borders in 1976, my "Scottishness" did not develop until *after* I left high school, owing to politics and social engineering. We did not study anything about being Scottish* at either primary or high school. (Well, we

---

* This won't be the case with every Scottish person. You may have had a different or exactly the same experience. It depends on the time, the region, the council and the educational peccadilloes of your Headmaster/mistress.

might have been taught at primary school how Robert the Bruce escaped and was protected by a spider). But while we learnt about WWII and the Kings and Queens of England at high school, and read plays in mediaeval English and recited Shakespeare until we were blue in the face, we didn't read John Barbour's epic masterpiece *The Brus* (*The Bruce*), one of the first Scottish texts still available. I have no memory of it, but a school friend informs me that we did read *one* Scottish book at high school, *Sunset Song*, by Lewis Grassic Gibbon, so there's *that*, I suppose—but in the words of John Lydon, "ever get the feeling you've been cheated?" As Scottish pupils we should have been taught Scottish history, had been made to read Scottish authors until we could recite large passages of text (like I can just about do with *Julius Caesar* to this day). Even the Scottish horror anthologies I managed to get a hold of were by English editors like Peter Haining and Ron Chetwynd-Hayes. Their Englishness seemed to me (at least) a big part of some weird English plot to suppress Scottish involvement in all aspects of Scottish life.

My Scottish reading came in dribs and drabs, in my late teens. *Tales, Legends and Historical Reminiscences of the Scottish Covenanters* (1862) by Ellen Jane Guthrie, Allan Cunningham's *Traditional Tales of the English and Scottish Peasantry* (1822) as mentioned above, *Weird Tales* from 1888, an uncredited anthology which includes the much anthologised "The Tapestried Chamber" by Sir Walter Scott amongst some other fine reading. The breakthrough for me came when I read *Strange Case of Dr. Jekyll and Mr. Hyde*. I was twenty, rough camping, and staying in a tent by Persie Loch and decided that evening to foolishly (or perhaps appropriately!) read it. It frightened whatever daylight remained out of me, more than any Stephen King or James Herbert had. My reading tastes were still to be refined and sophisticated, but that was the book that solidified my love of horror, I'm sure of it. The very next day I took myself to a second-hand bookshop and bought all of the Robert Louis Stevenson I could carry, and the more of his works I read and the further north I travelled, the more Scottish I felt. I then left Scotland and went to live in England, where I've remained for nearly thirty years, but those tales dug in deep.

Aware of having revealed all of my youthful hang-ups, this *is* a Scottish book, but it's for *everyone*. Every young person coming to the stories that drive *Scotland the Strange*, hello, you're most welcome. To every jaded horror fan who has read the same stories anthologised over and over, hello—there's some stuff in here I don't think you've read before. I've even managed to source two more stories translated from Gaelic, much like I did in *Celtic Weird*. As this is a Scottish anthology, there are several tales written in the Scots tongue—for those non-natives willing to tackle the harder examples, there are some good Scots dictionaries online. Never move past a word until you understand it. Yet, while some of the stories might be challenging, I don't want it to feel like homework—embrace it.

As we move into an uncertain future, and who knows if Scottish independence will be a part of that, let's rejoice for the moment with the one thing that binds us. The stories we told and the stories we've yet to tell.

JOHNNY MAINS, 2023

A NOTE FROM THE PUBLISHER

The original short stories reprinted in the British Library classic fiction series were written and published in a period ranging across the nineteenth and twentieth centuries. There are many elements of these stories which continue to entertain modern readers; however, in some cases there are also uses of language, instances of stereotyping and some attitudes expressed by narrators or characters which may not be endorsed by the publishing standards of today. We acknowledge therefore that some elements in the stories selected for reprinting may continue to make uncomfortable reading for some of our audience. With this series British Library Publishing aims to offer a new readership a chance to read some of the rare material of the British Library's collections in an affordable format, to enjoy their merits and to look back into the worlds of the past two centuries as portrayed by their writers. It is not possible to separate these stories from the history of their writing and as such the following stories are presented as they were originally published with one edit to the text and with minor edits made for consistency of style and sense. We welcome feedback from our readers, which can be sent to the following address:

British Library Publishing
The British Library
96 Euston Road
London, NW1 2DB
United Kingdom

Scotland the Strange *is dedicated to my high school librarian, Anne Taitt. She tilled the soil and planted the seeds.*

THE HUNT OF EILDON

James Hogg

James Hogg, "the Ettrick Shepherd" (1770–1835), was one of the most influential and admired writers of his day. He was born in Ettrick, Selkirkshire to Robert Hogg and Margaret (née Laidlaw), an acclaimed collector of Scottish ballads. It was said that Margaret's father, Will o' Phawhope, was the last man in the Border country to be able to communicate with fairies.

Upon writing "Donald Macdonald" in 1803, Hogg was recruited to collect ballads for Scott's *Minstrelsy of the Scottish Border*. This was swiftly followed by his first publication, "The Mountain Bard" in 1805. Hogg met Wordsworth and Byron in the Lake District in 1811, the year of the Great Comet, and challenged the latter to a swimming race, which according to some sources he won. Wordsworth didn't think that Hogg was a poet and felt offended when Hogg was compared to him. He wrote that Hogg was "undoubtedly a man of original genius, but of coarse manners and low and offensive opinions."

By 1817, Hogg was seen as the foremost expert of Scottish ballads and the Highland Society of Scotland commissioned him to produce *Jacobite Relics*: a two-volume collection of songs related to the Jacobite rising. The first volume was published in 1819 under the title *The Jacobite Relics of Scotland; Being the Songs, Airs, and Legends, of the Adherents to the House of Stuart*.

His greatest work was published anonymously in 1824. *The Private Memoirs and Confessions of a Justified Sinner* was presented as if it were a found document and offered to a new readership by an unnamed editor. It concerns Gil-Martin, the "sinner" who believes he is guaranteed salvation by God and can kill everyone he believes who has been damned. Way ahead of its time, it has been often cited as a direct influence on Stevenson's *The Master of Ballantrae* (1889) and more obliquely on his earlier *Strange Case of Dr. Jekyll and Mr. Hyde* (1886).

Hogg "paid the debt of nature" from bilious fever, jaundice and a paralytic stroke. He was buried in Ettrick Kirk.

"The Hunt of Eildon" is a little-known Hogg tale from *The Brownie of Bodsbeck and Other Tales*. It has rarely been anthologised, and was something I first came across as a teenager in an anthology called *The Devil's Coven: Classic Stories of Scottish Witchcraft* edited by Angus Black (1972). Sir Walter Scott may have called it "ridiculous"*, but I heartily disagree; I think it's a wild fairy tale, and as I grew up under the shadow of the Eildons, a fitting one.

---

* James Hogg—*Anecdotes of Scott* (Edinburgh University Press, 1999).

"I HOPE the king will not hunt today," said Gale, as he sat down on the top of the South Eildon, and stretched out his lazy limbs in the sun. "If he keep within doors today with his yelping beagles, I shall have one day's peace and ease; and my lambs shall have one day's peace and ease; and poor Trimmy shall have one day's peace and ease too. Come hither to me, Trimmy, and tell me what is the reason that you will not hunt with the king's two beagles?"

Trimmy came near, laid her paw on her master's knee, and looked him in the face, but she could not tell him what was the reason that she would not hunt with the king's two beagles, Mooly and Scratch.

"I say, tell me my good Trimmy, what you ail at these beautiful hounds? You wont to be the best follower of a track in all the Merse and Leader; but now, whenever you hear the sound of the horn, and the opening swell of the harriers, you take your tail between your legs and set off for home, as there were something on the hill that were neither good nor cannie. You are a very sensible beast, Trimmy, but you have some strange fancies and prejudices that I cannot comprehend."

Trimmy cocked her ears, and looked towards the Abbey, then at her master, and then at the Abbey again.

"Ah! I fear you hear them coming that you are cocking your ears at that rate. Then if that be the case, good morning to you, Trimmy."

It was neither the king nor his snow-white beagles that Trimmy winded, but poor Croudy, Gale's neighbour shepherd, who was coming sauntering up the brae, with his black lumpish dog at his foot, that was fully as stupid as himself, and withal as good-natured. Croudy was never lifting his eyes from the ground, but moving on as if he had been enumerating all the little yellow flowers that grew on the hill. Yet it was not for want of thought that Croudy was walking in that singular position, with his body bent forward, and the one ear turned down towards the ground, and the other up. No, no! for Croudy was trying to think all that he could; and all that he could do he could make nothing of it. Croudy had seen and heard wonderful things! "Bless me and my horn!" said he, as he sat down on a stone to rest himself, and try if he could bring his thoughts to any rallying point. It was impossible—they were like a hive of bees when the queen is taken from their head.

He took out the little crooked ewe-horn that he kept as a charm; he had got it from his mother, and it had descended to him from many generations; he turned it round in the one hand, and then round in the other hand—he put it upon his finger and twirled it. "Bless me an' my horn!" said he again. Then leaning forward upon his staff, he looked aslant at the ground, and began to moralise. "It is a growing world—ay—the gerse grows; the lambs eat it—they grow—ay—we eat them—we grow—there it goes!—men, women, dogs, bairns, a' eat—a' grow; the yird eats up a'—it grows—men eat women—they grow—what comes o' them?—Hoh! I'm fixed now!—I'm at the end o' my tether.—I might gang up the hill to Gale, an' tell him what I hae seen an' what I hae heard; but I hae four great fauts to that chiel. In the first place, he's a fool—good that! In the second place, he's a scholar, an' speaks English—bad! In the third place, he likes the women—warst ava!—and, fourthly and lastly, he misca's a' the words, and ca's the streamers the Roara Boriawlis—ha! ha!—Wha wad converse wi' a man, or wha *can* converse wi' a man, that ca's the streamers the Roara Boriawlis? Fools hae aye something about them no like ither fock! Now, gin I war to gang to sic a man as that, an' tell him that I heard a dog speakin', and another dog answering it, what wad he say? He wad speak English; sae ane wad get nae sense out o' him. If I war to gang to the Master o' Seaton an' tak my aith, what wad he say? Clap me up i' the prison for a daft man an' a fool. I couldna bide that. Then again, if we lose our king—an' him the last o' the race—Let me see if I can calculate what wad be the consequence?

4

The English—Tut! the English! wha cares for them? But let me see now—should the truth be tauld or no tauld?—That's the question. What's truth? Ay, there comes the crank! Nae man can tell that—for what's truth to ane is a lee to another—Mumps, ye're very hard on thae fleas the day—Truth?—For instance; gin my master war to come up the brae to me an' say, 'Croudy, that dog's useless,' that wadna be truth to me—But gin I war to say to him, 'Master, I heard a dog speak, an' it said sae an' sae; an' there was another dog answered it, an' it said sae an' sae,' that wad be truth to me; but then it wadna be truth to him—Truth's just as it is ta'en—Now, if a thing may be outher truth or no truth, then a' things are just the same—No—that disna haud neither—Mumps, ye're no gaun to leave a sample o' thae fleas the day, man—Look up, like a farrant beast—have ye nae pity on your master, nor nae thought about him ava, an' him in sic a plisky?—I wadna be just sae like a stump an' I war you, man—Bless me an' my horn! here's the Boriawlis comin' on me—here's the northern light."

"Good-morrow to you, Croudy."

"Humph!"

"You seem to be very thoughtful and heavy-hearted today, honest Croudy. I fear pretty Pery has given you a bad reception last night."

"Humph!—women!—women!"

"I hope she did not mention the kiln-logie, Croudy? That was a sad business! Croudy; some men are ill to know!"

"See, whaten white scares are yon, Gale, aboon the Cowdyknowes an' Gladswood linn? Look ye, they spread an' tail away a' the gate to the Lammer-Law—What ca' ye yon, Gale?"

"Some exhalation of the morning."

"What?—Bless me an' my horn! that's warst ava!—I thought it wad be some Boriawlis, Gale—some day Boriawlis; but I didna think o' aught sae high as this—ha! ha! ha! ha!"

Croudy went his way laughing along the side of the hill, speaking to Mumps one while, moralising about truth and the language of dogs and fairies another, and always between taking a hearty laugh at Gale. "Come away, Mumps," said he; "I can crack some wi' you, though ye're rather slow i' the uptake; but I can crack nane wi' a man that ca's the streamers a Roara Boriawlis, an' a white clud, an' Exaltation—Na, na, that will never do."

Croudy sauntered away down into the Bourgeon to be out of sight, and Gale went lightsomely away to the top of the North-east Eildon; and there, on one of the angles of the old Roman Camp, laid him down to enjoy the glorious prospect; and, sure, of all the lovely prospects in our isle, this is the most lovely. What must it have been in those days when all the ruins of monastery, tower, and citadel, which still make the traveller to stand in wonder and admiration, were then in their full splendour. Traveller! would you see Scotland in all its wild and majestic grandeur? sail along its western firths from south to north—Would you see that grandeur mellowed by degrees into softness? look from the top of Ben-Lomond—But would you see an amphitheatre of *perfect beauty*, where nothing is wanting to enrich the scene? seat yourself on the spot where Gale now lay, at the angle of the Roman Camp, on the top of the North-east Eildon.

Short time did he enjoy the prospect and the quiet in which he delighted. First the heads of two noblemen appeared on the hill beneath him, then came a roe by him at full speed. Trimmy would fain have hunted her, but as the shepherd deemed that the business was some way connected with the royal sport, he restrained her. The two noblemen some time thereafter sounded a bugle, and then in a moment the king and his attendants left the Abbey at full speed; and how beautiful was their winding ascent up the hill! The king had betted with the Earl of Hume and Lord Belhaven, seven steers, seven palfreys, seven deer-greyhounds, and seven gold rings, that his two snow-white hounds, Mooly and Scratch, would kill a roe-deer started on any part of the Eildon hills, and leave the Abbey walk with him after she was started. After the bet was fairly taken, the king said to the two noblemen, "You are welcome to your loss, my lords. Do you know that I could bet the half of my realm on the heads of these two hounds?"

The two lords held their peace, but they were determined to win if they could, and they did not blow the horn, as agreed on, immediately when the roe started, but sauntered about, to put off time, and suffer the trail to cool. The two hounds were brought up, and loosed at the spot; they scarcely shewed any symptoms of having discovered the scent. The king shook his head; and Hume, who loved the joke dearly, jeered the king about his wager, which his majesty only answered by speaking to one of the hounds that stood next to him. "Ah! Mooly, Mooly, if you deceive me, it is the first time; but I have another matter to think on than you this morning, Mooly." Mooly fawned on her royal master; jumped up at the stirrup, and took his foot playfully in her mouth, while Keryl, the king's steed, laid back his ears, and snapped at her, in a half-angry, half-playful mood. This done, Mooly turned her long nose to the wind; scented this way and that way, and then scampering carelessly over the brow of the hill, she opened in a tone so loud and so sprightly that it made all the Eildons sound in chorus to the music. Scratch joined with her elegant treble, and away they went like two wild swans, sounding over the hill.

"Trimmy! Trimmy! my poor Trimmy!" cried Gale, vexed and astonished; "Trimmy, halloo! hie, hunt the deer, Trimmy! Here, here, here!"

No; Trimmy would never look over her shoulder, but away she ran with all her might home to Eildon-Hall. "The plague be in the beast," said Gale to himself, "if ever I saw any thing like that! There is surely something about these two hounds that is scarcely right."

Round and round the hills they went side by side, and still the riders kept close up with them. The trail seemed to be warm, and the hounds keen, but yet no deer was to be discovered. They stretched their course to the westward, round Cauldshields Hill, back over Bothendean Moor, and again betook them to the Eildons; still no deer was to be seen! The two hounds made a rapid stretch down towards Melrose; the riders spurred in the same direction. The dogs in a moment turning short, went out between the two eastern hills, distancing all the riders, whom they left straggling up the steep after them as they could, and when these came over the height there was a fine roe-deer lying newly slain, and the two snow-white hounds panting and rolling themselves on the grass beside her. The king claimed his wager, but Hume objected, unless his majesty could prove that it was the same deer that they had started at the same place in the morning. The king had the greatest number of voices in his favour, but the earl stood to his point. "Is it true, my liege lord," said an ancient knight to the king, "that these two beautiful hounds have never yet been unlieshed without killing their prey?"

"Never," returned the king.

"And is it equally true," continued the old knight, "that to this day they have never been seen kill either roe, deer, or any other creature?"

"That is a most extraordinary circumstance," said the king; "pause until I recollect—No; I do not know that any eye hath ever yet seen them take their prey."

"I heard it averred last night," said the old man, "that if they are kept sight of for a whole day the deer is never seen, nor do they ever catch any thing; and that the moment they get out of sight, there the deer is found slain, nobody knows how. I took note of it, and I have seen it this day verified. Pray, is this a fact, my liege?"

"I never before thought of it, or noted it," said the king; "but as far as my memory serves me, I confess that it has uniformly been as you say."

"Will your majesty suffer me to examine these two hounds?" said the old man. "Methinks there is something very odd about them—Sure there was never any animal on earth had eyes or feet such as they have."

The two beagles kept aloof, and pretended to be winding some game round the top of the hill.

"They will not come now," said the king; "you shall see them by and by."

"If consistent with your majesty's pleasure," continued the aged knight, "where—how—or when did you get these two hounds?"

"I got them in a most extraordinary way, to be sure!" replied the king, in a thoughtful and hesitating mood.

"Your majesty does not then chuse to say how, or where, or from whom it was that you had them?" said the old knight.

The king shook his head.

"I will only simply ask this," continued he; "and I hope there is no offence.—Is it true that you got these hounds at the very same time that the beautiful Elen, and Clara of Rosline, were carried off by the fairies?"

8

The king started—fixed his eyes upon the ground—raised his hands, and seemed gasping for breath. All the lords were momentarily in the same posture; the query acted on them all like an electrical shock. The old man seemed to enjoy mightily the effect produced by his insinuations—He drew still nearer to the king.

"What is it that troubles your majesty?" said he. "What reflections have my simple questions raised in your mind?—Your majesty, I am sure, can have no unpleasant reflections on that score?"

"Would to the Virgin Mary that it were even so!" said the king.

"How is it possible," continued the officious old man, "that any thing relating to two dogs can give your majesty trouble? Pray tell us all about them—Who was it you got them from?"

"I do not know, and if I did—"

"Would you know him again if you saw him?"

The king looked at the old man, and held his peace.

"Did you buy them, or borrow them?" continued he.

"Neither!" was the answer.

"What then did you give in exchange for them?"

"Only a small token."

"And pray, if your majesty pleases, what might that token be?"

"Who dares to ask that?" said the king, with apparent trouble of mind.

"Would you know your pledge again if you saw it?" said the old man, sarcastically.

"Who are you, sir?" said the king, proudly, "that dares to question your sovereign in such a manner?"

"Who am I!" said the old man. "That is a good jest! That is such a question to ask at one who has scarcely ever been from your side, since you were first laid in your cradle!"

"I know the face," said the king, "but all this time I cannot remember who you are.—My Lord of Hume, do you know who the reverend old gentleman is?" And in saying this his majesty turned a little aside with the earl.

"Do I know who he is?" said Hume. Yes, by Saint Lawrence I do—I know him as well as I do your majesty. Let me see—It is very singular that

I cannot recollect his name—I have seen the face a thousand times—Is he not some abbot, or confessor, or—No—Curse me, but I believe he is the devil!"

The earl said this in perfect jocularity; because he could not remember the old man's name; but when he looked at the king, he perceived that his eyes were fixed on him in astonishment. The earl's, as by sympathy, likewise settled by degrees into as much seriousness as they were masters of, and there the two stood for a considerable time, gazing at one another, like two statues.

"I was only saying so in jest, my liege," said Hume; "I did not once think that the old gentleman was the devil. Why are you thoughtful?"

"Because, now when I think of it, he hinted at some things which I am certain no being on earth knew of, save myself, and another, who cannot possibly divulge them."

They both turned slowly about at the same instant, curious to take another look of this mysterious old man; but when fairly turned round they did not see him.

"What has become of the old man," said the king, "that spoke to me just now?"

"Here, sire!" said one.

"Here!" said another.

"Here!" said a third; all turning at the same time to the spot where the old man and his horse stood, but neither of them were there.

"How is this?" said the king, "that you have let him go from among you without noting it?"

"He must have melted into air, he and his horse both," said they; "else he could not otherwise have left us without being observed."

The king blessed himself in the name of the Holy Virgin, and all the chief saints in the calendar. The Earl of Hume swore by the greater part of them, and cursed himself that he had not taken a better look at the devil when he was so near him, as no one could tell if ever he would have such a chance again. Douglas said he hoped there was little doubt of that.

CHAPTER II

The hunt was now over, and Gale's lambs were all scattered abroad; he threw off his coat and tried to gather them, but he soon found that, without the assistance of Trimmy, it was impossible; so he was obliged to go home and endeavour to persuade her again out to the hill, by telling her that Mooly and Scratch had both left it. Trimmy then came joyfully, and performed in half an hour what her master could not have effected before night.

When he had gotten them all collected, and settled at their food, he went away in the evening to seek for his friend Croudy, to have some amusement with him. He found him lying in a little hollow, conversing with himself, and occasionally with Mumps, who paid very little attention to what he said. He now and then testified his sense of the honour intended to him, by giving two or three soft indolent strokes with his tail upon the ground, but withall neither lifted his head nor opened his eyes. Gale addressed his friend Croudy in a jocund and rallying manner, who took no notice of it, but continued to converse with Mumps.

"Ye're nae great gallaunt, after a' now, Mumps. Gin I had been you, man, an' had seen sic twa fine beasts as Mooly an' Scratch come to our hills, I wad hae run away to them, an' fiddled about them, an' smelt their noses, an' kissed them, an' cock-it up my tail on my rigging wi' the best o' them; but instead o' that, to tak the pet an' rin away far outbye, an' there sit turnin up your nose an' bow-wowing as ye war a burial-boding!—hoo, man, it is very bairnly like o' ye! Humph! fools do ay as they are bidden! Ye're nae fool, Mumps, for ye seldom do as ye're bidden."

"Tell me, Croudy," said Gale, "does Mumps really run away in a panic when he perceives the king's hounds?"

"*Panic when he perceives the king's hounds!* Are ye gaun to keep on at bletherin' English? Tell me, ye see—for if ye be, I'm gaun to clatter nane to ye."

"Dear Croudy, I have often told you that there is not such a thing as English and Scotch languages; the one is merely a modification of the other, a refinement as it were"—

"Ay, an *exaltation* like—ation! ation! I'm sure nae Scot that isna a fool wad ever let that sound, *ation*, come out o' his mouth. Mumps, what say ye tilt?"

"But, Croudy, I have news to tell you that will delight you very much; only, ere I begin, tell me seriously, Does your dog really run off when he sees or hears the king's two white hounds?"

"Really he does—Is that ony wonder? D'ye think Mumps sic a fool as no to ken a witch by a brute beast?"

"What do you mean to insinuate, Croudy?"

"*Sinuate*—What's that?"

"I mean, What would you infer when you talk of witches? I have some strange doubts about these dogs myself."

"Can you keep a secret?"

"Yes, if it is worth keeping."

"At ony rate, swear that if ever you do tell it, it is not to be in English. Nane o' your *awlis's* an' *ations* in it. Gale, I hae the maist wonderfu' story to tell ye that ever happened sin' Nimrod first gaed out to the hunting wi' a bull-dog an' a pouchfu' stanes. Ye see, yesterday at morn, when the hunt began, I clamb up into the Eildon tree, an' haid mysel' amang the very thickest o' its leaves, where I could see every thing, but naething could see me. I saw the twa white hounds a' the gate, but nae appearance of a deer; an' aye they came nearer an' nearer to me, till at last I saw a bonny, braw, young lady, a' clad i' white, about a hunder paces frae me, an' she was aye looking back an' rinning as gin she wantit to be at the Eildon tree. When she saw the hounds comin on hard behind her, she cried out; but they soon o'ertook her, threw her down, an' tore her, an' worried her; an' I heard her makin' a noise as gin she had been laughin' ae while an' singin' another, an' O I thought her sang was sweet; it was something about the fairies. Weel, this scene, sae contrair to a' nature, didna end here, for I heard the tae dog sayin' to the tither, in plain language,—'Wha's this has been the deer today?' An it answered again an' said, 'Lady Marrion of Coomsley, ye may see by her goud rings; she is the twenty-third, and our task will soon be dune.'

'Sister, read me my riddle,' said the first.

'I ate my love an' I drank my love,
    An' my love she gae me light;
  An' the heart o' the deer may lie right near
    Where it lay yesternight.'

'Ha! that's nae riddle!' said the other; 'little does some wat what they're to eat an' what they're to drink the night! Can ye tell me, sister, if the wicked deed will be done?—Will the king die tonight?

'The poison's distill'd, and the monk is won,
  And tonight I fear it will be done.
  Hush!—hush!—we are heard an' seen;
  Wae be to the ears, and wae be to the een!'

"An wi' that, they rowed themsels on the bonny corpse; and when I lookit again, there was a fine, plump, bausined roe-deer lying, an' the blude streamin' frae her side; an' down comes the king an' his men, an' took her away hame to their supper."

"Now, Croudy, of all the tales I ever heard that is the most improbable and unnatural! But it is too singular and out of the common course of nature for you to have framed it; and besides, I never knew you to tell a manifest lie—Are you certain that you did not dream it?"

"How could I dream on the top of a tree? Ye may either believe it or no as ye like—it's a' true."

"I was sure there was something more than ordinary about these dogs; but what to make of your story I know not. Saint Waldave be our shield! Do you think the king and his nobles have been feasting upon changed human creatures all this while? There is something in the whole business so revolting to human nature, a man cannot think of it! It seems, too, that there is a plot against the life of the king—What shall we do in this?—The fairies have again been seen at the Eildon Tree, that is certain; and it is said some more young people are missing."

"They'll soon hae us a' thegither—I like that way o' turnin' fock into deers an' raes, and worrying them, warst ava—Mumps, lad, how wad ye like to be turned into a deer, an' worried an' eaten?—Aigh, man! ye *wad* like it ill! I think I see how ye wad lay yoursel out for fear—Ha, ha! I wad like to see ye get a bit hunt, man, if I thought ye wad win away wi' the life—I wad like to see ye streek yoursel for aince."

"I wonder, Croudy, after seeing such a sight as you have just now described, that you can descend from that to speak such nonsense."

"Tongues maun wag—an' when they gang it's no for naething—It's a queer thing speaking!—Mumps, ye can speak nane, man—It's no for want of a tongue, I'm sure."

"Let us consider what's to be done—The king should be warned."

"I dinna see what's to hinder you to speak, Mumps, as weel as ony white beagle i' the country."

"I have it—I will go home directly and tell pretty Pery—she will apprise the abbot, and we shall have the two hounds, Mooly and Scratch, burnt at the stake tomorrow."

"You tell Pery? No; that will never do; for you will speak English—That tale winna tell in English; for the twa witches, or fairies, or changed fock, or whatever they may be, didna speak that language themsels—sin' the thing is to be tauld, I'll rather tell Pery mysel, if it is the same thing to you."

This Pery was a young volatile maiden at Eildon-Hall, who was over head and ears in love with Gale. She would have given the whole world for him; and in order to tease him somewhat, she had taken a whim of pretending to be in love with Croudy. Croudy hated all the women, and more particularly Pery, who had been the plague of his life; but of late he had heard some exaggerated accounts of the kind sentiments of her heart respecting him, which had wonderfully altered Croudy, although he still kept up as well as he could the pretence of disliking the sex. He went to Pery that evening as she was gathering in some clothes from the bushes, and desired her, with a most important face, to meet him at the Moss Thorn in half an hour, for he had something to tell her that would surprise her.

"Indeed and that I will with all my heart, Croudy," said she; "how glad I am that I have got you this length! I can guess what your secret will be."

"Ye can do nae sic thing," said Croudy, "nor nae woman that ever was born."

"I'll wager three kisses with you, Croudy, at the Old Moss Thorn, that I do," returned she.

Croudy hung his head to one side, and chuckled, and crowed, and laid on the ground with his staff; and always now and then cast a sly look-out at the wick of his eye to Pery.

"It's a queer creature a woman," said Croudy—"very bonny creature though!"

"Well, Croudy, I'll meet you at the Moss Thorn," said Pery, "and pay you your wager too, provided you have either spirit to ask, or accept of it when offered."

Croudy went away laughing till his eyes blinded with tears, and laying on the ground with his stick.—"I watna what I'll do now," said he to himself, "little impudent thing that she is!—She's eneugh to pit a body mad!—Mumps—O, man, ye're an unfarrant beast!—Three kisses at the Moss Thorn!—I wish I had this meeting by!—Mumps, I never saw sic an unfeasible creature as you, man, when ane thinks about a bonny woman—A woman!—What is a woman?—Let me see! —'Tis no easy to ken!—But I ken this—that a ewe lamb is a far nicer, bonnier, sweeter, innocenter, little creature than a toop lamb. Oh! I wish it war night, for I'm no weel ava!—Mumps, ye're a perfect blockhead, man!"

Precisely while this was going on at Eildon-Hall, there were two ladies met hurriedly on the Abbey Walk. No one knew who they were, or whence they came, but they were lovely beyond expression, although their eyes manifested a kind of wild instability. Their robes were white as snow, and they had that light, elegant, sylph-like appearance, that when they leaned forward to the evening air, one could hardly help suspecting that they would skim away in it like twin doves.

"Sister," said the one, "haste and tell me what we are to do?"

"There is much to do tonight," said the other. "That clown who saw us, and heard us speak, will blab the news; and then, think what the consequences may be! He must be silenced, and that instantly."

"And tell me," said the first, "is the plot against the king's life to be put in execution tonight?"

"I fear it is," answered the other; "and the abbot, his own kinsman, is in it."

"Alas, sister, what shall we do! Give me Philany's rod, and trust the clown to me. But do you make all possible haste, and find your way into the banquet hall, and be sure to remain there in spite of all opposition."

The two sisters parted; and she that got the wand from the other repaired straight to the Moss Thorn, where honest Croudy, and his dog Mumps, were lying at a little distance from each other; the one very busy biting for fleas, that he supposed had made a lodgment among his rough matted hair, and the other conversing with himself about the properties of women, fairies, and witches. All of a sudden he beheld this beautiful angelic creature coming towards him, which made his heart thrill within him.

"Saint Mary be my guide!" exclaimed Croudy to himself; "saw ever ony body the like o' yon? I declare Pery has dressed hersel like a princess to come an' speak to me!—An' to think o' me kissing a creature like yon! I maun do it, too, or else I'll never hear the end o't.—Och! what will I do!—I'll lie down an' pretend to be sleepin."

Croudy drew his plaid up over his face, stretched out his limbs, and snored as in a profound sleep. The fair lady came up, gave him three strokes with her wand, and uttered certain words at every stroke; and, lo! the whole mortal frame of Croudy was in five seconds changed into that of a huge bristly boar! The transformation was brought about so suddenly, and Mumps was so much engaged, that he never once noticed, in the slightest degree, till all was over, and the lady had withdrawn. Let any man judge of the honest colley's astonishment, when, instead of his master, he beheld the boar standing hanging his ears, and shaking his head at him. He betook himself to immediate flight, and ran towards the house faster than ever he ran in his life, yelping all the way for perfect fright. Croudy was very little better himself. At first he supposed that he was in a dream, and stood a long time considering of it, in hopes the fantasy would go off; but on seeing the consternation of Mumps, he looked first to the one side, and then to the other, and perceiving his great bristly sides and limbs, he was seized with indescribable terror, and fled at full speed. It is well known what a ridiculous figure a hog makes at any time when frightened, and exerting itself to escape from the supposed danger—there is not any thing so calculated to make one laugh—his stupid apprehension of some approaching mischief—the way that he fixes his head and listens—gives a grunt like the crack of a musket, and breaks away again. Every one who has witnessed such a scene, will acknowledge, that it is a masterpiece of the ludicrous. Consider, then, what it would be to see one in such a fright as this poor beast was, and trying to escape from himself; running grunting over hill and dale, hanging out his tongue with fatigue, and always carrying the object of his terror along with him. It was an ineffectual exertion of mind to escape from matter; for, though Croudy's form and nature were changed, he still retained the small and crude particles of the reasoning principle which he had before. All feelings else were, however, for the present swallowed up in utter dismay, and he ran on without any definitive aim, farther than a kind of propensity to run to the end of the world. He did not run a great way for all that; for he lost his breath in a very short time; but even in that short time, he run himself into a most imminent danger.

Squire Fisher of Dernaway Tower had a large herd of cows—they were all standing in the loan, as the milking green is called in that country, and the maidens were engaged in milking them, singing the while in full chorus, (and a sweet and enlivening chorus it was, for the evening was mild and serene), when down comes this unearthly boar into the loan, all fatigued as he was, gaping and running on without stop or stay. The kine soon perceived that there was something super-human about the creature, for even the most dull of animals have much quicker perceptions than mankind in these matters; and in one moment they broke all to the gate as they had been mad, overturning the milk, maidens, and altogether. The boar ran on; so did the kine, cocking their heads and roaring in terror, as if every one of them had been bewitched, or possessed by some evil spirit. It was a most dismal scene!—The girls went home with the rueful tidings, that a mad boar had come into the loan, and bitten the whole herd, which was all run off mad, along with the furious and dreadful animal. The dogs were instantly closed in for fear of further danger to the country; and all the men of the village armed themselves, and sallied out to surround and destroy this outrageous monster.

It chanced, however, that the boar in his progress ran into a large field of strong standing corn, which so impeded his course that he fell down breathless, and quite exhausted; and thus he lay stretched at full length, panting in a furrow, while all the men of the country were running round and round him, every one with a sword, spear, or fork, ready to run into his body.

Croudy, or the Boar, as it is now more proper to designate him, got here some time to reflect. He found that he was transformed by witch-craft or enchantment, and as he had never looked up from under his plaid during the moments of his transformation, he conceived it to have been the beautiful and wicked Pery that had wrought this woful change upon him; therefore he had no hopes of regaining his former shape, save in her returning pity and compassion; and he had strong hopes that she would ere long relent, as he had never wilfully done her any ill. Pery knew nothing about the matter; but actually went up with a heart as light as a feather to have some sport with Croudy at the Old Thorn; and when she found that he was not there, she laughed and went home again, saying to herself, that she knew he durst not stand such an encounter.

The poor boar arose from his furrow in the midst of the field of corn, as soon as it was daylight next morning, and with a heavy and forlorn heart went away back to the Old Moss Thorn, in hopes that the cruel Pery would seek him there, and undo the enchantment. When he came, he discovered honest Mumps lying on the very spot where he had last seen his master in his natural shape. He had sought it again over night, notwithstanding the horrible fright that he had got, for he knew not where else to find his master; and stupid as he was, yet, like all the rest of his species, he lived only in his master's eye. He was somewhat alarmed when he saw the boar coming slowly toward him, and began first to look over the one shoulder, and then over the other, as if meditating an escape; but, seeing that it came grunting in such a peaceable and friendly manner, Mumps ventured to await the issue, and by the time the monster approached within twenty paces of him, this faithful animal went cowering away to meet him, prostrated himself at the boar's feet, and showed every symptom of obedience and affection. The boar, in return, patted him with his cloven hoof, and stroked him with his bristly cheek. Matters were soon made up—thenceforward they were inseparable.

The boar lay all that day about the Moss Thorn, and Mumps lay in his bosom, but no pitying damsel, witch, or fairy, came near him. He grew extremely hungry the evening, and was deeply distressed what to do for food, for he pitied Mumps more than himself. At length he tried to plough up the earth with his nose, as he remembered of having seen swine do before, but at that he made small progress, doing it very awkwardly, and with great pain to his face. Moreover, for all his exertion, he found nothing to eat, save one or two moss-corns, and a ground walnut, with which he was obliged to content himself; and, for his canine friend, there was nothing at all.

Next morning he saw his neighbour servants seeking for him, and calling his name, but he could make them no answer, save by long and mournful sounds between a grunt and groan. He drew near to several of them, but they regarded him in no other light than as a boar belonging to some one in the neighbourhood, straying in the fields. His case was most deplorable; but as he still conceived there was one who knew his situation well, he determined to seek her. He went down to Eildon-Hall, with the faithful Mumps walking close by his side—tried to work his way into the laundry, but being repulsed, he waited with patience about the doors for an opportunity to present himself before Pery. She came out at length, and went away singing to the well. The boar followed, uttering the most melancholy sounds that ever issued from the chest of distressed animal. Pery could not help noticing him a little. "What strange animal can this be?" said she to herself; but perceiving that Mumps too was following her, her attention was soon directed solely to him.

"Alas, poor Mumps," said she, "you are famishing. What can be become of your master?"

The boar laid his ungraceful foot softly on that of Pery, looked ruefully in her face, and uttered a most melancholy sound; as much as to say, "You know well what is become of him! Have you no pity nor remorse in your heart?"

It was impossible Pery could comprehend this. She judged, like others, that the animal had strayed from home, and was complaining to her for food. She looked at him, and thought him a very docile and valuable swine, and one that would soon be ready for the knife. He was astonished at her apparent indifference, as well as moved with grief and vengeance, seeing the abject state to which she had reduced him; and in his heart he cursed the whole sex, deeming them all imps of Satan, witches, and enchantresses, each one. He followed her back to the house.

"Come in, Mumps," said she, "and you shall have your breakfast for the sake of him you belonged to, whatever is become of him, poor fellow!"

The boar ran forward, and kneeled at her feet moaning, on which she kicked him, and drove him away, saying, "What does the vile beast want with me? Mumps, come you in and get some meat, honest brute."

Mumps would not come in, but when the boar was expelled, turned back with him, looking very sullen. She brought him out a bicker of cold parritch mixed with milk, but he would not taste them until the boar had first taken his share; after which they went and lay down in the yard together, the dog in the boar's bosom. Thus did they continue for many days. At length the master of Eildon had the boar cried at the church-door, and at the cross of Melrose, and as no one appeared to claim him, he put him up for slaughter.

CHAPTER III

But to return from this necessary digression.—The king and his nobles had a banquet in the Abbey that night on which Croudy was changed, and it was agreed by all present, that the venison of the roe-deer of Eildon exceeded in quality that of any other part of the kingdom. The king appeared thoughtful and absent during the whole of the evening; and at mass, it was observed that he was more fervent in his devotions than ever he was wont to be. The words of the old mysterious stranger—his sudden disappearance—the rumours of fairies and witchcrafts that were abroad, together with another vision which he had seen, but not yet disclosed, preyed upon his mind, as it was little wonder they should, and made him apprehend that every step he took was on enchanted ground. The hound, Mooly, had slipt into the banquet-hall at the time of vespers, and neither soothing, threatening, nor the lash, would drive her hence. She clung to the king's foot until he took pity on her, and said, "Cease, and let the poor animal stay, since she insists on it. I will not have her maltreated for the fault of those who have the charge of her, and should have put her better up." So Mooly got leave to remain, and kept her station the whole night without moving.

The glass circulated until a late hour. At length the king said, "My lords, I crave a cup full to the brim, which I mean to dedicate to the health of a lady, whom I think I saw yesterday morning; the mentioning of whose name will a little astonish you."

"My royal son and sire," said the abbot, "for your majesty is both, in the general acceptation of the terms, shall it not be of your far-famed Malmsey that you will drink this beloved toast?"

"If you so please," said his majesty.

"Ralpho," said the abbot, "here is the key. You alone know where the portion of old Malmsey is to be found among his majesty's stores here deposited; bring one bottle only to his majesty, and pour it carefully yourself."

Ralpho obeyed; poured out the wine till the cup was full, and turned the remainder into a sewer. The king then arose, and lifting his cup on high—"My lords," said he, "I give you the fairest, the loveliest, and the most angelic maid that ever Scotland bred—I give you Elen of Rosline."

Every one started at the name till the wine was spilled all around the table. Astonishment was in every look, for the king had said he had seen her yesterday at morn. "To the bottom," cried the king.

Every one drank off his cup with avidity, anxious to hear the explanation. The king kept the position in which he stood until he saw every cup drained, and then brought his slowly and gracefully to his lips, with the intention of emptying it at one draught. But the moment that it reached them, Mooly sprung up, snatched the cup and wine out of his hand, and threw them on the floor.

"Strike the animal dead," cried one.

"Kick her out of the hall," said another.

"Take her out and let her be hung up," cried a third.

Mooly cowered at her royal master's feet, as if begging pardon, or begging to remain.

"Let her alone," said the king; "let us see what the beast means, and if she persists in the outrage."

He filled his cup of the wine before him, and brought it slowly to his head in the same manner as he did before. He even took it away and brought it back several times, in order to see if she would be provoked to do the like again. But no!—Mooly appeared perfectly satisfied, and suffered her master to drink it off piece-meal. A certain consternation reigned in the royal apartment for some time; sharp arguments followed; and, in the mean time, Angus and the abbot were heard whispering apart, and the one said, "It must be accomplished this night, or abandoned for ever."

The nobles again took their seats, and the king appeared as formerly to be growing thoughtful and dejected.

"Pray cheer up your heart and be merry, my liege," said Douglas, "and let not the casual frolic of a pampered animal tend to cast down your majesty's spirits. Your majesty has not yet drank the extraordinary toast you proposed."

"But that I shall do presently," said the king.

"Ay," said the abbot, "and your majesty shall do it too in the wine of which I have heard your majesty so much approve. Fetch another bottle, Ralpho."

Ralpho brought it.—"I will pour for myself," said the king; and taking the bottle, he poured about one-half of it into his cup; again named the name of Elen of Rosline with rapturous enthusiasm, and again as he put the cup to his lips, Mooly sprung up, snatched the cup from his hand, and dashed it on the floor more furiously than before, and then cowered at her master's feet as if begging not to be struck.

"There is something more than ordinary in this," said the king, "and I will have it investigated instantly."

"There is nothing in it at all," said the abbot. "Pardon me, sire; but it is a fault in your majesty, for which I have grieved, and often done penance myself. You are, and have always been a visionary, and nothing will ever wean you from it. You make idols of these two animals; they have sometime been taught a number of pranks, and for one of these would you augur aught against the monastery, your nobles, or your majesty's own peace of mind?"

"Are you certain that is the genuine Old Malmsey wine, Ralpho?" said the king.

"I am certain, sire, it is the wine that was shown to me as such."

The king poured out the remainder that was in the bottle. "Drink thou that, Ralpho," said he, "and tell me if it be really and truly the genuine Malmsey."

Ralpho thanked his majesty, bowed, and drank off the cup without hesitation.

"Is it genuine, Ralpho?"

"I don't know, your majesty; I think it tastes a little of the earth."

The circle laughed at Ralpho's remark; and the conversation began again to grow general, when, some time thereafter, Ralpho, who was bustling about, sat down in a languid and sickly posture on one of the window seats. They looked at him, and saw that his face was becoming black.

"What is the matter, Ralpho?" said one.

"I do not know what is the matter with me," returned he; "I think I feel as if that wine were not like to agree with my stomach."

He fell into immediate convulsions, and in ten minutes he was lying a swollen and disfigured corpse.

Douglas was the first to cry out *treason*. He bolted the door, and stood inside with his sword drawn, vowing that he would search the soul of every traitor in the room. Angus's great power made the other lords to stand in awe of him; although it was obvious to them all, that he was at least as likely to have a hand in this as any other. Hume charged him boldly to his face with it, and made proffer to abide by the proof; but he pretended to receive the charge only with scorn and derision, as one which no reasonable man could suppose. The king was greatly affected, and, upon the whole, showed rather more apprehension on account of his personal safety, than was, perhaps, becoming in a sovereign. He cried out that "they were all of them traitors! and that he would rather be at the head of a band of moss-troopers, than be thus condemned to have such a set about him whom he could not trust."

After some expostulation he acquitted the Earl of Angus, more, it was thought, through fear, than conviction of his innocence; but from an inference, the most natural in the world, he fixed the blame on the abbot.

"My liege," said the reverend father, "I know no more how this has happened than the child that is unborn. There can be no doubt but that, instigated by some of your majesty's enemies, the wretch, Ralpho, has mixed the poison himself, and has met with the fate he justly deserved."

"No!" replied the king. "If that had been the case, he would not have been so ready in participating of the draught. I will not believe, but that there is a combination among you to take my life."

Every one protested his innocence more strenuously than another.

The abbot was seized; and said, in his justification, "That he would show his majesty the set of wine from which he had ordered Ralpho to bring it, and he was willing to drink a share of any bottle of it that they chose;" which he did.

But this did not convince the king. He sent off privately a messenger to assemble the Border Chiefs, and bring them to his rescue—took his two favourite hounds with him into his chamber, placed a strong guard, counted his beads, and retired to rest.

Every means were tried next day by the nobles to dispel his majesty's fears, and regain his confidence; and as nothing decisive could be produced against any one, they succeeded in some degree. New perplexities, however, continued to way-lay him, for he was throughout his whole life the prey of witches and evil spirits; and though he wrecked due vengeance on many, they still continued to harass him the more.

After high mass he had retired to his chamber to meditate, when the nobleman in waiting came in, and said, that a stranger wanted to speak with him on some urgent business. He was introduced, and any one may judge of the king's astonishment, when he saw that it was the identical old man who had spoken to him on the mountain, and vanished, the day before. The king's lip grew pale, and quivered as the stranger made his obeisance.

"Thou herald of danger, treason, and confusion, what seekest thou again with me?" said the king.

"I come, my liege," said he, "to seek redress for the injured, and justice on the offenders. Your two favourite hounds came last night to the houses of two widows in Newstead, and have carried off their two children from their bosoms, which they have doubtlessly devoured, as no traces of them can be found."

"Thou art a liar!" said the king, "and an inventor of lies, if not the father of them; for these two dogs were locked up with me in my chamber last night, and a guard placed on the door, so that what you aver is impossible."

"I declare to your majesty," said the stranger, "by the truth of that right hand, that I myself saw the two hounds at liberty this morning at daylight. I saw them come along the Monk's Meadow, carrying something across on their necks."

"It is easy to prove the falsehood of all that thou hast said," replied the king; "and thy malicious intent shall not go unpunished."

He then called in the guards, and bade them declare before that audacious stranger, if his two white hounds, Mooly and Scratch, were not in his chamber all the night. The guards were mute, and looked one to another.

"Why are you ashamed to declare the truth?" said the king to them. "Say, were the two hounds in my chamber all night, or were they not?"

The men answered, "that the hounds were certainly out. How it came they knew not, but that they were let in in the morning."

"There is a conspiracy among you again," said the king; "if not to deprive your king of life, to deprive that life of every kind of quiet and social comfort."

"I demand justice," said the stranger, "in the names of two weeping and distracted mothers! In the name of all that is right, and held dear among men! I demand that these two obnoxious and devouring animals be hung upon a tree, or burnt alive before the sun go down. Then shall the men of Scotland see that their sovereign respects their feelings and privileges, even though they run counter to his own pleasures."

"One of these dogs saved my life last night," said the king; "and it is very hard indeed that I should be compelled to do this. I will have better testimony; and if I find that these children have actually been devoured, (as most unlikely it is,) the depredators shall be punished."

The old man bowed, and was preparing to reply, when the knight in waiting entered hastily, and told the king that there was a woman in the outer court, crying bitterly for justice, and who was very urgent to speak with him. The king ordered that she should be admitted, and in a moment she stood before him, pale, shrivelled, hagard, and wild, and altogether such a figure as one scarcely can see, or could see, without the impression that she was scarce earthly. Her appearance was that of a lady of quality, of great age; she had large ear-rings, a tremendous ruff, a headdress of a thousand intricate flutings, projecting before and tapering upward behind, cork-heeled shoes, a low hoop, and a waist of length and stiffness, not to be described.

"Revenge! Revenge! my lord, O king!" cried she. "I crave justice of your majesty—justice, and nothing more. You have two hounds, that came into my house early this morning, and have devoured, or taken away my only daughter, my sole stay and hope in this world, and nothing is left but a part of her garments. These dogs have some power deputed to them that is not of thy giving, therefore grant me that I may see vengeance done upon them, and their bodies burnt at a stake before the going down of the sun."

"That is a true and worthy gentlewoman, my liege," said the old stranger; "and you may take her word for whatever she advances."

The ancient dame turned about—stared on the stranger with wild astonishment—dropped a low courtesy, and then said, "I crave you pardon, my lord and master. I noted not that you were so nigh. I hope your errand here coincides with mine."

"It does," said he; "there are more sufferers than one; and, by the head that bows to thee!—I swear by none greater—we shall have justice if it be in the land!"

"This is a combination," said the king; "I pay no regard to it. Bring witnesses to establish your charges, and you shall have justice done."

They went forth to bring their proof, and behold they had them all in the outer court. In the mean time the king sent for some men of the place to come, and made enquiry of them who the old dame was, and what was the character that she bore. They informed him that she was a noted witch, and kept the whole country in terror and turmoil, and that she had indeed an only daughter, who was an impious and malevolent minx, devoted to every species of wickedness.

"The wrinkled beldame shall be burnt at the stake," said the king. "It is proper that the land should be cleansed of these disturbers of its peace; as for that old stranger, I have my own surmises concerning him, and we shall find a way to deal with his subtilty."

He then sent for a reverend old friar of the name of Rubely, who was well versed in all the minutiæ of diablery and exorcism, whose skill had often been beneficial to the king in the trying and intricate parts of his duty that related to these matters, and with him he conferred on this important subject. Father Rubely desired the king to defer the further examination of these people for a very little while; and, in the mean time, he brought in a basin of holy water, consecrated seven times, and set apart for sacred uses, after which the examination went on, and a curious one it was. The old witch lady deposed, "That as she was lying pondering on her bed, and wide awake, about the dawn of the morning, she heard a curious and uncommon noise somewhere about the house: That, rising, she went out silently to discover what it could be, and to her utter astonishment, beheld the king's two hounds, Mooly and Scratch, spring from her daughter's casement, and in a short space a beautiful roe-deer followed them and bounded away to the Eildons: That she hasted to her daughter's apartment, and found that her darling was gone." The stories of the other two were exactly similar to one another, only that the one blamed one hound, and the other the other. It was as follows: "I was lying awake in the morning very early, with my son in my arms, when one of the king's hounds came into my house. I saw it, and wist not how it had got there. A short time after I heard it making a strange scraping and noise in the other end of the house, on which I arose to turn it out; but on going to the place from whence the sound seemed to come, I found nothing. I searched all the house, and called the hound by her name, but still could find nothing; and at last I lighted a candle and sought all the house over again, without being able to discover any traces of her. I went back to return to my bed, wondering greatly what had become of the animal; but having opened the door before to let her make her escape, I conceived that she had stolen off without my having perceived it. At that very instant, however, I beheld her coming softly out of the bed where I had left my child, and in a moment she was out at the door and away. I ran to the bed with the light in my hand, but my dear child was gone, and no part, not even a palm of his hand, remaining!"

Ques. "Was there any blood in the bed, or any symptoms of the child having been devoured?"

A. "No; I could discover none."

Q. "Did the hound appear to have any thing carrying in her mouth, or otherwise, when she escaped from the house?"

A. "No; I did not notice that she had any thing."

Q. "Was there any thing else in the house at the time; any other appearance that you could not account for?"

A. "Yes; there was something like a leveret followed her out at the door, but I paid no regard to it."

Q. "Was the child baptised in a Christian church?" (No answer.)

Q. "Were you yourself ever baptised in a Christian church?" (No answer.)

Q. "Why do you not answer to these things?"

A. "Because I see no connection that they have with the matter in question."

"None in the least," said the old stranger, who still kept by their side.

When the king heard that the answers of the two women were so exactly similar, though the one was examined before the other was brought in, he said,—"This is some infernal combination; they are all of them witches, and their friend there is some warlock or wizard; and they shall all be burnt at the stake together before the going down of the sun."

"It is a judgment worthy of such a monarch," said the stranger.

"Father Rubely," said the king, "you who know all the men in this part of my dominions, Do you know any thing of this old man, who refuseth to give account of himself?"

"I have often seen the face," said Rubely; "but I cannot tell at present from whence he is.—Pray, sir, are you not he who has supplied the monastery with cattle for these many moons?"

"I am the same," said the stranger; "And were they not the best that ever were furnished to the Abbey?"

"They were," said Rubely.

"Were they not exquisite and delicious above all food ever before tasted?" said the old man.

"They were indeed," said Rubely; "and I think I have heard it reported that no one ever knew from whence you brought these cattle."

"I knew myself," said the stranger, "and that was sufficient for me."

"I have heard of this before," said the king, "and I think I divine something of the matter. Tell me, I insist on it, from whence you brought these cattle?"

"I brought them from among the poor and the indigent," said the old man, "on whom kings and priests for ever feed. For Christian carrion, I provide food from among themselves."

"They shall all be worried and burnt at the stake," said the king; "and this man's torments shall be doubled."

"Have patience, my lord, O king," said Rubely, "and let us not destroy the reclaimable with those of whom there is no hope." Then going near to the first woman who had lost her son, he said to her,—"It is better to do well late than never—are you content to be baptised even now?"

The woman bowed consent. He put the same question to the other, who bowed likewise. The old man stood close by their side, and appeared to be in great trouble and wrath. Rubely brought his goblet of consecrated water, and, as he passed, he threw a portion of it on the wrinkled face of the old man, pronouncing, at the same time, the sacred words of baptism. The whole form and visage of the creature was changed in a moment to that of a furious fiend: He uttered a yell that made all the Abbey shake to its foundations, and forthwith darted away into the air, wrapt in flame; and, as he ascended, he heaved his right hand, and shook his fiery locks at his inquisitors. The old withered beldame yelped forth hysteric gigglings, something between laughing and shrieks—the king fell on his knees, clasped the rood and kissed it—the two women trembled—and even old Rubely counted his beads, and stood for a short space in mute astonishment. He next proposed trying the same experiment with the old witch lady, but she resisted it so furiously, with cursing and blasphemy, that they abandoned her to her fate, and had her burnt at St. Miles's Cross before the going down of the sun. It was said by some that the old stranger appeared among the crowd to witness her latter end; and that she stretched out her hands towards him, with loud supplications, but he only flouted and mocked at her, and seemed to enjoy the sport with great zest. When Father Rubely heard of this, he said that it would happen so to every one who sold themselves to be slaves of sin in the hour of their extremity.

The other two women confessed their sins, and received absolution. They acknowledged that they had been acquainted with the stranger for a long season; that he had often pressed them to sign and seal, which they had always declined, but that nevertheless he had such an influence over them, that he in a manner led them as he pleased; that at first they took him for a venerable apostle, but at length discovered that he was a powerful sorcerer, and could turn people into the shapes of such beasts as he pleased, but that they never knew he was the devil till then.

Friar Rubely assured them, that it was only such as slighted church-ordinances over whom he was permitted to exert that power, and in this the king passionately acquiesced. They confessed farther, that they were still greatly afraid of him, for that he could turn himself into any shape or form that he pleased; that he had often tempted them in the form of a beautiful young man; and there was nothing more common with him than to tempt men in the form of a lovely and bewitching woman, by which means he had of late got many of them into his clutches. When the king heard that, he counted his beads with redoubled fervency, and again kissed the rood, for it reminded him of a lovely vision he had seen of late, as well as some things of a former day. The women added, that the stranger had of late complained grievously of two mongrel spirits, who had opposed and coun-teracted him in every movement; and that they had done it so effectually, that, for every weak Christian that he had overcome and devoured, they had found means to destroy one of his servants, or emissaries, so that his power in the land remained much upon a par as in former times, although his means and exertions had both been increased sevenfold.*

A consultation of holy men was next called, and measures adopted for the recovery of the two children. There it was resolved, that prayers should be offered up for them in seven times seven holy chapels and cells at the same instant of time, and the like number of masses said, with all due solemnity; and that then it would be out of the power of all the spirits of the infernal regions—all of them that were permitted to roam the earth, or any of their agents, to detain the children longer, into whatever shape or form they might change them. But for these solemnities some delay was necessary.

CHAPTER IV

Great was the consumpt of victuals at the Abbey during the stay of the royal visitor!—the parsimonious brethren were confounded, and judged

---

* From several parts of this traditionary tale it would appear, that it is a floating fragment of some ancient allegorical romance, the drift of which it is not easy to comprehend.

that the country would to a certainty be eaten up, and a dearth of all the necessaries of life ensue on the Border. When they beheld the immense droves of bullocks—the loads of wild hogs and fallow-deer that arrived daily from the royal forests of Ettrick and the mountains of the Lowes, together with the flocks of fat black-headed wedders,—they pressed their hands upon their lank sides, looked at their spare forms, and at one another; but not daring to make any verbal remarks, they only shaked their heads, and looked up to heaven!

Victuals were again wearing short. Gudgel, the fat caterer for that immense establishment, was out riding from morn till even in search of fat things; he delighted in the very sight of a well-fed sleek animal; it was health to his stomach, and marrow to his bones. It was observed, that, whenever he came in sight of one, he stroaked down his immense protuberance of paunch with both hands, and smacked his lips. He had been out the whole day, and was very hungry; and when hungry, he enjoyed the sight of a fat animal most. Gudgel certainly fed by the eye as well as the mouth; for it was noted, that when he was very hungry, he would have given the yeomen any price for a well-fed beast.

He had been out the whole day—had procured but little stuff, and that not of the first metal—but, on his way home, he heard of a fine well-fed boar at Eildon-Hall; so he rode off the road, and alighted to take a look of him. In a little triangular inclosure, at one corner of the yard, there he beheld the notable boar lying at his ease, with Mumps in his bosom. Of the dog he took no notice, but the sight of the boar exhilarated him; he drew in a great mouthful of breath, closed his lips, puffed out his cheeks, and made his two hands descend with a semi-circular sweep slowly down over the buttons of his doublet. It is impossible to tell how much the sight of such a carcase delighted Gudgel!—Immoderately fat himself, his eye feasted on every thing that was so; he could not even pass by a corpulent man, nor a pampered overgrown matron, without fixing a keen glance upon them, as if calculating exactly, or to a nearness, how much they would weigh, sinking offal.

"Oh, gracious heaven! what a fine hog! Goodman Fletcher, could you think of putting such a delicious morsel as that by your masters? For shame, goodman, not to let me know before this time of such a prize as this!—The very thing!—No words: the hog is mine. Name your price— Good security, Goodman Fletcher—a king and a priest—I am so glad I have found him—I'll have him slaughtered, and cut neatly up, as I shall direct, before I leave the house."

A piece of sad news this for the poor boar! (Croudy the shepherd, that once was.) When Gudgel pronounced the last sentence, the animal sprung to his feet, gave a great snuff, and grunted out a moan that would have pierced any heart but Gudgel's. "St. Elijah!" said he, "what a fine animal!" and gave him a lash with his whip as he rose. Mumps snarled, and tried to bite the voluptuary in return for the unprovoked attack on his master.

Precisely about the same time that Gudgel alighted at Eildon-Hall, the two lovely and mysterious sisters met at their accustomed place in the Abbey Walk, for it chanced to be the few minutes of their appearance in mortal frame. Their eyes had still the wild unearthly dash of sublimity in them; and human eye could not scan to which state of existence they pertained, but their miens were more beautiful and serene than when they last met.

"I give you joy, dear sister," said the one, "of our happy release! Our adversary is baffled and driven from his usurped habitation—Our woeful work of annihilation will henceforth cease, for the evil principle shall not, as we dreaded, prevail in this little world of man, in which we have received for a time a willing charge. Say what more is to be done before we leave these green hills and the Eildon Tree."

"Much is yet to be done, my beloved Ellen," answered the other. "As I was this day traversing the air in the form of a wild swan, I saw the Borderers coming down in full array, with a Chieftain of most undaunted might at their head. We must find means to warn the haughty Douglas, else they will cut his whole retinue to pieces; and the protector of the faithful must not fall into the hands of such men as these."

"He hath preyed on the vitals of his subjects," said she that spoke first; and as she spoke she fixed her eyes on the ground in a thoughtful attitude.

"It is meet he should," said the other—"And think ye he will not meet with his guerdon better where he is than among these freemen of the Border? Think not so seriously of this matter, for it will not abide a thought—from the spider to the king, all live upon one another!—What numbers one overgrown reptile must devour, to keep the balance of nature in equipoise!"

The two lovely sisters, as she spoke this, held each other by the hand; their angelic forms were bent gently forward, and their faces toward the ground; but as they lifted these with a soft movement towards heaven, a tear was glistening in each eye. Whether these had their source from the fountain of human feelings, or from one more sublimed and pure, no man to this day can determine.

"And then what is to become of the two little changelings?" said the last speaker. "All the spells of priests and friars will avail nought without our aid.—And the wild roe-deer?—And the boar of Eildon? He, I suppose, may take his fate—he is not worthy our care farther.—A selfish grovelling thing, that had much more of the brute than the man (as he should be) at first—without one principle of the heart that is worthy of preservation."

"You are ever inclined to be severe," said the other. "If you but saw the guise in which he is lying with his faithful dog. I think your heart would be moved to pity."

"If I thought there was one spark of the heavenly principle of gratitude in his heart, even to his dog," said she, "I would again renovate his frame to that image which he degraded; but I do not believe it.—Mere selfishness, because he cannot live without his dog."

"Here is Philamy's rod," answered the other, "go, and reconnoitre for yourself, and as you feel so act."

She took the golden wand, and went away toward Eildon-Hall; but her motion over the fields was like a thing sailing on the wind. The other glided away into the beechen grove, for there were voices heard approaching.

"Let us proceed to business, Goodman Fletcher," said Gudgel. "I insist on seeing that fine animal properly slaughtered, blooded, and cut up, before I go away. I have a man who will do it in the nicest style you ever beheld." The boar looked pitifully to Gudgel, and moaned so loud that Mumps fell a howling. "And I'll tell you what we'll do," continued Gudgel; "we'll have his kidneys roasted on a brander laid on the coals, and a stake cut from the inside of the shoulder.—How delicious they will be!—Pooh! I wish they were ready just now—But we'll not be long—And we'll have a bottle of your March beer to accompany them.—Eh? Your charge may well afford that, goodman—Eh?"

The boar made a most determined resistance; and it was not till after he was quite spent, and more hands had been procured, that he was dragged at last forcibly to the slaughter-house, and laid upon the killing-stool, with ropes tied round his legs; these they were afraid were scarcely strong enough, and at the request of the butcher, Pery lent her garters to strengthen the tie. Never was there a poor beast in such circumstances! He screamed so incessantly that he even made matters worse. His very heart was like to break when he saw Pery lend her garters to assist in binding him. Mumps was very sorry too; he whined and whimpered, and kissed his braying friend.

The noise became so rending to the ears, that all who were present retired for a little, until the monster should be silenced. The butcher came up with his bleeding-knife, in shape like an Andro Ferrara, and fully half as long—felt for the boar's jugular vein, and then tried the edge and point of his knife against his nail—"He has a hide like the soal of a shoe," said the butcher; "I must take care and sort him neatly." And so saying he went round the corner of the house to give his knife a whet on the grinding-stone.

At that very instant the beautiful angelic nymph with the golden rod came into the courtyard at Eildon-Hall, and hearing the outrageous cries in the slaughter-house, she looked in as she was passing, that being the outermost house in the square. There she beheld the woful plight of the poor boar, and could not help smiling; but when she saw honest Mumps standing wagging his tail, with his cheek pressed to that of the struggling panting victim, and always now and then gently kissing him, her heart was melted with pity. The dog cast the most beseeching look at her as she approached, which when she saw her resolution was fixed. She gave the monster three strokes with her wand, at each of which he uttered a loud squeak; but when these were done, and some mystic words of powerful charm uttered, in half a quarter of a minute there lay—no bristly boar—but the identical Croudy the shepherd! in the same garb as when transformed at the Moss Thorn; only that his hands and feet were bound with straw ropes, strengthened and secured by the cruel Pery's red garters.

"Bless me an' my horn!" said Croudy, as he raised up his head from the spokes of the killing-stool; "I believe I'm turned mysel again!—I wad like to ken wha the bonny queen is that has done this; but I'm sair mistaen gin I didna see the queen o' the fairies jink by the corner. I wonder gin the bloody hash will persist in killing me now. I'm fear'd Gudgel winna can pit aff wantin' his pork steaks. May Saint Abednego be my shield, gin I didna think I fand my ears birstling on a brander!"

The butcher came back, singing to himself the following verse, to the tune of *Tibby Fowler*, which augured not well for Croudy.

> "Beef stakes and bacon hams
> I can eat as lang's I'm able;
> Cutlets, chops, or mutton pies,
> Pork's the king of a' the table."

As he sung this he was still examining the edge of his knife, so that he came close to his intended victim, without once observing the change that had taken place.

"Gude e'en t'ye, neighbour," said Croudy.

The butcher made an involuntary convulsive spring, as if a thunder-bolt had struck him and knocked him away about six yards at one stroke. There he stood and stared at what he now saw lying bound with the ropes and garters, and the dog still standing by. The knife fell out of his hand—his jaws fell down on his breast, and his eyes rolled in their sockets.—"L—d G—d!" cried the butcher, as loud as he could roar, and ran through the yard, never letting one bellow abide another.

The servants met him, asking what was the matter—"Was he cut? Had he sticked or wounded himself?"

He regarded none of their questions; but dashing them aside, ran on, uttering the same passionate ejaculation with all the power that the extreme of horror could give to such a voice. Gudgel beheld him from a window, and meeting him in the entry to the house, he knocked him down. "I'll make you stop, you scoundrel," said he, "and tell me what all this affray means."

"O L—d, sir! the boar—the boar!" exclaimed the butcher as he raised himself with one arm from the ground, and defended his head with the other.

"The boar, you blockhead!" said Gudgel,—"what of the boar? Is he not like to turn well out?"

"He turns out to be the devil, sir—gang an' see, gang an see," said the butcher.

Gudgel gave him another rap with his stick, swearing that they would not get their brandered kidneys, and pork steak from the inside of the shoulder, in any reasonable time, by the madness and absurdity of that fellow, and waddled away to the slaughter-house as fast as his posts of legs could carry him. When he came there, and found a booby of a clown lying bound on the killing-stool, instead of his highly esteemed hog, he was utterly confounded, and wist not what to say, or how to express himself. He was in a monstrous rage, but he knew not on whom to vend it, his greasy wits being so completely bemired, that they were incapable of moving, turning, or comprehending any thing farther than a grievous sensation of a want not likely to be supplied by the delicious roasted kidneys, and pork steak from the inside of the shoulder. He turned twice round, puffing and gasping for breath, and always apparently looking for something he supposed he had lost, but as yet never uttering a distinct word.

The rest of the people were soon all around him—the Goodman, Pery, Gale, and the whole household of Eildon-Hall were there, all standing gaping with dismay, and only detained from precipitate flight by the presence of one another. The defrauded Gudgel first found expression—"Where is my hog, you scoundrel?" cried he, in a tone of rage and despair.

"Ye see a' that's to the fore o' him," said Croudy.

"I say, where is my hog, you abominable caitiff?—You miserable wretch!—you ugly whelp of a beast!—tell me what you have made of my precious hog?"

"Me made o' him!" said Croudy, "I made naething o' him; but some ane, ye see, has made a man o' him—It was nae swine, but me.—I tell ye, that ye see here a' that's to the fore o' him."

"Oh! oh!" groaned Gudgel, and he stroked down his immense flanks three or four times, every one time harder than the last. "Pooh! so then I am cheated, and betrayed, and deceived; and I shall have nothing to eat!—nothing to eat!—nothing to eat!—Goodman Fletcher, you shall answer for this;—and you, friend beast or swine, or warlock, or whatever you may be, shall not 'scape for nought;" and, so saying, he began to belabour Croudy with his staff who cried out lustily; and it was remarked somewhat in the same style and tenor, too, as he exhibited lately in a different capacity.

The rest of the people restrained the disappointed glutton from putting an end to the poor clown; and notwithstanding that appearances were strangely against him, yet, so well were they accustomed to Croudy's innocent and stupid face, that they loosed him with trembling hands, Pery being as active in the work as any, untying her red garters. "I know the very knots," said she,—"No one can tie them but myself."

"By the Rood, my woman! gin I war but up, I'll *knot* you weel eneuch," said Croudy; and if he had not been withheld by main force, he would have torn out her hair and her eyes. He, however, accused her of being a witch, and took witnesses on it; and said, he would make oath that she had changed him into a boar on such an evening at the Moss Thorn.

Pery only laughed at the accusation, but all the rest saw it in a different light. They all saw plainly that Croudy had been metamorphosed for a time by some power of witchcraft or enchantment—they remembered how Mumps had still continued to recognise and acknowledge him in that degraded state; and hearing, as they did, his bold and intrepid accusal of Pery, they all judged that it would stand very hard with her.

When Gudgel had heard all this, he seized the first opportunity of taking Pery aside, and proposed to her, for the sake of her own preservation, instantly to change the clown again; "And, as it is all one to you," said he, "suppose you make him a little fatter—if you do so, I shall keep your secret—if you do not, you may stand the consequences."

Pery bade him, "Look to himself,—keep the secret, or not keep it, as he chose;—there were some others, who should be nameless, that were as well worth changing as Croudy."

Gudgel's peril appeared to him now so obvious, and the consequences so horrible, that his whole frame became paralysed from head to foot. In proportion with his delight in killing and eating the fat things of the earth, did his mind revolt at being killed and eaten himself; and when he thought of what he had just witnessed, he little wist how soon it might be his fate. He rode away from Eildon-Hall a great deal more hungry and more miserable than he came. The tale, however, soon spread, with many aggravations; and the ill-starred Pery was taken up for a witch, examined, and committed to prison in order to stand her trial; and in the mean time the evidences against her were collected.

CHAPTER V
The Keylan Rowe

An' round, an' round, an' seven times round,
    An' round about the Eildon tree!
For there the ground is fairy ground,
    And the dark green ring is on the lea.

The prayers were pray'd, and the masses said,
    And the waning Moon was rising slow;
And ane dame sits at the Eildon-tree,
    Whose cheike is pale as April snow.

Ane cross is claspit in her hand,
    Ane other lyis on her breiste bone;
And the glaize of feire is on her ee,
    As she looks to the Eildon-stone.

And aye she sung her holy hymn;
    It was made to charm the elfin band,
And lure the little wilderit things,
    Whose dwelling is in Fairy-land.

And first she heard the horses' tread,
    Like drifting leaves come through the dell;
And then she heard their bridles ring,
    Like rain drops tinkling on a bell.

Then the wild huntsmen first came on,
    An' sic ane band was never seen!
Some wanted cheike, some wanted chin,
    And some had nouthir nose nor een;

One had ane ee in his forehead,
    That ee was like ane glaizit pole;
His breiste was like ane heck of hay;
    His gobe ane rounde and boral hole.

And ilk ane held ane bugle horn,
    And loud they toutit as they gaed by—
"Ycho! ycho! The Keylan Rowe!
    Hie to the weird-hill! huntsmen hie!

"The little wee hare o' Eildon Brae
    May trip it o'er the glen, O;
But nane shall bear the prize away,
    But Keylan and his men, O.

"Gil-Mouly's raid, and Keylan's Rowe,
    Shall sweep the moore and lea, O;
And the little wee hare o' Eildon Brae
    In heaven shall never be, O.

"O'er wizard ground, with horse and hound,
    Like rattling hail we'll bear, O—
Ycho! ycho! The Keylan Rowe!
    The quick and dead are here, O!"

Then came their collarit phantom tykis,
    Like ouf-dogs, an' like gaspin grews;
An' their crukit tungis were dry for blood,
    An' the red lowe firled at their flews;

Then came the troopis of the Fairy folke,
    And O they wore ane lovely hue!
Their robes were greine like the hollin leife,
    And thin as the web of the wiry dew.

And first went by the coal-black steedis,
    And then a troop o' the bonny bay;
And then the milk-white bandis came on,
    An' last the mooned and the merlit gray.

An', aye the song, an' the bridles rang,
    As they rode lightly rank an' file;
It was like the sound of ane maydenis voice
    Heard through the greene-wood many a mile.

"Hey, Gil-Mouly! Ho, Gil-Mouly!
    On we fly o'er steep and stile!
Hey, Gil-Mouly! Ho, Gil-Mouly!
    Hunt the hare another mile.

"Over fen and over fountain,
    Over downe and dusky lea;
Over moss, and moore, and mountain,
    We will follow, follow thee!

"O'er the dewy vales of even,
    Over tower and over tree;
O'er the clouds and clefts of heaven,
    We will follow, follow thee!

"Nae mair the dame shall young son rock,
    And sing her lilli-lu the while;
Hey, Gil-Mouly! Ho, Gil-Mouly!
    Hunt the hare another mile!"

The phantom huntsmen scaled the steeps,
    "Ycho! ycho! for Keylan's fame."
The Fairy barbs were light and fleet;
    The chirling echoes went and came.

The roe fled into the greine-woode,
    The dun deire boundit far away;
But nought wald serve the hunteris rude,
    But the little wee hare o' Eildon-Brae.

She heard, she knew, an' sped alone,
    Away, away, with panting breiste;
The fairy houndis are lilting on,
    Like Redwings wheepling through the mist.

Around, around the Eildons greine,
    Dashit the wild huntsmen furiouslye!
Och! sic ane night was never seine,
    Sin' Michael cleft these hills in three!

The sky was bright, and the dame beheld
    The brattling chace o'er moonlight brow;
Then in the darksome shade they rushit,
    With yelp, and yowle, and loud halloo.

O, but the little Fairy grews
    Swept lightly o'er the Eildon-Brae;
The houndis came youffing up behind,
    As fast as they could win their way.

And the wild huntsmen's gruesome tykis
    All urgit the chace, but stop or stande.
"Ycho! ycho! The Keylan Rowe!
    For earth, an' death, or Fairy-lande!"

The dame she claspit the halye roode,
    And dreddour wilde was in her ee;
And round, and round, and seven times round,
    And round about the Eildon-Tree!

The hunt still near and nearer drew—
    Weel moght the matronis herte be wae!
For hard they pressit, and aft they turnit
    The little wee hare o' Eildon-Brae.

They mouthit her aince, they mouthit her twice;
    Loud did she scream throu fear and dread;
That scream was like ane bairnyis cry
    Quhen it is piercit in cradle-bed.

But the dame behelde ane bonny hounde,
    White as the newly driftit snaw,
That close beside the leveret kept,
    And wore the elfin grews awa.

Hard did she toil the hare to save,
    For the little wee hare was sair foreworne;
And the ghaistly huntsmen gatherit on,
    With whoop, and whoo, and bugle-horne.

O but the hounde was hard bestedd!
    For round and round they harder press'd,—
At length, beneath the Eildon-Tree,
    The little wee leveret found its rest.

It sprung into the matronis lap,
    Wha row'd it in her kirtle gray;
And round, and round, came horse and hound,
    With snort, and neigh, and howl, and bay.

But the white hounde stood by her side,
    And wore them back full powerfullye;
And round, and round, and seven times round,
    And round about the Eildon-Tree!

They turn'd the hare within her arms
    A cockatrice and adder sterne;
They turn'd the hare within her arms
    A flittering reide het gaud o' ern.

But still within her kirtle row'd,
    She sung her hymn and held it fast;
And ere the seventh time round was won,
    Her child clung to his parent's breast.

"Ycho! ycho! The Keylan Rowe;"
    Away the fairy music sped,
"The day is lost, a maid has wonne,
    The babe maun lie amang the dead.

"The babe maun grow as grass has grown,
     And live, and die, and live anew,
Ycho! ycho! The Keylan Rowe
     Must vanish like the morning dew."

CHAPTER VI

As the beautiful fairy-dame, or guardian spirit, or whatever she was, had predicted, so it came to pass. The Borderers, alarmed at the danger of the king, came down a thousand strong, thinking to surprise Douglas, and take their monarch out of his hands by force; and they would have effected it with ease, had not the Earl received some secret intelligence of their design. No one ever knew whence he had this intelligence, nor could he comprehend or explain it himself, but it had the effect of defeating the bold and heroic attempt. They found him fully prepared—a desperate battle ensued—120 men were left dead on the field—and then things remained precisely in the same state as they had been before.

The court left Melrose shortly after—the king felt as if he stood on uncertain ground—a sort of mystery always hung around him, which he never could develope; but ere he went, he presided at the trial of the maiden Pery, who stood indicted, as the *Choronikkle of Mailros* bears, for being "Ane ranke wytche and enchaunteresse, and leigged hand and kneife with the devil."

A secret examination of the parties first took place, and the proof was so strong against the hapless Pery, that all hopes of escape vanished. There was Croudy ready to make oath to the truth of all that he had advanced with regard to his transmutation, and there were others who had seen her coming down from the Moss-Thorn at the very time that Croudy appeared to have been changed, just before he made his dashing entry into the loan among the cows; and even old Father Rubely had, after minute investigation, discovered the witch-mark, both on her neck and thumb-nail. The king would gladly have saved her, when he beheld her youth and beauty, but he had sworn to rid the country of witches, and no excuse could be found.

All the people of the country were sorry on account of Pery, but all believed her guilty, and avoided her, except Gale, who, having had the courage to visit her, tried her with the repetition of prayers and creeds, and found that she not only said them without hesitation, but with great devotional warmth; therefore he became convinced that she was not a witch. She told him her tale with that simplicity, that he could not disbelieve it, and withal confessed, that her inquisitors had very nearly convinced her that she was a witch; and that she was on the point of making a confession that had not the slightest foundation in truth. The shepherd was more enlightened than the worthy clergyman, as shepherds generally are, and accounted for this phenomenon in a truly philosophical way. Pery assented; for whatever Gale said sounded to her heart as the sweetest and most sensible thing that ever was said. She loved him to distraction, and adversity had subtilised, not abated the flame. Gale found his heart interested—he pitied her, and pity is allied to love. How to account for the transformation of Croudy, both were completely at a loss; but they agreed that it was the age of witchery, and no one could say what might happen! Gale was never from the poor culprit's side: He condoled with her—wept over her—and even took her in his arms, and impressed a tender kiss on her pale lips. It was the happiest moment of Pery's existence! She declared, that since she was pure in his eyes, she would not only suffer without repining, but with delight.

As a last resource, Gale sought out Croudy, and tried to work upon him to give a different evidence at the last and final trial; but all that he could say, Croudy remained obstinately bent on her destruction.

"It's needless for ye to waste your wind clatterin English, man," said Croudy, "for foul fa' my gab gin I say ony sic word. She didna only change me intil an ill-faurd he-sow, but guidit me shamefully ill a' the time I was a goossy—kickit me wi' her fit, an' yerkit me wi' a rung till I squeeled, and then leuch at me—An' warst ava, gae the butcher her gairtens to bind me, that he might get me bled, an' plottit, an' made into beef-steaks—de'il be on her gin I be nae about wi' her now!"

Gale, hoping that he would relent if he saw her woeful plight, besought of him to go and see her; but this he absolutely refused, for fear lest she should "turn him into some daft-like beast," as he expressed it. "Let her tak it," said he, "she weel deserves a' that she's gaun to get—the sooner she gets a fry the better—Odd, there's nae body sure o' himsel a minute that's near her—I never gang ower the door but I think I'll come in a goossy or a cuddy-ass—How wad ye like to gang plowin up the gittars for worms and dockan-roots wi' your nose, as I did!"

It was in vain that Gale assured him of her innocence, and told him how religious she was, and how well she loved him. Croudy remained obstinate.

"I wadna gie a boddle," said he, "for a woman's religion, nor for her love neither—mere traps for moudiworts. They may gar a fool like you trow that ae thing's twa, an' his lug half a bannock—Gin I wad rue an' save her life, it wadna be lang till I saw her carrying you out like a taed in the ernt-ings, an' thrawin ye ower the ass-midden."

Gale asked if he would save her, if she would pledge herself to marry him, and love him for ever?

"Me marry a witch!" said Croudy—"A bonny hand she would make o' me, sooth! Whenever I displeased her, turn me into a beast—But ilka woman has that power," added he with a grin,—"an' I fancy few o' them mislippin it. The first kind thought I ever had toward a woman made a beast o' me—an' it will do the same wi' every man as weel as me, gin he wist it. As she has made her bed, she may lie down. I shall fling a sprot to the lowe."

Gale was obliged to give him up, but in the deepest bitterness of soul he gave him his malison, which, he assured him, would not fall to the ground. Pery was tried, and condemned to be choaked and burnt at the stake on the following day; and Croudy, instead of relenting, was so much afraid of himself, that he was all impatience until the cruel scene should be acted. His behaviour had, however, been witnessed and detested by some of whom he was not aware; for that very evening, as he was on his way home, he beheld a nymph coming to meet him, whom he took for Pery, dressed in her Sunday clothes, for one of the mysterious maids had taken her form. He was terrified out of his wits when he beheld her at liberty, and falling flat on his face, he besought her, with a loud voice, to have mercy on him.

"Such as you have bestowed," said she; and giving him three strokes with her wand, he was changed into a strong brindled cat, in which form he remains to this day; and the place of his abode is no secret to the relater of this tale. He hath power one certain night in the year to resume his natural shape, and all the functions of humanity; and that night he dedicates to the relation of the adventures of each preceding year. Many a secret and unsuspected amour, and many a strange domestic scene, hath he witnessed, in his capacity of mouser, through so many generations; and a part of these are now in the hands of a gentleman of this country, who intends making a good use of them.

Poor Pery, having thus fallen a victim to the superstition of the times, she wist not how, was pitied and shunned by all except Gale, whom nothing could tear from her side; and all the last day and night that were destined for her to live, they lay clasped in each other's arms. While they were thus conversing in the most tender and affectionate way, Pery told her lover a dream that she had seen the night before. She dreamed, she said, that they were changed into two beautiful birds, and had escaped away into a wild and delightful mountain, where they lived in undecaying happiness and felicity, and fed on the purple blooms of the heath.

"O that some pitying power—some guardian angel over the just and the good, would but do this for us!" said Gale, "and release my dearest Pery from this ignominious death!" and as he said this, he clasped his beloved maiden closer and closer in his arms. They both wept, and, in this position, they sobbed themselves sound asleep.

Next morning, before the rising of the sun, two young ladies, beautiful as cherubs, came to the jailor, and asked admittance to the prisoner, by order of the king. The jailor took off his bonnet, bowed his grey head, and opened to them. The two lovers were still fast asleep, locked in each other's arms, in a way so endearing, and at the same time so modest, that the two sisters stood for a considerable time bending over them in delightful amazement.

"There is a delicacy and a pathos in this love," said the one, "into which the joys of sense have shed no ingredient. As their innocence in life hath been, so shall it remain;" and kneeling down, she gave three gentle strokes with her small golden rod, touching both with it at a time. The two lovers trembled, and seemed to be in slight convulsions; and in a short time they fluttered round the floor two beautiful moor-fowl, light of heart, and elated with joy. The two lovely and mysterious visitors then took them up, wrapt them in their snowy veils, and departed, each of them carrying one; and coming to Saint Michael's Cross, they there dismissed them from their palms, after addressing them severally as follows:

> "Hie thee away, my bonny moor-hen!
> Keep to the south of the Skelf-hill Pen;
> Blithe be thy heart, and soft thy bed,
> Amang the blooms of the heather so red.
> When the weird is sped that I must dree,
> I'll come and dwell in the wild with thee.
> Keep thee afar from the fowler's ken—
> Hie thee away, my bonny moor-hen."

> "Cock of the mountain, and king of the moor,
> A maiden's bennison be thy dower;
> For gentle and kind hath been thy life,
> Free from malice, and free from strife.
> Light be thy heart on the mountain grey,
> And loud thy note at the break of day.
> When five times fifty years are gone,
> I'll seek thee again 'mong the heath alone,
> And change thy form, if that age shall prove
> An age that virtue and truth can love.
> True be thy love, and far thy reign,
> On the Border dale, till I see thee again."

When the jailor related what had happened, it may well be conceived what consternation prevailed over the whole country. The two moor-fowl were soon discovered on a wild hill in Tiviotdale, where they have remained ever since, until last year, that Wauchope shot the hen. He suspected what he had done, and was extremely sorry, but kept the secret to himself. On viewing the beauty of the bird, however, he said to himself,—"I believe I have liked women as well as any man, but not so well as to eat them; however, I'll play a trick upon some, and see its effect." Accordingly he sent the moor-hen to a friend of his in Edinburgh, at whose table she was divided among a circle of friends and eaten, on the 20th of October 1817, and that was the final end of poor Pery, the Maid of Eildon. The effect on these gentlemen has been prodigious—the whole structure of their minds and feelings has undergone a complete change, and that grievously to the worse; and even their outward forms, on a near inspection, appear to be altered considerably. This change is so notorious as to have become proverbial all over the New Town of Edinburgh. When any one is in a querulous or peevish humour, they say,—"He has got a wing of Wauchope's moor-hen."

The cock is still alive, and well known to all the sportsmen on the Border, his habitation being on the side of Caret Rigg, which no moor-fowl dares to approach. As the five times fifty years are very nearly expired, it is hoped no gentleman will be so thoughtless as wantonly to destroy this wonderful and mysterious bird, and we may then live to have the history of the hunting, the fowling, fishing, and pastoral employments of that district, with all the changes that have taken place for the last two hundred and fifty years, by an eye-witness of them.

The king returned towards Edinburgh on the 14th of September, and on his way had twelve witches condemned and burnt at the Cross of Leader, after which act of duty his conscience became a good deal lightened, and his heart cheered in the ways of goodness; he hoped, likewise, to be rid of the spells of those emissaries of Satan that had beleaguered him all his life.

After they had passed the Esk, his two favourite white hounds were missing; the huntsmen judged them to be following some track, and waited till night, calling them always now and then aloud by their names. They were however lost, and did not return, nor could they ever be found, although called at every Cross in the kingdom, and high rewards offered.

On that very eve Elen and Clara of Rosline returned to their native halls, after having been lost for seven weeks. They came to the verge of the tall cliff towards the east, from whence they had a view of the stately towers of Rosline, then in their pride of baronial strength. The sun had shed his last ray from the summit of the distant Ochils; the Esk murmured in obscurity far below their feet; its peaceful bendings here and there appeared through the profusion of woodland foliage, uniting the brightness of crystal with the hues of the raven. All the linns and woody banks of the river re-echoed the notes of the feathered choir. To have looked on such a scene, one might have conceived that he dwelt in a world where there was neither sin nor sorrow; but, alas! the imperfections of our nature cling to us; they wind themselves round the fibres of the conscious heart, so that no draught of pure and untainted delight can ever allay its immortal earnings. How different would such a scene appear to perfect and sinless creatures, whose destiny did not subject them to the terrors of death, and the hideous and mouldy recesses of the grave! Were it possible for us to conceive that two such beings indeed looked on it, we might form some idea of their feelings, and even these faint ideas would lend a triple grandeur and beauty to such an evening, and indeed to every varied scene of nature, on which our eyes chanced to rest.

"Sister," said Clara, "we are again in sight of our native home, and the walks of our days of innocence; say, are our earthly forms and affections to be resumed, or are our bonds with humanity to be broken for ever? You have now witnessed the king of Scotland's private life—all his moods, passions, and affections—are you content to be his queen, and sovereign of the realm?"

"Sooner would I be a worm that crawls among these weeds, than subject myself to the embraces, humours, and caprices of such a thing—A king is a block, and his queen a puppet—happiness, truth, and purity of heart are there unknown—Mention some other tie to nature, or let us bid it adieu for ever without a sigh."

"We have a widowed mother, beautiful, affectionate, and kind."

"That is the only bond with mortality which I find it difficult to break, for it is a wicked and licentious world—snares were laid for us on every side—our innocence was no shield—and, sister, do not you yet tremble to think of the whirlpool of conflicting passions and follies from which we were so timeously borne away?"

The lovely Clara bowed assent; and away they went hand in hand once more to visit and embrace their earthly parent. They found her in the arms of a rude and imperious pirate, to whom she had subjected herself and her wide domains. They found themselves step-daughters in the halls that of right belonged to them, and instead of fond love and affection, regarded with jealousy and hate. Short and sorrowful was their stay; they embraced their mother once again; bade her farewell with looks of sorrow, and walking out to the fairy ring in the verge of the wood, vanished from the world for ever. It is said, that once in every seven years their forms are still to be seen hovering nigh to the ruins of Rosline. Many are the wild and incomprehensible traditions that remain of them over the country, and there are likewise some romantic scraps of song, besides the verses that are preserved in the foregoing chapter, which are supposed to relate to them. Many have heard the following verses chaunted to a tune resembling a dirge:

"Lang may our king look,
      An' sair mot he rue;
For the twin flowers o' Rosline
      His hand shall never pu'.
Lie thy lane, step-dame;
      An' liefu' be thy lair;
For the bonny flowers o' Rosline
      Are gane for evermair."

*   *   *   *

52

"O tell nae the news in the kitchen,
    An' tell nae the news in the ha',
An' tell nae the news in the hee hee tower
    Amang our fair ladies a'.
How damp were the dews o' the gloamin',
    How wet were her hose and her shoon;
Or wha met wi' fair Lady Rosline
    By the ee light o' the moon!"

*   *   *   *

"Douglas has lost his bassonet,
    The king his hawk, and milk-white hound;
And merry Maxwell has taen the bent,
    And its hey! and its ho! for the English ground!"

*   *   *   *

"When seven lang years were come an' gane,
    By yon auld castle wa';
There she beheld twa bonny maids
    A playing at the ba;
But wha shall speak to these fair maids
    Aneath the waning moon;
O they maun dree a waesome weird,
    That never will be doone!"

*   *   *   *

THE MURDER HOLE

Catherine Sinclair

Catherine Sinclair (17 April 1800–6 August 1864) was a novelist, children's author and philanthropist who is credited with the discovery that the author of the Waverley Novels was Sir Walter Scott. She was born at 6 Charlotte Square in Edinburgh, now known as Bute House, the official residence of Scotland's First Minister. Her father was Sir John Sinclair, editor of one of the most quoted historical sources, *The Statistical Account of Scotland* (1791–99).

Living in Edinburgh she would travel to London each year during "the season" where she was claimed by all of the fashionable circles of the day. But it was Edinburgh where her presence was most keenly felt. She provided soup kitchens for the poor, subsidised institutions for both underprivileged girls and boys, supplied cabbies with taxi shelters, and launched a campaign to furnish the city with public benches that are still in use to this day. A pamphlet called *Modern Superstitions* was published in 1857. She also founded the very first public drinking fountain in Edinburgh in 1859.

She died at her brother's residence and after her death a subscription was raised to construct a memorial. This gothic spire is located near her childhood home in Queen's Street, on the corner of Albyn Place and North Charlotte Street.

"The Murder Hole" is a little-known story, originally published anonymously in *Blackwood's Magazine* in 1829 and one I originally came across in Marjorie Bowen's *More Great Tales of Horror* (1935) during my formative years. Once read it's never forgotten, and pray you never fall down a small unassuming hole hidden by the long grass.

Ah, frantic Fear!
I see, I see thee near;
I know thy hurried step, thy hagard eye!
Like thee I start, like thee disorder'd fly!

COLLINS

I N a remote district of country belonging to Lord Cassillis, between
Ayrshire and Galloway, about three hundred years ago, a moor of
apparently boundless extent stretched several miles along the road,
and wearied the eye of the traveller by the sameness and desolation of its
appearance; not a tree varied the prospect—not a shrub enlivened the eye
by its freshness—nor a native flower bloomed to adorn this ungenial soil.
One "lonesome desert" reached the horizon on every side, with nothing to
mark that any mortal had ever visited the scene before, except a few rude
huts that were scattered near its centre; and a road, or rather pathway, for
those whom business or necessity obliged to pass in that direction. At length,
deserted as this wild region had always been, it became still more gloomy.
Strange rumours arose, that the path of unwary travellers had been beset
on this "blasted heath," and that treachery and murder had intercepted the
solitary stranger as he traversed its dreary extent. When several persons,
who were known to have passed that way, mysteriously disappeared, the
inquiries of their relatives led to a strict and anxious investigation; but
though the officers of justice were sent to scour the country, and examine
the inhabitants, not a trace could be obtained of the persons in question,
nor of any place of concealment which could be a refuge for the lawless or
desperate to horde in. Yet, as inquiry became stricter, and the disappearance
of individuals more frequent, the simple inhabitants of the neighbouring

hamlet were agitated by the most fearful apprehensions. Some declared that the death-like stillness of the night was often interrupted by sudden and preternatural cries of more than mortal anguish, which seemed to arise in the distance; and a shepherd one evening, who had lost his way on the moor, declared he had approached three mysterious figures, who seemed struggling against each other with supernatural energy, till at length one of them, with a frightful scream, suddenly sunk into the earth.

Gradually the inhabitants deserted their dwellings on the heath, and settled in distant quarters, till at length but one of the cottages continued to be inhabited by an old woman and her two sons, who loudly lamented that poverty chained them to this solitary and mysterious spot. Travellers who frequented this road now generally did so in groups to protect each other; and if night overtook them, they usually stopped at the humble cottage of the old woman and her sons, where cleanliness compensated for the want of luxury, and where, over a blazing fire of peat, the bolder spirits smiled at the imaginary terrors of the road, and the more timid trembled as they listened to the tales of terror and affright with which their hosts entertained them.

One gloomy and tempestuous night in November, a pedlar-boy hastily traversed the moor. Terrified to find himself involved in darkness amidst its boundless wastes, a thousand frightful traditions, connected with this dreary scene, darted across his mind—every blast, as it swept in hollow gusts over the heath, seemed to teem with the sighs of departed spirits— and the birds, as they winged their way above his head, appeared, with loud and shrill cries, to warn him of approaching danger. The whistle with which he usually beguiled his weary pilgrimage died away into silence, and he groped along with trembling and uncertain steps, which sounded too loudly in his ears. The promise of Scripture occurred to his memory, and revived his courage. "I will be unto thee as a rock in the desert, and as an hiding-place in the storm." *Surely*, thought he, *though alone, I am not forsaken*; and a prayer for assistance hovered on his lips.

A light now glimmered in the distance which would lead him, he conjectured, to the cottage of the old woman; and towards that he eagerly bent his way, remembering as he hastened along, that when he had visited it the year before, it was in company with a large party of travellers, who had beguiled the evening with those tales of mystery which had so lately filled his brain with images of terror. He recollected, too, how anxiously the old woman and her sons had endeavoured to detain him when the other travellers were departing; and now, therefore, he confidently anticipated a cordial and cheering reception. His first call for admission obtained no visible marks of attention, but instantly the greatest noise and confusion prevailed within the cottage. They think it is one of the supernatural visitants of whom the old lady talks so much, thought the boy, approaching a window, where the light within shewed him all the inhabitants at their several occupations; the old woman was hastily scrubbing the stone floor, and strewing it thickly over with sand, while her two sons seemed with equal haste to be thrusting something large and heavy into an immense chest, which they carefully locked. The boy, in a frolicsome mood, thoughtlessly tapped at the window, when they all instantly started up with consternation so strongly depicted on their countenances, that he shrunk back involuntarily with an undefined feeling of apprehension; but before he had time to reflect a moment longer, one of the men suddenly darted out at the door, and seizing the boy roughly by the shoulder, dragged him violently into the cottage. "I am not what you take me for," said the boy, attempting to laugh, "but only the poor pedlar who visited you last year." "Are you *alone?*" inquired the old woman, in a harsh deep tone, which made his heart thrill with apprehension. "Yes," said the boy, "I am alone *here*; and alas!" he added, with a burst of uncontrollable feeling, "I am alone in the wide world also! Not a person exists who would assist me in distress, or shed a single tear if I died this very night." "*Then* you are welcome!" said one of the men with a sneer, while he cast a glance of peculiar expression at the other inhabitants of the cottage.

It was with a shiver of apprehension, rather than of cold, that the boy drew towards the fire, and the looks which the old woman and her sons exchanged, made him wish that he had preferred the shelter of any one of the roofless cottages which were scattered near, rather than trust himself among persons of such dubious aspect. Dreadful surmises flitted across his

brain; and terrors which he could neither combat nor examine impercep-
tibly stole into his mind; but alone, and beyond the reach of assistance, he
resolved to smother his suspicions, or at least not increase the danger by
revealing them. The room to which he retired for the night had a confused
and desolate aspect; the curtains seemed to have been violently torn down
from the bed, and still hung in tatters around it—the table seemed to have
been broken by some violent concussion, and the fragments of various
pieces of furniture lay scattered upon the floor. The boy begged that a light
might burn in his apartment till he was asleep, and anxiously examined the
fastenings of the door; but they seemed to have been wrenched asunder on
some former occasion, and were still left rusty and broken.

It was long ere the pedlar attempted to compose his agitated nerves
to rest; but at length his senses began to "steep themselves in forgetful-
ness," though his imagination remained painfully active, and presented
new scenes of terror to his mind, with all the vividness of reality. He fancied himself again wandering on the heath, which appeared to be peopled
with spectres, who all beckoned to him not to enter the cottage, and as he
approached it, they vanished with a hollow and despairing cry. The scene
then changed, and he found himself again seated by the fire, where the
countenances of the men scowled upon him with the most terrifying malig-
nity, and he thought the old woman suddenly seized him by the arms, and
pinioned them to his side. Suddenly the boy was startled from these agitated slumbers, by what sounded to him like a cry of distress; he was broad
awake in a moment, and sat up in bed,—but the noise was not repeated,
and he endeavoured to persuade himself it had only been a continuation
of the fearful images which had disturbed his rest, when, on glancing at
the door, he observed underneath it a broad red stream of blood silently
stealing its course along the floor. Frantic with alarm, it was but the work
of a moment to spring from his bed, and rush to the door, through a chink
of which, his eye nearly dimmed with affright he could watch unsuspected
whatever might be done in the adjoining room.

His fear vanished instantly when he perceived that it was only a *goat*
that they had been slaughtering; and he was about to steal into his bed

again, ashamed of his groundless apprehensions, when his ear was arrested by a conversation which transfixed him aghast with terror to the spot.

"This is an easier job than you had yesterday," said the man who held the goat. "I wish all the throats we've cut were as easily and quietly done. Did you ever hear such a noise as the old gentleman made last night! It was well we had no neighbour within a dozen of miles, or they must have heard his cries for help and mercy."

"Don't speak of it," replied the other; "I was never fond of bloodshed."

"Ha! ha!" said the other, with a sneer, "you say so, do you?"

"I do," answered the first, gloomily; "the Murder Hole is the thing for me—*that* tells no tales—a single scuffle—a single plunge—and the fellow's dead and buried to your hand in a moment. I would defy all the officers in Christendom to discover any mischief *there*."

"Ay, Nature did us a good turn when she contrived such a place as that. Who that saw a hole in the heath, filled with clear water, and so small that the long grass meets over the top of it, would suppose that the depth is unfathomable, and that it conceals more than forty people who have met their deaths there?—it sucks them in like a leech!"

"How do you mean to dispatch the lad in the next room?" asked the old woman in an under tone. The elder son made her a sign to be silent, and pointed towards the door where their trembling auditor was concealed; while the other, with an expression of brutal ferocity, passed his bloody knife across his throat.

The pedlar boy possessed a bold and daring spirit, which was now roused to desperation; but in any open resistance the odds were so completely against him, that flight seemed his best resource. He gently stole to the window, and having by one desperate effort broke the rusty bolt by which the casement had been fastened, he let himself down without noise or difficulty. This betokens good, thought he, pausing an instant in dreadful hesitation what direction to take. This momentary deliberation was fearfully interrupted by the hoarse voice of the men calling aloud, "*The boy has fled—let loose the blood-hound!*" These words sunk like a death-knell on his heart, for escape appeared now impossible, and his nerves seemed to melt away like wax in a furnace. Shall I perish without a struggle! thought he, rousing himself to exertion, and, helpless and terrified as a hare pursued by its ruthless hunters, he fled across the heath. Soon the baying of the blood-hound broke the stillness of the night, and the voice of its masters sounded through the moor, as they endeavoured to accelerate its speed,—panting and breathless the boy pursued his hopeless career, but every moment his pursuers seemed to gain upon his failing steps. The hound was unimpeded by the darkness which was to him so impenetrable, and its noise rung louder and deeper on his ear—while the lanterns which were carried by the men gleamed near and distinct upon his vision.

At his fullest speed, the terrified boy fell with violence over a heap of stones, and having nothing on but his shirt, he was severely cut in every limb. With one wild cry to Heaven for assistance, he continued prostrate on the earth, bleeding, and nearly insensible. The hoarse voices of the men, and the still louder baying of the dog, were now so near, that instant destruction seemed inevitable,—already he felt himself in their fangs, and the bloody knife of the assassin appeared to gleam before his eyes,—despair renewed his energy, and once more, in an agony of affright that seemed verging towards madness, he rushed forward so rapidly that terror seemed to have given wings to his feet. A loud cry near the spot he had left arose on his ears without suspending his flight. The hound had stopped at the place where the Pedlar's wounds bled so profusely, and deeming the chase now over, it lay down there, and could not be induced to proceed; in vain the men beat it with frantic violence, and tried again to put the hound on the scent,—the sight of blood had satisfied the animal that its work was done, and with dogged resolution it resisted every inducement to pursue the same scent a second time. The pedlar boy in the meantime paused not in his flight till morning dawned—and still as he fled, the noise of steps seemed to pursue him, and the cry of his assassins still sounded in the distance. Ten miles off he reached a village, and spread instant alarm throughout the neighbourhood—the inhabitants were aroused with one accord into a tumult of indignation—several of them had lost sons, brothers, or friends on the heath, and all united in proceeding instantly to seize the old woman and her sons, who were nearly torn to pieces by their violence. Three gibbets were immediately raised on the moor, and the wretched culprits confessed before their execution to the destruction of nearly fifty victims in the Murder Hole which they pointed out, and near which they suffered the penalty of their crimes. The bones of several murdered persons were with difficulty brought up from the abyss into which they had been thrust; but so narrow is the aperture, and so extraordinary the depth, that all who see it are inclined to coincide in the tradition of the country people that it is unfathomable. The scene of these events still continues nearly as it was 300 years ago. The remains of the old cottage, with its blackened walls, (haunted of course by a thousand evil spirits,) and the extensive moor, on which a more modern *inn* (if it can be dignified with such an epithet) resembles its predecessor in every thing but the character of its inhabitants; the landlord is deformed, but possesses extraordinary genius; he has himself manufactured a violin, on which he plays with untaught skill,—and if any *discord* be heard in the house, or any *murder* committed in it, *this* is his only instrument. His daughter (who has never travelled beyond the heath) has inherited her father's talent, and learnt all his tales of terror and superstition, which she relates with infinite spirit; but when you are led by her across the heath to drop a stone into that deep and narrow gulf to which our story relates,—when you stand on its slippery edge, and (parting the long grass with which it is covered) gaze into its mysterious depths,—when she describes, with all the animation of an *eye witness*, the struggle of the victims grasping the grass as a last hope of preservation, and trying to drag in their assassin as an expiring effort of vengeance,—when you are told that for 300 years the clear waters in this diamond of the desert have remained untasted by mortal lips, and that the solitary traveller is still pursued at night by the howling of the blood-hound,—it is *then only* that it is possible fully to appreciate the terrors of THE MURDER HOLE.

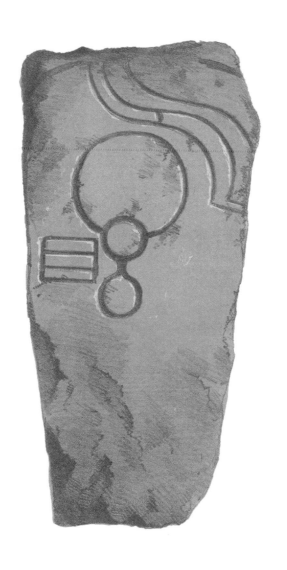

THE DOOM OF SOULIS

&

THE SEVEN LIGHTS

John Mackay Wilson

John Mackay Wilson *was* the Scottish Borders. He was born on 15 August 1804 to John Wilson from Duns and Jane Wison, from Tweedmouth, England. He started in the book trade when he was eleven. Clearly blessed with the gift of the gab, at fifteen he had managed to talk his employer, William Lochhead, Printers of Berwick, into printing a run of 100 copies of his poem "A Glance at Hinduism". He travelled in his twenties, producing well-received plays, but a life on the road is a hard one and Wilson found that he was often penniless and threw himself upon his friend's mercy to help him out. That changed when he arrived in Berwick and became the editor of the *Berwick Advertiser* in 1832. He began his *Tales of the Borders* in 1834, publishing local stories, myths and legends. They caught on, became a sensation and were soon published in a broadsheet. They had run for 48 issues before John died in 1835, two weeks after suffering a burst blood vessel. *Wilson's Historical, Traditionary and Imaginative Tales of the Border* continued being published in Weekly editions, priced three half-pence, edited by his brother James, with John's wife getting the proceeds.

"The Seven Lights" is a tale of haunting fate, whereas "The Doom of Soulis" concerns a wizard and contains one of my favourite paragraphs which begins:

> "'What!—*the wood comes!*' cried Soulis, and his cheek became pale, and he thought on the words of the demon—'*Beware of a coming wood!*'"

In this part of the tale Lord Soulis is attacked by people bearing rowan branches, with rowan known in mythology as a protection against witches. You can imagine eighty people walking through the trees towards Soulis, carrying their branches, ready to cave his skull in…

THE DOOM OF SOULIS

They roll'd him up in a sheet of lead—
A sheet of lead for a funeral pall;
They plunged him in the cauldron red,
And melted him—lead, bones, and all.

LEYDEN

A GAZETTEER would inform you that Denholm is a village beautifully situated near the banks of the Teviot, about midway between Jedburgh and Hawick, and in the parish of Cavers; and perhaps, if of modern date, it would add, it has the honour of being the birthplace of Dr. Leyden. It was somewhat early on a summer morning, a few years ago, that a young man, a stranger, with a fishing-rod in his hand, and a creel fastened to his shoulders, entered the village. Standing in the midst of it, and looking around—"This, then," thought he, "is the birthplace of Leyden—the son of genius—the martyr of study—the friend of Scott!"

The stranger proceeded up the Teviot, oftentimes thinking of Leyden, of all that he had written, and occasionally repeating passages aloud. He almost forgot that he had a rod in his hand, and his eyes did anything but follow the fly.

About midday he sat down on the green bank to enjoy his sandwich, and he also placed by his side a small flask. But he had not sat long, when a venerable old man saluted him with:

"Here's a bonnie day, sir."

The old man stood as he spoke. There was something prepossessing in his appearance. He had a weather-beaten face, with thin white hair; blue eyes, that had lost something of their former lustre; his shoulders were rather bent; and he seemed a man who was certainly neither rich nor affluent, but who was at ease with the world, and the world was at ease with him.

They entered into conversation, and they sat down together. The old man appeared exactly one of those characters you will occasionally find whose mind is filled with the traditions of the Borders, and still coloured by, and half believing in, their ancient superstitions. The thoughts of the young stranger still running upon Leyden, he turned to the elder, after they had sat together for some time, and said:

"Did you know Dr. Leyden, sir?"

"Ken him!" said the old man; "fifty year ago I've wrought day's wark beside his father for months together."

They continued their conversation for some time, and the younger inquired of the elder if he were acquainted with Leyden's ballad of *Lord Soulis*."

"Why, I hae heard a verse or twa o' the ballad, sir," said the old man; "but I'm sure everybody kens the story. However, if ye're no perfectly acquaint wi' it, I'm sure I'm willing to let ye hear it wi' great pleasure; and a remarkable story it is—and just as true, sir, ye may tak my word on't, as that I'm raising this bottle to my lips."

So saying, the old man raised the flask to his mouth, and, after a regular fisher's draught, added:

"Weel, sir, I'll let ye hear the story about Lord Soulis. You have no doubt heard of Hermitage Castle, which stands upon the river of that name, at no great distance from Hawick. In the days of the great and good King Robert the Bruce that castle was inhabited by Lord Soulis. He was a man whose very name spread terror far and wide; for he was a tyrant and a sorcerer. He had a giant's strength, an evil eye and a demon's heart, and he kept his *familiar* locked in a chest. He ruled over his vassals with a rod of iron. From the banks of Tweed, Teviot and the Jed, with their tributaries, to beyond the Lothians, an incessant cry was raised against him to Heaven and to the King. But his life was protected by a charm, and mortal weapons could not prevail against him.

"He was a man of great stature, and his person was exceeding powerful. He had also royal blood in his veins, and laid claim to the crown of Scotland, in opposition to the Bruce. But two things troubled him: and the one was, to place the crown of Scotland on his head; the other, to possess the hand of a fair and rich maiden, named Marion, who was about to wed with Walter, the young heir of Branxholm, the stoutest and the boldest youth on all the wide Borders. Soulis was a man who was not only of a cruel heart, but it was filled with forbidden thoughts; and, to accomplish his purpose, he went down into the dungeon of his castle, in the dead of night, that no man might see him perform the 'deed without a name.' He carried a small lamp in his hand, which threw around a lurid light, like a glow-worm in a sepulchre; and as he went, he locked the doors behind him. He carried a cat in his arms; behind him a dog followed timidly, and before him, into the dungeon, he drove a young bull, that had 'never nipped the grass.' He entered the deep and gloomy vault, and, with a loud voice, he exclaimed:

"'Spirit of darkness! I come!'

"He placed the feeble lamp upon the ground, in the middle of the vault; and with a pick-axe, which he had previously prepared, he dug a pit, and buried the cat alive; and as the poor suffocating creature mewed, he exclaimed the louder:

"'Spirit of darkness! come!'

"He then leaped upon the grave of the living animal, and, seizing the dog by the neck, he dashed it violently against the wall, towards the left corner where he stood, and, unable to rise, it lay howling long and piteously on the floor. Then did he plunge his knife into the throat of the young bull, and, while its bellowing mingled with the howling of the dying dog, amidst what might be called the blue darkness of the vault, he received the blood in the palms of his hands, and he stalked around the dungeon, sprinkling it in a circle, and crying with a loud voice:

"'Spirit of darkness! hear me!'

"Again he digged a pit, and, seizing the dying animal, he hurled it into the grave, feet upwards; and again he groaned, while the sweat stood on his brow: 'Come, spirit! come!'

"He took a horseshoe, which had lain in the vault for years, and which was called, in the family, the *spirit's shoe*, and he nailed it against the door, so that it hung obliquely; and as he gave the last blow to the nail, again he cried:

"'Spirit, I obey thee! come!'

"Afterwards, he took his place in the middle of the floor, and nine times he scattered around him a handful of salt, at each time exclaiming:

"'Spirit! arise!'

"Then did he strike thrice nine times with his hand upon a chest which stood in the middle of the floor, and by it was the pale lamp, and at each blow he cried:

"'Arise, spirit! arise!'

"Therefore, when he had done these things, and cried twenty-and-seven times, the lid of the chest began to move, and a fearful figure, with a red cap upon its head, and which resembled nothing in heaven above, or on earth beneath, rose, and with a hollow voice inquired:

"'What want ye, Soulis?'

"'Power, spirit! power!' he cried, 'that mine eyes may have their desire, and that every weapon formed by man may fall scathless on my body, as the spent light of a waning moon!'

"'Thy wish is granted, mortal!' groaned the fiend; 'tomorrow eve young Branxholm's bride shall sit within thy bower, and his sword return bent from thy bosom, as though he had dashed it against a rock. Farewell! invoke me not again for seven years, nor open the door of the vault, but then knock thrice upon the chest, and I will answer thee. Away! follow thy course of sin, and prosper; *but beware of a coming wood!*'

"With a loud and sudden noise, the lid of the massy chest fell, and the spirit disappeared, and from the floor of the vault issued a deep sound, like the reverbing of thunder. Soulis took up the flickering lamp, and, leaving the dying dog still howling in the corner, whence he had driven it, he locked the iron door, and placed the huge key in his bosom.

"He rode forth in the morning, with twenty of his chosen men behind him; and by the side of Teviot he beheld fair Marion, the betrothed bride of young Walter, the heir of Branxholm, riding forth with her maidens, and pursuing the red deer.

"'By this token, spirit!' muttered Soulis joyously, 'thou hast not lied—tonight young Branxholm's bride shall sit within my bower!'

"He dashed the spur into the side of his fleet steed, and, although Marion and her attendants forsook the chase, and fled, as they perceived him, yet, as though his *familiar* gave speed to his horse's feet, in a few seconds he rode by the side of Marion, and, throwing out his arm, he lifted her from the saddle.

"She screamed, she struggled wildly, but her strength was feeble as an insect's web in his terrible embrace. He held her upon the saddle before him.

"'Marion!—fair Marion!' said the wizard and ruffian lover, 'scream not—struggle not—be calm, and hear me. I love thee, pretty one!—I love thee!' and he rudely raised her lips to his. 'Fate hath decreed thou shalt be mine, Marion, and no human power shall take thee from me, and thy fair cheek shall rest upon a manlier bosom than that of Branxholm's beardless heir.' Thus saying, and still grasping her before him, he again plunged his spurs into his horse's sides, and he and his followers rode furiously towards Hermitage Castle.

"He locked the gentle Marion within a strong chamber, he

'Woo'd her as the lion woos his bride.'

And now she wept, she wrung her hands; she implored him to save her, to restore her to liberty; and again, finding her tears wasted and her prayers in vain, she defied him, she invoked the vengeance of Heaven upon his head; and, at such moments, the tyrant and the reputed sorcerer stood awed and stricken in her presence. For there is something in the majesty of virtue, and the holiness of innocence, as they flash from the eyes of an injured woman, which deprives guilt of its strength, and defeats its purpose, as though Heaven lent its power to defend the weak.

"But, wearied with importunity, and finding his threats of no effect, on the third night that she had been within his castle, he clutched her in his arms, and, while his vassals slept, he bore her to the haunted dungeon, that the spirit might throw its spell over her, and compel her to love him. He unlocked the massy door. The faint howls of the dog were still heard from the corner of the vault. He placed the lamp upon the ground. He held Marion to his side, and her terror had almost mastered her struggles. He struck his clenched hand upon the huge chest—he cried aloud: 'Spirit! come forth!'

"Thrice he repeated the blow—thrice he uttered aloud his invocation. But the spirit arose not at his summons. Marion knew the tale of his sorcery—she knew and believed it—and terror deprived her of consciousness. On recovering, she found herself again in the strong chamber where she had been confined, but Soulis was not with her. She strove to calm her fears, she knelt down and told her beads, and she begged that her Walter might be sent to her deliverance.

"It was scarce daybreak when the young heir of Branxholm, whose bow no man could bend, and whose sword was terrible in battle, with twice ten armed men arrived before Hermitage Castle, and demanded to speak with Lord Soulis. The warder blew his horn, and Soulis and his attendants came forth and looked over the battlement.

"'What want ye, boy,' inquired the wizard chief, 'that, ere the sun be risen, ye come to seek the lion in his den?'

"'I come,' replied young Walter boldly, 'in the name of our good King, and by his authority, to demand that ye give into my hands, safe and sound, my betrothed bride, lest vengeance come upon thee.'

"'Vengeance, beardling!' rejoined the sorcerer; 'who dare speak of vengeance on the house of Soulis?—or whom call ye king? The crown is mine— thy bride is mine, and thou also shalt be mine; and a dog's death shalt thou die for thy morning's boasting.

"'To arms!' he exclaimed, as he disappeared from the battlement, and within a few minutes a hundred men rushed from the gate.

"Sir Walter's little band quailed as they beheld the superior force of their enemies, and they were in dread also of the sorcery of Soulis. But hope revived when they beheld the look of confidence on the countenance of their young leader, and thought of the strength of his arm, and the terror which his sword spread.

"As hungry tigers spring upon their prey, so rushed Soulis and his vassals upon Sir Walter and his followers. No man could stand before the sword of the sorcerer. Antagonists fell as impotent things before his giant strength. Even Walter marvelled at the havoc he made, and he pressed forward to measure swords with him. But, ere he could reach him, his few followers who had escaped the hand of Soulis and his host fled, and left him to maintain the battle single-handed. Every vassal of the sorcerer, save three, pursued them; and against these three, and their charmed lord, young Walter was left to maintain the unequal strife. But, as they pressed around him, 'Back!' cried Soulis, trusting to his strength and to his charm; 'from my hand alone must Branxholm's young boaster meet his doom. It is meet that I should give his head as a toy to my bride, fair Marion.'

"'Thy bride, fiend!' exclaimed Sir Walter; 'thine!—now perish!' and he attacked him furiously.

"'Ha! ha!' cried Soulis, and laughed at the impetuosity of his antagonist, while he parried his thrusts; 'take rushes for thy weapon, boy; steel falls feckless upon me.'

"'Vile sorcerer!' continued Walter, pressing upon him more fiercely, 'this sword shall sever thy enchantment.'

"Again Soulis laughed; but he found that his contempt availed him not, for the strength of his enemy was equal to his own, and, in repelling his fierce assaults, he almost forgot the charm which rendered his body invulnerable. They fought long and desperately, when one of the followers of Soulis, suddenly and unobserved, thrusting his spear into the side of Sir Walter's horse, it reared, stumbled, and fell, and brought him to the ground.

"'An arrow-schot*!' exclaimed Soulis. 'Wherefore, boy, didst thou presume to contend with me?' And, suddenly springing from his horse, he

---

* When cattle died suddenly, it was believed to be by an arrow-shot—that is, shot or struck down by the invisible dart of a sorcerer.

pressed his iron heel upon the breast of his foe, and turning also the point of his sword towards his throat, 'Thou shalt not die yet,' said he; and turning to the three attendants who had not followed in the pursuit, he added, 'Hither—bind him fast and sure.' Then did the three hold him on the ground, and bind his hands and his feet, while Soulis held his naked sword over him.

"'Coward and wizard!' exclaimed Walter, as they dragged him within the gate, 'ye shall rue this foul treachery.'

"'Ha! ha! vain boasting boy!' returned Soulis, 'thou indeed shalt rue thy recklessness.'

"He caused his vassals to bear Walter into the strong chamber where fair Marion was confined, and, grasping him by the neck, while he held his sword to his breast, he dragged him towards her, and said, sternly, 'Consent thee now, maiden, to be mine, and this boy shall live; refuse, and his head shall roll before thee on the floor as a plaything.'

"'Monster!' she exclaimed, and screamed aloud, 'would ye harm my Walter?'

"'Ha! my Marion!—Marion!' cried Walter, struggling to be free. And, turning his eyes fiercely upon Soulis—'Destroy me, fiend,' he added, 'but harm not her.'

"'Think on it, maiden,' cried the sorcerer, raising his sword; 'the life of thy bonnie bridegroom hangs upon thy word. But ye shall have until midnight to reflect on it. Be mine, then, and harm shall not come upon him or thee; but a man shall be thy husband, and not the boy whom he hath brought to thee in bonds.'

"'Beshrew thee, vile sorcerer!' rejoined Walter. 'Were my hands unbound, and unarmed as I am, I would force my way from thy prison, in spite of thee and thine!'

"Soulis laughed scornfully, and again added, 'Think on it, fair Marion.'

"Then did he drag her betrothed bridegroom to a corner of the chamber, and, ordering a strong chain to be brought, he fettered him against the wall; in the same manner, he fastened her to the opposite side of the apartment—but the chains with which he bound her were made of silver.

"When they were left alone, 'Mourn not, sweet Marion,' said Walter, 'and think not of saving me—before tomorrow our friends will be here to thy rescue; and, though I fall a victim to the vengeance of the sorcerer, still let me be the bridegroom of thy memory.'

"Marion wept bitterly, and said that she would die with him.

"Throughout the day, the spirit of Lord Soulis was troubled, and the fear of coming evil sat heavy on his heart. He wandered to and fro on the battlements of his castle, anxiously looking for the approach of his retainers who had followed in pursuit of the followers of Branxholm's heir. But the sun set, and the twilight drew on, and still they came not; and it was drawing towards midnight when a solitary horseman spurred his jaded steed towards the castle gate. Soulis admitted him with his own hand into the courtyard; and, ere the rider had dismounted, he inquired of him hastily, and in a tone of apprehension:

"'Where be thy fellows, knave?—and why come alone?'

"'Pardon me, my lord,' said the horseman falteringly, as he dismounted; 'thy faithful bondsman is the bearer of evil tidings.'

"'Evil, slave!' exclaimed Soulis, striking him as he spoke; 'speak ye of evil to me? What of it?—where are thy fellows?'

"The man trembled, and added: 'In pursuing the followers of Branxholm, they sought refuge in the wilds of Tarras, and being ignorant of the winding paths through its bottomless morass, horses and men have been buried in it—they who sank not fell beneath the swords of those they had pursued, and I only have escaped.'

"'And wherefore did ye escape, knave?' cried the fierce sorcerer; 'why did ye live to remind me of the shame of the house of Soulis?' And, as he spoke, he struck the trembling man again.

"He hurried to the haunted dungeon, and again performed his incantations, with impatience in his manner and fury in his looks. Thrice he violently struck the chest, and thrice he exclaimed, impetuously:

"'Spirit! come forth!—arise and speak with me!'

"The lid was lifted up, and a deep and angry voice said: 'Mortal! wherefore hast thou summoned me before the time I commanded thee? Was not thy wish granted? Steel shall not wound thee—cords bind thee—hemp hang thee—nor water drown thee. Away!'

"'Stay!' exclaimed Soulis—'add, nor fire consume me!'

"'Ha! ha!' cried the spirit, in a fit of horrid laughter, that made even the sorcerer tremble. *Beware of a coming wood!*' And, with a loud clang, the lid of the chest fell, and the noise as of thunder beneath his feet was repeated.

"'Beware of a coming wood!' muttered Soulis to himself; 'what means the fiend?'

"He hastened from the dungeon without locking the door behind him, and as he hurried from it he drew the key from his bosom, and flung it over his left shoulder, crying: 'Keep it, spirit!'

"He shut himself up in his chamber to ponder on the words of his *familiar*, and on the extirpation of his followers; and he thought not of Marion and her bridegroom until daybreak, when, with a troubled and a wrathful countenance, he entered the apartment where they were fettered.

"'How now, fair maiden?' he began; 'hast thou considered well my words?—wilt thou be my willing bride, and let young Branxholm live?—or refuse, and look thy fill on his smooth face as his head adorns the point of my good spear?'

"'Rather than see her thine,' exclaimed Walter, 'I would thou shouldst hew me in pieces, and fling my mangled body to your hounds.'

"'Troth! and 'tis no bad thought,' said the sorcerer; 'thou mayest have thy wish. Yet, boy, ye think that I have no mercy: I will teach thee that I have, and refined mercy too. Now, tell me truly, were I in thy power as thou art in mine, what fate would ye award to Soulis?'

"'Then truly,' replied Walter, 'I would hang thee on the highest tree in Branxholm Woods.'

"'Well spoken, young Strong-bow,' returned Soulis; 'and I will show thee, though ye think I have no mercy, that I am more merciful than thou. Ye would choose for me the highest tree, but I shall *give thee the choice of the tree from which you may prefer your body to hang*, and from whose top the owl may sing its midnight song, and to which the ravens shall gather for a feast. And thou, pretty face,' added he, turning to Marion, 'sith you will not, even to save him, give me thine hand, i' faith, if I may not be thy husband, I will be thy priest, and celebrate your marriage, for I will bind your hands together, and ye shall hang on the next branch to him.'

"'For that I thank thee,' said the undaunted maiden.

"He then called together his four remaining armed men, and placing halters round the necks of his intended victims they were dragged forth to the woods around the Hermitage, where Walter was to choose the fatal tree.

"Now a deep mist covered the face of the earth, and they could perceive no object at the distance of half-a-bowshot before them; and ere he had approached the wood where he was to carry his merciless project into execution—

"'The wood comes towards us!' exclaimed one of his followers.

"'What!—*the wood comes!*' cried Soulis, and his cheek became pale, and he thought on the words of the demon—'*Beware of a coming wood!*'—and, for a time, their remembrance, and the forest that seemed to advance before him, deprived his arm of strength, and his mind of resolution, and before his heart recovered, the followers of the house of Branxholm, to the number of fourscore, each bearing a tall branch of a rowan-tree in their hands, as a charm against his sorcery, perceived, and raising a loud shout, surrounded him.

"The cords with which the arms of Marion and Walter were bound were instantly cut asunder. But, although the odds against him were as twenty to one, the daring Soulis defied them all. Yea, when his followers were overpowered, his single arm dealt death around.

"Now, there was not a day passed that complaints were not brought to King Robert, from those residing on the Borders, against Lord Soulis, for his lawless oppression, his cruelty, and his wizard-craft. And, one day, there came before the monarch, one after another, some complaining that he had brought diseases on their cattle, or destroyed their houses by fire, and a third, that he had stolen away the fair bride of Branxholm's heir, and they stood before the King, and begged to know what should be done with him. Now, the King was wearied with their importunities and complaints, and he exclaimed, peevishly and unthinkingly, '*boil him, if you please, but let me hear no more about him.*' But,

> "'It is the curse of kings to be attended
> By slaves that take their humour for a warrant';

and, when the enemies of Soulis heard these words from the lips of the King, they hastened away to put them into execution; and with them they took a wise man, one who was learned in breaking the spells of sorcery, and with him he carried a scroll, on which was written the secret wisdom of Michael the Wizard; and they arrived before Hermitage Castle while its lord was contending single-handed against the retainers of Branxholm, and their swords were blunted on his buckler, and his body received no wounds. They struck him to the ground with their lances; and they endeavoured to bind his hands and his feet with cords, but his spells snapped them asunder as threads.

"'Wrap him in lead,' cried the wise man, 'and boil him therewith, according to the command of the King; for water and hempen cords have no power over his sorcery.'

"Many ran towards the castle, and they tore the lead from the turrets, and they held down the sorcerer, and rolled the sheets around him in many folds, till he was powerless as a child, and the foam fell from his lips in the impotency of his rage. Others procured a cauldron, in which it was said many of his incantations were performed, and the cry was raised:

"'Boil him on the Nine-stane rig!'

"And they bore him to where the stones of the Druids are to be seen till this day, and the two stones are yet pointed out from which the cauldron was suspended. They kindled piles of faggots beneath it, and they bent the living body of Soulis within the lead; and thrust it into the cauldron, and, as the flames arose, the flesh and the bones of the wizard were consumed in the boiling lead. Such was the doom of Soulis.

"The King sent messengers to prevent his hasty words being carried into execution, but they arrived too late.

"In a few weeks there was mirth, and music, and a marriage feast in the bowers of Branxholm, and fair Marion was the bride."

THE SEVEN LIGHTS

JOHN M'Pherson was a farmer and grazier in Kintyre—a genuine Highlander. In person, though of rather low stature than otherwise, he was stout, athletic, and active; bold and fearless in disposition, warm in temper, friendly, and hospitable—this last to such a degree that his house was never without as many strangers and visitors of different descriptions, as nearly doubled his own household.

To the vagrant beggar his house and meal-chest were ever open; and to no one, whatever his condition, were a night's quarters ever refused. M'Pherson's house, in short, formed a kind of focus, with a power to draw towards itself all the misery and poverty in the country within a circle whose diameter might be reckoned at somewhere about twenty miles. The wandering mendicant made it one of his regular stages, and the traveller of better degree toiled on his way with increased activity, that he might make it his quarters for the night.

Fortunately for the character and credit of M'Pherson's hospitality, his wife was of an equally kind and generous disposition with himself; so that his absences from home, which were frequent, and sometimes long, did not at all affect the treatment of the stranger under his roof, or make his welcome less cordial.

But the hospitality exercised at Morvane, which was the name of M'Pherson's farm, sometimes, it must be confessed, led to occasional small depredations—such as the loss of a pair of blankets, a sheet, or a pair of stockings, carried off by the ungrateful vagabonds whom he sometimes sheltered. There were, however, one pair of blankets abstracted in this way, that found their road back to their owner in rather a curious manner.

The morning was thick and misty, when the thief (in the case alluded to) decamped with his booty, and continued so during the whole day, so that no object, at any distance, however large, could be seen. After toiling for several hours, under the impression that he was leaving Morvane far behind, the vagabond, who was also a stranger in the country, approached a house, with the stolen blankets snugly and carefully bundled on his back, and knocked at the door, with the view of seeking a night's quarters, as it was now dusk. The door was opened; but by whom, think you, good reader? Why, by M'Pherson!

The thief, without knowing it, had landed precisely at the point from which he had set out. Being instantly recognised, he was politely invited to walk in. To this kind invitation, the thief replied by throwing down the blankets, and taking to his heels—thus making, with his own hands, a restitution which was very far from being intended. Poor M'Pherson, however, did not get all his stolen blankets back in this way.

This, however, is a digression. To proceed with our tale. One night, when M'Pherson was absent, attending a market at some distance, an elderly female appeared at the door, with the usual demand of a night's lodging, which, with the usual hospitality of Morvane, was at once complied with. The stranger, who was a remarkably tall woman, was dressed in widow's weeds, and of rather respectable appearance; her deportment was grave, even stern, and altogether she seemed as if suffering from some recent affliction.

During the whole of the early part of the evening she sat before the fire, with her face buried between her hands, heedless of what was passing around her, and was occasionally observed rocking to and fro, with that kind of motion that bespeaks great internal anguish. It was noticed, however, that she occasionally stole a look at those who were in the apartment with her; and it was marked by all (but whether this was merely the effect of imagination, for all *felt* that there was something singular and mysterious about the stranger, or was really the case, we cannot decide) that, in these furtive glances, there was a peculiarly wild and appalling expression. The stranger spoke none, however, during the whole night; but continued, from time to time, rocking to and fro in the manner already described. Neither could she be prevailed upon to partake of any refreshment, although repeatedly pressed to do so. All invitations of this kind she declined, with a wave of the hand, or a melancholy, yet determined inclination of the head. In words she made no reply.

The singular conduct of this woman threw a damp over all who were present. They felt chilled, they knew not how; and were sensible of the influence of an indefinable terror, for which they could not account. For once, therefore, the feeling of comfort and security, of which all were conscious who were seated around M'Pherson's cheerful and hospitable hearth, was banished, and a scene of awe and dread supplied its place.

No one could conjecture who this strange personage was, whence she had come, nor whither she was going; nor were there any means of acquiring this information, as it was a rule of the house—one of M'Pherson's special points of etiquette—that no stranger should ever be questioned on such subjects. All being allowed to depart as they came, without question or inquiry, there was never anything more known at Morvane, regarding any stranger who visited it, than what he himself chose to communicate.

Under the painful feelings already described, the inmates of M'Pherson's house found, with more than usual satisfaction, the hour for retiring to rest arrive. The general attention being called to this circumstance by the hostess, everyone hastened to his appointed dormitory, with an alacrity which but too plainly showed how glad they were to escape from the presence of the mysterious stranger who, however, also retired to bed with the rest. The place appointed for her to sleep in, was the loft of an outbuilding, as there was no room for her accommodation within the house itself; all the spare beds being occupied.

We have already said that M'Pherson was from home on the evening of which we are speaking, attending a market at some distance. He, however, returned shortly after midnight. On arriving at his own house, he was much surprised, and not a little alarmed, to perceive a window in one of the outhouses blazing with light (it was that in which the stranger slept), while all around and within the house was as silent as the tomb. Afraid that some accident from fire had taken place, he rode up to the building, and standing up in his stirrups—which brought his head on a level with the window—looked in, when a sight presented itself that made even the stout heart of M'Pherson beat with unusual violence.

In the middle of the floor, extended on her pallet, lay the mysterious stranger, surrounded by seven bright and shining lights, arranged at equal distances—three on one side of the bed, three on the other, and one at the head. M'Pherson gazed steadily at the extraordinary and appalling sight for a few seconds, when three of the lights suddenly vanished. In an instant afterwards, two more disappeared, and then another. There was now only that at the head of the bed remaining. When this light had alone been left, M'Pherson saw the person who lay on the pallet, raise herself slowly up, and gaze intently on the portentous beam, whose light showed, to the terrified onlooker, a ghastly and unearthly countenance, surrounded with dishevelled hair, which hung down in long, thick, irregular masses over her pale, clayey visage, so as almost to conceal it entirely. This light, like all the others, at length suddenly disappeared, and with its last gleam the person on the couch sank down with a groan that startled M'Pherson from the trance of horror into which the extraordinary sight had thrown him. He was a bold and fearless man, however; and, therefore, though certainly appalled by what he had seen, he made no outcry, nor evinced any other symptom of alarm. He resolutely and calmly awaited the conclusion of the extraordinary scene; and when the last light had disappeared, he deliberately dismounted, led his horse into the stable, put him up, entered the house without disturbing any one, and slipped quietly into bed, trusting that the morning would bring some explanation of the mysterious occurrence of the night; but resolving, at the same time that, if it should not, he would mention the circumstance to no one.

On awaking in the morning, M'Pherson asked his wife what strangers were in the house, and how they were disposed of, and particularly, who it was that slept in the loft of the outhouse. He was told that it was a woman in widow's dress, of rather a respectable appearance, but whose conduct had been very singular. M'Pherson inquired no further, but desired that the woman might be detained till he should see her, as he wished to speak with her.

On some one of the domestics, however, going up to her apartment, shortly after, to invite her to breakfast, it was found that she was gone, no one could tell when or where, as her departure had not been seen by any person about the house.

Baulked in his intention of eliciting some explanation of the extraordinary circumstance of the preceding night, from the person who seemed to have been a party to it, M'Pherson became more strengthened in the resolution of keeping the secret to himself, although it made an impression upon him which all his natural strength of mind could not remove.

At this precise period of our story, M'Pherson had three sons employed in the herring fishing, a favourite pursuit in its season, because often a lucrative one, of those who live upon or near the coasts of the West Highlands.

The three brothers had a boat of their own; and, desirous of making their employment as profitable as possible, they, though in sufficiently good circumstances to have hired assistance, manned her themselves, and, with laudable industry, performed all the drudgery of their laborious occupation with their own hands.

Their boat, like all the others employed in the business we are speaking of, by the natives of the Highlands, was wherry-rigged; her name—she was called after the betrothed of the elder of the three brothers—*The Catherine*. The *take* of herrings, as it is called, it is well known, appears in different seasons in different places, sometimes in one loch, or arm of the sea, sometimes in another.

In the season to which our story refers, the fishing was in the sound of Kilbrannan, where several scores of boats, and amongst those that of the M'Phersons, were busily employed in reaping the ocean harvest. When the take of herrings appears in this sound, Campbelton Loch, a well-known harbour on the west coast of Scotland, is usually made the headquarters—a place of rendezvous of the little herring fleet—and to this loch they always repair when threatened with a boisterous night, although it was not always that they could, in such circumstances, succeed in making it.

Such a night as the one alluded to, was that that succeeded the evening on which M'Pherson saw the strange lights that form the leading feature of our tale. Violent gusts of wind came in rapid succession down the sound of Kilbrannan; and a skifting rain, flung fitfully but fiercely from the huge black clouds as they hurried along before the tempest that already raged above, swept over the face of the angry sea, and seemed to impart an additional bitterness to the rising wrath of the incipient storm. It was evident, in short, that what sailors call a "dirty night" was approaching; and, under this impression, the herring boats left their station, and were seen, in the dusk of the evening in question, hurrying towards Campbelton Loch. But the storm had arisen in all its fury long before the desired haven could be gained. The little fleet was dispersed. Some succeeded, however, in making the harbour; others, finding this impossible, ran in for the Saddle and Carradale shores, and were fortunate enough to effect a landing. All, in short, with the exception of one single boat, ultimately contrived to gain a place of shelter of some kind. This unhappy exception was *The Catherine*. Long after all the others had disappeared from the face of the raging sea, she was seen struggling alone with the warring elements, her canvas down to within a few feet of her gunwale, and her keel only at times being visible. The gallant brothers who manned her, however, had not yet lost either heart or hope, although their situation at this moment was but too well calculated to deprive them of both. Gravely and steadily, and in profound silence, they kept each by his perilous post, and endeavoured to make the land on the Campbelton side; but, finding this impossible, they put about, and ran before the wind for the island of Arran, which lay at the distance of about eight miles. But alarmed, as they approached that rugged shore, by the tremendous sea which was breaking on it, and which would have instantly dashed their frail bark to pieces, they again put about, and made to windward. While the hardy brothers were thus contending with their fate, a person mounted on horseback was seen galloping wildly along the Carradale shore, his eyes ever and anon turned towards the struggling boat with a look of despair and mortal agony. It was M'Pherson, the hapless father of the unfortunate youths by whom she was manned. There were others, too, of their kindred, looking, with failing hearts, on the dreadful sight; for all felt that the unequal contest could not continue long, and that the boat must eventually go down.

Amongst those who were thus watching, with intense interest and speechless agony, the struggle of the doomed bark, was Catherine, the beloved of the elder of the brothers, who ran, in wild distraction, along the shore, uttering the most heart-rending cries. "Oh, my Duncan!" she exclaimed, stretching out her arms towards the pitiless sea. "Oh, my beloved, my dearest, come to me, or allow me to come to you that I may perish with you!" But Duncan heard her not, although it was very possible he might see her, as the distance was not great.

There were, at this moment also, several persons on horseback, friends of the young men, galloping along the shore, from point to point, as the boat varied her direction, in the vain and desperate hope of being able to render, though they knew not how, some assistance to the sufferers. But the distracted father, urged on by the wild energy of despair, outrode them all, as they made, on one occasion, for a rising ground near Carradale, from whence a wider view of the sea could be commanded. For this height M'Pherson now pushed, and gained it just in time to see his gallant sons, with their little bark, buried in the waves. He had not taken his station an instant on the height, when *The Catherine* went down, and all on board perished.

The distracted father, when he had seen the last of his unfortunate sons, covered his eyes with his hands, and for a moment gave way to the bitter agony that racked his soul. His manly breast heaved with emotion, and that most affecting of all sounds, the audible sorrowing of a strong man, might have been heard at a great distance. It was, however, of short continuance. M'Pherson prayed to his God to strengthen him in this dread hour of trial, and to enable him to bear with becoming fortitude the affliction with which it had pleased Him to visit him; and the distressed man derived comfort from the appeal.

"My brave, my beautiful boys!" he said, "you are now with your God, and have entered, I trust, on a life of everlasting happiness." Saying this, he rode slowly from the fatal spot from which he had witnessed the death of his children. It was at this moment, and while musing on the misfortune that had befallen him, that the strange occurrence of the preceding night recurred, for the first time, to M'Pherson's mind. It was obtruded on his recollection by the force of association.

"Can it be possible," he inquired of himself, "that the appearances of last night can have any connection with the dreadful events of today? It must be so," he said; "for three of the lights of my eyes, three of the guiding stars of my life, have been this day extinguished." Thus reasoned M'Pherson; and, in the mysterious lights which he had seen, he saw that the doom of his children had been announced. But there were seven, he recollected, and his heart sunk within him as he thought of the three gallant boys who were still spared to him. One of them, the youngest, was at home with himself, the other two were in the Army—soldiers in the 42nd Regiment, which then boasted of many privates of birth and education. M'Pherson, however, still kept the appalling secret of the mysterious lights to himself, and determined to await, with resignation, the fulfilment of the destiny which had been read to him, and which he now felt convinced to be inevitable.

The gallant regiment to which M'Pherson's sons belonged was, at this period, abroad on active service. It was in America, and formed a part of the army which was employed in resisting the encroachments of the French on the British territories in that quarter.

The 42nd had, during the campaigns in the western world of that period—viz. 1754 and 1758,—distinguished themselves in many a sanguinary contest, for their singular bravery and general good conduct; and the fame of their exploits rung through their native glens, and was spread far and wide over their hills and mountains; for dear was the honour of their gallant regiment to the warlike Highlanders. Many accounts had arrived, from time to time, in the country, of their achievements, and joyfully were they received. But, on the very day after the loss of *The Catherine*, a low murmur began to arise, in that part of the country which is the scene of our story, of some dreadful disaster having befallen the national regiment. No one could say of what nature this calamity was; but a buzz went round, whose ominous whispering of fearful slaughter made the friends of the absent soldiers turn pale. Mothers and sisters wept, and fathers and brothers looked grave and shook their heads. The rumour bore that, though there had been no loss of honour, there had been a dreadful loss of life. Nay, it was said that the regiment had made a mighty acquisition to its fame, but that it had been dearly bought.

At length, however, the truth arrived, in a distinct and intelligible shape. The well-known and sanguinary affair of Ticonderoga had been fought; and, in that murderous contest, the 42nd Regiment, which had behaved with a gallantry unmatched before in the annals of war, had suffered dreadfully—no less than forty-three officers, commissioned and non-commissioned, and six hundred and three privates having been killed and wounded in that corps alone.

To many a heart and home in the Highlands did this disastrous, though glorious intelligence, bring desolation and mourning; and amongst those on whom it brought these dismal effects, was M'Pherson of Morvane.

On the third day after the occurrence of the events related at the outset of our narrative, a letter, which had come, in the first instance, to a gentleman in the neighbourhood, and who also had a son in the 42nd, was put into M'Pherson's hands, by a servant of the former.

The man looked feelingly grave as he delivered it, and hurried away before it was opened. The letter was sealed with black wax. Poor M'Pherson's hand trembled as he opened it. It was from the captain of the company to which his sons belonged, informing him that both had fallen in the attack on Ticonderoga. There was an attempt in the letter to soothe the unfortunate father's feelings, and to reconcile him to the loss of his gallant boys, in a lengthened detail of their heroic conduct during the sanguinary struggle. "Nobly," said the writer, "did your two brave sons maintain the honour of their country in the bloody strife. Both Hugh and Alister fell— their broadswords in their hands—on the very ramparts of Ticonderoga, whither they had fought their way with a dauntlessness of heart, and a strength of arm, that might have excited the envy and admiration of the son of Fingal."

In this account of the noble conduct of his sons the broken-hearted father did find some consolation. "Thank God!" he exclaimed, though in a tremulous voice, "my brave boys have done their duty, and died as became their name, with their swords in their hands, and their enemies in their front." But there was one circumstance mentioned in the letter, that affected the poor father more than all the rest—this was the intimation, that the writer had, in his hands, a sum of money and a gold brooch, which his son Alister had bequeathed, the first to his father, the latter to his mother, as a token of remembrance. "These," he said, "had been deposited with him by the young man previous to the engagement, under a presentiment that he should fall."

When he had finished the perusal of the letter, M'Pherson sought his wife, whom he found weeping bitterly, for she had already learned the fate of her sons. On entering the apartment where she was, he flung his arms around her, in an agony of grief, and, choking with emotion, exclaimed, that two more of his fair lights had been extinguished by the hand of heaven. "One yet remains," he said, "but that, too, must soon pass away from before mine eyes. His doom is sealed; but God's will be done."

"What mean ye, John?" said his sobbing wife, struck with the prophetic tone of his speech—"is the measure of our sorrows not yet filled? Are we to lose him, too, who is now our only stay, my fair-haired Ian. Why this foreboding of more evil—and whence have you it, John?" she said, now looking her husband steadfastly in the face; and with an expression of alarm that indicated that entire belief in supernatural intelligence regarding coming events, then so general in the Highlands.

Urged by his wife, who implored him to tell her whence he had the tidings of her Ian's approaching fate, M'Pherson related to her the circumstance of the mysterious lights.

"But there were seven, John," she said, when he had concluded—"how comes that?—our children were but six." And immediately added, as if some fearful conviction had suddenly forced itself on her mind—"God grant that the seventh light may have meant me!"

"God forbid!" exclaimed her husband, on whose mind a similar conviction with that with which his wife was impressed, now obtruded itself for the first time; that conviction was, that he himself was indicated by the seventh light. But neither of the sorrowing pair communicated their fears to the other.

Two days subsequent to this, the fair hair of Ian was seen floating on the surface of a deep pool, in the water of Bran; a small river that ran past the house of Morvane. By what accident the poor boy had fallen into the river, was never ascertained. But the pool in which his body was found was known to have been one of his favourite fishing stations. One only of the mysterious lights now remained without its counterpart; but this was not long wanting. Ere the week had expired, M'Pherson was killed by a fall from his horse, when returning from the funeral of his son, and the symbolical prophecy was fulfilled—and thus concludes the story of "The Seven Lights."

THE DEVIL OF GLENLUCE

Eliza Lynn Linton

Eliza Lynn Linton (10 February 1822–14 July 1898) was a Cumbrian-born author and Britain's first female salaried journalist. Her mother died shortly after Eliza was born and she was raised by her strict father, the Rev. James Lynn. Her unhappy childhood helped to instil a determination to be independent and succeed under her own merits. After moving to London she produced her debut novel, *Azeth, the Egyptian* (1847), though it wasn't until the release of her third novel, *Realities* (1851), that she became notable. The book was a biting critique of Victorian values which argued for better treatment of the poor and challenged the low status of women in society. However, later in life she became a staunch critic of female suffrage, claiming it had a detrimental impact on society. Controversy continued with her best-selling novel *The True History of Joshua Davidson, Christian and Communist* (1872), which accused the Church of England of hypocrisy and abuse. In 1896 she was the first woman to become a member of The Society of Authors and served on various committees. She died of pneumonia in 1898 having created an extensive body of work.

"The Devil of Glenluce" comes from Eliza's 1861 collection *Witch Stories*. It's an interesting piece, one that Eliza fleshed out more than the other "reportings" in the book. I think it was something she had a lot of fun writing.

I N 1654 one Gilbert Campbell was a weaver in Glenluce, a small village not far from Newton Stewart. Tom, his eldest son, and the most important personage in the drama, was a student at Glasgow College; and there was a certain old blaspheming beggar, called Andrew Agnew—afterwards hanged at Dumfries for his atheism, having said, in the hearing of credible witnesses, that "there was no God but salt, meal, and water"—who every now and then came to Glenluce to ask alms. One day old Andrew visited the Campbells as usual, but got nothing; at which he cursed and swore roundly, and forthwith sent a devil to haunt the house, for it was soon after this refusal that the stirs began, and the connection was too apparent to be denied. For what could they be but the malice of the devil sent by old Andrew in revenge? Young Tom Campbell was the worst beset of all, the demon perpetually whistling and rioting about him, and playing him all sorts of diabolical and malevolent tricks. Once, too, Jennet, the young daughter, going to the well, heard a whistling behind her like that produced by "the small slender glass whistles of children," and a voice like the damsel's, saying, "I'll cast thee, Jennet, into the well! I'll cast thee, Jennet, into the well!" About the middle of November, when the days were dark and the nights long, things got very bad. The foul fiend threw stones in at the doors and windows, and down the chimney head; cut the warp and threads of Campbell's loom; slit the family coats and bonnets and hose and shoon into ribbons; pulled off the bed-clothes from the sleeping children, and left them cold and naked, besides administering sounding slaps on those parts of their little round rosy persons usually held sacred to the sacrifices of the rod; opened chests and trunks, and strewed the contents over the floor; knocked everything about, and ill-treated bairn and brother; and, in fact, persecuted the whole family in the most merciless manner. The weaver sent his children away, thinking their lives but barely safe, and *in their absence there were no assaults whatever*—a thing to be specially noted. But on the minister's representing to him that he had done a grievous sin in thus withdrawing them from God's punishments, they were brought back again in contrition. Only Tom was left behind, and nothing ensued until Tom appeared; but unlucky Tom brought back the devil with him, and then there was no more peace to be had.

On the Sunday following Master Tom's return, the house was set on fire—the devil's doing: but the neighbours put the flames out again before much damage had ensued. Monday was spent in prayer; but on Tuesday the place was again set on fire, to be again saved by the neighbours' help. The weaver, in much trouble, went to the minister, and besought him to take back that unlucky Tom, whom the devil so cruelly followed and molested; which request he, after a time, "condescended to," though assuring the weaver that he would find himself deceived if he thought that the devil would quit with the boy. And so it proved; for Tom, having now indoctrinated some of his juniors with the same amount of mechanics and legerdemain as he himself possessed, managed that they should be still sore troubled—the demon cutting their clothes, throwing peats down the chimney, pulling off turf and "feal" from the roof and walls, stealing their coats, pricking their poor bodies with pins, and raising such a clamour that there was no peace or rest to be had.

The case was becoming serious. Glenluce objected to be made the headquarters of the devil; and the ministers convened a solemn meeting for fast and humiliation; the upshot of which was that weaver Campbell was led to take back his unlucky Tom, with the devil or without him. For this was the point at issue in the beginning; the motive of which is not hard to be discovered. Whereupon Tom returned; but as he crossed the threshold he heard a voice "forbidding him to enter that house, or any other place where his father's calling was exercised." Was Tom, the Glasgow student, afraid of being made a weaver, consent or none demanded? In spite of the warning voice he valiantly entered, and his persecutions began at once. Of course they did. They were tremendous, unheard of, barbarous; in fact, so bad that he was forced to return once more for a time to the minister's house; but his imitator or disciple left behind carried on business in his absence. On Monday, the 12th day of February, the demon began to speak to the family, who, nothing afraid, answered quite cheerily: so they and the devil had long confidential chats together, to the great improvement of mind and morals. The ministers, hearing of this, convened again, and met at weaver Campbell's, to see what they could do. As soon as they entered, Satan began: "Quum literatum is good Latin," quoth he. These were the first words of the Latin rudiments, as taught in the grammar-school. Tom's classical knowledge was coming into play.

After a while he cried out, "A dog! a dog!" The minister, thinking he was alluded to, answered, "He thought it no evil to be reviled of him;" to which Satan replied civilly, "It was not you, sir, I spoke to: I meant the dog there;" for there was a dog standing behind backs. They then went to prayer, during which time Tom—or the devil—remained reverently silent; his education being not yet carried out to the point of scoffing. Immediately after prayer was ended, a counterfeit voice cried out, "Would you know the witches of Glenluce? I will tell of them," naming four or five persons of indifferent repute, but one of whom was dead. The weaver told the devil this, thinking to have caught him tripping; but the foul fiend answered promptly, "It is true she is dead long ago, but her spirit is living with us in the world."

The minister replied, saying, "Though it was not convenient to speak to such an excommunicated and inter-communed person, 'the Lord rebuke thee, Satan, and put thee to silence. We are not to receive information from thee, whatsoever fame any person goes under. Thou art seeking but to seduce this family, for Satan's kingdom is not divided against itself.'" After which little sparring there was prayer again; so Tom did not take much by this move.

All the while the young Glasgow student was very hardly holden, so that there was more prayer on his special behalf. The devil then said, on their rising, "Give me a spade and a shovel, and depart from the house for seven days, and I will make a grave and lie down in it, and shall trouble you no more."

The good man Campbell answered, "Not so much as a straw shall be given thee, through God's assistance, even though that would do it. God shall remove thee in due time." Satan cried out, impudently, "I shall not remove for you. I have my commission from Christ to tarry and vex this family." Says the minister, coming to the weaver's assistance, "A permission thou hast, indeed; but God will stop it in due time." Says the demon, respectfully, "I have, sir, a commission which perhaps will last longer than yours." And the minister died in the December of that year, says Sinclair. Furthermore, the demon said he had given Tom his commission to keep. Interrogated, that young gentleman replied in an off-hand way, that "he had had something put into his pocket, but it did not tarry." They then began to search about for the foul fiend, and one gentleman said, "We think this voice speaks out of the children." The foul fiend, very angry at this—or Master Tom frightened—cries out, "You lie! God shall judge you for your lying; and I and my father will come and fetch you to hell with warlock thieves." So the devil discharged (forbade) the gentleman to speak anything, saying, "Let him that hath a commission speak (meaning the minister), for he is the servant of God." The minister then had a little religious controversy with the devil, who answered at last, simply, "I knew not these scriptures till my father taught me them." Nothing of all this disturbing the easy faith of the audience, they, through the minister, whom alone he would obey, conjured him to tell them who he was; whereupon he said that he was an evil spirit come from the bottomless pit of hell, to vex this house, and that Satan was his father. And then there appeared a naked hand, and an arm from the elbow downward, beating on the floor till the house did shake again, and a loud and fearful crying, "Come up, father! come up, father! I will send my father among ye! See! there he is behind your backs!"

Says the minister, "I saw, indeed, a hand and an arm, when the stroke was given and heard."

Says the devil, "Saw ye that? It was not my hand, it was my father's; my hand is more black in the loof."

"Oh!" said Gilbert Campbell, in an ecstasy, "that I might see thee as well as I hear thee!"

"Would ye see me?" says the foul thief. "Put out the candle, and I shall come but* the house among you like fire-balls; I shall let ye see me indeed."

Alexander Bailie of Dunraget said to the minister, "Let us go ben,† and see if there is any hand to be seen." But the demon exclaimed, "No! let him (the minister) come ben alone: he is a good honest man: his single word may be believed." He then abused Mr. Robert Hay, a very honest gentleman, very ill with his tongue, calling him witch and warlock: and a little while after, cried out, "A witch! a witch! there's a witch sitting upon the ruist! take her away." He meant that there was a hen sitting on one of the rafters. They then went to prayer again, and, when ended, the devil cried out, "If the good man's son's prayers at the College of Glasgow did not prevail with God, my father and I had wrought a mischief here ere now." Ah, Master Tom, did you then know so much of prayer and the inclining of the counsels of God?

Alexander Bailie said, "Well, I see you acknowledge a God, and that prayer prevails with him, and therefore we must pray to God, and commit the event to him." To whom the devil replied, having an evident spite against Alexander Bailie, "Yea, sir, you speak of prayer, with your broad-lipped hat" (for the gentleman had lately gotten a hat in the fashion with broad lips); "I'll bring a pair of shears from my father's which shall clip the lips of it a little." And Alexander Bailie presently heard a pair of shears go clipping round his hat, "which he lifted, to see if the foul thief had meddled with it."

Then the fiend fell to prophesying. "Tom was to be a merchant, Bob a smith, John a minister, and Hugh a lawyer," all of which came to pass. Turning to Jennet, the good man's daughter, he cried, "Jennet Campbell, Jennet Campbell, wilt thou cast me thy belt?"

Quoth she, "What a widdy would thou do with my belt?"

"I would fain," says he, "fasten my loose bones together."

---

* To the outer room.

† To the inner room.

A younger daughter was sitting "busking her puppies" (dressing her puppets, dolls), as young girls are used to do. He threatens to "ding out her harns," that is, to brain her; but says she quietly, "No, if God be to the fore," and so falls to her work again. The good wife having brought out some bread, was breaking it, so that every one of the company should have a piece. Cries he, "Grissel Wyllie! Grissel Wyllie! give me a piece of that haver bread. I have gotten nothing this day but a bit from Marritt," that is, as they speak in the country, Margaret. The minister said to them all, "Beware of that! for it is sacrificing to the devil!" Marritt was then called, and inquired if she had given the foul fiend any of her haver bread. "No," says she; "but when I was eating my due piece this morning, something came and clicked it out of my hands."

The evening had now come, and the company prepared to depart; the minister, and the minister's wife, Alexander Bailie of Dunraget, with his broad-lipped hat, and the rest. But the devil cried out in a kind of agony—

"Let not the minister go! I shall burn the house if he goes." Weaver Campbell, desperately frightened, besought the minister to stay; and he, not willing to see them come to mischief, at last consented. As he turned back into the house, the devil gave a great gaff of laughing, saying, "Now, sir! you have done my bidding!" which was unhandsome of Tom—very.

"Not thine, but in obedience to God, have I returned to bear this man company whom thou dost afflict," says the minister, nowise discomposed, and not disdaining to argue matters clearly with the devil.

Then the minister "discharged" all from speaking to the demon, saying, "that when it spoke to them they must only kneel and pray to God." This did not suit the demon at all. He roared mightily, and cried, "What! will ye not speak to me? I shall strike the bairns, and do all manner of mischief!" No answer was returned; and again the children were slapped and beaten on their rosy parts—where children are accustomed to be whipped. After a while this ended too, and then the fiend called out to the good-wife, "Grissel, put out the candle!"

"Shall I do it?" says she to the minister's wife.

"No," says that discreet person, "for then you shall obey the devil."

Upon which the devil shouted, with a louder voice, "Put out the candle!" No one obeyed, and the candle continued burning. "Put out the candle, I say!" cries he, more terribly than before. Grissel, not caring to continue the uproar, put it out. "And now," says he, "I will trouble you no more this night." For by this time I should suppose that Master Tom was sleepy, and tired, and hoarse.

Once again the ministers and gentlemen met for prayer and exorcism; when it is to be presumed that Tom was not with them, for everything was quiet; but soon after the stirs began again, and Tom and the rest were sore molested. Gilbert Campbell made an appeal to the Synod of Presbyters, a committee of whom appointed a special day of humiliation in February, 1656, for the freeing of the weaver's house from this affliction. In consequence whereof, from April to August, the devil was perfectly quiet, and the family lived together in peace. But after this the mischief broke out again afresh. Perhaps Tom had come home from college, or his father had renewed his talk of settling him firmly to his own trade: whatever the cause, the effect was certain, the devil had come back to Glenluce.

One day, as the good-wife was standing by the fire, making the porridge for the children, the demon came and snatched the "tree-plate," on which was the oat-meal, out of her hand, and spilt all the meal. "Let me have the tree-plate again," says Grissel Wyllie, very humbly; and it came flying back to her. "It is like if she had sought the meal too she might have got it, such is his civility when he is intreated," says Sinclair. But this would have been rather beyond even Master Tom's power of legerdemain. Things after this went very ill. The children were daily thrashed with heavy staves, and every one in the family underwent much personal damage; until, as a climax, on the eighteenth of September, the demon said he would burn the house down, and did, in fact, set it on fire. But it was put out again, before much damage was done.

After a time—probably by Tom's going away, or becoming afraid of being found out—the devil was quieted and laid for ever; and Master Tom employed his intellect and energies in other ways than terrifying his father's family to death, and making stirs which went by the name of demoniac.

This account is taken almost verbatim from an article of mine in "All the Year Round;" and if a larger space has been given to this than to many other stories, it is because there was more colouring, and more distinctness in the drawing, than in anything else that I have read. Though scarcely belonging to a book on witches, there is yet a hook and eye, if a very slender one, in the fact that the old beggar, Andrew Agnew, was hanged; and we may be sure that it was not only his atheism, but also his naughty tricks with Satan, and his connection with the devil of Glenluce, that helped to fit the hangman's rope round his neck. There are many other stories of haunted houses, notably, Mr. Monpesson's at Tedworth caused by the Demon Drummer, and the Woodstock Devil who harried the Parliamentary Commissioners to within an inch of their lives, and others to the full as interesting; but there is no hook and eye with them—nothing by which they can be hung on to the sad string of witches, or witchcraft murders. Baxter has two or three such stories; and the curious in such matters will find a large amount of interesting matter in the various works referred to at the foot of the pages; matter which could not be introduced here, because of its not belonging strictly to the subject in hand. I do not think that any candid or unprejudiced person will fail in seeing the dark shadow of fraud and deceit flung over every such account remaining. The importance of which, to me, is the evident and distinct likeness between these stories and the marvels going on now in modern society.

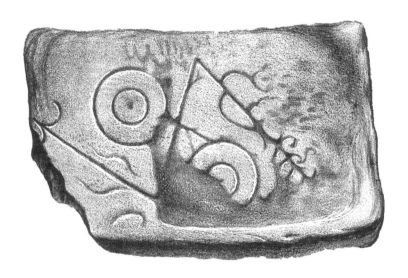

THE CAVERN OF STEENFOLL: A SCOTTISH LEGEND

Wilhelm Hauff
Translated by S. Mendel

Wilhelm Hauff (29 November 1802–18 November 1827) was a German author whose education came from the books in his grandfather's library after the death of his father. His novels include *The Memoirs of Satan* (1825/26), which sees the Devil touring contemporary Germany, and the lightly written *Fantasies in the Bremer Tavern* (1827). Hugely popular in his homeland, he styled one of his last books,*Lichtenstein: Romantic Saga from the History of Württemberg* on the Gothic romances of Scottish author Sir Walter Scott. Hauff died of typhoid fever only months after marrying his cousin Luise Hauff.

Posthumous collections translated into English include *The Caravan: A Collection of Popular Tales* (1881), *Hauff's Tales* (1886), from which the following story comes and *The Little Glass Man and Other Stories* (1894). "The Cavern of Steenfoll: A Scottish Legend" is a bonkers tale told from a stranger's view of Scotland.

MANY years ago there lived upon one of the rocky islands of Scotland two fishermen in happy concord. They were both unmarried, had no relatives, and although they were differently engaged in their common work, yet it supported them both. They were nearly of the same age, but there was as much resemblance between them in person and character as there is between an eagle and a sea-calf.

Kaspar Strumpf was a short, stout man, with a broad, fat, full-moon face, kind laughing eyes, to whom cares and sorrows were unknown. He was not merely stout, but also sleepy and lazy, and therefore it fell to his lot to attend to the housework, cooking and baking, the netting of nets for catching fish for their own use and for sale, as well as tilling a part of their little ground.

His companion was quite the reverse; he was tall and thin, had a bold hook-nose and fiery eyes, and known to be the most active and courageous fisherman, the most venturesome climber after birds and down, the most industrious field-labourer on the islands, as well as being the most greedy money-maker in the market-place of Kirkwall; but as his goods were of the best quality, and he was honest in his transactions, everybody liked to deal with him, and Will Hawk (this was the name given him by his fellow-countrymen) and Kaspar Strumpf, with whom the former, in spite of his greediness, gladly shared his hard earned gain, not merely lived well, but were also in a fair way of reaching a certain stage of opulence.

It was not, however, wealth alone after which Hawk's greedy mind was striving; he was bent upon acquiring wealth, and as he soon learned to perceive that in the usual way of industry he could not get rich so quickly, the idea at last occurred to him that he must obtain his wealth by some extraordinary chance of fortune, and this thought having once taken possession of his powerful working mind, nothing else found room in it, and he began to talk to Kaspar Strumpf about it as a certain thing. The latter, to whom all that Hawk said was regarded as Gospel, related it to his neighbours, and soon the rumour spread—Will Hawk had really either sold himself to the Evil One for gold, or he had at least received an offer for it, from the prince of the lower regions.

Although at first Hawk ridiculed these rumours, yet gradually he delighted in the idea that some genius might reveal to him some day a treasure, and he no longer contradicted whenever his fellow-countrymen taunted him with it. He still carried on his business, but with less zeal, and often lost a great deal of time, which he formerly spent in catching fish, and other useful pursuits, in aimlessly looking out for some adventure, by which he might suddenly become rich. As ill-luck would have it, he was one day standing on the lonely shore, and looking with uncertain hope upon the moving sea, as if his great fortune were to come thence, when a great wave which had uprooted a quantity of weeds and stones, rolled a yellow ball—a ball of gold—to his feet.

Will stood there as if bewitched; his hopes had not been empty dreams; the sea had presented gold to him, beautiful bright gold, probably the remains of a heavy bar, which the waves had rubbed down on the bottom of the sea until it became the size of a bullet. And now he clearly perceived that at one time, somewhere on this shore, a richly-laden ship must have foundered, and that he was selected to fetch out the buried treasures from the depths of the sea. This was henceforth his sole longing; to endeavour to carefully conceal his discovery even from his friend, in order that others might not spy it out; he neglected everything else, and spent days and nights on this shore, but he did not throw out a net after fish, but a drag, which he himself had made, for gold. But he found nothing but poverty; he earned nothing more himself, and Kaspar's sleepy exertions were not sufficient to maintain them both. In searching for greater treasures, not merely did the gold which he had found disappear, but gradually also the whole property of the bache-lors. But as Strumpf had silently allowed Hawk formerly to earn the greater part of his food, he now also allowed, silently and without grumbling, his aimless activity to deprive him of it, and it was just this gentle endurance of his friend which spurred on the other more strongly to continue his restless search for riches. But what made him still more active was, that whenever he lay down to rest, and his eyes closed in slumber, somebody whispered a word in his ears, which, although he appeared to hear it very distinctly, and which always seemed to him the same, yet he could never remember. True he did not know what this circumstance, however strange it was, might have to do with his present endeavours; but on a mind like that of Will Hawk everything made an impression; and even this mysterious whispering strengthened him in the belief that a great fortune awaited him, which he hoped to find in one single heap of gold.

One day a storm surprised him on the shore where he had found the golden ball, the violence of which urged him to seek refuge in a cavern near. This cavern which was called by the inhabitants the cavern of Steenfoll, consists of a long subterranean passage which has two outlets into the sea, giving a free passage to the foaming waves which worked their way through, continually with loud roars. This cavern was only accessible in one place, and that through a crevice from above, which was, however, seldom entered by any one except naughty boys. In addition to the peculiar dangers of the place, it was also known to be haunted by ghosts.

Will let himself down with difficulty, and took his place about twelve feet from the surface upon a projecting stone, and under an overhanging piece of rock, the roaring waves under his feet, and the raging storm over his head, when he sank into the usual train of thought about the foundered ship, and what sort of a ship it might have been; for in spite of all his inquiries from even the oldest of the inhabitants, he had been unable to obtain any news about the place where the ship had foundered.

How long he had sat in that manner he did not know himself; but when he awoke at last from his dreams he discovered that the storm had passed. He was about to ascend again when he heard a voice from beneath, and the word "Car-mil-han" was quite distinct to his ears. Terrified, he started up and looked down into the empty abyss. "Great God!" he exclaimed, "that is the word which has tormented me in my sleep! For Heaven's sake what can be the meaning of it?" "Car-mil-han!" it sighed once more up out of the cavern, when he had already one foot out of the crevice, and he fled like a hunted deer towards his hut.

Will was, however, no coward; he was merely unprepared for the affair; and besides, his greediness for money was too strong in him for a semblance of danger to frighten him from continuing his dangerous course. Once when he was fishing for treasures with his drag very late at night, by moonlight, opposite the cavern of Steenfoll, it stuck fast suddenly on something. He pulled with all his might, but the mass remained immovable. In the meantime the wind rose, dark clouds covered the sky, his boat rocked terribly, and threatened to upset; but Will was not so easily baffled, he kept on pulling and pulling until the resistance yielded, and feeling no weight, he believed his rope was broken. But just as the clouds were about to cover the moon, a round black mass appeared on the surface, and the tormenting word Car-mil-han resounded. He was about to seize it quickly, but just as quickly as he stretched out his arm towards it, it disappeared in the darkness of the night and the impending storm compelled him to seek shelter under an adjacent rock.

Here he fell asleep from fatigue, again to suffer those torments which an unchecked power of imagination and his restless longing after riches caused him to endure during the daytime. The first beams of the rising sun were now falling upon the quiet surface of the sea when Hawk awoke. He was again about to go to his accustomed work when he saw something coming towards him from a distance. He soon recognised it to be a boat which contained a human figure; but what excited his greatest surprise was that the boat went along without sails or rudder, and with the bows turned towards the shore, and the figure sitting in it did not seem in the least concerned about the rudder, if indeed it had one. The boat came nearer and nearer, and stopped at last close to Will's boat. The person in it now appeared to be a little shrivelled-up old man, dressed in yellow linen, and with a red nightcap, standing upright, with his eyes closed, and sitting there, immovable, like a dried-up corpse. After having vainly called to him and pushed him, he was about to fasten a rope on the boat to pull it away, when the little man opened his eyes, and began to move in such a way that he filled even the bold fisherman with terror.

"Where am I?" he asked, in Dutch, after a deep sigh. Hawk, who had learned something about the language from the Dutch herring-fishers, told him the name of the island, and asked who he was and what had brought him here.

"I have come to look for the Carmilhan."

"The Carmilhan? For heaven's sake! what is that?" cried the fisherman eagerly.

"I do not answer questions which are put to me in this way," replied the little man, evidently terrified.

"Well," exclaimed Hawk, "what is the Carmilhan?"

"The Carmilhan is nothing now, but once upon a time it was a beautiful ship laden with more gold than any other ship has ever carried."

"Where did it run aground, and when?"

"It happened a hundred years ago; where, I do not know exactly; I have come to look for the place and to fish up the lost gold; if you will assist me we will share the treasure with each other."

"With all my heart, only tell me what I must do?"

"What you have to do requires courage; you most go just before midnight to the most barren and lonely place on the island, accompanied by a cow, which you must kill there, and get some one to wrap you up in her fresh hide. Your companion must then lay you down on the ground, and leave you. Before the clock strikes one you will know where the treasures of the Carmilhan are buried."

"In this way the old Engrol was ruined both in body and soul!" cried Will with terror. "You are the evil spirit," he continued, whilst rowing away hastily, "away with you! I will have nothing to do with you."

The little man gnashed his teeth, abused him, and sent curses after him; the fisherman, however, who had seized both his oars, was soon out of his hearing, and after having rowed round a rock was also out of sight. The discovery, however, that the evil spirit endeavoured to profit by his greediness and to allure him with gold into his clutches, made no impression on the beguiled fisherman; on the contrary, he thought he was able to turn to advantage the communication of the little yellow man, without selling himself to the evil one; and as he continued to fish for gold on the barren shore, he neglected the wealth which the large shoals of fish offered to him in other parts of the sea, as well as all other means on which he had formerly employed his energies, and sank day after day, together with his companion, into deeper poverty, until at last they often stood in need of the necessaries of life.

But although this ruin must be ascribed entirely to Hawk's stubbornness and vain desire, and the support of both now alone fell on Kaspar Strumpf, yet the latter never reproached him in the slightest degree; nay, he still showed the same submissiveness, the same confidence in his better judgment, as at the time when he had succeeded in all his undertakings; this circumstance increased Hawk's sufferings very much, but induced him all the more to seek for gold, because he hoped thereby to recompense his friend for his present deprivation. At the same time the fiendish whisperings of the word Carmilhan still tormented him in his sleep. In short, necessity, disappointed expectations, and greediness brought him at last to a kind of frenzy, so that he finally resolved to do that which the little man had advised him, although he was fully aware according to the old tradition that he was giving himself over with it to the powers of darkness.

All Kaspar's representations to the contrary were in vain. Hawk only became the more furious the more the other entreated him to abstain from his desperate intention. The good-natured, weak-minded man at last consented to accompany him and help him to accomplish his design. Both their hearts were painfully moved when they put a rope round the horns of a beautiful cow, the last of their remaining property, which they had reared from a calf, and which they had always refused to sell, because they could not bear to see her in strange hands. The evil spirit, however, who had mastered Will now stifled all better feeling in him, and Kaspar was unable to resist him in anything.

It was in the month of September, the long evenings of a Scotch winter had begun. The dark clouds of evening rolled heavily before the boisterous wind and rose like icebergs in the whirling stream, deep shadows filled the ravines between the mountains and the damp turf marshes, and the gloomy beds of the streams appeared dark and terrible like dreadful gulfs. Hawk went first, Strumpf followed, shuddering at his own boldness, and tears filled his dim eyes as often as he looked at the poor animal which went so confidentially and unconsciously towards speedy death, which it was to receive from that hand which had hitherto given it food. With difficulty they reached the narrow and marshy mountain-valley which was covered with moss and heath, with large stones, and surrounded by a rocky chain of mountains which was lost in the grey mist, and whither the foot of man seldom strayed. They approached a large stone on the unsafe ground which was in the centre, and from which a frightened eagle flew upwards screaming.

The poor cow lowed gently, as though she recognised the terrors of the place, and her impending fate; Kaspar turned away in order to wipe away his tears which were flowing in torrents. He looked down through the crevice of the rock by which they had come up, and whence the distant surges of the sea were heard, and then up to the mountain tops upon which the clouds as black as coal had settled, and out of which was heard from time to time a deep murmuring. On turning round to Will the latter had already tied the poor cow to a stone, and with uplifted hatchet was about to strike down the good animal.

This was too much for his resolution to acquiesce in the will of his friend. With his hands clasped he threw himself upon his knees. "For heaven's sake, Will Hawk!" he exclaimed in a voice of despair, "spare yourself, spare the cow. Spare yourself and me. Spare your soul. Spare your life! If you must tempt God wait until tomorrow, and sacrifice rather any other animal than our beloved cow!"

"Kaspar, are you mad?" cried Will like a madman, whilst he was still holding up his hatchet ready for action. "Shall I spare the cow and die of hunger?"

"You shall not die of hunger," replied Kaspar, in a resolute manner, "as long as I have hands you shall not die of hunger. I will work for you from morning until night, only do not forfeit your soul's salvation, and do grant me the poor animal's life."

"Then take the hatchet and split my head," exclaimed Hawk, in a despairing tone. "I shall not stir from this place until I have what I want. Can you raise the treasures of the Carmilhan for me? Can your hands earn more than the barest necessaries of life? but they can terminate my misery—come and let me be the sacrifice."

"Will, if you kill the cow, you kill me. It makes no difference to me, I only care for your salvation. Alas! this is, as you are aware, the altar of the Picts, and the sacrifice which you are anxious to offer belongs to the prince of darkness."

"I do not know anything about such things," exclaimed Hawk, laughing wildly, like one who is determined to be ignorant of anything that might divert him from his resolution. "Kaspar, you are mad, and make me mad—but there," he continued, throwing away the hatchet and picking up the knife from the stone, as if he would kill himself, "there keep the cow instead of me!"

Kaspar was immediately by his side, snatched the murderous weapon from his hand, seized the hatchet, lifted it up high into the air, and brought it down so powerfully upon the head of the beloved animal that it fell dead at its master's feet without moving.

Lightning, accompanied by a thunderclap, followed this rash act, Hawk staring at his friend as a man would do at a child having ventured to do what he himself would not have dared. Strumpf, however, did not seem to be either frightened at the thunder or disconcerted at the rigid surprise of his companion, and without saying a word attacked the cow and commenced to pull off the hide. On Will having recovered a little, he assisted him in this work, but with as evident a dislike as he had before been eager to see the sacrifice completed. During this work the thunderstorm had increased in fury, the thunder resounded amid the mountains, and terrible flashes of lightning were winding around the stone and over the moss of the ravine, whilst the winds, which had not yet attained to their height, filled the valley beneath and the sea-shore with terrible howlings. When the hide had at last been pulled off, both fishermen were already drenched to the skin. They spread the hide on the ground, and Kaspar enveloped and tied Hawk firmly in it, just as he had been instructed by him. It was only after this had been accomplished that the poor fellow broke the silence, and looking pitifully at his foolish friend, asked him in a trembling voice: "Is there anything I can do for you, Will?"

"Nothing more," replied the other, "Farewell!"

"Farewell," replied Kaspar, "God be with you, and pardon you as I do."

These were the last words Will heard from him, for the next moment he had disappeared in the ever-increasing darkness, and at the same moment one of the most terrible thunderstorms Will had ever heard burst forth. It commenced with lightning, which showed Hawk not merely the mountains and rocks in his immediate neighbourhood, but also the valley beneath him, with the foaming sea, and the rocky islands which lay scattered in the creek, among which he believed he saw the appearance of a large quaint-looking and dismantled ship, which also again disappeared instantly in the most intense darkness. The claps of thunder became quite deafening. A number of pieces of rock rolled down the mountain and threatened to kill him. The rain came down in such torrents, that the narrow marshy valley was flooded in a moment with a high flood, and soon came up to Will's shoulders; fortunately, however, Kaspar had placed him with the upper part of his body upon an elevation, or else he would have been drowned at once. The water still rose higher and higher, and the more Will strove to extricate himself from his dangerous position, the more tightly the hide held him. In vain he called for Kaspar, who was far away. He dared not call upon God in his danger, and he was seized with terror as he was about to call upon the powers of darkness, to whom he felt he had surrendered himself.

The water had by this time almost penetrated his ears, and nearly touched his lips. "I am lost!" he exclaimed, as he felt a shower coming down upon his face—but at the same moment he heard a faint sound in his ear resembling that of a near waterfall, and immediately his mouth was again free! The flood had made its way through the stones, and as the rain ceased somewhat at the same time, and the clouds disappeared, his despair also vanished, and a ray of hope seemed to return to him. Although he felt exhausted just like one fighting with death, and ardently wishing to be released from his captivity, yet the aim of his despairing longing had not yet been attained, and with the disappearance of the imminent danger so also avarice returned into his bosom with all its fury. Being convinced, however, that he was obliged to persevere in his position in order to attain his object, he kept quiet, and sank from cold and exhaustion into a deep sleep.

He might have been asleep for nearly two hours when a cold wind, passing over his face, and the rushing like that of approaching sea-waves awoke him out of his happy self-forgetfulness. The sky had again become darkened, a flash of lightning, like the one which had caused the first storm, once more illuminated the whole country round, and he believed he saw again the strange boat, which was now close to the Steenfoll-cliff, suspended upon a great wave and then suddenly shoot into the abyss. He was still staring after the phantom, for an incessant lightning kept the sea illuminated, when all of a sudden a water spout the height of a mountain, poured out of the valley, throwing him with such might against a rock that he became senseless. When he came to himself again, the thunderstorm had passed, the sky was serene, but the sheet lightning still continued. He lay close to the foot of the mountains, which surrounded this valley, and he felt so bruised that he was scarcely able to move. He heard the quiet sound of the surges, and amongst them solemn music like church hymns; these strains were at first so weak that he thought it to be a delusion. But they were heard ever and again, and every time more distinctly and nearer, and it seemed to him at last as if he could recognise in them the chanting of a psalm which he had heard in the last summer on board a Dutch herring smack.

At last he even seemed to recognise voices, and it appeared to him as if he even heard the words of that hymn. The voices were now in the valley, and after he had pushed himself to a stone with difficulty, upon which to lay his head, he actually saw a procession of human figures from whom this music proceeded, and which was making its way straight towards him. Sorrow and anxiety were depicted on the people's faces whose clothes seemed to be dripping wet. They were now close to him, and their singing ceased. At the head were several musicians, followed by a number of sailors, and behind these walked a tall, strong man, clad in old-fashioned dress richly embroidered with gold, a sword at his side, and a long, thick Spanish reed with a golden knob in his hand. On his left walked a servant boy, who gave his master a long pipe from time to time, out of which he smoked in a solemn manner, and then went on his way. He stood still right in front of Will, and other less splendidly dressed men placed themselves at his side, all having pipes in their hands, less costly than that which was carried after the stout man. Behind these latter, other persons took their places, amongst them several women, some of them having children in their arms, or leading them by the hand, all in costly but quaint dress. A crowd of Dutch sailors closed the procession, each one of whom had his mouth filled with tobacco, and a little brown pipe between his teeth, which he smoked in gloomy silence.

The fisherman looked with terror on this strange assembly; the expectation, however, of that which was to happen, kept up his courage. They thus stood round him for a long time, and the smoke of their pipes rose like a cloud over them, through which the stars blinked. The circle drew closer and closer round Will, the smoking increased more furiously, the cloud which rose from their mouths and pipes became more dense. Hawk was a courageous and audacious man; he had prepared himself for extraordinary things, but as this enormous crowd always came nearer and nearer to him, as if they would smother him with numbers, he lost courage, large drops of perspiration bathed his forehead, and he expected to die of fear. His fright may be imagined, when he was about to turn his eyes, he saw sitting upright and stiff close to his head the little yellow man, just as he had seen him for the first time, only now as if to mock the whole assembly, he too had a pipe in his mouth. In the agony of death which now seized him, he called out, turning towards the chief:

"In the name of him whom you serve, who are you, and what do you require of me?"

The tall man puffed three times in a more solemn manner than before, then gave his pipe to his servant, and replied with terrible coldness: "I am Alfred Franz van der Swelder, captain of the ship Carmilhan from Amsterdam, which foundered on this rocky shore with all on board, on its way homeward from Batavia: these are my officers and passengers, and those my brave sailors, who were all drowned with me. Why did you call us up from our dwellings in the deep sea? Why did you disturb our rest?"

"I should like to know where the treasures of the Carmilhan are buried."

"At the bottom of the sea."

"Where?"

"In the cavern of Steenfoll."

"How shall I get them?"

"A goose dives into the abyss for a herring; are not the treasures of the Carmilhan worth as much?"

"How much of it shall I get?"

"More than you will ever be able to spend."

The little yellow man grinned, and the whole assembly burst out laughing.

"Have you finished?" asked the captain further.

"I have. Farewell!"

"Farewell, till we meet again," replied the Dutchman on the point of going away; the musicians again went in front and the whole procession went away in the same order in which it had come, and with the same solemn chanting, which became quieter and more indistinct with the distance, until at last after some time the noise was lost entirely in the surges. Will now used his remaining strength to free himself from his fetters, and succeeded at last in freeing one arm, with which he severed the rope which bound him, and at last rolled himself entirely out of the hide. Without turning round, he hastened towards the hut and found poor Kaspar Strumpf lying on the floor in rigid unconsciousness. With difficulty he brought him round, and the good man cried for joy on seeing his old friend again, whom he had thought lost. This gleam of happiness, however, soon vanished again on hearing from him what a despairing undertaking he was now bent upon.

"I would rather throw myself into hell than look any longer at these naked walls and this misery; whether you follow or not, I shall go."

With these words Will took a torch, with flint and steel, and a rope, and then hastened away. Kaspar ran after him as quickly as he could, and found him already standing on the piece of rock on which he had formerly found protection against the storm, and ready to let himself down by the rope into the roaring black abyss. Finding all his representation to the madman useless, he got ready to descend after him; Hawk, however, ordered him to stay where he was, and to hold the rope. With terrible exertion, to which only the blindest avarice could give courage and strength, Hawk climbed down the cavern, and at last found himself upon a projecting piece of rock, under which black waves tipped with wreaths of white foam, dashed forward. He looked about him eagerly, and at last saw something sparkling in the water just under him. He put down the torch, threw himself down and seized something heavy which he brought up. It was a little iron box full of gold pieces. He told his companion what he had found; he would not, however, listen to his entreaties to be satisfied with it, and ascend again. Hawk thought this was only the first result of his great exertions. He threw himself down once more—a loud laughter resounded from the sea, and Will Hawk was never seen again.

Kaspar went home alone, quite a changed man. The strange sensations which his weak head and sensitive heart suffered, unsettled his mind. He let everything belonging to him go to ruin, and wandered about day and night, staring vacantly before him, pitied and avoided by all his former acquaintances. A fisherman is said to have recognised Will Hawk on a stormy night amidst the crew of the Carmilhan, near the shore, and Kaspar Strumpf also disappeared on the same night. People looked for him everywhere, but no one has ever been able to find a trace of him. But the legend says, that he, together with Hawk, had often been seen amongst the crew of the phantom ship, which has ever since appeared at regular times near the cavern of Steenfoll.

TICONDEROGA

Robert Louis Stevenson

Robert Lewis Balfour Stevenson was born on 13 November 1850 in Edinburgh to father Thomas Stevenson, a foremost lighthouse engineer, and mother, Margaret Isabella. Robert's childhood was wracked with extreme illness, something that would haunt him into his adult years. Too sick to stay at his first primary school, he was educated by tutors. He loved writing and would dictate stories to his mother and nurse before he could write. His father paid to have Robert's first publication, *The Pentland Rising: A Page of History, 1666*, produced on the 200th anniversary of the event.

At eighteen, Robert changed "Lewis" to "Louis". In 1867 Stevenson entered the University of Edinburgh as a science student; he lost interest and turned his sights instead on Scottish history and French literature. His father was upset that Robert did not want to join the family business, but was firm that if Robert wanted to become a writer, a safety net was needed. It was agreed that Robert should practise law. During the summer he would travel to France and write, publishing his first works of travel writing during this time. When he left the University it was with a law degree at twenty-four years old.

He travelled abroad and, when in Paris, met an American magazine writer, Fanny Osbourne. They were together for two years before Fanny was forced to return to America to her husband. Robert headed after her a year later, making the arduous journey from Glasgow to New York on a steamer, before taking the train out to California. When he arrived he was near death. The journey had broken him. They married in 1880 in San Francisco, once Fanny had received her divorce.

From 1880 to 1889 Stevenson wrote his most popular works: *Treasure Island* in 1883, "The Body Snatcher" in 1885, *Kidnapped* and *Strange Case of Dr. Jekyll and Mr. Hyde* in 1886 and, inspired by Robert Marryat's *The Phantom Ship* (1839), *The Master of Ballantrae* in 1889.

Stevenson died of a brain haemorrhage on 3 December 1894, and was interred at the top of Mount Vaea, Apia, Samoa. His legacy is as one of Scotland's most fearless and original writers.

"Ticonderoga: A Legend of the West Highlands" is a poem by Stevenson, first published by *Scribner's* in 1887. It's one of ghostly revenge and is often lost amongst Stevenson's other works.

This is the tale of the man
　　Who heard a word in the night
In the land of the heathery hills,
　　In the days of the feud and the fight.
By the sides of the rainy sea,
　　Where never a stranger came,
On the awful lips of the dead,
　　He heard the outlandish name.
It sang in his sleeping ears,
　　It hummed in his waking head:
The name—Ticonderoga,
　　The utterance of the dead.

On the loch-sides of Appin,
  When the mist blew from the sea,
A Stewart stood with a Cameron:
  An angry man was he.
The blood beat in his ears,
  The blood ran hot to his head,
The mist blew from the sea,
  And there was the Cameron dead.

"O, what have I done to my friend,
  O, what have I done to mysel',
That he should be cold and dead,
  And I in the danger of all?
Nothing but danger about me,
  Danger behind and before,
Death at wait in the heather
  In Appin and Mamore,
Hate at all of the ferries
  And death at each of the fords,
Camerons priming gunlocks
  And Camerons sharpening swords."

But this was a man of counsel,
  This was a man of a score,
There dwelt no pawkier Stewart
  In Appin or Mamore.

He looked on the blowing mist,
  He looked on the awful dead,
And there came a smile on his face
  And there slipped a thought in his head.

Out over cairn and moss,
  Out over scrog and scaur,
He ran as runs the clansman
  That bears the cross of war.
His heart beat in his body,
  His hair clove to his face,
When he came at last in the gloaming
  To the dead man's brother's place.
The east was white with the moon,
  The west with the sun was red,
And there, in the house-doorway,
  Stood the brother of the dead.

"I have slain a man to my danger,
  I have slain a man to my death.
I put my soul in your hands,"
  The panting Stewart saith.
"I lay it bare in your hands,
  For I know your hands are leal;
And be you my targe and bulwark
  From the bullet and the steel."

Then up and spoke the Cameron,
  And gave him his hand again:
"There shall never a man in Scotland
  Set faith in me in vain;
And whatever man you have slaughtered,
  Of whatever name or line,

By the bread of life and the steel of war,
    I make your quarrel mine.
I bid you in to my fireside,
    I share with you house and hall;
It stands upon my honour
    To see you safe from all."

It fell in the time of midnight,
    When the fox barked in the den
And the plaids were over the faces
    In all the houses of men,
That as the living Cameron
    Lay sleepless on his bed,
Out of the night and the other world,
    Came in to him the dead.

"My blood is on the heather,
    My bones are on the hill;
There is joy in the home of ravens
    That the young shall eat their fill.
My blood is poured in the dust,
    My soul is spilled in the air;
And the man that has undone me
    Sleeps in my brother's care."

"I'm wae for your death, my brother,
    But if all of my house were dead,
I couldnae withdraw the plighted hand,
    Nor break the word once said."

"O, what shall I say to our father,
    In the place to which I fare?
O, what shall I say to our mother,

Who greets to see me there?
And to all the kindly Camerons
    That have lived and died long-syne—
Is this the word you send them,
    Fause-hearted brother mine?"

"It's neither fear nor duty,
    It's neither quick nor dead
Shall gar me withdraw the plighted hand,
    Or break the word once said."

Thrice in the time of midnight,
    When the fox barked in the den,
And the plaids were over the faces
    In all the houses of men,
Thrice as the living Cameron
    Lay sleepless on his bed,
Out of the night and the other world
    Came in to him the dead,
And cried to him for vengeance
    On the man that laid him low;
And thrice the living Cameron
    Told the dead Cameron, no.

"Thrice have you seen me, brother,
    But now shall see me no more,
Till you meet your angry fathers
    Upon the farther shore.
Thrice have I spoken, and now,
    Before the cock be heard,
I take my leave for ever
    With the naming of a word.
It shall sing in your sleeping ears,
    It shall hum in your waking head,

The name—Ticonderoga,
  And the warning of the dead."

Now when the night was over
  And the time of people's fears,
The Cameron walked abroad,
  And the word was in his ears.

"Many a name I know,
  But never a name like this;
O, where shall I find a skilly man
  Shall tell me what it is?"

With many a man he counselled
  Of high and low degree,
With the herdsmen on the mountains,
  And the fishers of the sea.
And he came and went unweary,
  And read the books of yore,
And the runes that were written by men of old
  On stones upon the moor.
And many a name he was told,
  But never the name of his fears—
Never, in east or west,
  The name that rang in his ears:
Names of men and of clans,
  Names for the grass and the tree,
For the smallest tarn in the mountains—
  The smallest reef in the sea:
Names for the high and low,
  The names of the crag and the flat;
But in all the land of Scotland,
  Never a name like that.

II

And now there was speech in the south,
    And a man of the south that was wise,
A periwig'd lord of London,
    Called on the clans to rise.
And the riders rode, and the summons
    Came to the western shore,
To the land of the sea and the heather,
    To Appin and Mamore.
It called on all to gather
    From every scrog and scaur,
That loved their fathers' tartan
    And the ancient game of war.

And down the watery valley
    And up the windy hill,
Once more, as in the olden time,
    The pipes were sounding shrill;
Again in highland sunshine
    The naked steel was bright;
And the lads, once more in tartan,
    Went forth again to fight.

"O why should I dwell here
    With a weird upon my life,
When the clansmen shout for battle
    And the war-swords clash in strife?
I cannae joy at feast,
    I cannae sleep in bed,
For the wonder of the word
    And the warning of the dead.
It sings in my sleeping ears,

It hums in my waking head,
The name—Ticonderoga,
    The utterance of the dead.
Then up, and with the fighting men
    To march away from here,
Till the cry of the great war-pipe
    Shall drown it in my ear!"

Where flew King George's ensign
    The plaided soldiers went:
They drew the sword in Germany,
    In Flanders pitched the tent.
The bells of foreign cities
    Rang far across the plain:
They passed the happy Rhine,
    They drank the rapid Main.
Through Asiatic jungles
    The Tartans filed their way,
And the neighing of the war-pipes
    Struck terror in Cathay.

"Many a name have I heard," he thought,
    "In all the tongues of men,
Full many a name both here and there,
    Full many both now and then.
When I was at home in my father's house
    In the land of the naked knee,
Between the eagles that fly in the lift
    And the herrings that swim in the sea,
And now that I am a captain-man
    With a braw cockade in my hat—
Many a name have I heard," he thought,
    "But never a name like that."

III

There fell a war in a woody place,
  Lay far across the sea,
A war of the march in the mirk midnight
  And the shot from behind the tree,
The shaven head and the painted face,
  The silent foot in the wood,
In a land of a strange outlandish tongue
  That was hard to be understood.

It fell about the gloaming
  The general stood with his staff,
He stood and he looked east and west
  With little mind to laugh.

"Far have I been and much have I seen
  And kent both gain and loss,
But here we have woods on every hand
  And a kittle water to cross.
Far have I been and much have I seen
  But never the beat of this;
And there's one must go down to that waterside
  To see how deep it is."

It fell in the dusk of the night
  When unco things betide,
The skilly captain, the Cameron,
  Went down to that waterside.
Canny and soft the captain went;
  And a man of the woody land,
With the shaven head and the painted face,
  Went down at his right hand.

It fell in the quiet night,
  There was never a sound to ken;
But all of the woods to the right and the left
  Lay filled with the painted men.

"Far have I been and much have I seen
  Both as a man and boy,
But never have I set forth a foot
  On so perilous an employ."

It fell in the dusk of the night
  When unco things betide,
That he was aware of a captain-man
  Drew near to the waterside.
He was aware of his coming
  Down in the gloaming alone;
And he looked in the face of the man,
  And lo! the face was his own.

"This is my weird," he said,
  "And now I ken the worst;
For many shall fall the morn,
  But I shall fall with the first.
O you of the outland tongue,
  You of the painted face,
This is the place of my death;
  Can you tell me the name of the place?"

"Since the Frenchmen have been here
  They have called it Sault-Marie;
But that is a name for priests,
  And not for you and me.
It went by another word,"

Quoth he of the shaven head:
"It was called Ticonderoga
    In the days of the great dead."

And it fell on the morrow's morning,
    In the fiercest of the fight,
That the Cameron bit the dust
    As he foretold at night;
And far from the hills of heather,
    Far from the isles of the sea,
He sleeps in the place of the name
    As it was doomed to be.

"DEATH TO THE HEAD THAT WEARS NO HAIR!"

David Grant

David Grant (1823–1886) was a poet, born in Affrusk, Upper Banchory. He had a happy childhood, which he spent writing rude verse. He left home at twenty-four and studied at Aberdeen Grammar School and proceeded to Marischal College, but ill-health stopped him from completing more than two years there. He became a teacher in Stonehaven, then moved to Morayshire and became the editor of the *Elgin Courier*. When he took up the post of Master at Canisbay Parochial School, he sent prose and verse to the Aberdeen Herald—they would publish him till his death. Grant moved between Glasgow, Sheffield and London, always teaching and making himself known in literary circles. It was during this time that *Metrical Poems and Other Tales* was published. The following tale, "Death to the Head that Wears No Hair!" was serialised in *Aberdeen Free Press* before it was collected in the posthumous *Scotch Stories* in 1888. It's cheeky, it's funny, it's weird and encapsulates Scots humour. David died suddenly in 1886, leaving a wife and two children. He is an author who has been largely lost to the mists of time but should be at the front of any Scots revival.

TOWARDS the end of the summer of 18—, the Rev. Dr. Woodcross, Her Majesty's Inspector of Schools for the Highlands and Isles of Scotland, received instructions to proceed to the Shetland Islands and make a careful report of the state of elementary education in those remote parts of Her Majesty's dominions.

The mission was one which the Inspector would have been glad to remit to his assistant, a much younger man, for he was by no means fond of the rough seas of the far North at so advanced a period of the year.

Moreover, a former experience in the same region had taught him that the Shetlanders were not very partial to Governmental officials generally, and that the lower orders of them looked, at that time, with special disfavour on the threatened interference with their educational affairs.

The Doctor could not forget how, on the occasion of his first visit in an official capacity, the islanders seemed to have considerable difficulty in distinguishing between him and the officers of Excise—gentlemen who appeared to be very obnoxious to them.

As he was being ferried from one island to another, he had been at some pains to make the nature of his business clear to the crew of the boat, and to point out the benefits likely to arise from a liberal education; but he failed completely to carry conviction to the minds of his auditors whose opinions were summed up and clenched, so to speak by the skipper in the following words:—

"I've heard say that education is a good thing, and it may be so in some respects; but this I'm well sure of, it's not a necessary—for there's a hand that can neither read nor write" (at the same time extending one of his sledgehammer fists) "but it can pull an oar or kill a cod with any hand in Shetland."

The Lairds of Shetland were not more favourable to an extended education than the owner of the "hand that could neither read nor write," for they were aware that it would lead, in the long run, to a demand for better schools and school-houses, and a consequent tax upon their pockets.

It was further in the Doctor's recollection that the ministers of the Established Church were also in favour of letting matters educational in Shetland slide, because they saw in the introduction of the "grants-in-aid" the beginning of an interference which would seriously diminish their control over the schools in their parishes, if not ultimately abolish it altogether.

These considerations would have had slight influence with the Doctor at almost any other time, but during the previous spring and summer he had added on to his official duties the preparation of some school-books, which had cost him no small labour and thought. He was consequently in a condition, mental and physical, which would have made a less arduous and unpopular mission much more acceptable.

However, the orders of my Lords of the Committee of Council on Education were peremptory. Dr. Woodcross was personally to make a careful inspection of the state of education in the Shetlands, and lay before my Lords a report based upon his own observations. Obedience was imperative.

Accordingly the Rev. Doctor went on board the steamer "Prince Consort" at Aberdeen, and in due course found himself safely landed at Lerwick, the chief town of the Shetland Islands.

During his tour of inspection the Doctor received various unmistakable indications of the unpopularity of his mission, and he was therefore well pleased when he had finished collecting the information which he considered necessary to enable him to draw up the required report.

Not that he had had any real reason to dread personal violence, or had experienced serious personal discourtesy, far from it; but still he had felt that he was among those who had but little goodwill towards the object of his visit; and in addition to this he was, in consequence of the extra strain of work during the spring and summer, out of sorts, nervous, and subject at the time to those vague, groundless apprehensions which so frequently supervene on mental exhaustion.

It was thus with a feeling of relief that he returned to Lerwick to await the arrival of the steamer which would convey him back to Aberdeen.

The Doctor had not taken time during his tour to see anything of Shetland society, although he had been urgently requested to partake of the hospitality of several ministers and proprietors. But when his inspection was completed, and he found that he would have to wait for the steamer several days at Lerwick, he recollected that, on his way north, he had formed the acquaintance of a Mr. Swanson, a passenger like himself on board of the "Prince Consort," and that this gentleman had given him a very pressing invitation to pay him a visit.

Mr. Swanson resided in the mainland, at a distance of only a mile and a half from the town, and as he had proved himself an intelligent and agreeable travelling companion, the Doctor thought he could not more pleasantly pass a spare evening than in enjoying his society and hospitality.

Having despatched a note on the previous day to apprise Mr. Swanson of his intended visit, the Doctor set out from the chief hotel in Lerwick early on a November afternoon, and, after a leisurely walk of three-quarters of an hour's duration, arrived at his destination, the residence of the proprietor of Westercliffe.

Westercliffe House, called more frequently Westercliffe Castle by courtesy, was a large, grey, gloomy-looking mansion, of a nondescript style of architecture, overlooking the melancholy waters of the Northern Ocean, whose long, rolling billows were to be seen that evening breaking in sheets of foam upon the rugged edges of the rock-bound coast.

The mansion stood about 200 yards back from the shore, facing inland, and the cliffs behind it ran sheer down three or four hundred feet to meet the incessant shock of the wildly-moaning surge.

In front of the house, and towards the right and left, the land rose so high as to limit the view to a semicircle of less than a quarter of a mile in radius, within which no other human habitation was visible.

In the frame of mind in which the Doctor then was, the melancholy, solitary grandeur of the place impressed him with an awe and superstitious dread which had well-nigh compelled him to return to Lerwick without paying his intended visit.

He had, however, as was before mentioned, sent word to Mr. Swanson to expect him, and therefore he shook off, as far as possible, his nervous feeling, and marched boldly up to the door.

He was warmly welcomed by his host and hostess, and introduced to five or six other gentlemen who had been invited to meet him, and he soon began to feel more at ease.

The early part of the evening was passed in general conversation, and, although a few allusions were made to the Doctor's mission in its professional sense, yet those were sufficient to show him that it was not very warmly approved by any member of the company, the laws of hospitality alone preventing them from giving expression in terms more pithy to their real sentiments on the subject.

The Doctor would therefore gladly have limited his visit to a protracted call, but that his host and hostess would not hear of. They said that the evening was particularly fine, that the moon would be up between nine and ten o'clock, and, in conjunction with the northern lights, would make the night as clear as day; and, besides, good care should be taken to see Dr. Woodcross within sure reach of Lerwick.

There was no resisting such hospitality, and the Doctor could think of no good excuse for refusing it.

As the evening wore on the company were served with a plentiful repast, which, for want of a more fitting name, may be termed a "tea supper."

Previously there had been no lack of "drams," but as soon as supper was fairly over, whisky-punch was introduced in all its glory.

Toast-drinking then began, and numerous northern stories of perilous adventures by sea and land were related.

The Doctor was himself a capital story-teller, and he was not slow to exercise his gifts that night, but his stock consisted for the most part of probable, lively, and ludicrous incidents, while the narratives related by his host and the other guests were chiefly of a supernatural, horrible, and blood-curdling character.

When the night was pretty far advanced, a thick-set, harsh-featured man on the Doctor's left hand told a thrilling tale concerning the tragic death of an unpopular exciseman, who was related to have been first brutally tortured and finally precipitated over a cliff into the sea by a band of daring smugglers, who could not, however, be convicted of the crime.

The Doctor had from the first felt an instinctive dislike of the thick-set man, and shuddered with horror at the tale which he had related with such a thrilling minuteness of detail.

According to the laws of Shetland conviviality, the last story-teller could either call on another for a story or toast, or he might propose a toast himself, and in the exercise of his right the thick-set man demanded full bumpers for a toast.

The Doctor was a moderate drinker at all times, and on that occasion he had contrived to drink several toasts with one glass of punch, a proceeding which did not seem to meet the approval of either his host or of his fellow-guests.

The thick-set man, in particular, had rallied him somewhat boisterously on his abstemiousness.

To avoid importunities, therefore, the Doctor was careful to replenish his glass to this particular toast as requested.

The thick-set man, having filled himself a brimmer, sprang to his feet, and said that he had a toast to propose which, he believed, every man in that company would honour with a glass filled to the brim and drained to the bottom.

Here he paused, appeared to Dr. Woodcross to fix his eyes on him, and gave forth in a stentorian voice as a toast—

“Death to the Head that Wears no Hair!”

The Doctor threw a rapid glance round the company, and observed that the head of every individual in it save his own was supplied with an abundant natural covering of hair. His, the mirror over the mantelpiece showed him as bare as the back of his own hand.

The observation startled him, and a sudden thrill of dread ran through his entire frame. He could hear his own heart beat, and feel that chill, crawling sensation of the flesh which dread horror inspires.

He believed himself a doomed man. His was "the head that wore no hair;" the only bald head in the company, and doubtless he was the person whose death was so tragically denounced by the thick-set ruffian on his left.

As the events of a lifetime are said to be condensed into the struggling moments of a drowning person, so did every suspicious circumstance connected with his unpopular mission flash across the doctor's mind, magnified ten, twenty, a hundred-fold by terror.

There was not a single doubt left in his mind but that his destruction had been determined, pre-arranged, and would speedily be executed.

At that lone house, in that remote region, he could easily be murdered, and his body made away with, without any suspicion of foul play being awakened in the minds of his dearest friends.

He might be beaten to death with the bludgeon-like walking-sticks, which he had observed in the entrance hall; starved to death in one of the dungeons which doubtless existed under the *quasi* castle; or he might be precipitated over the cliffs, like the unpopular exciseman, and justice might never overtake the perpetrators of the horrible crime.

It could easily be given out that he had fallen over the rocks into the sea on his way back to Lerwick, and none out of that company would doubt the truth of the statement.

In that company the scowl of a fixed hostile determination appeared on every countenance. All in it were his enemies. None would intercede for him, none would compassionate him.

Under plea of household duties the hostess had retired, and there were thus only men of stern, relentless purpose to be dealt with.

Resistance was hopeless, mercy scarce to be dreamt of.

But while these thoughts were flashing with electric swiftness through the mind of the doomed man, the glasses were slowly, steadily rising.

Should he drink or dash his glass to the floor?

What! Drink to his own destruction. No; but he would drink to sharpen his wits, to deaden his terror, to nerve him to meet his fate like a man.

Like the rest around the board, he raised the glass to his lips, and this time he drained the contents to the last drop.

Deafening cheers followed the act, but the Doctor sank back into his chair pale as a "sheeted ghost."

Happily his agitation was quite unobserved.

On the contrary, the thick-set man actually slapped him on the back, and complimented him vociferously for having emptied his glass to the last toast "like a jolly good fellow."

"But what does it all mean?" gasped the bewildered Inspector.

"Why," said his neighbour, "the toast is well known to every Shetlander, but you as a stranger are quite excusable for not having understood it, and I owe you an apology for introducing it without a suitable explanation. You must know that here in Shetland we are all more or less interested in the fishing trade, and as the head of the fish has no hair on it, and the more fish that are caught and die so much the better for our interests. 'Death to the head that wears no hair' is a toast which always commands full bumpers in our convivial meetings."

Dr. Woodcross thanked the thick-set man for his explanation, which he considered perfectly satisfactory. Having, however, had quite enough conviviality for that evening, he soon started for Lerwick under a suitable guide, and arrived at the hotel at which he was putting up, with "the head that wore no hair" perfectly safe on its owner's shoulders.

Of course, nobody would have known of the mistake into which the Doctor had fallen, but he was fond of a good story, and used to tell this one with much dramatic effect as long as he lived, in order, as he would say, to illustrate the fact that, under certain mental conditions, a person may convert the most innocuous circumstances into causes of the most serious apprehension.

THE GHOSTS OF CRAIG-AULNAIC

Anonymous

"The Ghosts of Craig-Aulnaic" may have an anonymous author, but its editor, Charles John Tibbitts, oversaw many books of folklore, collecting tales from Scotland, Germany, Ireland, England, Russia, Scandinavia and Asia. Tibbitts was also the editor of the *Weekly Dispatch*, a prominent newspaper that ran from 1801–1961. During his tenure, in 1901, he was found guilty of perverting "the due course of justice" in a child cruelty case and sentenced to six weeks' imprisonment alongside his co-conspirator, a "crime investigator" called Charles Windust.

Our simple ghost tale, set in Banffshire, sees the poor farmer James Gray simply trying to tend to his sheep. He has his ear bent in every direction by two "celebrated" ghosts. The story includes a loss of fine savoury fish.

T WO celebrated ghosts existed, once on a time, in the wilds of Craig-Aulnaic, a romantic place in the district of Strathdown, Banffshire. The one was a male and the other a female. The male was called Fhuna Mhoir Ben Baynac, after one of the mountains of Glenavon, where at one time he resided; and the female was called Clashnichd Aulnaic, from her having had her abode in Craig-Aulnaic. But although the great ghost of Ben Baynac was bound by the common ties of nature and of honour to protect and cherish his weaker companion, Clashnichd Aulnaic, yet he often treated her in the most cruel and unfeeling manner. In the dead of night, when the surrounding hamlets were buried in deep repose, and when nothing else disturbed the solemn stillness of the midnight scene, oft would the shrill shrieks of poor Clashnichd burst upon the slumberer's ears, and awake him to anything but pleasant reflections.

But of all those who were incommoded by the noisy and unseemly quarrels of these two ghosts, James Owre or Gray, the tenant of the farm of Balbig of Delnabo, was the greatest sufferer. From the proximity of his abode to their haunts, it was the misfortune of himself and family to be the nightly audience of Clashnichd's cries and lamentations, which they considered anything but agreeable entertainment.

One day as James Gray was on his rounds looking after his sheep, he happened to fall in with Clashnichd, the ghost of Aulnaic, with whom he entered into a long conversation. In the course of it he took occasion to remonstrate with her on the very disagreeable disturbance she caused himself and family by her wild and unearthly cries—cries which, he said, few mortals could relish in the dreary hours of midnight. Poor Clashnichd, by way of apology for her conduct, gave James Gray a sad account of her usage, detailing at full length the series of cruelties committed upon her by Ben Baynac. From this account, it appeared that her living with the latter was by no means a matter of choice with Clashnichd; on the contrary, it seemed that she had, for a long time, lived apart with much comfort, residing in a snug dwelling, as already mentioned, in the wilds of Craig-Aulnaic; but Ben Baynac having unfortunately taken into his head to pay her a visit, took a fancy, not to herself, but her dwelling, of which, in his own name and authority, he took immediate possession, and soon after he expelled poor Clashnichd, with many stripes, from her natural inheritance. Not satisfied with invading and depriving her of her just rights, he was in the habit of following her into her private haunts, not with the view of offering her any endearments, but for the purpose of inflicting on her person every torment which his brain could invent.

Such a moving relation could not fail to affect the generous heart of James Gray, who determined from that moment to risk life and limb in order to vindicate the rights and avenge the wrongs of poor Clashnichd, the ghost of Craig-Aulnaic. He, therefore, took good care to interrogate his new *protégée* touching the nature of her oppressor's constitution, whether he was of that *killable* species of ghost that could be shot with a silver sixpence, or if there was any other weapon that could possibly accomplish his annihilation. Clashnichd informed him that she had occasion to know that Ben Baynac was wholly invulnerable to all the weapons of man, with the exception of a large mole on his left breast, which was no doubt penetrable by silver or steel; but that, from the specimens she had of his personal prowess and strength, it were vain for mere man to attempt to combat him. Confiding, however, in his expertness as an archer—for he was allowed to be the best marksman of the age—James Gray told Clashnichd he did not fear him with all his might,—that *he* was a man; and desired her, moreover, next time the ghost chose to repeat his incivilities to her, to apply to him, James Gray, for redress.

It was not long ere he had an opportunity of fulfilling his promises. Ben Baynac having one night, in the want of better amusement, entertained himself by inflicting an inhuman castigation on Clashnichd, she lost no time in waiting on James Gray, with a full and particular account of it. She found him smoking his *cutty*, for it was night when she came to him; but, notwithstanding the inconvenience of the hour, James needed no great persuasion to induce him to proceed directly along with Clashnichd to hold a communing with their friend, Ben Baynac, the great ghost. Clashnichd was stout and sturdy, and understood the knack of travelling much better than our women do. She expressed a wish that, for the sake of expedition, James Gray would suffer her to bear him along, a motion to which the latter agreed; and a few minutes brought them close to the scene of Ben Baynac's residence. As they approached his haunt, he came forth to meet them, with looks and gestures which did not at all indicate a cordial welcome. It was a fine moonlight night, and they could easily observe his actions. Poor Clashnichd was now sorely afraid of the great ghost. Apprehending instant destruction from his fury, she exclaimed to James Gray that they would be both dead people, and that immediately, unless James Gray hit with an arrow the mole which covered Ben Baynac's heart. This was not so difficult a task as James had hitherto apprehended it. The mole was as large as a common bonnet, and yet nowise disproportioned to the natural size of the ghost's body, for he certainly was a great and a mighty ghost. Ben Baynac cried out to James Gray that he would soon make eagle's meat of him; and certain it is, such was his intention, had not the shepherd so effectually stopped him from the execution of it. Raising his bow to his eye when within a few yards of Ben Baynac, he took deliberate aim; the arrow flew—it hit—a yell from Ben Baynac announced the result. A hideous howl re-echoed from the surrounding mountains, responsive to the groans of a thousand ghosts; and Ben Baynac, like the smoke of a shot, vanished into air.

Clashnichd, the ghost of Aulnaic, now found herself emancipated from the most abject state of slavery, and restored to freedom and liberty, through the invincible courage of James Gray. Overpowered with gratitude, she fell at his feet, and vowed to devote the whole of her time and talents towards his service and prosperity. Meanwhile, being anxious to have her remaining goods and furniture removed to her former dwelling, whence she had been so iniquitously expelled by Ben Baynac, the great ghost, she requested of her new master the use of his horses to remove them. James observing on the adjacent hill a flock of deer, and wishing to have a trial of his new servant's sagacity or expertness, told her those were his horses—she was welcome to the use of them; desiring that when she had done with them, she would inclose them in his stable. Clashnichd then proceeded to make use of the horses, and James Gray returned home to enjoy his night's rest.

Scarce had he reached his arm-chair, and reclined his cheek on his hand, to ruminate over the bold adventure of the night, when Clashnichd entered, with her "breath in her throat," and venting the bitterest complaints at the unruliness of his horses, which had broken one-half of her furniture, and caused her more trouble in the stabling of them than their services were worth.

"Oh! they are stabled, then?" inquired James Gray. Clashnichd replied in the affirmative. "Very well," rejoined James, "they shall be tame enough tomorrow."

From this specimen of Clashnichd, the ghost of Craig-Aulnaic's expertness, it will be seen what a valuable acquisition her service proved to James Gray and his young family. They were, however, speedily deprived of her assistance by a most unfortunate accident. From the sequel of the story, from which the foregoing is an extract, it appears that poor Clashnichd was deeply addicted to propensities which at that time rendered her kin so obnoxious to their human neighbours. She was constantly in the habit of visiting her friends much oftener than she was invited, and, in the course of such visits, was never very scrupulous in making free with any eatables which fell within the circle of her observation.

One day, while engaged on a foraging expedition of this description, she happened to enter the Mill of Delnabo, which was inhabited in those days by the miller's family. She found his wife engaged in roasting a large gridiron of fine savoury fish, the agreeable smell proceeding from which perhaps occasioned her visit. With the usual inquiries after the health of the miller and his family, Clashnichd proceeded with the greatest familiarity and good-humour to make herself comfortable at their expense. But the miller's wife, enraged at the loss of her fish, and not relishing such unwelcome familiarity, punished the unfortunate Clashnichd rather too severely for her freedom. It happened that there was at the time a large caldron of boiling water suspended over the fire, and this caldron the enraged wife overturned in Clashnichd's bosom!

Scalded beyond recovery, she fled up the wilds of Craig-Aulnaic, uttering the most melancholy lamentations, nor has she been ever heard of since.

THE STAG-HAUNTED STREAM

Mrs. Campbell of Dunstaffnage

Frustratingly, without a first name for Mrs. Campbell, the full identity of this author may forever remain anonymous. As the book was edited by Archibald Campbell (1846–1913), there may be scope to suggest that Mrs Campbell could be a close relative. Answers on a postcard, please!

I n the ages gone by, when chiefs were wont to seek for fame, glory, and, perchance, wealth in foreign climes, a great man departed from the Western land, bound on some such errand. His noble wife, six years before, had left him a widower, she having been stricken with a terrible plague which raged throughout the land. Their only child, Morag, survived, and she was her father's joy. "Where," said he, "can I leave my child when I quit my home for a time?" After having thought over this matter, he recollected his kinsman, Fillan More, and he decided to leave his daughter under the shelter of his roof, where she would be watched over by his wife, and cheered by his happy household; there, thought he, she will grow in stature and in mind, and acquire all necessary feminine accomplishments, and grow into a vigorous woman. He noticed that there was a pallor on her cheek, not usual in a Highland girl, and that her gait lacked the elasticity of perfect health. No sooner had he thought the matter out than he acted on the decision arrived at, and he wrote to his kinsman, and all was arranged for the reception of Morag. She parted in sorrow from her father, but he assured her it was not for long, and was able to inspire some feeling of comfort in the poor child's heart; for child she was, as yet being but thirteen years of age when this took place. Morag soon became as one of the family. She joined both boys and girls in all their amusements, and before many months were over she was the picture of a healthy, happy girl.

Time slipped away. Years passed without her father returning, though Morag often heard of his ever-increasing prosperity, and of his many noble and daring deeds.

The two sons, Dermid and Cailean, were Morag's devoted slaves, and would encounter any peril to procure for her the accomplishment of her wishes; and, as might be expected, before either of them were aware of it, the hearts of both the young fellows were given to Morag.

She was now in her seventeenth year, and of surpassing beauty of form and disposition. It was long before she realised that for either of them she had other than sisterly love, but circumstances occurred causing Dermid to unburden his heart and speak of his feelings, and poor Morag felt she could have sympathised with his brother had he approached with such words.

It was the old tale, so often to be renewed, of the course of true love seldom running smooth, and in this case it ended in a dire calamity.

The subject came up, and a bitter quarrel took place. The first tragedy that darkened the world was again to be repeated. There, on the mountainside lay Cailean, slain by his brother, the heather and the moss dyed crimson with his life-blood. And Morag! who can portray her feelings? She wept and wept, until her tears formed a stream down the side of Ben Cruachan, and from its waters her lover reappeared in the form of a stag, which may to this day be seen near that water in the early hours of autumnal mornings.

—1895—

THE TWO SISTERS AND THE CURSE

Translated by
Rev. John Gregorson Campbell

John Gregorson Campbell (1836–1891), was a Scottish folklorist and Free Church minister in Tiree. Gregorson transcribed the stories as they were told to him with minimal comments, a trait not followed by other Christian ministers who often held their parishioners' tales and myths with nothing but contempt. His books included *Clan Traditions and Popular Tales of the Western Highlands and Islands* (1895), *Superstitions of the Highlands and Islands of Scotland* and *Witchcraft and Second Sight in the West Highlands*, all of which were published in the years after his death.

TWO sisters were living in the same township on the south side of Mull. One of them who was known as Lovely *Mairearad*[1] had a fairy sweetheart, who came where she was, unknown to anyone, until one day she confided the secret to her sister, who was called Ailsa[2] (*Ealasaid*), and told her how she dearly loved her fairy sweetheart. "And now, sister," she said, "you will not tell any one." "No," her sister answered, "I will not tell any one; that story will as soon pass from my lips as it will from my knee (*o'm ghlùn*)"; but she did not keep her promise; she told the secret of the fairy sweetheart to others, and when he came again, he found that he was observed, and he went away and never returned, nor was he seen or heard of ever after by any one in the place. When the lovely sister came to know this, she left her home and became a wanderer among the hills and hollows, and never afterwards came inside of a house door, to stand or sit down, while she lived. Those who herded cattle (*ag uallach threud*) tried frequently to get near her and persuade her to return home, but they never succeeded further than to hear her crooning a melancholy song in which she told how her sister had been false to her, and that the wrong done to her would be avenged on the sister or her descendants, if a fairy (*neach sìth*) has power. On hearing that Ailsa was married, she repeated, "Dun Ailsa is married and has a son Torquil, and the evil will be avenged on her or on him (*phòs, phòs Ealasaid Odhar*,[3] *&c.*)." What she hummed in her mournful song was:—

My mother's place is deserted, empty and cold,
My father, who loved me, is asleep in the tomb,
Friendless and solitary I wander through the fields,
Since there is none in the world of my kindred

But a sister without pity.
She asked, and I told, out of the fulness of my joy;
There was none nearer of kin to know my secret;
But I felt, and this brought the tears to my eyes,
      (*lit.*, raindrip on my sight),
That a story comes sooner from the lip than from the knee.

She was then heard to utter these wishes:—

May nothing on which you have set your expectations ever grow,
Nor dew ever fall on your ground.
May no smoke rise from your dwelling,
In the depth of the hardest winter,
May the worm be in your store,
And the moth under the lid of your chests.
If a fay-being has power,
Revenge will be taken though it may be on your descendants.

Tha suidheag mo mhàthar gu fàs, falamh, fuar,
Tha m' athair 'thug luaidh dhomh 'n a shuain fo 'n lic.
Gun daoine gun duine na raoin tha mi 'siubhal,
'S gun 's an t-saoghal do 'm chuideachd
Ach piuthar gun iochd.
Dh' iarr ise 's thug mise do mheud mo thoil-inntinn;
'S mi gun neach 'bu dìsle g' an innsinn mo rùn;
Ach dh' fhairich mi sid 's thug e snidh' air mo léirsinn
Gur luaithe 'thig sgeul o 'n bheul na o 'n ghlùn.

An sin thuirt i na guidheachan so:—

"Na-na-chinn 's na-na-chuir thu t-ùidh,
'S na-na-shil an driùchd ad shlios,
'S na-na-rug ad bhothan smùid

160

Ann an dùlachd crùth an crios;⁴
Gu 'n robh a' chnuimheag ann ad stòr
'S an leòmann fo bhòrd do chist';
Ma tha cumhachd aig neach sìth,
Dìolar ge b' ann air do shliochd."

Ailsa (*Ealasaid*) married, and had one son. In some way her afflicted sister
heard of this, and she then added to her song:—

Dun Ailsa has married,
And she has a son Torquil.
Brown-haired Torquil who can climb the headland
And bring the seal off the waves,
The sickle in your hand is sharp,
You will in two swaths reap a sheaf.

Phòs, phòs Ealasaid Odhar,
'S tha mac aice—Torcuil.
Torcuil donn 'dhìreadh sròin,
'S a bheireadh ròn bhàrr nan stuadh,
Bu sgaiteach do chorran 'n ad dhòrn
'S dheanadh tu dhà dhlòth an sguab.

Whatever gifts the brown-haired only child of her sister was favoured with,
besides others, he was a noted reaper, but this gift proved fatal to him (*dh'
fhòghainn e dha*). When he grew up to manhood, he could reap as much as
seven men, and none among them could compete with him. He was then
told that a strange woman was seen coming to the harvest fields in autumn,
after the reapers had left, and that she would reap a field before daylight
next morning, or any part of the ripe corn that the reapers could not finish
that day, and in whatever field she began, she left the work of seven reapers,
finished, after her. She was known as the Maiden of the Cairn (*Gruagach⁵ a'
chùirn*), from being seen to come out of a cairn over opposite. One evening

then, brown-haired Torquil, who desired to see her at work, being later than usual of returning home, on looking back saw her beginning in his own field. He returned, and finding his sickle where he had put it away, he took it with him, and after her he went. He resolved to overtake her and began to reap the next furrow, saying, "You are a good reaper or I will overtake you;" but the harder he worked, the more he saw that instead of getting nearer to her, she was drawing further away from him, and he then called out to her,

"Maiden of the cairn, wait for me, wait for me." (*'Ghruagach a' chùirn, fuirich rium, fuirich rium.*)

She said, answering him,

"Handsome brown-haired youth, overtake me, overtake me." (*'Fhleasgaich a' chuil-duinn, beir orm, beir orm.*)

He was confident that he would overtake her, and went on after her till the moon was darkened by a cloud; he then called to her,

"The moon is clouded (*lit.* smothered by a cloud), delay, delay." (*Tha 'ghealach air a mùchadh fo neòil, fuirich rium, fuirich rium.*)

"I have no other light but her, overtake me, overtake me," she said.

He did not, nor could he, overtake her, and on seeing again how far she was in advance of him, he said, "I am weary with yesterday's reaping, wait for me, wait for me." She answered, "I ascended the round hill of steep summits (*màm cas nan leac*), overtake me, overtake me;" but he could not. He then said, "My sickle would be the better of being sharpened (*air a bhleath*), wait for me, wait for me." She answered, "My sickle will not cut garlic, overtake me, overtake me." At this she reached the head of the furrow, finished reaping, and stood still where she was, waiting for him. When he reached the head of his own furrow, he caught the last handful of corn,[6] to keep it, as was the custom, it being the "Harvest Maiden" (*a' mhaighdean-bhuana*), and stood with it in one hand and the sickle in the other. Looking at her steadily in the face, he said,

"You have put the old woman far from me, and it is not my displeasure you deserve." (*Chuir thu a' chailleach fada uam's cha b' e mo ghruaim a thoill thu.*)[7]

She said,

"It is an evil thing early on Monday to reap the harvest maiden." (*'S dona 'n ni* (var., *mì-shealbhach*) *moch Di-luain dol a bhuain maighdein.*)

On her saying this, he fell dead on the field and never more drew breath. The Maiden of the Cairn was never afterwards seen, nor heard of; and that was how the sister's wishes ended.

NOTES

1. This name is sometimes rendered in English, Margaret. Erraid Isle (*Eilean earraid*) is in the Sound of Iona, south of Mull.
2. The rock of Ailsa in the firth of Clyde is called in Gaelic *Creag Ealasaid*, and *Ealasaid a' chuain* (Ailsa of the sea). A round grey rock lying near the shore in Mannal, south side of Tiree, is called *Sgeir Ealasaid*, the Ailsa rock. The name *Ealasaid* is in English also as Elizabeth and Elspeth.
3. *Odhar*, dun or grey, is applied to cattle; as, *bò mhaol odhar*, a dun hornless cow; *gabhar mhaol odhar*, a grey goat: it is sometimes used as an expression of contempt, as *creutair odhar*, a dun creature. The diminutive of *odhar*, *odhrag*, is a pet name for a cow.
4. The words of the first four lines of "the wishes," are, as regards their form in the Gaelic text, almost unintelligible; they merely represent the sounds uttered by the reciter, without being correct either in form or composition. The sounds belonging to the first line might, for instance, have been represented thus:—'*Na ana-chìnnt 's 'n a an-shocair dhuit d' ùidh*: perhaps the utterance was intentionally ambiguous.—(Ed.)
5. *Gruagach*, the supernatural being, in this instance was said to be a woman; but *gruagach* usually meant a chief.
6. There was a custom at one time, that the last handful of corn that was cut, and which finished the harvest, was taken home by the reaper, who was usually the youngest person in the family who could reap. The bunch was tastefully decorated and kept, at least till the following year, as the harvest maiden.
7. It was also a custom in other times for old women to go about asking charity, and if infirm, they were carried about from house to house and villages, and whoever was last in a township to finish the reaping of his corn had to maintain one that year, and the same thing might happen to him the next year. When the run-rig system was common, the last furrow of corn was sometimes left standing as no one could be got to own it, through fear of having to keep the old woman for a year.

THE OUTGOING OF THE TIDE

John Buchan

John Buchan (28 August 1875–11 February 1940) was a novelist and politician. He was born in Kirkcaldy and spent his summers with his grandparents in the Scottish Borders. He was awarded a scholarship to the University of Glasgow at seventeen then moved to Brasenose College in Oxford in 1895, which coincided with his first novel, *Sir Quixote of the Moors*. In 1910 he wrote his first major novel, *Prester John*, a South African set adventure novel. He wrote for the British War Propaganda Bureau during the Great War and was sent out to the Western Front in 1916, attached to the Intelligence Section. During this period his most famous novel, *The Thirty-Nine Steps*, was published. Buchan moved to Canada in 1935 and spent his last years there before suffering a head injury, caused by a stroke. He died aged 64, having written twenty-eight novels (one published posthumously) forty-four works of non-fiction, eleven biographies, four poetry collections and five short story collections (one published posthumously). "The Outgoing of the Tide" is a tale that feels lost amongst Buchan's oeuvre, but it's one that's worth rescuing. It was originally published in *The Atlantic Monthly* in 1902. I discovered it in my twenties when I read it in a distressed paperback of *The Watcher by the Threshold*, published by the mighty Digit Books. Said to be from the unpublished notes of the Reverend John Dennistoun, "Tide" is about a tryst set to take place on Beltane's Eve.

From the unpublished Remains of the Reverend John Dennistoun,
sometime minister of the Gospel in the parish of Caulds,
and author of Satan's Artifices against the Elect.

"Between the hours of twelve and one, even at the turning of the tide."

MEN come from distant parts to admire the tides of Solloway, which race in at flood and retreat at ebb with a greater speed than a horse can follow. But nowhere are there queerer waters than in our own parish of Caulds at the place called the Sker Bay, where between two horns of land a shallow estuary receives the stream of the Sker. I never daunder by its shores, and see the waters hurrying like messengers from the great deep, without solemn thoughts and a memory of Scripture words on the terror of the sea. The vast Atlantic may be fearful in its wrath, but with us it is no clean open rage, but the deceit of the creature, the unholy ways of quicksands when the waters are gone, and their stealthy return like a thief in the night watches. But in the times of which I write there were more awful fears than any from the violence of nature. It was before the day of my ministry in Caulds, for then I was a bit callant in short clothes in my native parish of Lesmahagow; but the worthy Doctor Chrystal, who had charge of spiritual things, has told me often of the power of Satan and his emissaries in that lonely place. It was the day of warlocks and apparitions, now happily driven out by the zeal of the General Assembly. Witches pursued their wanchancy calling, bairns were spirited away, young lassies selled their souls to the evil one, and the Accuser of the Brethren in the shape of a black tyke was seen about cottage doors in the gloaming. Many and earnest were the prayers of good Doctor Chrystal, but the evil thing, in spite of his wrestling, grew and flourished in his midst. The parish stank of idolatry, abominable rites were practised in secret, and in all the bounds there was no one had a more evil name for this black traffic than one Alison Sempill, who bode at the Skerburnfoot.

The cottage stood nigh the burn in a little garden with lilyoaks and gro-sart bushes lining the pathway. The Sker ran by in a linn among hollins, and the noise of its waters was ever about the place. The highroad on the other side was frequented by few, for a nearer-hand way to the west had been made through the Lowe Moss. Sometimes a herd from the hills would pass by with sheep, sometimes a tinkler or a wandering merchant, and once in a long while the laird of Heriotside on his grey horse riding to Gledsmuir. And they who passed would see Alison hirpling in her garden, speaking to herself like the ill wife she was, or sitting on a cutty-stool by the doorside with her eyes on other than mortal sights. Where she came from no man could tell. There was some said she was no woman, but a ghost haunting a mortal tenement. Others would threep she was gentrice, come of a perse-cuting family in the west, that had been ruined in the Revolution wars. She never seemed to want for siller; the house was as bright as a new preen, the yaird better delved than the manse garden; and there was routh of fowls and doos about the small steading, forbye a wheen sheep and milk-kye in the fields. No man ever saw Alison at any market in the countryside, and yet the Skerburnfoot was plenished yearly in all proper order. One man only worked on the place, a doited lad who had long been a charge to the parish, and who had not the sense to fear danger or the wit to understand it. Upon all other the sight of Alison, were it but for a moment, cast a cold grue, not to be remembered without terror.

It seems she was not ordinarily ill-faured, as men use the word. She was maybe sixty years in age, small and trig, with her grey hair folded neatly under her mutch. But the sight of her eyes was not a thing to forget. John Dodds said they were the een of a deer with the devil ahint them, and indeed they would so appal an onlooker that a sadden unreasoning terror came into his heart, while his feet would impel him to flight. Once John, being overtaken in drink on the roadside by the cottage, and dreaming that he was burning in hell, woke, and saw the old wife hobbling towards him. Thereupon he fled soberly to the hills, and from that day became a quiet-living, humble-minded Christian. She moved about the country like a wraith, gathering herbs in dark loanings, lingering in kirkyairds, and casting a blight on innocent bairns. Once Robert Smillie found her in a ruinous kirk on the Lang Muir where of old the idolatrous rites of Rome were practised. It was a hot day, and in the quiet place the flies buzzed in crowds, and he noted that she sat clothed in them as with a garment, yet suffering no discomfort. Then he, having mind of Beelzebub, the god of flies, fled without a halt homewards; but, falling in the Coo's Loan, broke two ribs and a collar-bone, the whilk misfortune was much blessed to his soul. And there were darker tales in the countryside—of weans stolen, of lassies misguided, of innocent beasts cruelly tortured, and in one and all there came in the name of the wife of the Skerburnfoot.

It was noted by them that kenned best that her cantrips were at their worst when the tides in the Sker Bay ebbed between the hours of twelve and one. At this season of the night the tides of mortality run lowest, and when the outgoing of these unco waters fell in with the setting of the current of life, then indeed was the hour for unholy revels. While honest men slept in their beds, the auld rudas carlines took their pleasure. That there is a delight in sin no man denies, but to most it is but a broken glint in the pauses of their conscience. But what must be the hellish joy of those lost beings who have forsworn God and trysted with the Prince of Darkness, it is not for a Christian to say. Certain it is that it must be great, though their master waits at the end of the road to claim the wizened things they call their souls. Serious men, notably Gidden Scott in the Back of the Hill and Simon Wauch in the Sheiling of Chasehope, have seen Alison wandering on the wet sands, dancing to no earthly music, while the heavens, they said, were full of lights and sounds which betokened the presence of the Prince of the Powers of the Air. It was a season of heart-searching for God's saints in Caulds, and the dispensation was blessed to not a few.

It will seem strange that in all this time the Presbytery was idle, and no effort was made to rid the place of so fell an influence. But there was a reason, and the reason, as in most like cases, was a lassie. Forbye Alison there lived at the Skerburnfoot a young maid, Ailie Sempill, who by all accounts was as good and bonnie as the other was evil. She passed for a daughter of Alison's, whether born in wedlock or not I cannot tell; but there were some said she was no kin to the auld witch-wife, but some bairn spirited away from honest parents. She was young and blithe, with a face like an April morning and a voice in her that put the laverocks to shame. When she sang in the kirk folk have told me that they had a foretaste of the music of the New Jerusalem, and when she came in by the village of Caulds old men stottered to their doors to look at her. Moreover, from her earliest days the bairn had some glimmerings of grace. Though no minister would visit the Skerburnfoot, or if he went, departed quicker than he came, the girl Ailie attended regular at the catechising at the Mains of Sker. It may be that Alison thought she would be a better offering for the devil if she were given the chance of forswearing God, or it may be that she was so occupied in her own dark business that she had no care of the bairn. Meanwhile the lass grew up in the nurture and admonition of the Lord. I have heard Doctor Chrystal say that he never had a communicant more full of the things of the Spirit. From the day when she first declared her wish to come forward to the hour when she broke bread at the table, she walked like one in a dream. The lads of the parish might cast admiring eyes on her bright cheeks and yellow hair as she sat in her white gown in the kirk, but well they knew she was not for them. To be the bride of Christ was the thought that filled her heart; and when at the fencing of the tables Doctor Chrystal preached from Matthew nine and fifteen, "Can the children of the bride-chamber mourn, as long as the bridegroom is with them?" it was remarked by sundry that Ailie's face was liker the countenance of an angel than of a mortal lass.

It is with the day of her first communion that this narrative of mine begins. As she walked home after the morning table she communed in secret and her heart sang within her. She had mind of God's mercies in the past: how He had kept her feet from the snares of evil-doers which had been spread around her youth. She had been told unholy charms like the seven south streams and the nine rowan berries, and it was noted when she went first to the catechising that she prayed "Our Father which wert in heaven," the prayer which the ill wife Alison had taught her, meaning by it Lucifer, who had been in heaven and had been cast out therefrom. But when she had come to years of discretion she had freely chosen the better part, and evil had ever been repelled from her soul like Gled water from the stones of Gled brig. Now she was in a rapture of holy content. The drucken bell—for the ungodly fashion lingered in Caulds—was ringing in her ears as she left the village, but to her it was but a kirk bell and a goodly sound. As she went through the woods where the primroses and the whitethorn were blossoming, the place seemed as the land of Elam, wherein there were twelve wells and threescore and ten palm trees. And then, as it might be, another thought came into her head, for it is ordained that frail mortality cannot long continue in holy joy. In the kirk she had been only the bride of Christ; but as she came through the wood, with the birds lilting and the winds of the world blowing, she had mind of another lover.

For this lass, though so cold to men, had not escaped the common fate. It seemed that the young Heriotside, riding by one day, stopped to speir something or other, and got a glisk of Ailie's face, which caught his fancy. He passed the road again many times, and then he would meet her in the gloaming or of a morning in the field as she went to fetch the kye. "Blue are the hills that are far away" is an owercome in the countryside, and while at first on his side it may have been but a young man's fancy, to her he was like the god Apollo descending from the skies. He was good to look on, brawly dressed, and with a tongue in his head that would have wiled the bird from the tree. Moreover, he was of gentle kin, and she was a poor lass biding in a cot-house with an ill-reputed mother. It seems that in time the young man, who had begun the affair with no good intentions, fell honestly in love, while she went singing about the doors as innocent as a bairn, thinking of him when her thoughts were not on higher things. So it came about that long ere Ailie reached home it was on young Heriotside that her mind dwelt, and it was the love of him that made her eyes glow and her cheeks redden.

Now it chanced that at that very hour her master had been with Alison, and the pair of them were preparing a deadly pit. Let no man say that the devil is not a cruel tyrant. He may give his folk some scrapings of unhallowed pleasure; but he will exact tithes, yea of anise and cummin, in return, and there is aye the reckoning to pay at the hinder end. It seems that now he was driving Alison hard. She had been remiss of late, fewer souls sent to hell, less zeal in quenching the Spirit, and above all the crowning offence that her bairn had communicated in Christ's kirk. She had waited overlong, and now it was like that Ailie would escape her toils. I have no skill of fancy to tell of that dark collogue, but the upshot was that Alison swore by her lost soul and the pride of sin to bring the lass into thrall to her master. The fiend had bare departed when Ailie came over the threshold to find the auld carline glunching by the fire.

It was plain she was in the worst of tempers. She flyted on the lass till the poor thing's cheek paled. "There you gang," she cried, "troking wi' thae wearifu' Pharisees o' Caulds, whae daurna darken your mither's door. A bonnie dutiful child, quotha! Wumman, hae ye nae pride?—no even the mense o' a tinkler lass?" And then she changed her voice, and would be as soft as honey. "My puir wee Ailie! was I thrawn till ye? Never mind, my bonnie. You and me are a' that's left, and we maunna be ill to ither." And then the two had their dinner, and all the while the auld wife was crooning over the lass. "We maun 'gree weel," she says, "for we're like to be our lee-lane for the rest o' our days. They tell me Heriotside is seeking Joan o' the Croft, and they're sune to be cried in Gledsmuir kirk."

It was the first the lass had heard of it, and you may fancy she was struck dumb. And so with one thing and other the auld witch raised the fiends of jealousy in that innocent heart. She would cry out that Heriotside was an ill-doing wastrel, and had no business to come and flatter honest lassies. And then she would speak of his gentle birth and his leddy mother, and say it was indeed presumption to hope that so great a gentleman could mean all that he said. Before long Ailie was silent and white, while her mother rhymed on about men and their ways. And then she could thole it no longer, but must go out and walk by the burn to cool her hot brow and calm her thoughts, while the witch indoors laughed to herself at her devices.

For days Ailie had an absent eye and a sad face, and it so fell out that in all that time young Heriotside, who had scarce missed a day, was laid up with a broken arm and never came near her. So in a week's time she was beginning to hearken to her mother when she spoke of incantations and charms for restoring love. She kenned it was sin; but though not seven days syne she had sat at the Lord's table, so strong is love in a young heart that she was on the very brink of it. But the grace of God was stronger than her weak will. She would have none of her mother's runes and philters, though her soul cried out for them. Always when she was most disposed to listen some merciful power stayed her consent. Alison grew thrawner as the hours passed. She kenned of Heriotside's broken arm, and she feared that any day he might recover and put her stratagems to shame. And then it seems that she collogued with her master and heard word of a subtler device. For it was approaching that uncanny time of year, the festival of Beltane, when the auld pagans were wont to sacrifice to their god Baal. In this season warlocks and carlines have a special dispensation to do evil, and Alison waited on its coming with graceless joy. As it happened, the tides in the Sker Bay ebbed at this time between the hours of twelve and one, and, as I have said, this was the hour above all others when the powers of darkness were most potent. Would the lass but consent to go abroad in the unhallowed place at this awful season and hour of the night, she was as firmly handfasted to the devil as if she had signed a bond with her own blood. For there, it seemed, the forces of good fled far away, the world for one hour was given over to its ancient prince, and the man or woman who willingly sought the spot was his bond-servant for ever. There are deadly sins from which God's people may recover. A man may even communicate unworthily, and yet, so be it he sin not against the Holy Ghost, he may find forgiveness. But it seems that for this Beltane sin there could be no pardon, and I can testify from my own knowledge that they who once committed it became lost souls from that day. James Deuchar, once a promising professor, fell thus out of sinful bravery and died blaspheming; and of Kate Mallison, who went the same road, no man can tell. Here, indeed, was the witch-wife's chance, and she was the more eager, for her master had warned her that this was her last chance. Either Ailie's soul would be his, or her auld wrinkled body and black heart would be flung from this pleasant world to their apportioned place.

Some days later it happened that young Heriotside was stepping home over the Lang Muir about ten at night—it being his first jaunt from home since his arm had mended. He had been to the supper of the Forest Club at the Cross Keys in Gledsmuir, a clamjamfry of wild young blades who passed the wine and played at cartes once a fortnight. It seems he had drunk well, so that the world ran round about and he was in the best of tempers. The moon came down and bowed to him, and he took off his hat to it. For every step he travelled miles, so that in a little he was beyond Scotland altogether and pacing the Arabian desert. He thought he was the Pope of Rome, so he held out his foot to be kissed, and rolled twenty yards to the bottom of a small brae. Syne he was the King of France, and fought hard with a whin-bush till he had banged it to pieces. After that nothing would content him but he must be a bogle, for he found his head dunting on the stars and his legs were knocking the hills together. He thought of the mischief he was doing to the auld earth, and sat down and cried at his wickedness. Then he went on, and maybe the steep road to the Moss Rig helped him, for he began to get soberer and ken his whereabouts.

On a sudden he was aware of a man linking along at his side. He cried "A fine night," and the man replied. Syne, being merry from his cups, he tried to slap him on the back. The next he kenned he was rolling on the grass, for his hand had gone clean through the body and found nothing but air.

His head was so thick with wine that he found nothing droll in this. "Faith, friend," he says, "that was a nasty fall for a fellow that has supped weel. Where might your road be gaun to?"

"To the World's End," said the man; "but I stop at the Skerburnfoot."

"Bide the night at Heriotside," says he. "It's a thought out of your way, but it's a comfortable bit."

"There's mair comfort at the Skerburnfoot," said the dark man.

Now the mention of the Skerburnfoot brought back to him only the thought of Ailie and not of the witch-wife, her mother. So he jaloused no ill, for at the best he was slow in the uptake.

The two of them went on together for a while, Heriotside's fool head filled with the thought of the lass. Then the dark man broke silence. "Ye're thinkin' o' the maid Ailie Sempill," says he.

"How ken ye that?" asked Heriotside.

"It is my business to read the herts o' men," said the other.

"And who may ye be?" said Heriotside, growing eerie.

"Just an auld packman," said he—"nae name ye wad ken, but kin to mony gentle houses."

"And what about Ailie, you that ken sae muckle?" asked the young man.

"Naething," was the answer—"naething that concerns you, for ye'll never get the lass."

"By God, and I will!" says Heriotside, for he was a profane swearer.

"That's the wrong name to seek her in, anyway," said the man.

At this the young laird struck a great blow at him with his stick, but found nothing to resist him but the hill wind.

When they had gone on a bit the dark man spoke again. "The lassie is thirled to holy things," says he. "She has nae care for flesh and blood, only for devout contemplation."

"She loves me," says Heriotside.

"Not you," says the other, "but a shadow in your stead."

At this the young man's heart began to tremble, for it seemed that there was truth in what his companion said, and he was ower drunk to think gravely.

"I kenna whatna man ye are," he says, "but ye have the skill of lassies' hearts. Tell me truly, is there no way to win her to common love?"

"One way there is," said the man, "and for our friendship's sake I will tell it you. If ye can ever tryst wi' her on Beltane's Eve on the Sker sands, at the green link o' the burn where the sands begin, on the ebb o' the tide when the midnight is bye but afore cockcrow, she'll be yours, body and soul, for this world and for ever."

And then it appeared to the young man that he was walking his lone up the grass walk of Heriotside, with the house close by him. He thought no more of the stranger he had met, but the word stuck in his heart.

It seems that about this very time Alison was telling the same tale to poor Ailie. She cast up to her every idle gossip she could think of. "It's Joan o' the Croft," was aye her owercome, and she would threep that they were to be cried in kirk on the first Sabbath of May. And then she would rhyme on about the black cruelty of it, and cry down curses on the lover, so that her daughter's heart grew cauld with fear. It is terrible to think of the power of the world even in a redeemed soul. Here was a maid who had drunk of the well of grace and tasted of God's mercies, and yet there were moments when she was ready to renounce her hope. At those awful seasons God seemed far off and the world very nigh, and to sell her soul for love looked a fair bargain. At other times she would resist the devil and comfort herself with prayer; but aye when she woke there was the sore heart, and when she went to sleep there were the weary eyes. There was no comfort in the goodliness of spring or the bright sunshine weather, and she who had been wont to go about the doors lightfoot and blithe was now as dowie as a widow woman.

And then one afternoon in the hinder end of April came young Heriotside riding to the Skerburnfoot. His arm was healed, he had got him a fine new suit of green, and his horse was a mettle beast that well set off his figure. Ailie was standing by the doorstep as he came down the road, and her heart stood still with joy. But a second thought gave her anguish. This man, so gallant and braw, would never be for her; doubtless the fine suit and the capering horse were for Joan o' the Croft's pleasure. And he in turn, when he remarked her wan cheek and dowie eyes, had mind of what the dark man said on the muir, and saw in her a maid sworn to no mortal love. Yet the passion for her had grown fiercer than ever, and he swore to himself that he would win her back from her phantasies. She, one may believe, was ready enough to listen. As she walked with him by the Sker water his words were like music to her ears, and Alison within-doors laughed to herself and saw her devices prosper.

He spoke to her of love and his own heart, and the girl hearkened gladly. Syne he rebuked her coldness and cast scorn upon her piety, and so far was she beguiled that she had no answer. Then from one thing and another he spoke of some true token of their love. He said he was jealous, and craved a token to ease his care. "It's but a small thing I ask," says he; "but it will make me a happy man, and nothing ever shall come atween us. Tryst wi' me for Beltane's Eve on the Sker sands, at the green link o' the burn where the sands begin, on the ebb o' the tide when midnight is bye but afore cockcrow. For," said he, "that was our forbears' tryst for true lovers, and wherefore no for you and me?"

The lassie had grace given her to refuse, but with a woeful heart, and Heriotside rode off in black discontent, leaving poor Ailie to sigh her lone. He came back the next day and the next, but aye he got the same answer. A season of great doubt fell upon her soul. She had no clearness in her hope, nor any sense of God's promises. The Scriptures were an idle tale to her, prayer brought her no refreshment, and she was convicted in her conscience of the unpardonable sin. Had she been less full of pride she would have taken her troubles to good Doctor Chrystal and got comfort; but her grief made her silent and timorous, and she found no help anywhere. Her mother was ever at her side, seeking with coaxings and evil advice to drive her to the irrevocable step. And all the while there was her love for the man riving in her bosom and giving her no ease by night or day. She believed she had driven him away and repented her denial. Only her pride held her back from going to Heriotside and seeking him herself. She watched the road hourly for a sight of his face, and when the darkness fell she would sit in a corner brooding over her sorrows.

At last he came, speiring the old question. He sought the same tryst, but now he had a further tale. It seemed he was eager to get her away from the Skerburnside and auld Alison. His aunt, the Lady Balcrynie, would receive her gladly at his request till the day of their marriage. Let her but tryst with him at the hour and place he named, and he would carry her straight to Balcrynie, where she would be safe and happy. He named that hour, he said, to escape men's observation for the sake of her own good name. He named that place, for it was near her dwelling, and on the road between Balcrynie and Heriotside, which fords the Sker Burn. The temptation was more than mortal heart could resist. She gave him the promise he sought, stifling the voice of conscience; and as she clung to his neck it seemed to her that heaven was a poor thing compared with a man's love.

Three days remained till Beltane's Eve, and throughout the time it was noted that Heriotside behaved like one possessed. It may be that his conscience pricked him, or that he had a glimpse of his sin and its coming punishment. Certain it is that, if he had been daft before, he now ran wild in his pranks, and an evil report of him was in every mouth. He drank deep at the Cross Keys, and fought two battles with young lads that had angered him. One he let off with a touch on the shoulder, the other goes lame to this day from a wound he got in the groin. There was word of the procurator-fiscal taking note of his doings, and, troth, if they had continued long he must have fled the country. For a wager he rode his horse down the Dow Craig, wherefore the name of the place is the Horseman's Craig to this day. He laid a hundred guineas with the laird of Slipperfield that he would drive four horses through the Slipperfield loch, and in the prank he had his bit chariot dung to pieces and a good mare killed. And all men observed that his eyes were wild and his face grey and thin, and that his hand would twitch as he held the glass, like one with the palsy.

The eve of Beltane was lown and hot in the low country, with fire hanging in the clouds and thunder grumbling about the heavens. It seems that up in the hills it had been an awesome deluge of rain, but on the coast it was still dry and lowering. It is a long road from Heriotside to the Skerburnfoot. First you go down the Heriot Water, and syne over the Lang Muir to the edge of Mucklewhan. When you pass the steadings of Mirehope and Cockmalane you turn to the right and ford the Mire Burn. That brings you on to the turnpike road, which you will ride till it bends inland, when you keep on straight over the Whinny Knowes to the Sker Bay. There, if you are in luck, you will find the tide out and the place fordable dryshod for a man on a horse. But if the tide runs, you will do well to sit down on the sands and content yourself till it turn, or it will be the solans and scarts of the Solloway that will be seeing the next of you.

On this Beltane's Eve the young man, after supping with some wild young blades, bade his horse be saddled about ten o'clock. The company were eager to ken his errand, but he waved them back. "Bide here," he says, "and birl the wine till I return. This is a ploy of my own on which no man follows me." And there was that in his face as he spoke which chilled the wildest, and left them well content to keep to the good claret and the soft seat and let the daft laird go his own ways.

Well and on, he rode down the bridle-path in the wood, along the top of the Heriot glen, and as he rode he was aware of a great noise beneath him. It was not wind, for there was none, and it was not the sound of thunder, and aye as he speired at himself what it was it grew the louder till he came to a break in the trees. And then he saw the cause, for Heriot was coming down in a furious flood, sixty yards wide, tearing at the roots of the aiks, and flinging red waves against the drystone dykes. It was a sight and sound to solemnise a man's mind, deep calling unto deep, the great waters of the hills running to meet with the great waters of the sea. But Heriotside recked nothing of it, for his heart had but one thought and the eye of his fancy one figure. Never had he been so filled with love of the lass, and yet it was not happiness but a deadly secret fear.

As he came to the Lang Muir it was geyan dark, though there was a moon somewhere behind the clouds. It was little he could see of the road, and ere long he had tried many moss-pools and sloughs, as his braw new coat bare witness. Aye in front of him was the great hill of Mucklewhan, where the road turned down by the Mire. The noise of the Heriot had not long fallen behind him ere another began, the same eerie sound of burns crying to ither in the darkness. It seemed that the whole earth was overrun with waters. Every little runnel in the bog was astir, and yet the land around him was as dry as flax, and no drop of rain had fallen. As he rode on the din grew louder, and as he came over the top of Mirehope he kenned by the mighty rushing noise that something uncommon was happening with the Mire Burn. The light from Mirehope sheiling twinkled on his left, and had the man not been dozened with his fancies he might have observed that the steading was deserted and men were crying below in the fields. But he rode on, thinking of but one thing, till he came to the cot-house of Cockmalane, which is nigh the fords of the Mire.

John Dodds, the herd who bode in the place, was standing at the door, and he looked to see who was on the road so late.

"Stop," says he, "stop, Laird Heriotside. I kenna what your errand is, but it is to no holy purpose that ye're out on Beltane Eve. D'ye no hear the warning o' the waters?"

And then in the still night came the sound of Mire like the clash of armies.

"I must win over the ford," says the laird quietly, thinking of another thing.

"Ford!" cried John in scorn. "There'll be nae ford for you the nicht unless it be the ford o' the river Jordan. The burns are up, and bigger than man ever saw them. It'll be a Beltane's Eve that a' folk will remember. They tell me that Gled valley is like a loch, and that there's an awesome folk drooned in the hills. Gin ye were ower the Mire, what about crossin' the Caulds and the Sker?" says he, for he jaloused he was going to Gledsmuir.

And then it seemed that that word brought the laird to his senses. He looked the airt the rain was coming from, and he saw it was the airt the Sker flowed. In a second, he has told me, the works of the devil were revealed to him. He saw himself a tool in Satan's hands, he saw his tryst a device for the destruction of the body, as it was assuredly meant for the destruction of the soul, and there came on his mind the picture of an innocent lass borne down by the waters with no place for repentance. His heart grew cold in his breast. He had but one thought, a sinful and reckless one—to get to her side, that the two might go together to their account. He heard the roar of the Mire as in a dream, and when John Dodds laid hands on his bridle he felled him to the earth. And the next seen of it was the laird riding the floods like a man possessed.

The horse was the grey stallion he aye rode, the very beast he had ridden for many a wager with the wild lads of the Cross Keys. No man but himself durst back it, and it had lamed many a hostler lad and broke two necks in its day. But it seemed it had the mettle for any flood, and took the Mire with little spurring. The herds on the hillside looked to see man and steed swept into eternity; but though the red waves were breaking about his shoulders and he was swept far down, he aye held on for the shore. The next thing the watchers saw was the laird struggling up the far bank, and casting his coat from him, so that he rode in his sark. And then he set off like a wildfire across the muir towards the turnpike road.

Two men saw him on the road and have recorded their experience. One was a gangrel, by name M'Nab, who was travelling from Gledsmuir to Allerkirk with a heavy pack on his back and a bowed head. He heard a sound like wind afore him, and, looking up, saw coming down the road a grey horse stretched out to a wild gallop and a man on its back with a face like a soul in torment. He kenned not whether it was devil or mortal, but flung himself on the roadside, and lay like a corp for an hour or more till the rain aroused him. The other was one Sim Doolittle, the fish hawker from Allerfoot, jogging home in his fish cart from Gledsmuir fair. He had drunk more than was fit for him, and he was singing some light song, when he saw approaching, as he said, the pale horse mentioned in the Revelations, with Death seated as the rider. Thoughts of his sins came on him like a thunderclap, fear loosened his knees, he leaped from the cart to the road, and from the road to the back of a dyke. Thence he flew to the hills, and was found the next morning far up among the Mire Craigs, while his horse and cart were gotten on the Aller sands, the horse lamed and the cart without the wheels.

At the tollhouse the road turns inland to Gledsmuir, and he who goes to Sker Bay must leave it and cross the wild land called the Whinny Knowes, a place rough with bracken and foxes' holes and old stone cairns. The toll-man, John Gilzean, was opening his window to get a breath of air in the lown night when he heard or saw the approaching horse. He kenned the beast for Heriotside's, and, being a friend of the laird's, he ran down in all haste to open the yett, wondering to himself about the laird's errand on this night. A voice came down the road to him bidding him hurry; but John's old fingers were slow with the keys, and so it happened that the horse had to stop, and John had time to look up at the gash and woeful face.

"Where away the nicht sae late, laird?" says John.

"I go to save a soul from hell," was the answer.

And then it seems that through the open door there came the chapping of a clock.

"Whatna hour is that?" asks Heriotside.

"Midnicht," says John, trembling, for he did not like the look of things.

There was no answer but a groan, and horse and man went racing down the dark hollows of the Whinny Knowes.

How he escaped a broken neck in that dreadful place no man will ever tell. The sweat, he has told me, stood in cold drops upon his forehead; he scarcely was aware of the saddle in which he sat; and his eyes were stelled in his head, so that he saw nothing but the sky ayont him. The night was growing colder, and there was a small sharp wind stirring from the east. But, hot or cold, it was all one to him, who was already cold as death. He heard not the sound of the sea nor the peesweeps startled by his horse, for the sound that ran in his ears was the roaring Sker Water and a girl's cry. The thought kept goading him, and he spurred the grey till the creature was madder than himself. It leaped the hole which they call the Devil's Mull as I would step over a thistle, and the next he kenned he was on the edge of the Sker Bay.

It lay before him white and ghastly, with mist blowing in wafts across it and a slow swaying of the tides. It was the better part of a mile wide, but save for some fathoms in the middle where the Sker current ran, it was no deeper even at flood than a horse's fetlocks. It looks eerie at bright midday when the sun is shining and whaups are crying among the seaweeds; but think what it was on that awesome night with the powers of darkness brooding over it like a cloud. The rider's heart quailed for a moment in natural fear. He stepped his beast a few feet in, still staring afore him like a daft man. And then something in the sound or the feel of the waters made him look down, and he perceived that the ebb had begun and the tide was flowing out to sea.

He kenned that all was lost, and the knowledge drove him to stark despair. His sins came in his face like birds of night, and his heart shrank like a pea. He knew himself for a lost soul, and all that he loved in the world was out in the tides. There, at any rate, he could go too, and give back that gift of life he had so blackly misused. He cried small and soft like a bairn, and drove the grey out into the waters. And aye as he spurred it the foam should have been flying as high as his head; but in that uncanny hour there was no foam, only the waves running sleek like oil. It was not long ere he had come to the Sker channel, where the red moss-waters were roaring to the sea, an ill place to ford in midsummer heat, and certain death, as folks reputed it, at the smallest spate. The grey was swimming, but it seemed the Lord had other purposes for him than death, for neither man nor horse could drown. He tried to leave the saddle, but he could not; he flung the bridle from him, but the grey held on, as if some strong hand were guiding. He cried out upon the devil to help his own, he renounced his Maker and his God; but whatever his punishment, he was not to be drowned. And then he was silent, for something was coming down the tide.

It came down as quiet as a sleeping bairn, straight for him as he sat with his horse breasting the waters, and as it came the moon crept out of a cloud and he saw a glint of yellow hair. And then his madness died away and he was himself again, a weary and stricken man. He hung down over the tides and caught the body in his arms, and then let the grey make for the shallows. He cared no more for the devil and all his myrmidons, for he kenned brawly he was damned. It seemed to him that his soul had gone from him and he was as toom as a hazel shell. His breath rattled in his throat, the tears were dried up in his head, his body had lost its strength, and yet he clung to the drowned maid as to a hope of salvation. And then he noted something at which he marvelled dumbly. Her hair was drookit back from her clay-cold brow, her eyes were shut, but in her face there was the peace of a child. It seemed even that her lips were smiling. Here, certes, was no lost soul, but one who had gone joyfully to meet her Lord. It may be in that dark hour at the burnfoot, before the spate caught her, she had been given grace to resist her adversary and flung herself upon God's mercy.

And it would seem that it had been granted, for when he came to the Skerburnfoot there in the corner sat the weird-wife Alison, dead as a stone and shrivelled like a heather birn.

For days Heriotside wandered the country or sat in his own house with vacant eye and trembling hands. Conviction of sin held him like a vice:

he saw the lassie's death laid at his door, her face haunted him by day and night, and the word of the Lord dirled in his ears telling of wrath and punishment. The greatness of his anguish wore him to a shadow, and at last he was stretched on his bed and like to perish. In his extremity worthy Doctor Chrystal went to him unasked and strove to comfort him. Long, long the good man wrestled, but it seemed as if his ministrations were to be of no avail. The fever left his body, and he rose to stotter about the doors; but he was still in his torments, and the mercy-seat was far from him. At last in the back end of the year came Mungo Muirhead to Caulds to the autumn communion, and nothing would serve him but he must try his hand at this storm-tossed soul. He spoke with power and unction, and a blessing came with his words, the black cloud lifted and showed a glimpse of grace, and in a little the man had some assurance of salvation. He became a pillar of Christ's Kirk, prompt to check abominations, notably the sin of witchcraft; foremost in good works; but with it all a humble man, who walked contritely till his death. When I came first to Caulds I sought to prevail upon him to accept the eldership, but he aye put me by, and when I heard his tale I saw that he had done wisely. I mind him well as he sat in his chair or daundered through Caulds, a kind word for every one and sage counsel in time of distress, but withal a severe man to himself and a crucifier of the body. It seems that this severity weakened his frame, for three years syne come Martinmas he was taken ill with a fever, and after a week's sickness he went to his account, where I trust he is accepted.

ASSIPATTLE AND THE MESTER STOORWORM

Elizabeth W. Grierson

Elizabeth W. Grierson was born in Hawick in 1869, the second daughter of farmer Andrew Grierson. Predominantly a children's writer, her books included *The Children's Book of Edinburgh*, *Children's Tales from Scottish Ballads*, *The Children's Book of Celtic Stories*, *Vivian's Lesson* and *The Scottish Fairy Book* which includes "The Milk-White Doo"—a story which I selected for my 2022 anthology *Celtic Weird*. Grierson acknowledged that her work owed much to the four-volume collection *Popular Tales of the Western Highlands* by John Francis Campbell (1862), but here she did herself a disservice. She imbued her folklore tales with a true sense of wonder, tapping into the Lowlands of Scotland in particular, teasing out many of its hidden supernatural inhabitants. She was dedicated to two churches for the last forty years of her life, Old St. Pauls in Edinburgh and St. Cuthbert's, Hawick, and undertook many trips abroad as a missionary. Working and writing till the end of her life, she died in 1943.

"Assipattle and the Mester Stoorworm" is one of those romps you can imagine being read to children at night during the Edwardian era. It is sly, abundantly humorous, and if you have children, choose a suitably dark and stormy evening to sit by them and read a full-on Scottish fairy tale! And if you don't have children, grab a cuppa and delight yourself!

I N far bygone days, in the North, there lived a well-to-do farmer, who had seven sons and one daughter. And the youngest of these seven sons bore a very curious name; for men called him Assipattle, which means, "He who grovels among the ashes."

Perhaps Assipattle deserved his name, for he was rather a lazy boy, who never did any work on the farm as his brothers did, but ran about the doors with ragged clothes and unkempt hair, and whose mind was ever filled with wondrous stories of Trolls and Giants, Elves and Goblins.

When the sun was hot in the long summer afternoons, when the bees droned drowsily and even the tiny insects seemed almost asleep, the boy was content to throw himself down on the ash-heap amongst the ashes, and lie there, lazily letting them run through his fingers, as one might play with sand on the sea-shore, basking in the sunshine and telling stories to himself.

And his brothers, working hard in the fields, would point to him with mocking fingers, and laugh, and say to each other how well the name suited him, and of how little use he was in the world.

And when they came home from their work, they would push him about and tease him, and even his mother would make him sweep the floor, and draw water from the well, and fetch peats from the peat-stack, and do all the little odd jobs that nobody else would do.

So poor Assipattle had rather a hard life of it, and he would often have been very miserable had it not been for his sister, who loved him dearly, and who would listen quite patiently to all the stories that he had to tell; who never laughed at him or told him that he was telling lies, as his brothers did.

But one day a very sad thing happened—at least, it was a sad thing for poor Assipattle.

For it chanced that the King of these parts had one only daughter, the Princess Gemdelovely, whom he loved dearly, and to whom he denied nothing. And Princess Gemdelovely was in want of a waiting-maid, and as she had seen Assipattle's sister standing by the garden gate as she was riding by one day, and had taken a fancy to her, she asked her father if she might ask her to come and live at the Castle and serve her.

Her father agreed at once, as he always did agree to any of her wishes; and sent a messenger in haste to the farmer's house to ask if his daughter would come to the Castle to be the Princess's waiting-maid.

And, of course, the farmer was very pleased at the piece of good fortune which had befallen the girl, and so was her mother, and so were her six brothers, all except poor Assipattle, who looked with wistful eyes after his sister as she rode away, proud of her new clothes and of the rivlins which her father had made her out of cowhide, which she was to wear in the Palace when she waited on the Princess, for at home she always ran barefoot.

Time passed, and one day a rider rode in hot haste through the country bearing the most terrible tidings. For the evening before, some fishermen, out in their boats, had caught sight of the Mester Stoorworm, which, as everyone knows, was the largest, and the first, and the greatest of all Sea-Serpents. It was that beast which, in the Good Book, is called the Leviathan, and if it had been measured in our day, its tail would have touched Iceland, while its snout rested on the North Cape.

And the fishermen had noticed that this fearsome Monster had its head turned towards the mainland, and that it opened its mouth and yawned horribly, as if to show that it was hungry, and that, if it were not fed, it would kill every living thing upon the land, both man and beast, bird and creeping thing.

For 'twas well known that its breath was so poisonous that it consumed as with a burning fire everything that it lighted on. So that, if it pleased the awful creature to lift its head and put forth its breath, like noxious vapour, over the country, in a few weeks the fair land would be turned into a region of desolation.

As you may imagine, everyone was almost paralysed with terror at this awful calamity which threatened them; and the King called a solemn meeting of all his Counsellors, and asked them if they could devise any way of warding off the danger.

And for three whole days they sat in Council, these grave, bearded men, and many were the suggestions which were made, and many the words of wisdom which were spoken; but, alas! no one was wise enough to think of a way by which the Mester Stoorworm might be driven back.

At last, at the end of the third day, when everyone had given up hope of finding a remedy, the door of the Council Chamber opened and the Queen appeared.

Now the Queen was the King's second wife, and she was not a favourite in the Kingdom, for she was a proud, insolent woman, who did not behave kindly to her step-daughter, the Princess Gemdelovely, and who spent much more of her time in the company of a great Sorcerer, whom everyone feared and dreaded, than she did in that of the King, her husband.

So the sober Counsellors looked at her disapprovingly as she came boldly into the Council Chamber and stood up beside the King's Chair of State, and, speaking in a loud, clear voice, addressed them thus:

"Ye think that ye are brave men and strong, oh, ye Elders, and fit to be the Protectors of the People. And so it may be, when it is mortals that ye are called on to face. But ye be no match for the foe that now threatens our land. Before him your weapons be but as straw. 'Tis not through strength of arm, but through sorcery, that he will be overcome. So listen to my words, even though they be but those of a woman, and take counsel with the great Sorcerer, from whom nothing is hid, but who knoweth all the mysteries of the earth, and of the air, and of the sea."

Now the King and his Counsellors liked not this advice, for they hated the Sorcerer, who had, as they thought, too much influence with the Queen; but they were at their wits' end, and knew not to whom to turn for help, so they were fain to do as she said and summon the Wizard before them.

And when he obeyed the summons and appeared in their midst, they liked him none the better for his looks. For he was long, and thin, and awesome, with a beard that came down to his knee, and hair that wrapped him about like a mantle, and his face was the colour of mortar, as if he had always lived in darkness, and had been afraid to look on the sun.

But there was no help to be found in any other man, so they laid the case before him, and asked him what they should do. And he answered coldly that he would think over the matter, and come again to the Assembly the following day and give them his advice.

And his advice, when they heard it, was like to turn their hair white with horror.

For he said that the only way to satisfy the Monster, and to make it spare the land, was to feed it every Saturday with seven young maidens, who must be the fairest who could be found; and if, after this remedy had been tried once or twice, it did not succeed in mollifying the Stoorworm and inducing him to depart, there was but one other measure that he could suggest, but that was so horrible and dreadful that he would not rend their hearts by mentioning it in the meantime.

And as, although they hated him, they feared him also, the Council had e'en to abide by his words, and pronounced the awful doom.

And so it came about that, every Saturday, seven bonnie, innocent maidens were bound hand and foot and laid on a rock which ran into the sea, and the Monster stretched out his long, jagged tongue, and swept them into his mouth; while all the rest of the folk looked on from the top of a high hill—or, at least, the men looked—with cold, set faces, while the women hid theirs in their aprons and wept aloud.

"Is there no other way," they cried, "no other way than this, to save the land?"

But the men only groaned and shook their heads. "No other way," they answered; "no other way."

Then suddenly a boy's indignant voice rang out among the crowd. "Is there no grown man who would fight that Monster, and kill him, and save the lassies alive? I would do it; I am not feared for the Mester Stoorworm."

It was the boy Assipattle who spoke, and everyone looked at him in amazement as he stood staring at the great Sea-Serpent, his fingers twitching with rage, and his great blue eyes glowing with pity and indignation.

"The poor bairn's mad; the sight hath turned his head," they whispered one to another; and they would have crowded round him to pet and comfort him, but his elder brother came and gave him a heavy clout on the side of his head.

"Thou fight the Stoorworm!" he cried contemptuously. "A likely story! Go home to thy ash-pit, and stop speaking havers"; and, taking his arm, he drew him to the place where his other brothers were waiting, and they all went home together.

But all the time Assipattle kept on saying that he meant to kill the Stoorworm; and at last his brothers became so angry at what they thought was mere bragging, that they picked up stones and pelted him so hard with them that at last he took to his heels and ran away from them.

That evening the six brothers were threshing corn in the barn, and Assipattle, as usual, was lying among the ashes thinking his own thoughts, when his mother came out and bade him run and tell the others to come in for their supper.

The boy did as he was bid, for he was a willing enough little fellow; but when he entered the barn his brothers, in revenge for his having run away from them in the afternoon, set on him and pulled him down, and piled so much straw on top of him that, had his father not come from the house to see what they were all waiting for, he would, of a surety, have been smothered.

But when, at supper-time, his mother was quarrelling with the other lads for what they had done, and saying to them that it was only cowards who set on bairns littler and younger than themselves, Assipattle looked up from the bicker of porridge which he was supping.

"Vex not thyself, Mother," he said, "*for I could have fought them all if I liked*; ay, and beaten them, too."

"Why didst thou not essay it then?" cried everybody at once.

"Because I knew that I would need all my strength when I go to fight the Giant Stoorworm," replied Assipattle gravely.

And, as you may fancy, the others laughed louder than before.

Time passed, and every Saturday seven lassies were thrown to the Stoorworm, until at last it was felt that this state of things could not be allowed to go on any longer; for if it did, there would soon be no maidens at all left in the country.

So the Elders met once more, and, after long consultation, it was agreed that the Sorcerer should be summoned, and asked what his other remedy was. "For, by our troth," said they, "it cannot be worse than that which we are practising now."

But, had they known it, the new remedy was even more dreadful than the old. For the cruel Queen hated her step-daughter, Gemdelovely, and the wicked Sorcerer knew that she did, and that she would not be sorry to get rid of her, and, things being as they were, he thought that he saw a way to please the Queen. So he stood up in the Council, and, pretending to be very sorry, said that the only other thing that could be done was to give the Princess Gemdelovely to the Stoorworm, then would it of a surety depart.

When they heard this sentence a terrible stillness fell upon the Council, and everyone covered his face with his hands, for no man dare look at the King.

But although his dear daughter was as the apple of his eye, he was a just and righteous Monarch, and he felt that it was not right that other fathers should have been forced to part with their daughters, in order to try and save the country, if his child was to be spared.

So, after he had had speech with the Princess, he stood up before the Elders, and declared, with trembling voice, that both he and she were ready to make the sacrifice.

"She is my only child," he said, "and the last of her race. Yet it seemeth good to both of us that she should lay down her life, if by so doing she may save the land that she loves so well."

Salt tears ran down the faces of the great bearded men as they heard their King's words, for they all knew how dear the Princess Gemdelovely was to him. But it was felt that what he said was wise and true, and that the thing was just and right; for 'twere better, surely, that one maiden should

194

die, even although she were of Royal blood, than that bands of other maidens should go to their death week by week, and all to no purpose.

So, amid heavy sobs, the aged Lawman—he who was the chief man of the Council—rose up to pronounce the Princess's doom. But, ere he did so, the King's Kemper—or Fighting-man—stepped forward.

"Nature teaches us that it is fitting that each beast hath a tail," he said; "and this Doom, which our Lawman is about to pronounce, is in very sooth a venomous beast. And, if I had my way, the tail which it would bear after it is this, that if the Mester Stoorworm doth not depart, and that right speedily, after he have devoured the Princess, the next thing that is offered to him be no tender young maiden, but that tough, lean old Sorcerer."

And at his words there was such a great shout of approval that the wicked Sorcerer seemed to shrink within himself, and his pale face grew paler than it was before.

Now, three weeks were allowed between the time that the Doom was pronounced upon the Princess and the time that it was carried out, so that the King might send Ambassadors to all the neighbouring Kingdoms to issue proclamations that, if any Champion would come forward who was able to drive away the Stoorworm and save the Princess, he should have her for his wife.

And with her he should have the Kingdom, as well as a very famous sword that was now in the King's possession, but which had belonged to the great god Odin, with which he had fought and vanquished all his foes.

The sword bore the name of Sickersnapper, and no man had any power against it.

The news of all these things spread over the length and breadth of the land, and everyone mourned for the fate that was like to befall the Princess Gemdelovely. And the farmer, and his wife, and their six sons mourned also; all but Assipattle, who sat amongst the ashes and said nothing.

When the King's Proclamation was made known throughout the neighbouring Kingdoms, there was a fine stir among all the young Gallants, for it seemed but a little thing to slay a Sea-Monster; and a beautiful wife, a fertile Kingdom, and a trusty sword are not to be won every day.

So six-and-thirty Champions arrived at the King's Palace, each hoping to gain the prize.

But the King sent them all out to look at the Giant Stoorworm lying in the sea with its enormous mouth open, and when they saw it, twelve of them were seized with sudden illness, and twelve of them were so afraid that they took to their heels and ran, and never stopped till they reached their own countries; and so only twelve returned to the King's Palace, and as for them, they were so downcast at the thought of the task that they had undertaken that they had no spirit left in them at all.

And none of them dare try to kill the Stoorworm; so the three weeks passed slowly by, until the night before the day on which the Princess was to be sacrificed. On that night the King, feeling that he must do something to entertain his guests, made a great supper for them.

But, as you may think, it was a dreary feast, for everyone was thinking so much about the terrible thing that was to happen on the morrow, that no one could eat or drink.

And when it was all over, and everybody had retired to rest, save the King and his old Kemperman, the King returned to the great hall, and went slowly up to his Chair of State, high up on the dais. It was not like the Chairs of State that we know nowadays; it was nothing but a massive Kist, in which he kept all the things which he treasured most.

The old Monarch undid the iron bolts with trembling fingers, and lifted the lid, and took out the wondrous sword Sickersnapper, which had belonged to the great god Odin.

His trusty Kemperman, who had stood by him in a hundred fights, watched him with pitying eyes.

"Why lift ye out the sword," he said softly, "when thy fighting days are done? Right nobly hast thou fought thy battles in the past, oh, my Lord! when thine arm was strong and sure. But when folk's years number four score and sixteen, as thine do, 'tis time to leave such work to other and younger men."

The old King turned on him angrily, with something of the old fire in his eyes. "Wheest," he cried, "else will I turn this sword on thee. Dost thou think that I can see my only bairn devoured by a Monster, and not lift a finger to try and save her when no other man will? I tell thee—and I will swear it with my two thumbs crossed on Sickersnapper—that both the sword and I will be destroyed before so much as one of her hairs be touched. So go, an' thou love me, my old comrade, and order my boat to be ready, with the sail set and the prow pointed out to sea. I will go myself and fight the Stoorworm; and if I do not return, I will lay it on thee to guard my cherished daughter. Peradventure, my life may redeem hers."

Now that night everybody at the farm went to bed betimes, for next morning the whole family was to set out early, to go to the top of the hill near the sea, to see the Princess eaten by the Stoorworm. All except Assipattle, who was to be left at home to herd the geese.

The lad was so vexed at this—for he had great schemes in his head—that he could not sleep. And as he lay tossing and tumbling about in his corner among the ashes, he heard his father and mother talking in the great box-bed. And, as he listened, he found that they were having an argument.

"'Tis such a long way to the hill overlooking the sea, I fear me I shall never walk it," said his mother. "I think I had better bide at home."

"Nay," replied her husband, "that would be a bonny-like thing, when all the countryside is to be there. Thou shalt ride behind me on my good mare Go-Swift."

"I do not care to trouble thee to take me behind thee," said his wife, "for methinks thou dost not love me as thou wert wont to do."

"The woman's havering," cried the Goodman of the house impatiently. "What makes thee think that I have ceased to love thee?"

"Because thou wilt no longer tell me thy secrets," answered his wife. "To go no further, think of this very horse, Go-Swift. For five long years I have been begging thee to tell me how it is that, when thou ridest her, she flies faster than the wind, while if any other man mount her, she hirples along like a broken-down nag."

The Goodman laughed. "'Twas not for lack of love, Goodwife," he said, "though it might be lack of trust. For women's tongues wag but loosely; and

I did not want other folk to ken my secret. But since my silence hath vexed thy heart, I will e'en tell it thee.

"When I want Go-Swift to stand, I give her one clap on the left shoulder. When I would have her go like any other horse, I give her two claps on the right. But when I want her to fly like the wind, I whistle through the windpipe of a goose. And, as I never ken when I want her to gallop like that, I aye keep the bird's thrapple in the left-hand pocket of my coat."

"So that is how thou managest the beast," said the farmer's wife, in a satisfied tone; "and that is what becomes of all my goose thrapples. Oh! but thou art a clever fellow, Goodman; and now that I ken the way of it I may go to sleep."

Assipattle was not tumbling about in the ashes now; he was sitting up in the darkness, with glowing cheeks and sparkling eyes.

His opportunity had come at last, and he knew it.

He waited patiently till their heavy breathing told him that his parents were asleep; then he crept over to where his father's clothes were, and took the goose's windpipe out of the pocket of his coat, and slipped noiselessly out of the house. Once he was out of it, he ran like lightning to the stable. He saddled and bridled Go-Swift, and threw a halter round her neck, and led her to the stable door.

The good mare, unaccustomed to her new groom, pranced, and reared, and plunged; but Assipattle, knowing his father's secret, clapped her once on the left shoulder, and she stood as still as a stone. Then he mounted her, and gave her two claps on the right shoulder, and the good horse trotted off briskly, giving a loud neigh as she did so.

The unwonted sound, ringing out in the stillness of the night, roused the household, and the Goodman and his six sons came tumbling down the wooden stairs, shouting to one another in confusion that someone was stealing Go-Swift.

The farmer was the first to reach the door; and when he saw, in the starlight, the vanishing form of his favourite steed, he cried at the top of his voice:

"Stop thief, ho!
Go-Swift, whoa!"

And when Go-Swift heard that she pulled up in a moment. All seemed lost, for the farmer and his sons could run very fast indeed, and it seemed to Assipattle, sitting motionless on Go-Swift's back, that they would very soon make up on him.

But, luckily, he remembered the goose's thrapple, and he pulled it out of his pocket and whistled through it. In an instant the good mare bounded forward, swift as the wind, and was over the hill and out of reach of its pursuers before they had taken ten steps more.

Day was dawning when the lad came within sight of the sea; and there, in front of him, in the water, lay the enormous Monster whom he had come so far to slay. Anyone would have said that he was mad even to dream of making such an attempt, for he was but a slim, unarmed youth, and the Mester Stoorworm was so big that men said it would reach the fourth part round the world. And its tongue was jagged at the end like a fork, and with this fork it could sweep whatever it chose into its mouth, and devour it at its leisure.

For all this, Assipattle was not afraid, for he had the heart of a hero underneath his tattered garments. "I must be cautious," he said to himself, "and do by my wits what I cannot do by my strength."

He climbed down from his seat on Go-Swift's back, and tethered the good steed to a tree, and walked on, looking well about him, till he came to a little cottage on the edge of a wood.

The door was not locked, so he entered, and found its occupant, an old woman, fast asleep in bed. He did not disturb her, but he took down an iron pot from the shelf, and examined it closely.

"This will serve my purpose," he said; "and surely the old dame would not grudge it if she knew 'twas to save the Princess's life."

Then he lifted a live peat from the smouldering fire, and went his way.

Down at the water's edge he found the King's boat lying, guarded by a single boatman, with its sails set and its prow turned in the direction of the Mester Stoorworm.

"It's a cold morning," said Assipattle. "Art thou not well-nigh frozen sitting there? If thou wilt come on shore, and run about, and warm thyself, I will get into the boat and guard it till thou returnest."

"A likely story," replied the man. "And what would the King say if he were to come, as I expect every moment he will do, and find me playing myself on the sand, and his good boat left to a smatchet like thee? 'Twould be as much as my head is worth."

"As thou wilt," answered Assipattle carelessly, beginning to search among the rocks. "In the meantime, I must be looking for a wheen mussels to roast for my breakfast." And after he had gathered the mussels, he began to make a hole in the sand to put the live peat in. The boatman watched him curiously, for he, too, was beginning to feel hungry.

Presently the lad gave a wild shriek, and jumped high in the air. "Gold, gold!" he cried. "By the name of Thor, who would have looked to find gold here?"

This was too much for the boatman. Forgetting all about his head and the King, he jumped out of the boat, and, pushing Assipattle aside, began to scrape among the sand with all his might.

While he was doing so, Assipattle seized his pot, jumped into the boat, pushed her off, and was half a mile out to sea before the outwitted man, who, needless to say, could find no gold, noticed what he was about.

And, of course, he was very angry, and the old King was more angry still when he came down to the shore, attended by his Nobles and carrying the great sword Sickersnapper, in the vain hope that he, poor feeble old man that he was, might be able in some way to defeat the Monster and save his daughter.

But to make such an attempt was beyond his power now that his boat was gone. So he could only stand on the shore, along with the fast assembling crowd of his subjects, and watch what would befall.

And this was what befell!

Assipattle, sailing slowly over the sea, and watching the Mester Stoorworm intently, noticed that the terrible Monster yawned occasionally, as if longing for his weekly feast. And as it yawned a great flood of sea-water went down its throat, and came out again at its huge gills.

So the brave lad took down his sail, and pointed the prow of his boat straight at the Monster's mouth, and the next time it yawned he and his boat were sucked right in, and, like Jonah, went straight down its throat into the dark regions inside its body. On and on the boat floated; but as it went the water grew less, pouring out of the Stoorworm's gills, till at last it stuck, as it were, on dry land. And Assipattle jumped out, his pot in his hand, and began to explore.

Presently he came to the huge creature's liver, and having heard that the liver of a fish is full of oil, he made a hole in it and put in the live peat.

Woe's me! but there was a conflagration! And Assipattle just got back to his boat in time; for the Mester Stoorworm, in its convulsions, threw the boat right out of its mouth again, and it was flung up, high and dry, on the bare land.

The commotion in the sea was so terrible that the King and his daughter—who by this time had come down to the shore dressed like a bride, in white, ready to be thrown to the Monster—and all his Courtiers, and all the countryfolk, were fain to take refuge on the hill top, out of harm's way, and stand and see what happened next.

And this was what happened next.

The poor, distressed creature—for it was now to be pitied, even although it was a great, cruel, awful Mester Stoorworm—tossed itself to and fro, twisting and writhing.

And as it tossed its awful head out of the water its tongue fell out, and struck the earth with such force that it made a great dent in it, into which the sea rushed. And that dent formed the crooked Straits which now divide Denmark from Norway and Sweden.

Then some of its teeth fell out and rested in the sea, and became the Islands that we now call the Orkney Isles; and a little afterwards some more teeth dropped out, and they became what we now call the Shetland Isles.

After that the creature twisted itself into a great lump and died; and this lump became the Island of Iceland; and the fire which Assipattle had kindled with his live peat still burns on underneath it, and that is why there are mountains which throw out fire in that chilly land.

When at last it was plainly seen that the Mester Stoorworm was dead, the King could scarce contain himself with joy. He put his arms round Assipattle's neck, and kissed him, and called him his son. And he took off his own Royal Mantle and put it on the lad, and girded his good sword Sickersnapper round his waist. And he called his daughter, the Princess Gemdelovely, to him, and put her hand in his, and declared that when the right time came she should be his wife, and that he should be ruler over all the Kingdom.

Then the whole company mounted their horses again, and Assipattle rode on Go-Swift by the Princess's side; and so they returned, with great joy, to the King's Palace.

But as they were nearing the gate Assipattle's sister, she who was the Princess's maid, ran out to meet him, and signed to the Princess to lout down, and whispered something in her ear.

The Princess's face grew dark, and she turned her horse's head and rode back to where her father was, with his Nobles. She told him the words that the maiden had spoken; and when he heard them his face, too, grew as black as thunder.

For the matter was this: The cruel Queen, full of joy at the thought that she was to be rid, once for all, of her step-daughter, had been making love to the wicked Sorcerer all the morning in the old King's absence.

"He shall be killed at once," cried the Monarch. "Such behaviour cannot be overlooked."

"Thou wilt have much ado to find him, your Majesty," said the girl, "for 'tis more than an hour since he and the Queen fled together on the fleetest horses that they could find in the stables."

"But I can find him," cried Assipattle; and he went off like the wind on his good horse Go-Swift.

It was not long before he came within sight of the fugitives, and he drew his sword and shouted to them to stop.

They heard the shout, and turned round, and they both laughed aloud in derision when they saw that it was only the boy who grovelled in the ashes who pursued them.

"The insolent brat! I will cut off his head for him! I will teach him a lesson!" cried the Sorcerer; and he rode boldly back to meet Assipattle. For although he was no fighter, he knew that no ordinary weapon could harm his enchanted body; therefore he was not afraid.

But he did not count on Assipattle having the Sword of the great god Odin, with which he had slain all his enemies; and before this magic weapon he was powerless. And, at one thrust, the young lad ran it through his body as easily as if he had been any ordinary man, and he fell from his horse, dead.

Then the Courtiers of the King, who had also set off in pursuit, but whose steeds were less fleet of foot than Go-Swift, came up, and seized the bridle of the Queen's horse, and led it and its rider back to the Palace.

She was brought before the Council, and judged, and condemned to be shut up in a high tower for the remainder of her life. Which thing surely came to pass.

As for Assipattle, when the proper time came he was married to the Princess Gemdelovely, with great feasting and rejoicing. And when the old King died they ruled the Kingdom for many a long year.

BLACK-HAIRED JOHN
OF LEWIS, SAILOR

Translated by
Rev. James MacDougall

Rev. James MacDougall (1833–1906) was the self-professed "sometime Minister of Duror", Ballachulish. He was born in Craignish and was a tutor before entering college and becoming ordained. He roved the Highlands and islands as a missionary until he was told to present himself at the Parish of Duror. There he married the daughter of Mr. Cuthbert Cowan from Ayr and lived a happy life. He had a keen interest in superstition, specifically researching fairies, and wanted to make his mark in books. He edited the five-volume *Waifs and Strays of the Celtic Tradition* (1889–95), *Folk and Hero Tales* (1891), and the posthumous *Highland Fairy Legends* (1910) and *Folk Tales and Fairy Lore in Gaelic and English* (1910). "Black-Haired John of Lewis, Sailor" comes from the latter book. I've chosen it because I really enjoyed reading it, and when I read it again after letting it breathe for a few months, I knew that I had to include it. It also contains one of the funniest sentences I've ever come across in fiction—a shortcut if there ever was one to speed a story up.

A FISHER'S son was Black-haired John. When he was a little boy his father was drowned, and after that he was brought up by his uncle. He lived a short distance from the Great Anchorage (now Stornoway), in Lewis. There he used to fish, and see the vessels that frequented the Anchorage. He thus took a great liking for the sea, and at length no trade would please him but to be a sailor.

On a certain evening he saw a fine ship coming into the haven under full sail, and it seemed to him that never before had he seen a more beautiful sight. He sprang into his own little fishing boat, and before the ship's anchor reached the bottom, he was on board of her. He waited until her sails had been furled, and then he ascended one of the masts, and began to run out and in on the yards, and to climb the ropes as he saw the sailors do. The Captain noticed how bold and active he was, and as soon as he descended from the mast, he asked him whether he would like to be a sailor? Black John answered that there was nothing in the world he would like better.

"Go home, then," said the Captain, "and get thy father's leave, and tomorrow come ye here together; and if ye and I agree, I will let thee go away with me and learn sailoring." Black John said that his father was not living, but that he would ask his uncle for leave to go. That satisfied the Captain, and John went home in great haste.

Early next day he returned, running and leaping, and scarcely had he got on board when he said with joy that he had got his uncle's full permission to go with the ship. "And did he say nothing to thee about taking an engagement?" said the Captain. "O yes," answered John, "I am to bind myself to the ship for five years that I may learn seamanship aright." "And what did he say to thee about wages?" "He said that I was to get a half-penny at the end of the first month, two half-pennies at the end of the second month, and so doubling the wages of each succeeding month to the close of the five years."

The Captain laughed aloud at Black John's wages, and without thinking beforehand of what he was about to do, he said: "Thou shalt get that, my little hero," and John was then bound to the ship by a deed of indenture.

On the following day the ship sailed out of the Anchorage, and went on a long voyage to a far away country. She reached the seaport to which she was bound, and stayed a long time abroad, but at the end of four years she returned to England; and in the beginning of the fifth year of Black John's engagement, she arrived at the seaport to which she belonged.

Her owners came on board, and after welcoming the Captain they began to look over the ship.

Black John had grown into a fine lad and an excellent sailor. But he had not yet got a penny of his wages further than a shilling or two now and again when he happened to go ashore with the other sailors at the ports where they called. Nor did the Captain think of reckoning the sum to which the lad's wages would amount, until the owners came on board. Then one of them asked where did he get the sailor boy he had yonder? The Captain answered that he got him in the Island of Lewis. "And how long hast thou had him?" "I have had him more than four years." "And what wages art thou giving him? No doubt thou art giving him a good wage, for he is as clever a sailor as we have ever seen?" The Captain smiled and said: "Well, I have given him no wages yet, but he himself asked that he should be bound for five years, and that he should receive for wages a half-penny at the end of the first month, two half-pennies at the end of the second month, and so doubling the wage of each successive month to the end of the five years. And what he asked I promised him in a joke, and not with the intention of paying him according to his request." "Didst thou think beforehand of what thou wert going to do? Thou hast promised the lad more than the ship is worth, and more than she has earned since the first day she was launched." At first the Captain did not believe this; but when he saw it was true, he was struck with great shame and regret. At length he said: "What shall we do?" The owners answered: "There is only one thing thou canst do. Thou shalt go away on the next voyage without delay, and thou shalt take good care to keep a good distance from land on the last day of the lad's engagement. We will give thee in three bags all the money we possess. On the last day of his time at twelve o'clock, say to him that thou hast his wages in the bags, and that he will get them if he will then leave the ship with them; but if he will not, then after that thou shalt pay him as thou pleasest." The Captain said that, hard as it was for him to do that, he would try to do it.

As soon as the Captain got everything ready, he departed on the next sea voyage. He reached the place whither he was bound in safety, and having delivered his cargo, returned the way he came. Black John's time ran out before the ship had come in sight of land, and on the last day of his time the Captain offered him his wages on condition that he would leave the ship at once. "All right," said John. "If I get my wages I will leave the ship this moment, but wilt thou give me two hours of the carpenter's time to make a raft for me?" "Thou shalt get that, and wood too," said the Captain; for he was sorry to part with John, and willing to help him.

When the raft was ready it was lowered over the ship's side. John received as his wages one bag full of gold, another of silver, and a third of copper. He placed them unopened on the raft with a bag of biscuits and a bottle of drink, and he pushed the raft away from the side of the ship. The crew raised a shout three times at parting, and then the ship went off on her way.

Every minute she was going further away and night was coming. At length night fell, and the darkness took her out of his sight. Then poor John began to grow dejected, not knowing what would happen before the next day dawned. At last he thought he would see what stuff was in the bottle. He took a toothful from it, and felt that that had lightened his mind. About midnight sleep overpowered him and he did not awake till day was breaking. There was then a nice breeze of wind driving the raft before it. John passed three nights and three days on the raft. But on the evening of the third day he beheld land ahead of him, and in the darkening of the night the raft struck the shore in a bay, from margin of wave to border of wood, the very prettiest he had ever seen.

John the Sailor sprang ashore, glad that he had once more got the breadth of his soles of land under him. He took the bags with him to the top of the beach, where he hid them in the sand. He then drew the raft up to the border of the wood, for he said to himself: "There is no saying but that it may yet be useful to another man."

He then struck into the wood to see if he could fall in with a house where he might stay. But, though he travelled the night long, he saw neither house nor hald. About daybreak he gave a glance ahead of him, and saw a short distance off smoke ascending from the foot of a high precipice. He made straight for it, and what was there but a big black clumsy building like an old mill. He was ready to drop with fatigue and sleep, and so he walked in without leave asked or obtained.

A handsome woman sat at the fireside before him; and when she noticed him, she was much alarmed, for she was not accustomed to see travellers coming the way. In a short time, however, she gathered courage enough to ask him whence he came. He replied that he was a poor sailor who had swam ashore from a ship which sank far out at sea. She gave him food and drink, and begged of him to make haste and be gone from the house as quick as he could. He asked the reason, and she replied that seven robbers stayed in the house; and if they arrived before he left, they would not let him go with his life. He then asked when they would come. She answered that she expected them every minute. "Let them come, then," said John the Sailor. "Since I got in, I will not go out until I get a little wink of sleep." "Well," said the woman, "do as thou pleasest; but I fear thou shalt repent of not taking my advice." "Be that as it may, but in the meantime tell me where I can stretch myself and take a while of rest." The woman did that, and at once he was sound asleep.

He knew not how long he slept, but it was the loud talk of the robbers that awoke him. He heard them ask where he was. The woman told them that, and without a moment's delay they came where he was, and asked him what brought him there? He told them the reason, as he had told it to the woman. "Well," said one of them, "we are robbers, and we suffer no man who comes this way to escape alive." "Ha, ha!" said Black John, "how pleased I am that I have met with fellow-craftsmen of my own. Robbing was my trade in my native country till I was forced to flee, and betake myself to the sea. If you take me with you, I will promise to be as true as any one in the band."

"Thy appearance will do," said one of them, "and thy language proves thee to be courageous. We will give thee an opportunity to prove what thou canst do. Thou shalt get tomorrow to rest; but after that every one of us will take his own way, and he who brings home most spoil for three nights will be chief over the rest, and will have nothing to do but to take care of the house while his companions are away." This pleased John well, and he stayed at home till the first day of trial came.

Then he went off and took his own way, as did every one of the band. When night came he returned home with the little bag of copper which he had hidden near the shore; and none of the company had as much. He started off next day, and returned at night with the little bag of silver; and if he had done better than his comrades the first night, he did seven times better that day. On the third day he went out for the last time, and brought home the little bag of gold. He poured out all it contained on the floor, and asked if any of them had done better. They all answered that they had not; and as he was as good as his promise to them, they would be as good as their promise to him, and they made him chief over them all.

Next day the robbers went away to seek their fortune, while John stayed at home. As soon as he found himself alone he bethought him that he would search the house. He took down a big bunch of keys he saw hanging on a nail in the wall, and with them he opened every room in the house save one. The key of that one the woman had hidden, and she at first refused to part with it. However, when John told her that he was now chief, and that she must be obedient to him, she gave up the key.

Then he opened the door of the secret chamber, and saw before him a sight which made him shudder. A lady, as beautiful and as handsome as eye ever beheld, was hanging by her hair from a crook in the ceiling of the room, and the points of her toes were scarcely touching the floor. He sprang to where she was, unloosed her hair, and laid her down on the floor, seemingly dead. She was for a while in a swoon; but when she came out of it, he told her how he had come to that place, and then she told him the way she had been brought there. She was the daughter of the King of Spain. Two of the robbers were caught at the King's Castle, and because they were put to death by her father, the rest vowed that they would not rest till they were revenged upon him. The revenge they took was to seize her when she was taking a walk about the Castle, and carry her away to their own place, and torture her by leaving her hanging in the manner Black John had found her.

To shorten this part of the tale, they fled from the house of the robbers, taking with them as much as they could carry of gold and precious things, with food for the journey. They took the most unfrequented paths, until night came. They then beheld a shieling bothy before them, and made straight for it. They were not long in reaching it. They went in, and though they found it empty, it had seemingly been occupied shortly before. No matter, they resolved to pass the night there as well as they could. Some time after they entered they heard a murmur like the conversation of men outside the door. At first they thought it was the robbers. and that they were whispering to one another without. Soon, however, they understood that the small weak voices they were hearing came neither from the robbers nor from any earthly creatures. At length Black John sprang to his feet, saying that he would know presently from what, or from whom, the noises came. So he opened the door, but bold as he was, the sight before him startled him. Three human bodies, holding their heads between their hands stood before him. "Honest men," said John, "what do you want?" "We," replied they, "are a father and two sons who were murdered by robbers in this bothy, and buried behind the house; but, as every head was not placed with its own body, we find no rest. If thou wilt place our heads where they ought to be, perhaps we may yet do as much for thee." John replied that he would do as they asked him, if they would show him where the heads were, and where they would like them placed. They went with him, and he did everything as they directed him: and when all was over, they went out of sight.

Next day Black John and the King's daughter left the bothy, and they stopped not until they reached the nearest seaport. They married there, and set up an Inn with the gold they took from the house of the robbers. They were prosperous and happy there, till a war-ship came into the harbour. On board of this ship was the chief commander of the Spanish fleet, seeking the King's daughter, that he might win herself and half the kingdom; for this was the reward the King had promised to the commander on sea or on land who should find her, and bring her home in safety.

The commander came ashore with another officer, and of all places where did they call but at Black John's house? They were not long within when they formed an acquaintance with John and his wife. They recognised that she was the King's daughter, but they did not make that known. Before leaving they gave herself and her husband a friendly invitation to go out next day and see the ship. They both heartily accepted the invitation; but when the commander got them on board he set sail, and kept on his way, until he was a great distance from land. There he left poor Black John in a small boat without oar or sail, and went away.

John's predicament in the little boat was nearly as trying as it had been on the raft. He passed the rest of the day in dejection; but on the approach of night he saw a sight which gave him some little heartening, for the boat was keeping her bow pointing steadily in one direction with a good way on her. Then he noticed a bottle of strong drink in the forepart of the boat, and after taking a draught from it he fell asleep. As soon as he awoke next day, he looked every way but no land was in sight. Still the boat was making good way and holding her head in the same direction as on the night before. This gave him more courage; yet he felt the day long enough. At the approach of night he took another drink from the bottle, and fell asleep over it. On the third morning he looked ahead, and saw land far off, and the boat making straight for it. The painter was out ahead, and a hard pull on it; and what was still more wonderful, a strong wake before the furthest out end of the rope. But what, or who, was towing the boat, he could neither conceive nor understand.

At last she reached the shore, and three men went out of the sea before her, pulling her with the painter till they left her beyond the reach of the highest tide. These were the three men whose heads and trunks he had placed together behind the shieling bothy. As soon as they saw John's foot on land, they vanished out of sight.

The rest of the tale may be told in a few words. The King's daughter would not marry the commander who found her until every soldier and sailor in the kingdom was made to pass by under her window in her father's Castle. After going through many hardships, John reached the Castle last of all. He was just in time. The King's daughter knew him. They were again married, and if they are still living they are happy.

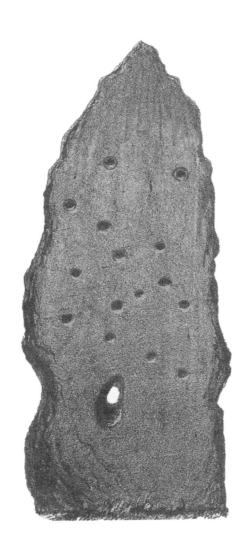

THE MOOR

Neil M. Gunn

Neil M. Gunn (8 November 1891–15 January 1973) was the seventh child of nine, and born in Dunbeath, Caithness, to his father James and mother Isabella. When Neil was 15 years old he was sent to London to work before being transferred to the Income Tax Department in Edinburgh. Afterwards he settled near Inverness and started writing, mainly short stories. His first novel, *The Grey Coast*, was published in 1926 and several historical novels followed, but it wasn't until the publication of *Highland River* in 1937, that he really entered the public eye. In 1941 he wrote *Young Art and Old Hector*, followed in 1944 by his best work, *The Green Isle of the Great Deep*, which featured characters Art and Hector from the previous book, but in a more fantastical totalitarian setting. He regretted not learning Gaelic and deliberately chose not to write in Scots so he would capture a bigger readership. This choice made him the greatest Highland writer to write in English—his ability to capture the Highland way of thinking as much as the Highland way of speech was the basis of his work. Towards the end of his life he drifted towards the philosophies of Zen Buddhism.

Gunn died after a short spell in hospital and the Neil Gunn International Fellowship was quickly created. Its first recipient, the Nobel-winning Heinrich Böll, visited universities in Glasgow and Stirling to give public lectures on the place of the writer in contemporary writing.

"The Moor", originally published in Gunn's collection *Hidden Doors* (1929), is a simple love story suffocating in a desolate peat bog. I think. It's the least supernatural of the offerings in this book, yet it suits the "weird" label the most. A tale, for me, that seems to change and twist with every reading.

A FEW miles back it had looked like a sea-anemone on a vast tidal ledge, but now, at hand, it rose out of the moor's breast like a monstrous nipple. The scarred rock, heather tufted, threw a shadow to his aching feet, and because he was young enough to love enchantment in words, he savoured slowly, "like the shadow of a great rock in a weary land." With a nameless shudder of longing he passed his tongue between his sticky lips. The wide Sutherland moor under the August sun was silent as a desert.

At a little pool by the rock-base he drank and then dipped his face.

From the top of the rocky outcrop the rest of his tramp unrolled before him like a painted map. The earth fell away to the far sea, with cottages set here and there upon it like toys, and little cultivated strips, green and brown, and serpentine dark hollows.

He kept gazing until the sandwich in his mouth would not get wet enough to swallow. Then his eyes rested on the nearest cottage of all.

The loneliness of that cottage was a thing to catch the heart. Its green croft was snared in the moor's outflung hand. In the green stood a red cow. Creaming in upon his mind stole the seductive thought of milk. Tasting it made a clacking sound in his mouth and he stopped eating.

As he neared the cottage the red cow stared at him, unmoving save for the lifeless switch of her tail. The cottage itself, with its grey curved thatch and pale gable-end, made no move. The moor's last knuckle shut off the world.

The heather had not yet stirred into bloom and, far as the eye could see, lay dark under the white sun. He listened for a sound… and in that moment of suspense it came upon him that the place was bewitched.

A dog barked and every sense leapt. The tawny brute came out at the front door, showing half-laughing teeth, twisting and twining, and in no time was at his back. He turned round, but still kept moving towards the door, very careful not to lift his eyes from those eyes, so that he nearly tumbled backwards over the doorstep... and was aware, with the beginnings of apologetic laughter, that he was in the presence of a woman. When he looked up, however, the laugh died.

Her eyes were gipsy dark. Perhaps she was twenty. Sunk in the darkness of her eyes were golden sun motes. Madonna of the adder-haunted moor. His confusion stared speechless. A tingling trepidation beset his skin. A tight drawn bodice just covered and repressed her breasts. Her beauty held the still, deep mesmerism of places at the back of beyond. She was shy, yet gazed at him.

The dry cup of his flesh filled with wine. Then his eyes flickered, shifted quickly; he veiled them, smiling, as though the rudeness of his bared emotion had gone forth unpardonably and touched her skin.

To his stammered request for milk, she smiled faintly, almost automatically, and disappeared.

Then he heard the beating of his heart. Through the warmth of his tired body swept a distinct heat. Excitement broke in spindrift. He smiled secretly to himself, absorbed.

When he caught himself listening at the door, however, he immediately bespoke the dog, inviting its approach with such a sudden snapping hand that the brute leapt back, surprised into a short growl. He awaited her appearance so alive and happy that he was poised in apprehension.

She brought the milk in a coarse tumbler. He barely looked at her face, as if good manners could not trust his instinct; but the last grain of thanks he concentrated in a glance, a word or two, a smile breaking into a laugh. She had covered somewhat the wide V gleam of her breast, had swept back her hair; but the rents, the burst seam under an arm, the whole covering for her rich young body was ragged as ever, ragged and extraordinarily potent, as if it sheathed the red pulse at white beauty's core. He said he would drink the milk sitting outside if she didn't mind. She murmured, smiled, withdrew.

He ate his lunch excitedly, nibbling at the sandwiches to make them last, throwing crusts to the dog. His mind moved in its bewilderment as in coloured spindrift, but underneath were eyes avid for the image of her body, only he would not let their stare fix. Not yet. Not now... Living here at the back of beyond... this secret moor... Extraordinary! The wave burst in happy excited spindrift... But underneath he felt her like a pulse and saw her like a flame—a flame going to waste—in the dark of the moor, this hidden moor. Attraction and denial became a tension of exquisite doubt, of possible cunning, of pain, of desire. His soul wavered like a golden jet.

As the last drop of the milk slid over, he heard a sound and turned—and stared.

A withered woman was looking at him, eyes veiled in knowingness. She said, "It's a fine day that's in it."

"Yes, isn't it!" He got to his feet.

She slyly looked away from him to the moor, the better to commune with her subtle thought. A wisp of grey hair fell over an ear. Her neck was sinewy and stretched, her chin tilted level from the stoop of her shoulders. The corners of her eyes returned to him. Just then the girl came to the door.

"It's waiting here, Mother." Through a veiled anxiety quietly, compellingly, she eyed the old woman.

"Are ye telling me?"

"Come on in."

"Oh, I'm coming." She turned to the young man and gave a little husky laugh, insanely knowing. The daughter followed her within, and he found himself with the thick glass in his hand staring at the empty doorway. "*She leuch*" rose a ballad echo, like a sunless shudder. A sudden desire to tiptoe away from that place seized him. My God! he thought. The blue of heaven trembled.

But he went to the door and knocked.

"This is the glass—" he began.

She smiled shyly, politely, and, taking the glass from his outstretched hand, smoothly withdrew.

His hand fell to his side. He turned away, going quietly.

Down between the cottages, the little cultivated strips green and brown, the serpentine dark hollows, he went jerkily, as though the whole place were indeed not earth, but a painted map, and he himself a human toy worked by one spring. Only it was a magic spring that never got unwound. Even in the hotel that overlorded the final cluster of cottages, the spring seemed wound up tighter than ever.

For privacy he went up and sat on his bed. "Lord, I cannot get over it!" he cried silently. He got off his bed and walked about the floor. This was the most extraordinary thing that had ever happened to him… without, as it were, quite happening to him.

Inspiration had hitherto thrilled from within. This was from without, and so vast were its implications that he could not feel them all at once in a single spasm of creation. He got lost in them and wandered back to his bed, whereon he lay full length, gazing so steadily that he sank through his body into a profound sleep.

He awoke to a stillness in his room so intense that he held his breath, listening. His eyes slowly turned to the window where the daylight was not so much fading as changing into a glimmer full of a moth-pale life, invisible and watchful. Upon his taut ear the silence began to vibrate with the sound of a small tuning fork struck at an immense distance.

His staring eyes, aware of a veiled face… focussed the face of the girl on the moor. The appeal of her sombre regard was so great that he began to tremble; yet far back in him cunningly he willed body and mind to an absolute suspense so that the moment might remain transfixed. Footsteps on the corridor outside smashed it, and all at once he was listening acutely to perfectly normal voices.

"Well, Mr. Morrison—you here? What's up now?"

"Nothing much. The old woman up at Albain—been certified."

"So I heard. Poor old woman. When are you lifting her?"

"Tomorrow."

"There's no doubt, of course, she is… ay, ay, very sad."

"Yes. There's the girl, too—her daughter. You'll know her?"

"Well—yes. But she's right enough. I mean there's nothing—there. A bit shy, maybe… like the heather. You know."

"I was wondering what could be done for her."

"Oh, the neighbours will look after her, I'm sure. She'll just have to go into service. We're fixed up for the season here now, or I…"

The footsteps died away, and the light in the bedroom withdrew itself still more, like a woman withdrawing her dress, her eyes, but on a lingering watchfulness more critical than ever, and now faintly ironic.

His body snapped into action and began restlessly pacing the floor, irony flicking over the face. Suddenly he paused… and breathed aloud— "The auld mither!" His eyes gleamed in a profound humour.

The exclamation made him walk as it were more carefully, and presently he came to the surface of himself some distance from the hotel and realised where he was going.

But now he cunningly avoided the other cottages and in a roundabout way came in over the knuckle of moor in the deepening dusk. The cow was gone and the cottage seemed more lonely than ever. Indeed, it crouched to the earth with rounded shoulders drawing its grey thatch about its awful secret. Only the pale gable-end gloomed in furtive watchfulness.

Grey-green oasis, dark moor, and huddled cottage were privy to the tragedy of their human children, and, he felt, inimical to any interference from without. Never before had he caught this living secretive intensity of background, although, as a young painter believing in vision, it had been his business to exploit backgrounds of all sorts.

The girl herself walked out from the end of the house, carrying two empty pitchers. On the soft turf her feet made no sound. Unlike her background she was not inimical but detached. And, as her slave, her background spread itself in quiet ecstasy under her feet.

By the time he joined her at the well she had her buckets full, and as he offered to carry them she lifted one in each hand. He pursued his offer, stooping to take them. The little operation brought their bodies into contact and their hands, so that there was a laughing tremble in his voice as he walked beside her, carrying the water. But at the doorway, which was reached in a moment, he set down the buckets and raised his cap.

As he went on into the moor, still smiling warmly as though she were beside him, he kept saying to himself that to have dallied or hesitated would have been unpardonable… yet not quite believing it… yet knowing it to be true.

He sat down on the moor, his heart aflame. The moor lost its hostility and became friendly. Night drew about them her dim purple skin. Silence wavered like the evening smoke of a prehistoric fire. The sense of translation grew in him… until the girl and himself went walking on the moor, on the purple, the rippled skin, their faces set to mountain crests and far dawns.

He tore his vision with a slow humour and, getting to his feet, shivered. As he returned by the cottage he saw her coming out of the byre-door and on a blind impulse went up to her and asked:

"Are you not lonely here?"

"No," she answered, with a smile that scarcely touched her still expression.

"Well—it does seem lonely—doesn't it?"

Her eyes turned to the moor and only by a luminous troubling of their deeps could he see that his words were difficult. She simply did not speak, and for several seconds they stood perfectly silent.

"I can understand," he broke through, "that it's not lonely either." But his awkwardness rose up and clutched him. If the thickening dusk saved his colour, it heightened her beauty in a necromantic way. Mistrust had not touched her, if tragedy had. A watchfulness, a profound instinct young and artless—yet very old.

The front door opened and her mother came peering on to the doorstep. In low quick tones he said:

"I'll come—tomorrow evening."

Her eyes turned upon his with a faint fear, but found a light deeper than sympathy.

By the time he got back to the hotel, his companion, Douglas Cunningham, had arrived, round about, with the motor-cycle combination.

"Sorry I'm so late. The beastly clutch kept slipping. I had the devil's own time of it."

"Had you?"

"Yes. We'll have to get down to it tomorrow… What happened?" Douglas looked at Evan shrewdly. "Seems to have lit you up a bit, anyhow!"

"Does it?"

Then Evan told him.

Douglas met his look steadily.

"You can't see?" probed Evan, finally. "The moor, the lonely cottage, the mad mother, and the daughter… My God, what a grouping! Can't you see—that it transcends chance? It has overwhelmed me."

"My dear chap, if you'd been in the ditch with a burst clutch and umpteen miles from nowhere you would have been, by analogy, completely pulverised."

Their friendly arguments frequently gathered a mocking hostility.

"You show me the clutch of your tinny motor bike," thrust Evan. "I show you the clutch of eternal or infernal life. I'm not proving or improving anything: I'm only showing you. But you can't see. Lord, you are blind. Mechanism, clutch, motor bike… these are the planets wheeling about your Cyclops glassy eye. You are the darling of evolution, the hope of your country, the proud son of your race. You are the *thing* we have arrived at!… By the great Cuchulain, is it any wonder that your old mother is being taken to a mad-house?"

"By which I gather that you have found the daughter's mechanism—fool-proof?"

Evan took a slow turn about the floor, then with hands in pockets stood glooming satanically. "I suppose," he said, "we have sunk as low as that."

Douglas eyed him warningly.

"Easy, Evan."

Evan nodded. "Whatever I do I must not go in off the deep end!" He suddenly sat down and over his closed fist on the table looked Douglas in the face. "Why shouldn't I go in off the deep end?"

Douglas turned from the drawn lips and kicked off his boots.

"You can go in off any damned end you like," he said.

And in bed, Evan could not sleep. To the pulse of his excitement parable and symbol danced with exquisite rhythm and to a pattern set upon the grey-green oasis of the croft, centring in the cottage… fertile matrix of the dark moor.

Vision grew and soon wholly obsessed him. He found in it a reality at once intoxicating and finally illuminating. A pagan freedom and loveliness, a rejuvenation, an immense hope… and, following after, the moods of reflection, of beauty, of race… to go into the moor not merely to find our souls but to find life itself—and to find it more abundantly.

But the following evening the little cottage presented quite another appearance. He came under its influence at the very first glance from the near moor crest. It had the desolate air of having had its heart torn out, of having been raped. A spiritless shell, its dark-red door pushed back in an imbecile gape. One could hear the wind in its emptiness. A sheer sense of its desolation overcame him. He could not take his eyes off it.

And presently an elderly woman came to the door, followed by the girl herself. They stood on the doorstep for a long time, then began slowly to walk up to the ridge beyond which lay the neighbours' cottages. But before they reached the ridge they stopped and again for a long time stood in talk. At last the elderly woman put out her hand and caught the girl's arm. But the girl would not go with her. She released herself and stepped back a pace, her body bending and swaying sensitively. The elderly woman stood still and straight, making her last appeal. The girl swayed away from that appeal also, turned and retreated. With hooded shawl her elder remained looking after her a moment, then like a woman out of the ages went up over the crest of the moor.

From his lair in the heather, Evan saw the door close, heard, so still the evening was, the clash and rattle of the latch. And with the door closed and the girl inside, the house huddled emptier than ever. His heart listened so intently that it caught the dry sound of her desolate thought… she was not weeping… her arms hung so bare that her empty hands kept plucking down her sleeves…

She came at his knock. The pallor of her face deepened the dark of her eyes. Their expressionlessness troubled and she stood aside to let him in. Only when they were by the fire in the gloom of the small-windowed kitchen did she realise what had happened.

But Evan did not feel awkward. He knew what he had to do like a man who might have imaginatively prepared himself for the test. He placed her chair at the other side of the fire but did not ask her to sit down. He sat down himself, however, and looking into the fire began to speak.

Sometimes he half turned with a smile, but for the most part kept his eyes on the burning peat, with odd silences that were pauses in his thought. He was not eager nor hurried; yet his gentleness had something fatal in it like the darkness of her mood. Sensitiveness that was as exquisite as pain transmuted pain to a haunted monotone.

She stood so still on the kitchen floor that in the end he dared not look at her. Nor did his immobility break when he heard her quietly sit down in the opposite chair, though the core of the fire quickened before his gaze.

Without moving, he started talking again. He did not use words that might appeal to a primitive intelligence. He spoke in the highest—the simplest—way he could to himself.

He looked at himself as a painter desiring to paint the moor. Why? He found himself dividing the world into spirit and mechanism. Both might be necessary, but spirit must be supreme. Why? Even if from no other point than this that it afforded the more exquisite delight. And the more one cultivated it the more varied and interesting life became, the deeper, the more charming, and, yes, the more tragical. Yes, the more tragical, thereby drawing spirit to spirit in a communion that was the only known warmth in all the coldness of space. And we needed that particular warmth; at moments one needed it more than anything else. Man's mechanism was a tiny flawed toy in the vast flawless mechanism of the universe. But this warmth of his was a thing unique; it was his own special creation… and in a way—who could say?—perhaps a more significant, more fertile, thing than even the creation of the whole mechanical universe…

As he thought over this idea for a time, he felt her eyes on his face. The supreme test of spirit would be that while not knowing his words it would yet understand him perfectly—*if it was there.*

"I do not know," he said at last, and repeated it monotonously. "Coming in over the moor there I saw you and the woman. Then there was the moor itself. And you in the cottage. I wish I could understand that. But I cannot understand it, any more than you—or the woman. Yet we understand it, too. And the woman could have helped you. Only you didn't want to be helped in her way yet." He paused, then went on slowly: "I can see that. It's when I go beyond that to my sitting here that it becomes difficult. For what I see is you who are the moor, and myself with the moor about me, and in us there is dawn, and out of the moor comes more of us... That sounds strange, but perhaps it is truer than if I said it more directly. For you and I know that we cannot speak to each other yet—face to face."

Then he turned his face and looked at her.

Her dark eyes were alight with tears that trickled in slow beads down her cheeks.

He gave his face to the fire again. *It was there.*

Quietly he got to his feet. "I'll make a cup of tea."

She also arose. "I'll make it."

It had grown quite dark in the kitchen. They stood very still facing the unexpected darkness. Caught by something in the heart of it, they instinctively drew together. He turned her face from it.

In the morning Douglas arrived at the cottage on the heels of the woman with the shawl. The woman had tried the door and found it locked. But her quick consternation lessened when she found the key under the thatch.

Douglas, grown oddly curious, waited for her to come out. She came, with a face as grey as the wall.

"She hasn't slept in her bed at all."

"Oh!" His lips closed.

The woman looked at him.

"Do you know...?"

"Not a thing," said Douglas. "Must have gone over the hills and far away. They've got a fine morning for it." And he turned and left her, his scoffing sanity sticking in his throat like a dry pellet.

GOOD BAIRNS

Dorothy K. Haynes

Dorothy K. Haynes (Dorothy Gray) was an author whose work progressively became more suited to the horror genre. Born in Lanark, 1918, her mother died in 1929 and her father, then unable to take care of her and her twin brother, sent them to the Episcopal Orphanage at Aberdour to be educated. Her first published work was at eleven in a local magazine, and her first novel, *Winter's Traces,* was published when she was 27. She won the Tom-Gallon Trust Award in 1947 for her short story "The Head" (although it was never published until 1972). Her first collection, *Thou Shalt Not Suffer a Witch*, was published by Methuen in 1949 alongside her novel *Robin Ritchie*—a weird "small town" book. Haynes really hit her stride in the seventies writing stories and selling reprints for the paperback horror anthologies that were doing the rounds, which included the *Fontana Book of Great Horror Stories* and the *Pan Book of Horror Stories*, amongst others. Dorothy was diagnosed with breast cancer and died in 1987.

This is her second appearance in one of my anthologies; her first was well received in *Celtic Weird*, and now, I feel that this book of Scottish stories would not be complete without one of her macabre masterpieces. "Good Bairns" is a traditional "everyday" horror tale, and one featuring children. I can feel your shudders already.

THEY were really frightened this time. A little mud, a little dust and perhaps an odd slit, was nothing to worry about, but this time they had gone too far. Up at the farm, hanging around to see what was going on, they had met Danny Beveridge. Danny had a dog, a big wild lump of a thing, of an excitability that was near hysteria. Between wrestling and pushing each other for the privilege of leading this creature by a rope, and encouraging, then evading the wild enthusiasm of the mongrel, there had been a general mess-up. Rab and Geordie landed in the muck heap, and came home stinking, inadequately wiped with grass, and soaked with water from unsuccessful cleansings.

Mrs. Donaldson met them at the stairhead, and cursed loud lest she should weep. "My God, what is it noo? They jerseys were just new washed and darned; an' what's tae dae wi' yer trousers? Where have ye *been*? It's sheer downright badness, the pair o' ye. And yer boots! Right ower the ankles wi' glaur, an' me here a' day trying tae keep the place decent. Where were ye?"

"Up at Beveridge's. The dug—"

"Yon brute ought tae be shot. Here, take a' thae off afore ye come near me. The stink's enough tae knock ye oot a mile away. Dinna pit them on the table, ye dirty wee midden! Honest to God, there's aye something. Could ye no' play decent? Clarted up there—"

"We never meant ony harm. Yon dug rolled us, an'—"

"Ye'd no business goin' near the dug. Here, oot o' the road till I get thir sinded through. The very day I want tae get on—"

Naked, silent, they slipped out of the way into the bedroom. "Come oot o' there!" she shrilled. "Ye'll need tae wash first, afore ye put on yer other claes. Here, I'll dae it for ye. It'll save time." She filled an enamel basin, soaped a flannel, and rubbed them down with much lathering of carbolic. "There's a towel, now; dry yersel's. The idea, me havin' tae bath grown laddies--"

"What'll we put on?" asked Geordie.

"It'll need tae be yer Sunday suits. Ye've nothing else."

"To play in?"

"Well, ye'll need tae. I cannie spring-clean wi' youse in the hoose. Some laddies I ken are a help tae their mithers—"

"We'll help," said Rab, dabbing gingerly at a bruise on his hip.

"You'll dae nothing of the sort. I wouldna hae a meenit's peace—just put on yer Sunday suits till yer other things dry. But mind ye, if you dare to come in wi' thae claes wasted—!"

"We'll mind them, honest. It was just yon dug—"

"Well, keep away frae Beveridge's. I'm no' in wi' Beveridge the noo, onyway; his milk's no' guid. Just go for a quiet walk, for once."

They lifted their Sunday suits from the box under the room bed. The bed was dismantled, a fascinating disarray of springs and irons and brass knobs, with the mattress propped against the chest of drawers, to air at the window. Pictures and dishes were stacked in piles on the floor. They put on clean shirts and socks, fresh and aired, and felt the cool slipperiness of stiff, new lining on their drawers and waistcoats. It was like Sunday. They sleeked their heads and presented themselves for their mother's approval.

She brushed her hair back with her wrist and nodded warningly. "All right now. Away you go till five o'clock, and mind you behave yourselves. Keep out o' the fields, and don't go messing about with water. Hurry up noo! Look at that clock! Keeping me back—"

They slipped out through the back kitchen, and shut the door quietly. The street was windy, spring dust driving in piles behind houses. They walked on the pavements, new shoes squeaking, their faces bland with the uncomfortable dignity of Sunday.

"Where'll we go?" said Rab.

"Dunno. Where *can* we go like this?"

"Kirk." It sounded like Hell.

"Come on an' we'll away an' see if Joe's in."

"Naw. Joe's too pansy."

"Well, what dae we look like, in this? We're just as pansy as him the day. Tell you what; we'll go down the river."

"Naw. We'd better no'."

"How no'?"

"We'll get wet."

"Och away, we'll no'. We'll just walk along the path. We dinna need tae go near the water."

"OK, but we'd better mind oorsel's."

"Och aye, we'll mind oorsel's!"

They climbed down the steep brae to the river bank, past the rubbish dump, and on to the riverside road. Here, the hedges were already green with brier. The thick vivid leaves curled like froth on the twigs, and hid nests and eggs and nervous, steadfast mother birds. Rab and Geordie hovered on the outskirts of these discoveries, standing ankle deep in a prickle of young nettles and grass. With grotesque care they lifted branches between finger and thumb, keeping cuffs from contact with anything that might fray or stain. There was no fun in it. All they were fit for, dressed like this, was a nice quiet walk with a hymn book.

They wandered on under a disconsolate sky. Behind the hedges, blossomed plum trees thrust up glorious branches, cold white against the green. On their left, the river showed in dull grey glimpses. In autumn they would come here, and wriggle through the hedge, and cup furtive hands round the gold globes of the fruit, sunny-ripe, with juice spurting between the teeth. They would eat till their stomachs ached with the acid-hot pain of too much fruit—but it was only April, and they daren't trespass an inch in Sunday suits.

Just as the road widened to a meadow, and swept the hedges back for further spaciousness, the sun came out. It picked out thick primroses, yellow as margarine, and it lit a touch of silver in the quick river. There were one or two cows moving in lazy aimlessness. The boys edged cautiously among the dung flops. Their shoes had only been worn twice, and the soles were still smooth.

They went down to the river, of course. There was no harm in that, just to watch the water. A stick whirled past, reared almost upright on the back of a white horse, plunged down and went on again in a swift glide. They watched it till it turned the deep corner beyond the bridge. "It'll sink noo," said Geordie.

"It'll no'. It's wood."

"Oh aye; I forgot. Here, I'm for a seat."

"Naw, dinna!" Rab pulled his young brother up. "You'll dirty yersel'! Here, let me dust you."

They pondered a moment in gloom. Then, behind them, they heard a cough, and turned their backs on the swift water to see who it was.

The cough was genuine, and not done to attract attention. It belonged to a little thin boy about four years old. It was his personal possession, a part of him. He coughed again, a shrill, irritating double syllable, "A-huh a-*huh*!" and finished up with a sniff. The boys stared at him, half amused, half annoyed at him for being so small and thin and unconcerned. The child stared back from his pointed face. Thin hair curled lightly on his head, and his eyes were large and blue, but he was not pretty. One hand held a bunch of primroses, the other trailed a stick. Once more he coughed, "A-huh a-*huh*!" and sniffed again.

The brothers exchanged glances. "What's yer name?" said Rab.

The boy stared.

"Come on, what's yer name?" Geordie advanced threateningly, but Rab pulled him back.

"Leave him alane. What's yer name, son?"

"Oliver."

"Eh?"

"Oliver." The voice was thin, but decidedly English.

"Where d'you stay?"

The primroses pointed uphill, the way they had come.

"What age are you?" The child did not answer, but coughed again.

Rab came a step nearer. A queer feeling, a desire to be cruel, and a shame in the desire, made the boys flush. "Wipe yer nose," said Rab. "No, dinna wipe it on yer hand, ye dirty wee tyke! Use yer hankie! Here, what are ye gatherin' flooers for? Yer mammy?"

Oliver nodded, and became suddenly fluent. "I've picked free bunches today. The first bunch, the stems were too small, and I had to frow them away." He smiled, and coughed again.

"Kid canna speak," said Geordie.

"Say 'three,'" he commanded.

"Free."

"See? He says 'free.'" They laughed loudly. "Say it again," said Geordie.

"Free." Not sure whether to laugh, the youngster coughed again. "A-huh a-*huh*!"

"You've an awful cold," said Rab, his nose screwed with irritation. "Can ye no' stop coughin'?"

"No." The infant shook his head. The brothers looked at each other for inspiration, wondering whether to pet or punish him for being so small and queer and different-spoken. He wasn't like other small boys. In silent, shamed agreement, they decided to experiment farther, to see how Oliver reacted.

"Can you fight?" said Geordie.

The little boy nodded eagerly.

"Come on, then." Geordie began to set up his guard and make furious preparations. Oliver looked round, worried. "I don't know where to put my flowers."

"Pit them on the grass."

"No. They might get trod on."

"Oh, here, gie's them, I'll haud them." Rab snatched the flowers, holding them contemptuously, heads down. "Get on, noo. Fight."

Oliver struck the first blow, a light babyish tap. Geordie dared not hit back, for fear he hit too hard. His fights were usually of the all-in variety, and he dared not attempt that here. Oliver stood still, smacking pettishly with a flat cold hand. "Here," said Rab, full of impatience, "here's yer flooers. Ye canna fight at a'."

"A-huh a-*huh*! Sniff."

"That's a terrible cough." Pity and curiosity made the boy's voice gentle. "You shouldna gather flooers here by yersel'. That's what makes ye so queer. Have ye no' got any pals?"

The boy shook his head and coughed.

"Can ye play tig?"

"No."

"That's whit's wrang wi ye, ye canna play. Ye've got tae—tae lead an *active* life. Come on, we'll take ye in hand till the holidays are by. Would ye like that, us comin' tae play every day?"

Oliver nodded.

"C'mon then. You try to catch us, an' say 'tig.' C'mon! Run hard!"

Racing and doubling with patronising slowness, they let themselves be caught, enjoying Oliver's pleasure in the game. Oliver coughed and choked and giggled. "Now *you* run away," said Rab. "Run quick; we're after you! Moo-oo! The coos'll get ye!"

It was better fun to chase him than to be chased. They roared after him, and let him have frights and narrow escapes, and drove him nearly hysterical. He was not sure whether to be frightened or amused, and the more he choked and coughed, the more the brothers carried him on, half in good will, half in a mood of reckless cruelty that comes to all boys. Once, converging on their prey, they collided and fell on the grass. They dusted themselves guiltily, and were more careful for a while.

It wasn't their fault. They were only chasing the boy, and his foot slipped on a smear of mud, and he fell into the water. It was so easily done. They hadn't meant to chase him into the river. Anybody could have fallen that way, anybody. One moment he was running and coughing, "A-huh a-*huh*!" and then he was up to his neck (he was so wee, and the river was so deep), thrashing about and gurgling with water splashing into his mouth.

"Let me—!" screamed Geordie, rushing down the bank, as white as a blanket.

"Geordie! Yer *suit*!"

The boy hesitated. He could have done nothing, anyway. Oliver was rushed away like a stick, round the bend under the bridge. He would drown there, in the deep black patch where the froth drifted like white sixpences.

The boys stood, swallowing, pale and quiet. "He—he—"

"It wasna us," said Rab.

"Is he away?"

"Ay, I think sae."

"It was that quick—we couldna ha' saved him, onywey."

"I ken. We'd ha' been drooned tae. Onyway, it wasna us. He went in himsel'."

"Ay. We couldna' ha' helped. It was his ain fault, carryin' on like yon, no' lookin' where he was goin'. It wasna us."

"Naw, Rab, come on hame."

"Ay. We'll no say we seen—him—?"

"Naw, Naebuddy needs tae ken. An', Rab—dinna—we'll no' even talk aboot him oorsel's—"

"We'll no' mention him. Here, there's his primroses. What'll we dae wi them?"

"Chuck them in the river."

The flowers were swirled away as soon as they touched the water. Geordie vomited on the path.

"Here, Geordie, come on. Calm doon. Here, we'll—we'll gather some flooers tae take hame."

"No, I couldna. It makes me sick tae think o' primroses—"

"I ken, but ye'll just need tae. Mother'll want tae ken what we've been daein'."

"Well, a'right, then." He rubbed his hand across his eyes, and bent among the frail pink stems.

Their tea was set in the back kitchen. Mrs. Donaldson, scrubbing through in the bedroom, did not know that they ate nothing. They had the table cleared for her when she came through.

"Are ye away oot again?" she asked, suspicion in her eyes, but her voice softened with gratitude.

"Naw. Mither, can we help ye? We'll no' get in the way, honest we'll no'. We want tae help."

"A'right then. I'll gie ye a chance." She brought out Brasso and rags, and watched their industrious heads bent close together as they rubbed and polished the taps and candlesticks. A jam-jar of primroses stood on the sink. The woman smiled and yawned. They were good bairns, when you took them the right way.

THE LASS WITH THE DELICATE AIR

Eileen Bigland

Eileen Pollard Bigland (29 May 1898–11 April 1970), was a travel writer and biographer. She was born in Edinburgh to a Russian mother and was the first European woman to travel the length of the Burma Road. While in China, she survived the first bombing of Chongqing (3 and 4 May 1939) in which 700 residents died and over 350 were injured. She wrote several books on her travels and would visit towns across the UK giving lectures on China and Russia. These talks were sanctioned and allowed by the Ministry of Information. She wrote biographies on Mary Shelley and Marie Corelli and edited *The Princess Elizabeth Gift Book* with Cynthia Asquith in 1935. Their friendship was a solid one; seventeen years after working together Cynthia would ask Eileen to write a short story for *The Second Ghost Book* (1952). That tale is reprinted here in a non-Asquith book for only the second time. "The Lass with the Delicate Air" is a love story, but one with a dead girl—and the war veteran who sees her knows she's dead but doesn't care. Not gruesome in the slightest, and that's what makes this tale a real treasure.

ARLY in 1949 I underwent a rather severe operation. Convalescence was a slow process and being an impatient sort of man I asked the specialist if he couldn't hurry matters along. A dour but kindly Scot, he said merely, "Humph! You know a deal about machinery, don't you?"

"I ought to—after all, I'm an engineer."

"Then you know that major repairs to a broken-down machine may take a considerable time?"

"Of course, but…"

"You're the machine," he interrupted drily, "and you've consistently over-worked yourself the past four years. Have you ever taken a holiday since you came back from the war?"

"Oh, a week-end here and there." I began to explain that after my long absence in North Africa and Italy my business had required every minute I could spend on it, but again he cut across my speech.

"And now you've let yourself in for a six months job." In blunt terms he told me that my only chance of regaining complete health lay in giving up work until the autumn. "You've got partners and you can afford it finan-cially," he ended abruptly.

He was right. Inwardly I had known, though I had refused to admit it, that both my mind and body were worn out, and now I felt strangely grateful for his confirmation. Despite difficult conditions business was flourishing and there was no reason why I should not leave the running of it to my colleagues. "But where could I go?" I asked feebly.

"Scotland—it's a soothing country though you may not believe it. You fish a bit, don't you, and can handle a gun? Take a wee house somewhere in the Highlands and live outdoors as much as possible." Ushering me to the door he added, "Try McTavish in Union Street, Inverness. He's a sound agent."

Feeling slightly bewildered I paused on the steps and looked up and down Harley Street. Perhaps if it had not been one of those cruelly brilliant April mornings when the light emphasises the dinginess of town houses I might not have accepted the specialist's advice, but as I blinked in the sunshine I thought suddenly of the shining firths of the north, the cloud-dappled hills, the scented forests of fir and pine. Four days later I reached Inverness, booked a room in the Station Hotel, and went in search of McTavish.

He was a pleasant elderly man, but he shook his head when I told him what I wanted. "I doubt there's nothing nearer than Nairnside," he said.

I replied eagerly that when stationed near Nairn early in the war I had developed quite an affection for the district, whereupon he looked relieved and suggested driving me there that very afternoon. We took the coast road that runs by the Moray Firth, turned inland at Gollanfield, climbed towards Cawdor woods and the wine-dark peat moss behind them. Glancing back I saw the silver stretch of water, the black humps of the soutars guarding the entrance to Cromarty harbour, the glittering white cap of Wyvis rising beyond. If the house mentioned by McTavish commanded such a view I'd take it at any price!

But it turned out to be a grim, small-windowed building set in a hollow ringed by trees so tall that all view was blotted out. McTavish was apologetic, and when I demanded if he knew of anywhere from which the firth and the Black Isle could be seen he eyed me warily. "Would you be afraid of ghosts?" he asked.

I burst out laughing. "Good heavens, no!"

"Well," his voice was hesitant, "there's Auchindoune; you get a rare view from its windows. But you see, during the '45 Rebellion it was a farmhouse where Charlie's men sheltered after Culloden. The red-coats caught and shot them—the marks are on the kitchen-garden wall to this day—and the crofters say that come the back-end of every year you'll hear the skirl of the pipes and the tramp of the clansmen's feet. Back in the war I sold the place to a rich man from Glasgow, but inside of three months he rushed into my office as if the devil were after him, roaring that the house was haunted, that he never wished to see it again, and that I could let it furnished at any rental I could get. I've let it twice," he added lugubriously, "but the folk didn't stay."

"Because of the ghosts of Charlie's men?" I asked idly.

A queerly evasive expression crossed McTavish's face. "Maybe," he said, "or maybe…" his voice tailed off.

But I wasn't in the mood to listen to any more superstitious nonsense and turned towards the car. "Let's have a look at it." As McTavish drove on up the hill I grinned at the notion of anyone asking a hard-headed, middle-aged business man like myself if he was afraid of ghosts.

Auchindoune was a square, comfortable-looking house, its garden well tended and gay with spring flowers, its big high-ceilinged rooms furnished with good solid stuff (whatever the man from Glasgow's failings he had had taste), and the view was superb. We were shown round by an old couple called Cameron who were resident caretakers and before our tour of inspection was over I said I would take the place for six months. While we discussed details Mrs. Cameron stood primly, hands crossed above her spotless white apron, but her husband regarded me suspiciously. "Would you be alone?" he demanded.

"Yes, I'm a bachelor. Maybe the house is too large for my needs but I like it. It has an—an air about it." Then I stopped aghast. Whatever had possessed me to say those last words?

"It has that," answered Cameron, and I fancied his expression was distinctly more favourable. "The wife could do for you."

So it was arranged and I settled into Auchindoune the following day. It was glorious weather and for the first week I saw little of the Camerons—which was just as well, I reflected, being aware that to the inhabitants of these parts anybody hailing from outside a twenty-mile radius was a foreigner, an enemy one to boot. Mrs. Cameron thawed first under compliments on her excellent cooking but I gave her husband a fairly wide berth until a morning when I came across him in the yard plaiting withy baskets and paused to inquire about trout-fishing prospects. He gave me particulars civilly enough, then shot a glance at some primroses in my buttonhole and jerked a thumb towards the rounded wooded hill at the back of the house. "Have you been up the Doune?"

I nodded. "It's my favourite after-breakfast walk. The air tastes like wine on the tongue up there, and as for the primroses in that mossy hollow on the top," I touched my buttonhole, "they're better than you'd find in most gardens."

A funny smile flickered on his lips and was gone. "Ay," he said softly, "they grow well for ones they love." But before I could ask his meaning he switched the subject back to fishing and, to my surprise, suggested accompanying me to the stream up on the peat moss that afternoon.

I soon discovered that where trout were concerned I was a tyro compared to Cameron. I found too that he was surprisingly well informed about world affairs, on which he discoursed at length. As we walked homewards he regaled me with legendary tales of fishermen in the far-off days of his youth, yet despite the friendliness in his soft Highland voice I could not rid myself of the feeling that behind his talk lay a certain hostility. This, I thought, was understandable enough. He was an old man, he loved Auchindoune, he resented its occupation by a mere Sassenach; when he grew more used to my company he would thaw as his wife had done.

After a delicious high tea (Mrs. Cameron had grilled our catch to perfection) I wandered up to my sittingroom on the first floor feeling happily, healthily tired and looking forward with an eagerness long forgotten to the reading of a new biography which had just arrived from the library. As I opened the door I heard a slight noise—like the swish of a woman's skirts—and drew back instinctively. Who on earth could be in my room? Not Mrs. Cameron, for I had just left her clearing the dining room table. I pushed the door wide. The room was empty, the long curtains by the open windows billowed in the breeze—then I smelt the fragrance of primroses and could have sworn that someone drifted past me.

"Pull yourself together," I muttered, closing the door sharply behind me. "You've been listening to too many tall Highland tales." Settling myself in my chair I opened my book but I hadn't read more than a few pages before another sound made me lift my head. Outside in the garden someone was whistling a sad, plaintive tune impossible to describe, for though the notes were soft and sweet they held a throbbing urgency so disturbing that I leapt to my feet and leaned far out over the window-sill.

There was nobody in sight. The garden lay dreaming under the pale evening sky, yet that inexpressibly poignant whistling rose on the still air from the lawn directly beneath me. Presently it grew fainter, as if the whistler was retreating round the corner of the house in the direction of the Doune, and suddenly I *knew* I had to follow, had to trace the origin of that tragic little tune. Reluctant that the Camerons should see me I crept downstairs, let myself out of the front door, and took the wooded path leading up the Doune. The whistling floated back to me, but though I broke into a half-trot and kept peering ahead through the young green branches of the mountain-ash I could see no sign of the whistler. Panting, my feet slipping on the smooth path, I gained the top of the hill at last and paused on the lip of the mossy hollow. Below me, bending above the primroses, was the figure of a girl in a faded blue print frock. For a moment I paused, feeling extraordinarily foolish. Whatever was this village lass, for such I judged her to be, going to think of a middle-aged stranger, breathless and red-faced, interrupting her primrose-picking? Besides, ten to one she had come to keep tryst with some local lad, probably the mysterious whistler, who would imagine I was pursuing his beloved. It was an infernally awkward situation but as I teetered on the lip of the hollow wondering how I could retreat without rousing her attention the girl lifted her head…

She had a face I had dreamed of sometimes but never encountered, its perfect oval shape framed in tumbled hair of bright chestnut. The eyes beneath the arched brows were grey and wide-set, the nose small and straight, the mouth generously curved. Even as I stared at her she stood erect, her hands full of starry blossoms, and I saw her dress was ragged, her slim feet bare and brown. Then she began to walk towards me, her every movement holding ineffable grace, and as she came closer I saw such anguish in her eyes that for a moment I could neither speak nor move.

Somehow I found my voice. "What is wrong? Do you want help?"

She made no answer but nodded slightly and for an instant I thought a smile touched her mouth. Only then did I notice her extreme pallor. "But you're ill," I babbled stupidly. "Look, sit down and rest, then tell me where you live and I will take you home," and I stepped forward to take her by the arm. What happened next made the blood freeze in my veins, for when I tried to grasp her elbow my hand closed upon itself—*there was no arm to take hold of.* Yet still in front of me, only about two feet away, stood this amazingly beautiful creature with the tortured eyes.

From somewhere in the distance I heard myself say hoarsely, "There are no such things as ghosts—you can't be one." She gave a second little nod, threw her arms wide in a gesture of despair so that the primroses scattered on the ground, and darted to the far lip of the hollow. So swiftly had she moved that by the time I had collected myself and scrambled after her she was running downhill through the trees. Strangely enough my spasm of fear had left me and as I followed the glint of her blue frock in the gathering dusk I remember murmuring confusedly, "Phantom or human: human or phantom she's in dreadful trouble. I've *got* to catch up with her and learn her story." But it was easier to say than to do, for there was no path this side of the Doune, and while I slithered and stumbled through the undergrowth the girl ahead skimmed along like a bird, her feet seeming scarcely to touch the ground.

My heart was pounding in my chest before she paused in her flight, rested her hand against the bole of a mountain-ash and gazed back at me out of those sorrowful grey eyes. When I neared her she threw back her head and looked upwards through the branches as though in search of something. I too looked up, then as quickly looked back—the girl had gone. Furiously I blundered on another hundred yards or so and found I had reached the edge of the wood. Before me the broad fields of Nairnside stretched in the twilight but strain my sight as I might I could catch no glimpse of a blue frock against their misty green. In that split second of time at the mountain-ash the girl had completely vanished.

Laboriously I clambered up the Doune again, arguing with myself as I went. She couldn't be a ghost, it was ridiculous nonsense even to imagine it. Ah, but she hadn't spoken and there was something about the lift of her head, the pallor of her skin, the incredible grace of her movements. Rubbish, ghosts didn't pick primroses… suddenly I stopped. Those primroses she had dropped, *there* was proof! I struggled on till I reached the mossy hollow, walked round it, went down on my knees and scanned the ground. There was still enough light but as an extra precaution I ran my hands over the moss. Not a single loose primrose could I find.

How long I crouched by the hollow I do not know, but by the time I swung down the hill towards Auchindoune a sickle moon hung high in the sky. From the shadowy drive Cameron's voice hailed me. "I've been waiting on Sutherland the keeper from Clunis who said he'd be over the night. Did you see him up the Doune, sir? A big man with a brown jacket and leggings."

Somehow I felt this visit of Sutherland to be a fiction and a wild, unreasoning anger filled me. "I saw nobody," I snapped, "goodnight!"

In my sittingroom I poured myself a large whisky and soda and took up my book. But the drink tasted bitter on my tongue and between my eyes and the printed page came the lovely oval face of the girl in blue. Was that old devil Cameron trying to witch me? Was I going daft? Was the girl real or was she a figment of the imagination induced perhaps by all those new-fangled drugs they had given me in hospital? Suddenly I jerked upright in the chair at a familiar melancholy sound. In two strides I was at the window. "Cameron," I shouted, "stop that confounded whistling!"

A minute or so later Mrs. Cameron put her head round the door. "Were you wanting something, sir?" she asked anxiously.

"No—yes—where's your husband?"

"In his bed this past half-hour, sir." Her russet-apple face creased into lines of such perplexity that I knew she was telling the truth. With a muttered apology I dismissed her and swallowed the rest of my drink at a gulp. There was, there must be, some perfectly reasonable explanation of the evening's happenings. In the morning I'd go into Inverness and ask McTavish exactly why the man from Glasgow and others had left Auchindoune. Not that I was afraid of… the glass slid from my hand and shivered to pieces in the empty fireplace. It had just come to me that I was far from being afraid. Whoever or whatever the girl in blue was I had fallen in love for the first time in my forty-three years.

I didn't go to Inverness the following day. Instead, like any love-sick boy, I spent the next three weeks haunting the Doune. I walked right round the base of the hill, climbed it from all angles, searched the tangles of blackberry, gorse and bog myrtle for possible caves or other hiding-places, sat for hours in the mossy hollow where the primroses grew; but not once did I see the girl whose beauty and anguish now so obsessed me that I thought of her by day and dreamed of her by night, nor did I hear the whistler's plaintive tune. Mrs. Cameron sighed over the tears and rents in my flannel trousers and her husband eyed me curiously when I refused to go fishing with him. People to whom I had been given introductions sent me invitations to which I returned evasive replies, and when a friend telegraphed saying he was in Inverness and would like to come and stay I flew into such a state of panic that I borrowed the Cawdor grocer's bicycle and pedalled the twelve miles into town to put him off.

After all it was McTavish who gave me the first clue. He arrived unexpectedly one afternoon and inquired so courteously about my comfort that I could do no less than ask him to tea. We chatted idly of this and that; then he said, "My Glasgow client is delighted you took the house."

Almost without volition I demanded, "What made him leave. What did he see here—'maybe Charlie's men, or maybe…?'" McTavish looked acutely uncomfortable. "It wasn't seeing exactly, it was—well—hearing. Mind you", he hurried on, "he was a skeery fellow and it's my opinion he gossiped too much with the Nairnside folk, but he said that come every new moon he heard whistling…"

But I was out of my chair and shaking him by the shoulder. "*Whistling!* From the garden, you mean?"

Poor McTavish cowered back. "I don't know, just whistling. Oh, sir, don't say you've heard it too?"

"I have," I said grimly, "but it's not driving me away, I want to find out its origin."

He shook his head. "There are always scores of stories about old houses like this but the people hereabouts are so close-mouthed that all I can find out is that about fifty years ago the farmer who lived here had a beautiful daughter who ran off with a tinker lad. Some say he got himself shot, others that he sickened and died. Anyway the girl went out of her mind with grief and didn't live long after him. I'd not be knowing any more," he finished feebly. "I've heard tell old Cameron has the whole history but when I asked him he swore he'd never heard of it."

At the moment the significance of that last remark escaped me—I was too busy trying to remember when there was a new moon, and before McTavish's car was out of the drive I was leafing the pages of my diary. The date was six days ahead.

Thereafter I lived for the new moon. During my first six days of waiting I kept away from the Doune and passed the long drowsy hours in the garden conning over in my mind the sparse information given me by McTavish. Several times I thought of eking this out by tactful questioning of the Cawdor villagers but I felt a strange reluctance to do so and a positive recoil from the idea of approaching Cameron on the subject, for somehow instinct told me he was antagonistic to the figure I had met with on the Doune; several times I tried to laugh myself out of the whole absurd business of imagining I was in love with a being, earthly or unearthly, whose appearance was heralded by a whistled tune but self-mockery did not work—I was too much in thrall, worldly individual though I was.

And the new moon did not fail me. Just after sunset I heard the whistling and, trembling with excitement, followed it up the Doune. There in the hollow was the girl in blue, but this time she stood facing me with outstretched arms, a smile on her lips. "So you've come back," I whispered, "come back because I love you so utterly, my very dear." But to my horror, as I stepped towards her the arms fell slackly to her sides and she stared at me sadly, shaking her head. The next moment she had fled down the far side of the hill and, as before, I raced after her, saw her rest her hand on the mountain-ash and gaze up into its branches, lost her entirely just short of the edge of the wood…

So elusive an encounter, yet as I walked homewards I was filled with an ecstasy not even the presence of Cameron in the yard could dispel.

June passed, and July, and half of August. Looking back it seems as if I dreamed through those two and a half months, waking only when the date on the calendar told me my love would return that night—then I would wait in a fever of impatience for the summer day to close. It had been April when I first saw her and I remember awakening on the morning of 16th August and thinking: "Tonight we shall meet again but this fifth time she will tell me what troubles her, and I shall destroy or exorcise whatever it may be, and she will stay warm and sweet in my arms."

But to my dismay her face was drawn with grief when I found her in the hollow and I shall never forget the piteous appeal in her grey eyes. As usual she ran from me and I followed, but when she reached the mountain-ash she not only looked up but pointed to the green berries beginning to cluster on its branches. I stepped forward, pointing also, and the sorrow died in her eyes and she nodded. Just for a minute she stood so close I could see the rise and fall of her breast, then suddenly she was gone and I was staring at the still bole of the tree…

That was the end of dreaming, for day and night I was haunted by the memory of her tragic face and by the knowledge that in some way I had failed to give her something she wanted desperately, something without which she was compelled to suffer time without end.

The moon was in its last quarter when Mrs. Cameron lingered after setting my luncheon dishes on the table. "If you please, sir, Cameron's asking could you come and see him."

I glanced up in bewilderment. "See him? Why, can't he come and see me?"

She gave a little snuffle. "He's been in his bed a week, sir. I had the Doctor out from Nairn. He says it's the pneumonia and gave me a fair talking-to for not sending for him earlier."

My sense of guilt must have shown in my flushed face. Ever since that April evening when he had told me that cock-and-bull story about a visit from Sutherland the keeper I had kept out of Cameron's way, spoken to him tersely when obliged. Then I had grown conscious that he kept a vigilant eye on me around the time of the new moon and been convinced of his enmity towards both myself and the girl of the Doune. For the past three weeks I had been so absorbed I had entirely failed to notice his disappearance from garden or yard. Now, looking at his wife's worried, wrinkled countenance, I felt all kinds of a cad.

"Of course I'll come," I said, giving her shoulder an awkward pat, "but why on earth didn't you tell me when he was first taken ill?"

"You looked gey sick yourself, sir." Then her voice dropped, "and Cameron said he thought you were against him."

So Cameron had been aware of my feelings and—what was it McTavish had said?—Cameron had the whole history of the farmer's daughter who had run away with a tinker lad. My lunch went untouched and despite the heat of the day I sat shivering in my chair. Was I on the fringe of discovering what ailed my unhappy love—and did I want to know the truth? For the first time in months the materialist in me came uppermost. These damned Highlanders had bewitched me with their hints of spooks and such-like nonsense and I was a fool ever to have meddled…

"Would you be ready now, sir?" said Mrs. Cameron from behind me.

I followed her along the stone passage leading to the kitchen quarters conscious only of the violent conflict in my mind. One side cried urgently to know the secret behind my lovely girl's wanderings: the other shied desperately away from any possible proof that she belonged to a world not our own, for selfishly it clung to the hope that some day, somehow, she and I might find normal human happiness together.

Mrs. Cameron pushed open a door. "In here, sir."

Cameron lay propped up on pillows in a wide bed. One glance sufficed to tell me he was very ill indeed and while I murmured conventional sympathy his faded eyes regarded me in mute entreaty. He waited until his wife had left us before saying in a thread-like whisper, "She came to you every new moon, didn't she?"

This time I could not lie. "Yes," I said.

He sighed. "She came to me but the once, yon was my punishment. Fifty years I've lived with my sin and before I go I must tell you the ways of it. Her name was Elspeth Munro and she lived here in Auchindoune. Such a delicate lass she was with her chestnut hair, and her big grey eyes, and her walk that was like running water. Her father Hamish was a hard man, set on his only child making a fine marriage, and when I came here from the Lochiel country and began to court her he was gey pleased."

His gnarled hands twitched restlessly on the white coverlet. "It's hard to believe, but I had money in those days, most of it made in ways I don't like to remember. A cattle and sheep dealer I was, but the real money came from distilling whisky—there wasn't a lad in the Cameron country who could jink the Excisemen as cleverly as I did. Well, I bought a farm over Culloden way, a lonely place with a barn just suited to my purpose, for I distilled the whisky in a hut up on the peat moss and stored the casks in the barn under the grain. The moment I set eyes on Elspeth I knew she was the lass for me and by the year's end we were betrothed. She hated me, I know that now. When I kissed her she fluttered in my arms like a bird—but I was a masterful man and a cruel one and I was set on bending her to my will. The wedding-day was fixed for September but the spring before a tinker came to my door asking for work. They called him Logie, a heigho-heugho lad he was with a gipsy face and a quick bright smile—and I gave him the job of minding my sheep up on the peat moss.

"I never heard a lad whistle like Logie. I used to hear it echoing down the glen of an evening, but what I didn't know was that Elspeth heard it too until the April night I found them lying in the hollow on the Doune top. I thrashed the lad within an inch of his life, took Elspeth home and told her father to keep her under lock and key till her wedding-day. She grew pale and wisht but I didn't care for she was like a fever in my blood and all I minded was to have her for my own. Come August a shepherd from the west told me Logie was working at Achnasheen and that was good news for it was a long journey from Nairnside at that time.

"We were married in Cawdor church, and I mind how beautiful Elspeth looked in her long white silk dress as she came up the aisle with her father. One sorrowful glance she gave me that went through me like a knife, but then the service began and all I thought of was the presents I would give her to win her round, to make her love me."

Cameron's thready voice petered out and he closed his eyes for a moment, then went on: "It was when we came out of the church that it happened. I could feel Elspeth trembling on my arm but I was so proud of showing her to the crowd that had gathered that I did not hear the whistling—at first. It was only when I was about to hand her into the fine carriage I had hired that she broke from me, and it was then I heard the tune that Logie had always whistled. The next instant Elspeth was running through the Castle gates and up the path leading through Cawdor woods to the peat moss, her dress kilted up above her knees, her long white veil streaming behind her. I started after her, but she moved too quick…" Cameron's head turned from side to side on the pillow and when he spoke again I had to bend closer to hear the words.

"Logie must have been waiting for her in the woods, but though Hamish and I searched for a week we never saw sign of them. I doubt it was my pride was hurt the most, but I wouldn't admit that. Back home I went, shut myself up, and drank my own whisky. Half fuddled I was all and every day, but never too drunk to walk up the Doune each night. It was there they had first loved each other and I had the feeling they'd come back so I always carried my gun. It was year to the day of my marriage I found them. They were sitting beneath a rowan tree and it broke my heart to see Elspeth, for she wore a ragged blue dress and had no shoes to her feet and she was burned as black as Logie. Laughing they were and teasing each other with great bunches of the scarlet berries. They neither saw nor heard me as I drew nearer and raised my gun.

"I mind the blood spurting from Logie's mouth, spattering his shirt with great red blotches, and Elspeth kneeling beside him. Then she lifted her head and when I saw the hate blazing from her eyes I was off down the hill like the coward I was. But I couldn't keep away. In the gloaming I went back. Elspeth had gone but Logie's body was still there and I carried it—I was a strong man then—up the Doune to the edge of the hollow. I covered him with bracken and went home for a spade. I knew I'd be safe, for not a single crofter would climb the Doune after dusk for fear of the ghosts of Charlie's men. Late that night I buried him—you'll mind what I told you, primroses grow well for those they love?

"Next day two of Hamish's men found Elspeth wandering on the Doune side and brought her home to Auchindoune. Her wits were gone and never a word did she say till the day I rode over to see her. Sane or mad I wanted to claim her as my wife but when she saw me she raised herself up in bed and pointed, 'Red as rowan berries', she said. 'Red as rowan berries,'"

The old man's head lolled forward. "There's little else to tell," he muttered. "She died three months later and they buried her in Cawdor churchyard. I aye think Hamish knew the truth for a year later he put the Excisemen on to me, but when I came out of gaol he too had died and all I wanted was to forget. I wasn't allowed to that. Everywhere I went I heard Logie's whistle and saw Elspeth's eyes. I tried to leave the place—something kept me tied to it. When I married I came here to Auchindoune for I thought maybe if I tended her home she'd forgive me. It didn't work out that way..." He slumped back, his breath coming in shallow gasps.

I leaned over him and gripped his shoulder. "Tell me, tell me, what is it that Elspeth wants so desperately?"

His eyelids flickered. "Red as rowan berries," he muttered, "red as rowan berries!"

Cameron died three days later. On the evening of the new moon I sat waiting in my sittingroom and on the table beside me lay a great sheaf of rowan branches aglow with scarlet berries. Presently I heard the sweet clear whistle float in from the garden and made my way out of the house and up the Doune. There she stood in the hollow, my lovely ghost, and when she saw what I bore in my arms a look of radiance overspread her face. I bent down and strewed the rowans on Logie's makeshift grave and as I straightened she stretched out her hands. I took them in my own and they were, I swear, warm living hands. I drew her towards me, and as we kissed I knew that for one wild, wonderful moment the real Elspeth Munro belonged to me; then she retreated, but now the colour glowed in her cheeks and as she reached the far lip of the hollow she turned and gave me a joyous wave of the hand…

Deliberately I extended my tenancy of Auchindoune for a further month and told McTavish I wished to rent it the following summer. But though I waited in the sittingroom on new moon evenings I never heard the whistle of Logie again, never saw the blue-clad Elspeth standing in the hollow. Sad though I was—for I shall always love her—I knew in my heart I had done the only thing possible, I had given her peace.

THE INHERITANCE

Simon Pilkington

Simon Pilkington (1938–2009) was a bit of a mystery. "The Inheritance" is the only genre short story written under that name and was originally published in Richard Davis' *Tandem Horror 2* in 1968. Without access to the payment files of that and the two other books the tale was reprinted in, it was pretty difficult to track him down. I had found another short story by a "Simon Pilkington" from 1967, titled "The Diversion", and published in *Blackwood's Magazine*. I then came across an advert from the 1980s in a tourism catalogue for Knockingham Lodge Hotel in Portpatrick, Stranraer. The owner back then was Simon Pilkington. I went with my hunch, phoned the hotel, who said they had owned the hotel for the last twenty years but hadn't heard from Simon in as long and didn't know where he was. Right at the end of the phone call the owner David Ibbertson said, "My wife has just mentioned that his stepson is the author Charles Cumming. Do you know him?"

One Twitter exchange with Charles Cumming (who also co-wrote the script for the fabulous *Plane* (2023)) later solved the mystery. Simon *is* the author of "The Inheritance", but, sadly, he died in 2009.

"The Inheritance" is a cracking story and I consider it one of the best horror stories of its type. Angus is off to meet his Uncle Cole on the Dracken Rock. With some saying Cole has grown horns and gallops with the goats, and others adamant that he gave his soul to the sea, who will Angus meet?

As Angus stepped through the door of the crowded drinking-house in Callach, every head turned towards him and silence fell in the room. The old, bearded fishermen moved aside to make room for him at the bar. They watched as he ordered his dram and laid a florin on the wood.

He did not mind their curiosity; it was natural in a place as remote as this where strangers from the mainland seldom, if ever, came. He turned and raised his glass.

"Good evening to you, gentlemen."

Gutturally, they murmured their acknowledgements, and some turned away to continue interrupted tales of fishing and the sea.

Angus addressed an old man standing near him. "Excuse me, sir," he said, "but is there a man here who would take me to the Dracken Rock?"

In the silence that followed they all turned to stare at him anew, and the man to whom he had spoken withdrew a little, looking uneasily to right and left.

Angus hesitated. "I can pay," he said.

He could hear the murmur of the sea beyond the harbour wall. Even the barman had set down the glass that he was polishing and was standing motionless.

He shrugged his shoulders and moved towards the peat fire. He pulled up a chair and sat twirling his glass between his palms. At length he looked up to see an old fisherman standing before him. The man studied him carefully through unblinking, watery eyes, then he said,

"So you are wanting to go to the Dracken Rock?"

Angus rose. "Yes, I am."

The old man nodded slowly. "It's a long while since a boat has been out there," he said. "I doubt if there's a man in all the Hebrides would take you." Behind him the room was watching and waiting.

"Why is that?" Angus asked.

"There are many reasons. Do you not know the Rock then?"

Angus shook his head. "I've never been to the islands before."

A second old fisherman joined the first. "What would you be wanting with the Dracken Rock?" he asked harshly.

Angus turned to him. "My uncle lives there."

"Your uncle lives there?"

"Yes."

"No one ever lived on the Rock but Cole Bartholemew," the old man answered defiantly.

"Cole Bartholemew is my uncle."

There was a general stirring in the room.

"You say Cole Bartholemew was your uncle?" the old man asked, incredulous.

"Yes."

"Cole Bartholemew has been dead these last ten years," the first old man said. The others exchanged glances and nodded.

Angus laughed. "I'm sorry to disappoint you all," he said, "but my uncle is alive. I have a letter from him here." He took a crumpled envelope from his pocket. "Here. I'll read it to you."

Several of the fishermen turned away but others stayed.

"Why don't they want to hear?" Angus asked.

"Read the letter," one of the men said quietly.

"My dear Angus," Angus read, "I am your mother's elder brother and you are my only living relative. You are to inherit the Dracken Rock. Come to see me before the winter storms if you can get away. I shall look for you. Your uncle, Cole Bartholemew." He folded the paper away. "There now, you see he is not dead."

One voice spoke above the murmuring. "May I ask you when you received the letter?"

"Three weeks ago. The postmark is Callach, October 2nd."

The fishermen looked at each other strangely.

"This is the work of the Devil," one said.

"Aye, it is the work of the Devil." They crossed themselves.

"But why?" Angus cried. "Here is the proof that he is alive." He brandished the letter.

"You still believe that your uncle is alive?" the first old man asked.

"Yes."

"Euan…" They turned towards a wizened, white-haired man who sat apart. "Euan, when was the last time a boat went out to the Rock?"

"Mine was the last," Euan said, looking at Angus.

"And when was that?"

"Six years ago this last July."

"And no boat has been since?" Angus cried.

"And no boat has been since," Euan answered.

"But…" Angus began, but the others moved away muttering and nodding their heads. The old man called Euan crossed the room and sat beside him.

"You are young," he said. "Do not concern yourself with the Dracken Rock and Cole Bartholemew."

"But he is my uncle."

"Was your uncle." Euan rested a veined hand on his knee. "Far be it from me to contradict a stranger, but I have seen the place where he lies."

"But then…"

"Nor would I speak ill of the dead," Euan went on slowly, "but it must be told that he was an evil man—as evil as Lucifer himself."

"How was he evil?" Angus asked.

Euan moved closer to the fire as if the memory chilled him. His old eyes stared into the glowing peat and he clasped and unclasped his hands. "Some say horns grew out of his skull; others that he ran on all fours, frisking and galloping with the wild goats among the rocks." He paused. "Had you never met your uncle?"

"No, never."

"Aye. That would explain your not knowing," Euan said. He gestured behind him. "He stood a head and shoulders above the tallest man here. His hair was like a beast's hair and he was as wild as the sea that cast him on to the Rock out of the Correvecan."

"What is the Correvecan?" Angus asked.

"Have you never heard tell of the Correvecan?"

"No."

Euan sighed. "The Correvecan is the whirl off the eastern coast of the Dracken Rock," he said. "It has claimed many a fine boat, and your Uncle Cole's was one of them. The story goes that the sea took pity on him and threw him up on the Rock."

"Then he is alive," Angus cried.

"When he came out of the sea," the old man went on, "his hair was as white as snow and he was mad with fear. He heard voices in the wind, and the voices told him that he owed the sea a debt."

"And what was the debt?" Angus asked disbelievingly.

"His life."

"His life?"

"Aye. The same sea that gave him life would take it away."

"And you have seen the place where he lies?"

"Aye."

"How long do you believe he lived on the Rock before his death?"

Euan frowned. "'Twould be well nigh seven years."

"And how did he live?"

"Only the good God knows that," Euan answered. "Or the Devil. I used to run the post and the provisions to the outer islands once a month, but Cole Bartholemew would take neither. He would stand on the cliff-top and wave me away, roaring in his great voice to leave him be. He wore goatskins for clothing."

"But is there no croft?" Angus asked.

"Aye, but 'tis a ruin. It was never lived in."

"And the goats?"

"From the Armada."

Angus smiled. "It's a tall tale if you ask me," he said.

"It's as true as I stand here," the old man replied.

The peat reddened in the downdraught from the chimney: the fishermen stood in groups looking at the floor. At length Angus asked,

"Tell me about the Correvecan, Euan."

"The Correvecan, aye—" the old man ran forefinger and thumb wisely over his chin "—there is a great hole in the sea-bed. When the wind and the tide are right the whirlpool forms. At first you would hardly notice it, then the waves on the edge whiten. The whole sea begins to turn until it is spinning at a great rate. You can hear the roar of it for miles. The water sucks towards the centre and the mouth opens to receive it."

"And Cole Bartholemew lived through that?"

"He did."

"Then how did he die?"

"The sea took him and buried him in the caves below the Rock."

"And you have seen the place?"

"Aye."

Angus looked the old man in the eye. "Forgive my disbelief," he said, "but I am not from the islands. On the mainland we do not accept superstition." Euan was about to break in, but Angus stayed him. "No, wait. I must have proof. Don't you understand? I have his letter. Who but he could have written it?"

Old Euan nodded slowly. "I have never been to the mainland and I am seventy-one years of age. When you live all your life with the sea, it reveals its secrets to you. I could tell you stranger tales than Cole Bartholemew's."

"Will you take me to the Dracken Rock, Euan?"

One of the men said, "You speak with the audacity of ignorance, boy."

Angus insisted. "Will you take me, Euan?"

There was a long silence, then Euan said, "I'll take you on one condition."

"And what is that?"

"That I do not set my foot upon the Rock. It is an evil place."

"Done!" said Angus triumphantly. He rose. Euan stopped him.

"There is one more thing. It's some way from the jetty up to the croft. I shall not wait for you."

"Then how shall I get back?" Angus cried in despair.

"On the first calm day I'll come for you."

"But how will I know the day?"

"You'll see the calm. You'll come to the cliff-top above the jetty and you'll look for me."

"I shall do it," Angus said.

Euan did not stir. Angus left him sitting by the fireside, made his way through the silent, bearded men and opened the door. He stood on the cobbles of the quay and felt the cold fingers of the wind in his hair. As he looked out to sea, lightning lit the horizon with a hellish glow. For one brief moment the outline of a gaunt rock was visible low in the west; then the darkness swept it from his sight.

"It's getting rough, isn't it?" Angus shouted.

"Aye." Old Euan scanned the darkening sky. "There's a big blow coming."

"How far to go?"

"Some way yet."

Spray lashed Angus' face. He cupped his hands. "Do you want to turn back, Euan?"

Euan looked at him with the faintest smile.

"For your own sake, I meant," Angus said.

"Are you afraid now?"

"Afraid you won't make it back, yes."

"Will you teach me about the sea, too, young man?"

Angus was silent, his eyes on the mounting crests.

"If 'twere a clear day, you'd see the Rock now," Euan called.

Angus nodded. The boat ploughed on. Some while later he shouted, "Where's the Correvecan?"

"Never you mind about the Correvecan. There'll be no whirl with the wind in the north."

Rain drummed on the torn waters, flattening the wave-tops. The swells, wind-furrowed and churning, swept awesomely by. The wind caught the thump of the diesel and hurled it contemptuously away.

Old Euan sat in his streaming oilskins in the stern, the tiller tight under his arm. He gestured with his head. "Do you hear?"

Angus listened. Nothing but the wind. Then it came to him: a dull booming.

"What is it?"

"The sea in the caves under the Rock."

Angus shivered. "That's an eerie sound if ever I heard one."

"Does it make you afraid?"

"Yes."

"It's not too late to turn about."

"Go on, Euan. Go on before I change my mind."

"And if your uncle is dead as I say he is, will you not be afraid to stay on the Rock alone?"

"If he was dead, of course I should be," Angus shouted.

"On your head be it then."

The booming was close at hand.

"You can see the Rock now," Euan called.

Angus saw black cliffs advancing through the columns of the rain, their feet white with tumultuous foam: the gaping jaws of caves sucked in the breakers and their mournful booming reverberated in the heart of the Rock.

"How do I get ashore?"

"Be patient, lad, be patient."

Euan nosed the boat forward until the rocks were close enough to touch. The cliffs parted to reveal an inlet no wider than the beam. The wind dropped to a whisper. The water lifted high, then sank down over the rock-tables, streaming the seaweed out like hair.

"Take the line and jump when you get the chance," Euan said.

Angus gripped his satchel. The boat heaved up and he sprang on to the jetty.

"You won't come with me?"

"Not if it was the last place on earth," Euan said. "Good luck. I'll be back for you when the storm abates."

Angus threw the line into the bow and waved. When the boat had gone he stood for a moment on the stones watching the sea; then he turned and made for the steps hewn out of the rock.

On the cliff-top the wind bullied him. In the gathering darkness a cairn pointed at the rushing sky. In the abyss behind the angry waves dashed themselves to death against the rocks.

The goat-track was muddy under the blackened heather. He sheltered in the lea of the cairn; the wind moaned plaintively through the piled stones. In the gloom he saw a square rock and ran towards it.

When the croft came into view he saw that it was no more than a ruin surrounded by crumbling walls. Bracing himself against the wind, he cupped his hands to his mouth.

"Uncle Cole."

His voice was whirled away. Streamers of mist fled past and the rain drove horizontally under his sou'wester.

He walked nearer, across grassy knolls strewn with rabbit-dung. Four walls of rough stone, windows like blind eyes and a slate roof gushing with water at the eaves. A startled goat rushed past him.

"Uncle Cole!"

The door opened and the outline of a man stood in the frame.

"Who's there?" The voice boomed like the water in the caves.

"It's Angus, your nephew." He approached the shadow. "You summoned me here."

"So I summoned you here, did I, Angus, my nephew?" The big man stepped forward. "Any nephew of mine is welcome here. Wait while I bring the lamp."

"You gave me quite a turn there," Angus said.

His uncle laughed. "You were believing the tales you've been hearing about me, I suppose?"

"Almost, yes."

"Come in."

Inside a peat fire burned low and it was warm. The earthen floor was thickly strewn with dry seaweed; the pods burst underfoot.

"So you are Angus." Uncle Cole held the lamp close. "Aye, I can see your mother in you."

"Can you?"

"You scarce believed your mother had a brother, did you?"

"Hardly."

Uncle Cole chuckled. "Sit you down then, and take off your wet things before you catch your death. How did you come here?"

"Old Euan brought me."

Uncle Cole nodded. "Aye, it would have been old Euan." He suddenly roared with laughter. "And did he tell you that I was dead?"

"They all did."

"What else did they tell you?"

When Angus had recounted one or two of the tales, the croft shook with Uncle Cole's laughter. When his mirth had subsided, he said,

"Well then, young Angus, what brings you to the Dracken Rock. Is it curiosity after your uncle's fate?"

"I came when I received your letter," Angus said.

Uncle Cole frowned. "Letter? I haven't set pen to paper for close on ten years."

"I have it here," Angus said.

"Show me then."

Angus took the crumpled note from his pocket. "Here."

Uncle Cole held the lamp close. The hand that held the paper was broad and covered with black hair. It was a fisherman's hand, rough as bark, with thick fingers and a thumb bent by labour. The head was massive and the hair grew thickly over the skull, as unkempt as a mane. His lips moved in his beard as he read.

"This is not my hand," he said at length.

"But it must be, Uncle Cole." Angus felt the strangeness of the man and was a little afraid.

"Unless I wrote it while I was asleep it is not my hand."

"Perhaps you have forgotten. It was written some time ago. The post-mark is October 2nd."

"Callach, October 2nd, aye… a month means nothing to me. I go by the seasons here. I have no calendar, no watch. I may have written it when the Correvecan was last in spate. I do strange things then." He paused and laid a hand on Angus' shoulder. "You think I'm mad, don't you?"

"I think you have lived too long alone. With nothing to remember you have no memory."

"They told you I was mad, didn't they?" Uncle Cole insisted.

"Yes."

"And if I tell you that this letter was written—how shall I say?—on my behalf, you would be believing them, eh?"

"How do you mean?"

"Written for me is what I mean."

"But there is no one here but you."

Uncle Cole nodded. "Aye, and I have no boat."

Angus looked up in alarm. Uncle Cole went to the fire and beckoned to him. "You'll be wanting to dry your wet things, will you not?"

They sat close to the fire and listened to the wind: a goat roasted on a spit. In the flickering light Angus could make out piled skins on a crude, wooden bunk. The shoulder-bone of an animal lay in the ashes at the corner of the hearth-stone and ancient nets festooned the walls.

"There's a great storm coming," Uncle Cole said.

"So Euan told me."

Uncle Cole spat, "Och, and what does Euan know about storms?"

"He should after fifty years as a fisherman."

"Aye, but does he know what it's like to live for years with only the storms for company and never the sound of a human voice, I wonder?"

"You could have had company. I was told you waved the mail-boat away."

"So I did, but they never came back to see whether I was dead or alive."

"Euan came."

Uncle Cole laughed. "And what did he tell you he found?"

"He said he had seen the place where you were lying."

"He lies. If that were so, I must have heaped the earth upon myself."

Angus nodded. "These old fisherfolk are full of superstitions."

Uncle Cole clapped him on the shoulder. "And you are above all that, coming as you do from the mainland, eh?"

"Yes."

"What are you, boy? Do you fish the sea?"

"I'm in the liquor trade in Glasgow."

Uncle Cole said nothing. There was a long silence then Angus asked,

"Is it true about the Correvecan?"

"Aye, what they say about the Correvecan is true."

"And is it true that it spewed you up on the Dracken Rock?"

"Aye, all true." Uncle Cole stared into the fire, rubbing his coarse hands. "There's a great storm coming," he said half to himself.

"Euan is coming back for me on the first calm day."

"Then he'll not be back for a week or more."

"Can it last that long?"

"Aye, and longer." The storm grew. The fury of the wind increased and from every quarter the sea raged at the cliffs, lifting its spray across the Rock.

"I've never known such weather," Angus said.

There was a clattering of hoofs on the bare rock outside the door, but Uncle Cole took no notice. "There's worse than this to come," he said.

"There's something outside the door," Angus said, trembling.

Uncle Cole listened. "It's only the beasts seeking shelter."

"What beasts?"

"Goats, boy, goats. There's no call to be afraid." He laughed suddenly, "They have cloven hoofs like the Devil but that is where the likeness ends."

He crossed the seaweed carpet and threw open the door. A wild-eyed ram stood uncertainly on the threshold, water streaming from its shaggy hair. The wind tore at Uncle Cole's hair and beard.

"Well, you black devil, are you coming in or nay?" he roared.

The ram hesitated, lowering his head at Angus.

"It's you he's afraid of," Uncle Cole shouted.

He bent forward. In a single movement he caught the brute by the horn and threw it clear across the room into the shadows under the nets. After that the rest followed, glancing warily at Angus as they passed him. Uncle Cole fastened the door. "Do you know why they come, Angus?" Angus shook his head. "They come because of the blow-hole."

"The blow-hole? What is that?"

"Did Euan not tell you about that then?"

"No."

"Ah, he should have told you about that. When it blows it is as if all the tortured souls in Hell were screaming." Uncle Cole pointed to the floor. "Beneath our feet there is a cave. I call it 'The Cathedral Cave'. On a still day the tide whispers in and out. It needs a storm like this to fill it to the dome." He bent forward. "The pressure can only escape through one funnel no wider than a man's shoulders. The sound of it can be heard ten miles out at sea."

"No wonder no one lives here," Angus said, "and the croft is a ruin."

Uncle Cole nodded sombrely.

"Why do you stay on the Rock?" Angus asked.

"I have my reasons and you'll hear them before you go."

That night, as he lay on the floor beneath the goatskins, Angus thought of the letter. He turned the words. "You are to inherit the Dracken Rock" over and over in his mind. Their meaning eluded him. He looked across to where Uncle Cole lay on his bunk beside the fire.

"Are you awake, Uncle Cole?" he called. The wind moaned and cried.

"Aye."

"What did you mean when you said I would inherit the Dracken Rock?"

"Are you still thinking on that?"

"Yes."

"I meant nothing by it."

"But you must have meant something."

"No doubt whoever wrote it meant something by it," Uncle Cole said quietly. When Angus was silent he went on, "It must have been written by the same voices I heard when I first came out of the Correvecan, the voices of those who had perished in the whirlpool. They told me that I owed them my life." He paused. "Whenever the debt is paid, you will inherit the Dracken Rock."

"I don't understand," Angus said.

Uncle Cole sighed. "Aye, how could you? They claimed that it was due to them that I left my boat and swam to the edge of the whirl."

"But…"

"Hear me out, Angus—" Uncle Cole's voice had risen—"and I'll tell you why I stay on the Rock.

"One night, three years ago, I heard their voices clearly, but they were not addressing me. One said, 'Cole Bartholemew still has his debt to pay': another said, 'His life will soon not be worth claiming. He is so alone he'll die ere long of misery': a third said, 'Let him alone and let the Rock take its toll of him. Give him the Spaniard's jewels and let him hoard them.' Then the wind blew away the words, and I saw the mouth of the 'Cathedral Cave'.

"In my dream I clambered down the rocks to where a small boat was tied. The oars were shipped and the sea lapped against the hull. I stepped aboard and rowed into the mouth of the cave. I lit the lamp that I had with me, but its light could not reach the walls or the roof. The sound of the sea was all about me and the shadows crowded in. As I steadied the boat with the oars one blade scraped the rock. I held the light aloft and saw the wall rising to a ledge. I took the painter and the lamp and reached the lip. Before me was a low entrance. I stooped and entered, holding the lamp before me. The passage wound for many yards, but the painter never left my hand.

"At length I came to a round chamber, dry and cluttered with the wreckage of the sea. An iron-bound chest lay there. I bent to lift it but it was as heavy as ten men. I knelt beside it and raised the lid. Golden suns and chalices lay one upon the other in disarray, but I put them aside, digging my fingers deeper into the treasure until I came upon the black pearls and held them to the light. Five strings fair enough for the throat of a Spanish princess.

"I bore them carefully back the way I had come. I let myself down into the waiting boat and rowed to the mouth of the cave. I tied the boat and climbed the rocks. When I reached the top, I looked back to find the boat had gone."

When Uncle Cole had finished, Angus was silent for a long time. "Well, Angus, do you believe the dream?"

"No, Uncle Cole, I don't believe it."

"You think I'm mad, don't you, boy?"

"No. It was just a dream."

"Are you quite sure, Angus?"

"Yes, I'm sure."

Uncle Cole got out of his bunk. "What do you think of this then?" He went to a corner and fetched a small wooden box. "Open the box, Angus."

Angus obeyed with trembling hands.

"Am I mad?" Uncle Cole asked him.

Angus took out the pearls. They lay in the palm of his hand and fell across his fingers. They were cool and smooth and he felt the sand in them.

"Do you see?" Uncle Cole said.

Angus nodded his head slowly. "I see them. They must be worth a fortune!"

"They are. Do you see why I stay here now?"

"But haven't you been back for the chalices?"

"How can I without a boat?"

"Have you no boat at all?"

"None."

"And before?"

"Never."

Uncle Cole put the box away, and for some time not a word was spoken. Later he said, "Can you hear the hole beginning to whisper?"

"It sounds like the sea breathing, doesn't it?"

"Aye. That's what it is—the sea breathing. It's tired of being cooped up in 'The Cathedral Cave' and is looking for the way out."

"Listen!" Angus sat up. The wind carried the long sigh to the croft; it passed over and away.

"Would you like to see?" Uncle Cole asked.

Outside the wind tore and battered them.

"This way, and follow me close," Uncle Cole shouted.

Soon Angus could make out the roaring gulf that marked the cliff's edge. It was the edge of the earth. Beyond a fearful tumult could be heard. The darkness was whitened by the torn surge of advancing combers; an unearthly incandescence hovered above each rearing crest. Angus dared not approach for fear the wind might lift him off his feet.

"Where's the hole?"

"Yonder," his uncle roared, pointing with his arm. "Come to the edge with me. It's the greatest sight your eyes will ever behold."

Angus clawed his way forward. His uncle was standing, legs braced, hair and beard flying, on the very brink. He reached down a hand. "Take my arm." Angus was lifted from the rock, and the wind flattened him against his uncle's chest. "Look down," he roared. "Those waves are seventy feet high. How would you like to be down there in that?"

A great wave heaved into a mountain, manes of spume smoking from its crest, and broke on the rocks with an earth-shaking rumble. A curtain of spray fountained from the depths, drenching the onlookers. The wind caught it and skimmed it away over the heights; then the water surged back, dropping sickeningly away to reveal the jagged base of the cliff.

"The next one will touch the hole," Uncle Cole roared.

As the giant unleashed its onslaught against the rocks, Angus felt the island quiver at the impact. An immense sound, prolonged and tormented, rent his eardrums; behind them the hole blasted skywards a solid pillar of foam.

Uncle Cole pushed him violently. "Back," he roared, "or we'll be deafened!"

The hole blew for three days and three nights until the storm was spent. During those terrible hours Angus lay motionless on the ground with the goatskins piled on his head. When the wind dropped, he covered his body with the skins and slept for a day and a night.

Angus awoke to find his uncle gone from his bunk. There was no sound in the croft and the door was open. The winter sun shone on the grassy knolls, goats bleated in the distance. He got up and stirred the glowing peat with his toe. He went outside and walked through the crumbling walls towards the cliff. Seaweed and rock fragments lay in the heather and the earth was still soft from the rain. He looked down at the bright sea, at the rocks dotted with cormorants and gulls. The water lapped at them gently, belying the violence of the storm.

He stood with his back to the cliff and called his uncle by name.

"Uncle Cole."

Beside the square rock some goats trotted off in alarm. Angus could see the full circle of the sea.

"Uncle Cole," he shouted.

There was no reply. He walked to the square rock and clambered to the summit. He called again,

"Uncle Cole!"

This time there was a faint answer. It came from beyond the cliffs.

"Ahoy, ahoy."

"Ahoy, ahoy," he shouted back. He jumped from the rock and ran across the heather. Approaching the island was Euan. When Angus reached the jetty, he was edging the boat into the inlet. "Are you all right?" he asked anxiously.

"A little deaf," Angus laughed. "Otherwise fine. It's good to see you again, Euan."

"It's fine to see you again," Euan said. "When I reached Callach they were all accusing me of murder."

"Why?" Angus laughed at the old man's consternation.

"Why! I tell you it's not many would have kept their sanity alone on the Rock in that storm."

"But I was not alone," Angus said.

"Aye, but for the goats you were though," Euan answered, "or will you be telling me that your Uncle Cole was here to bid you welcome?"

"Of course he was," Angus exclaimed. When Euan's face darkened, he said, "Don't tell me you don't believe me!"

"That's just what I am telling you," Euan said.

Angus threw up his hands. "He's up there as large as life."

"As life, you say?"

"Yes."

"Have you spoken with him?"

"Of course I have," Angus cried. "He opened the door to me himself."

"Now, now. Don't fret yourself," Euan said quietly.

"Are you surprised at me?"

"I am, to be frank."

"My uncle knows you, Euan. He knows you told me he was dead. He also said that he might well have been by now, and because of you. Why did you never call here?"

Euan did not answer. Instead he said, "You are an obstinate young man. No doubt it is a Bartholemew trait. Are you coming with me now?"

"Not until I've shown you that what I'm saying is true."

Euan lost his patience. "All right then. Go back up the cliff and bring your uncle to me. I'll not believe a word of your tale until I see him standing here before me on this jetty."

"Come with me then."

"I never would."

"That's because you don't want to be made a fool of, isn't it?" Angus shouted. "Uncle Cole wouldn't come down here to you. What are you afraid of, Euan?"

"I'm afraid of nothing, but I'll not come with you. This place is evil."

Angus jeered at him. "You're a superstitious old coward. You're afraid of Cole Bartholemew. You haven't called in for six years and you think he's dead. You're afraid you've murdered him, Euan."

Euan raised a hand. "That'll be enough. Very well, I'll come with you. I am afraid, I do admit, but I am more afraid for you."

"Nonsense."

"You'll be sorry, too," Euan said.

Angus turned and shouted up the cliff. "Uncle Cole!" There was no answer. "Uncle Cole. Come and meet Euan!" He turned to the old man who was making fast the boat. "He will have heard that."

At the top of the cliff Euan pointed. "I remember that cairn and the square rock beyond from my boyhood days."

"Come on," Angus said, impatiently.

"Stop a moment. Can you not sense the evil of the place?"

"No. You are imagining it."

"It was not here before Cole Bartholemew came."

They reached the square rock and looked down on the croft.

"Aye, and there's the ruin," Euan said. He glanced round apprehensively, "This is a terrible place indeed."

When they reached the grassy knolls strewn with rabbit-dung, Angus called, "Uncle Cole."

Uncle Cole's voice came from inside the croft. "Ah, there you are, Angus. I was wondering where you had hidden yourself."

"I've brought Euan with me." He turned to the old man. "There you are. What did I tell you?"

Euan smiled uneasily. "My hearing is not so good any more."

Angus took him by the shoulder and hurried him to the door. They went inside. Uncle Cole stood up as they entered, massive, his beard on his chest. He extended a calloused hand. "It's been a long time, Euan," he said.

Euan did not acknowledge the greeting. He stood and looked about him at the crumbling walls, at the blackened hearth-stones, at the gaping roof.

"Euan!" Angus' eyes were wide with fear. He caught the old man by the arm and pushed him roughly at Uncle Cole as he stood before the fire. Euan fell heavily against the mantel-shelf. He looked at Angus.

"I'll forgive you that. You'll be coming with me to Callach now, I think."

As Angus allowed himself to be led away, his face set in a hideous mask, Uncle Cole laughed and stirred the glowing peat with his hoof.

THE CURSE OF MATHAIR NAN UISGEACHAN

Angus Wolfe Murray

Angus Wolfe Murray (20 May 1937–15 January 2023) was a novelist and co-founder of Canongate Books. Born in Edinburgh, at five years old he lost his mother during WWII during an attack on the RMS *Laconia*. Although born into privilege, he hated snobbery and rejected much of his upbringing. His first novel, the nostalgic *The End of Something Nice* (1967) was highly acclaimed on its release. Telling the story of Jonathan and Jane who live on an estate with their wistful mother and dying father, the boy is sent off to boarding school. Jane falls off a cliff and lands on a gamekeeper who she kills, and it is down to their uncle, James, to try to maintain the estate. Sometimes violent, this is not a "horror" novel, but it's one of quiet horror.

Murray tried to write a follow-up, but found the process nigh-on impossible, ripping to shreds his manuscript. His second, more experimental work, *Resurrection Shuffle*, about a British rock and roll singer on tour in the US—the title coming from a song by Ashton, Gardner and Dyke—came out years later, in 1978, and was seen as a failure. By that time Canongate Books, a venture he ran with his wife Stephanie and the writer Bob Shure, was already up and running. He left soon after its formation, but was instrumental in bringing Alasdair Gray's phenomenal *Lanark* (1981) to the publisher, having fallen in love with an excerpt of the book he had read. In later years he ran a fine art removal business, played lots of cricket and was a film critic for *The Scotsman* and the website Eye For Film.

"The Curse of Mathair Nan Uisgeachan" was originally published in Giles Gordon's *Prevailing Spirits: A Book of Scottish Ghost Stories* in 1976, and reprinted in a 1996 variant of *Prevailing Spirits* titled *Scottish Ghost Stories*. The new edition is where I read it for the first time. It is high time the story had another champion, so I gladly carry the baton for it. This tale, much like Murray's debut novel, is set in the world of gentry, but has a good old dose of legend and butchery thrown in for good measure.

M y childhood was scattered and quite lonely. When asked, "Where are you from?", I answered, "Scotland", without much conviction. I enjoyed the nomadic independence of an emotional refugee. I was lucky.

My grandparents owned large estates in the Highlands. Fertile valley pastures were farmed or let to tenants and the rest divided into crofts, deer forests and moorland. At a tender age I was initiated to the rites of aristocratic modes and manners, what I should and should not do, who I should and should not speak to, what I must and must not wear, why it was forbidden to play with the gardener's son in the nursery but tolerated in the servants' hall. Once old enough to express my feelings I made my parents understand that I did not relish such restrictive practices. Memories of the castle marred the pleasure of Highland holidays, rooms cold and dusky even in the middle of the day, no central heating, a private electricity supply working off the burn and dungeons cold as caves oozing snail wine over pitted flags.

One of my aunts was drowned on the morning of her tenth birthday and both my uncles were killed in the war, a tragedy that deeply affected my grandparents. My mother admitted that other families suffered as much without resorting to extremes of morbid self-accusation.

"Perhaps the contrast was too great," she said. "As children we were especially happy."

There were five, all of whom excelled at one thing or another. London society of the '30s was dominated by their charm and beauty, and throughout those doomed and brilliant summers the castle was filled with friends from the south. There was shooting, fishing, stalking, sailing on the sea loch, endless games and parties.

I remember the shadows of trees lengthening across the leafy lawn in autumn and thinking that the castle itself would be swallowed in darkness so that the inner dark would meet the outer dark and together create a blackness unknown even in the vaults of Egypt. It was then that I became frightened and stayed close to the fire.

My grandfather died while I was still at Oxford. He was seventy-two. My cousin, Hugh, son of the eldest uncle, inherited. He was six years older than me and worked for a merchant bank in Toronto. He came home immediately, bringing his Canadian wife, Anne. My grandmother left and went to live in Aberdeenshire with my aunt Magda.

I heard snatches of gossip here and there. Anne's renovation of the castle, Hugh's plans for the estate, rumours of an interest in deer farming, something not attempted outside Scandinavia, causing disquiet amongst the local gentry who expected invitations to stalk during the season. Obviously Hugh was having none of that. It sounded encouraging.

Hugh had been brought up by his mother in Hampshire and had spent even less time in Scotland than I. An extraordinary likeness to his father upset my grandmother so much that instead of seeing him she wrote copious letters explaining everything that was going on so that he would know, if nothing else, the names of the estate workers and what jobs they did. Hugh told me later that he filed these letters without opening them so that when my grandfather died he brought them out and laid them across the floor of his flat in Toronto and opened every third one.

"I spent six and a half hours on that bloody floor," he said. "By the end I could tell you the name of the stonemason's son-in-law and why the joiner's wife couldn't have children. I knew who was a good worker, who was a bad worker, who poached salmon, who snared pheasants, what was planted in the garden, when and by whom, the condition of the cook's varicose veins before and after her operation. Of course, when I arrived and met them they were very impressed."

I contacted Hugh a week before leaving Oxford and asked whether I could stay for a summer at the shepherd's bothy on the loch. He thought it an excellent idea and said that I could stay for as long as I liked. He seemed genuinely pleased to hear from me.

Spring comes late in the Highlands and when it does it is less dramatic than the sensual bursting of wet buds in rural England. Winter hangs deep in the hills long into April and May and there are moments when you imagine the dead land will remain forever still. But when the green shoots push up through the white stalks and wild flowers pierce damp hussocks beside the river and along the shores of the loch it is more wondrous in its miracle because the need for reassurance is essential to combat the harsh realities. Beyond the castle towards the western regions the land is barren and bleak, fearful with a grandeur that defies beauty. The lost trees of the old forest lie white and rotting against the brown grass. Eagles and hoodies, deer and foxes live there; no people. Once this glen, and others like it, were filled with thriving communities. Now the heartland is a forgotten wilderness. Even in the eyes of crofters who reside at the outer reaches of the loch you can sense a wound going back so far, an agony of the soul unchecked by whisky, state charity or tourism. The dark lines of this nation's dead scar the earth, if not in fact, certainly in spirit. Even Hugh, the new laird and chief of the clan, knew that what existed once, a tribal system based on communal enterprise and sharing, owing all and yet owning all, had passed away. He was a rich man, a farmer. He played the role, wore the kilt.

"It is expected of me," he said.

I laughed, remembering my early lessons in the nature of duty.

Anne and Hugh had taken care over the work they had done at the castle. I felt the emphasis had changed. Anne, being Canadian, was free from the strictures of the English upper class. She was energetic and conscientious, eager to learn and understand. They had plans, not only for deer farming which had begun already on a limited scale, but for the renovation of derelict cottages and the building of chalets as holiday homes, the opening of a shop in the village to encourage weavers and potters and craftsmen of all sorts, and the possible construction of a deep freeze unit and smoking house so that salmon could be dressed and frozen direct from the river.

I settled into the bothy. Although an outsider I was surprised by the reception I received from so many of the estate workers who remembered my visits as a child. To them I was a member of the old family, more so than Hugh who appeared too modern with his ambitious ideas and foreign wife. I tried to reassure them by expressing my enthusiasm. They smiled, nodded, but remained suspicious. The situation was intriguing. I waited and watched. Spring faded into summer and the hot blue days when the wind fluttered in the trees and deer wandered to the river in the early evening filled with a timeless sense of life's slow evolution, trout jumping in the loch, martins diving and soaring about the eaves, bats jagged against the moon, the zing of insects, chirp of small birds in the reeds, midges rising out of the marshes like clouds of dusty pollen.

The bothy was four miles from the castle, up the track that followed the loch half its length along the northern shore. No shepherd had lived there since the war although the building remained strong with thick stone walls and a slate roof already green with moss. I had a Rayburn stove in which I burnt sticks and coal, and a room beyond with a bed and a chest of drawers and a cupboard. From my door I could see where the loch turned west in the shape of an L and the mountain cut sheer into the water. At that point, below the cliff, was the Mathair Nan Uisgeachan whirlpool, an extraordinary natural fault, capable of dragging down swimming stags. At the cliff face was a cavern leading to a narrow underwater channel and when the wind blew from the south-west the spin of the pool was wider than the length of a tall pine tree. Anne tried to persuade Hugh to let frogmen go down to discover the distance of the channel and where it emerged. Hugh would placate her with vague promises but I knew nothing would come of it.

My life adapted to the quiet run of the days. I dug a small vegetable garden at the front of the bothy and wired the sheep pen for chickens. I bought a second-hand chainsaw and an old van and spent the bright still afternoons when fishing was impossible cutting wood for the stove. Twice a week I dined at the castle and occasionally Anne and Hugh would picnic at the loch and we'd take the boat out. I did not question the relevance of my existence or allow myself to brood on the future. I was twenty-two, had spent the last fifteen years at schools and university. I knew I wanted to write and as the weeks passed became more and more convinced of what this should be. I kept a diary of thoughts and ideas that occurred to me during the day and soon a pattern emerged, two themes simultaneously recurring. The first was my impression of the land itself, the emptiness of the wilderness area. The second concerned the family, my mother's childhood filled with joy and promise, followed so fast by a desperate sadness. Somewhere these two themes connected.

Hugh spent his time in the estate office with Roger Cornish, my grandfather's factor. The difficulty of creating change in a system that had worked for years on the basis that every conversation must be prefaced with lengthy inquiries about the health of each member of a man's family was hard enough, especially for Hugh who understood the rudiments of North American efficiency. There was no sense of urgency, no desire for innovation. The soft underbelly of feudalism, combined with a romantic notion of clannish brotherhood, enhanced the status quo and made progress erratic. Roger had given up the struggle and was content to let things follow their own course. He was an Englishman whose ambitions did not extend far beyond his salmon rod, his twelve-bore and a full case of rare malt whisky. Locally he was well liked. He turned a blind eye to the evasions that were perpetrated in the name of the estate. "A little honest poaching never ruined a river," he would say. "And if the stalkers are selling the odd beast during hind season, God knows they aren't paid much!" As long as discretion was maintained and a certain restraint exercised, why make a fuss? It was only when outsiders intervened, poachers from the south with tins of Cimag and high velocity rifles, that Roger, the police and the stalkers acted together.

"That's as it should be," he told me. "We don't want the Mafia here."

"This *is* the Mafia," I said.

He poured another of his mature Highland malts and passed me the glass.

"You're in a unique position to observe the discrepancies of an archaic system," he said. "But don't get it into your head that change is always for the best. I know the problems of these people. They come and tell me. I know who is operating an illegal still, who is taking dole money and working jobs on the side. That's not important compared with retaining an understanding so that life can operate to the best advantage of all concerned. The Highlander is a proud and independent chap, cunning as a fox, I'll grant you, but he has to be, he knows that, and he takes care whom he trusts, if he trusts anyone. He trusts us, or rather uses us, but that's all right because I recognise his loyalty remains first towards himself and secondly towards the continuation of his way of life. You can't tell a Highlander what he *should* be doing, how much money he *should* be making. He won't listen. Why should he? Now Hugh is talking of putting up the crofters' rents. It's madness. I don't care how absurd it may seem to someone fresh out of Harvard, or wherever it was, but for the people themselves it's an insult because they feel that land belongs to them, which it did in the old days. And look at the politics. Where else do you find Liberals winning seats? Lloyd George is dead and gone. You wouldn't know it. The younger generation think they're anti-Establishment, *against* authority. The Highlander *invented* the word! You must accept that from the start or you'll find they're agin you."

Hugh was easing Roger out by taking more and more responsibility himself. He imported an accountant from Edinburgh to go through the books and advise on methods of improving office efficiency. Obviously money was being borrowed and not repaid, rents lapsed unaccountably, bad debts carried over for years without complaint, files disintegrated into a series of scrawled cross-references and notes from Roger written in an indecipherable hand on the sleeves of envelopes. Hugh called it "a miser's den of hoarded waste". The accountant stayed six weeks before departing in a state of nervous exhaustion. From this came the third theme of my prospective novel, also connected to the others by a thread of circumstantial invention, the Highlander's jealous hold on the property of his father, a communal distrust of visitors, disguised by guileful charm, passions lying at the heart of pride, already damaged by history and now directed towards the breakdown of progressive change.

Anne was forever arranging bazaars and charity evenings, organising the tourist shop, supervising the renovation of the cottages and planning sites for the chalets. Everything was contained in that bright smile, the *immediacy* of response, so that enthusiasms appeared less sincere than actual, encouraging noises to satisfy the curiosity of the natives. In June she caught a virulent flu bug and went to bed. Hugh asked me to drop by if I had the time and cheer her up. I did so. She talked of a belief in positive thinking, the act of creating atmosphere for constructive relationships, and confided that there were days when she came home and wept with frustration. I found her awkward, strangely uncertain.

"I guess I'm naive," she said. "But sometimes I want to stand on a table at one of those damned meetings and pull off my clothes just to *force* some kind of response."

She laughed.

"You must think I'm crazy," she said.

She was embarrassed.

"It sounds very sane to me," I said.

"Hugh would be devastated," she said.

I told her about my novel and the problems of the conflicting themes.

"You're *right*," she said. "I used to spend hours *marvelling* at that beautiful thing, you know? The mountains and the water and the sky. The peace of it. The real open *space*. It intoxicated me." She laughed again. "But when I walk alone with the dogs, which I do whenever I can, I recognise what you're saying. It's like I'm a stranger in a foreign land."

"You are," I said. "So am I."

"Sure, but then you feel this oppression."

"Yes."

"I feel it too, but differently. I feel *surrounded*. Like I'm not alone."

The good weather broke and the rain returned, dark grey days when clouds hung low over the hills, creeping into the glen like pillows of damp hay. Anne waited for me. It was always the same. I arrived for lunch and we spent the afternoons together, sitting in front of the fire in the drawing-room, talking or playing backgammon. She said that she had been sick more than once and often woke dizzy with nausea. Hugh was worried. Three weeks after the illness she seemed depressed and listless.

"I can't interest her in anything," he said.

One day as I was leaving the clouds lifted and sun glistened on the marsh reeds beside the road. Anne squeezed my arm.

"Let's go out," she said. "It's beautiful."

We took the dogs and walked along the edge of the loch, across the burn, over to the far side of the river. Water ran down the hill, through peat hags, under tussocks, breaking into pools. The sudden heat hatched a plague of midges that clung to our faces and hands. We began to climb.

"We mustn't go too far," I said. "You're tired."

She looked at me, the sun full on her cheeks. I was aware how pretty she was.

"You've changed," I said.

"People don't change," she said. "They adapt."

"What do you mean?"

"I adapt to you."

"That can't be good."

"It's good for me."

The silence embraced us, filling the air with feelings neither dared to express. I turned and looked back at the castle. She stood close to me now. Her arm touched the rib of my sweater.

"This is mad," I said.

"I know it's mad," she said.

I began to walk down the hill. She followed, her small delicate body moving easily over the sodden earth. We came to an open space of clear short grass on a mound beside the river. She stopped.

"I want to show you something," she said.

She called the dogs. They came bounding out of the peat hags, stopping at the edge of the grass.

"Come on!" she cried.

They circled us, whining, almost on their bellies.

"How did you know?" I asked.

"It's happened before," she said.

Across the river were the marshy flats leading to the road, and beyond the road, the castle, square and dark against the black trees. Suddenly I felt cold.

Hugh's car appeared round the curve at the edge of the wood. We crossed the river at the shallow ford and waded through the reeds. Midges whined in our ears again. We stood on the gravel path and waited, the dogs panting from their run, tongues dripping. I looked over the river at the grassy knoll.

"What do you think it is?" Anne said.

"I don't know," I said.

"I want to see you," she said.

"You *are* seeing me," I said.

"I want to see you tomorrow."

"Why?"

"Will you come?"

"I don't know. I don't know if I can."

"Please."

We heard Hugh shouting. The dogs scrambled through the rhododendrons, squealing for him. Anne and I walked up the drive. Hugh greeted us.

"How are you?" he called.

She smiled.

"It's time I stopped being an invalid," she said.

When I arrived the next day as arranged Anne acted as if nothing had happened. I felt confused and hurt. She bustled through lunch, impatient and nervous, busy with details and new plans. I made an excuse and returned to the bothy. I considered packing my suitcase, then and there, but something stopped me, the foolishness of it, the exaggeration on my part of an incident that existed only in my own mind. Escape would defeat its own purpose. Also, I had the notes of my novel. I would devote the remainder of the summer to that.

Two weeks later Hugh told me that Anne was pregnant.

"It'll make all the difference," he said.

"To what?" I asked.

Already my appreciation of Hugh was waning. He seemed more arrogant than enlightened, more narrow-minded than liberal. His views on what was good for the crofters and the estate did not coincide with local opinion, in fact constantly aggravated it. He wondered why jobs weren't completed on schedule, why everyone had to be told things three times, why the village policeman failed to catch poachers. I could have told him but he wouldn't have listened, and even if he had, wouldn't have believed me.

I walked alone in the hills, spent days fishing on the loch. The interference of mortality was an anachronism. The land was all land, the rocks all rocks. Man's insistence on making his presence felt, showing proof of his existence, was futile against the weight of this wilderness. My sadness, even anger, that communities once prospered in these glens altered as I began to realise that perhaps they did not prosper. Even the ruins of simple steadings were lost. Nothing remained. The silence was not a death in life as I had supposed but a life in death where every living creature was at war.

I worked on the book. It was slow. I felt restless. Why did the mountains oppress me? Why did I nurture five chickens in a wired sheep pen as if their survival was a personal victory?

Anne worried about my isolation.

"What is it?" she asked.

"I don't know," I said.

She was happy. These were the best days. She would create a sanctuary of love for her baby so that the world outside could be enjoyed with wonder and joy. Again I was struck by the sentimentality of the image.

"I was coming across the hill yesterday, on the other side of the river, and I saw you," I said.

"Yes," she said.

"Who was with you?"

"The dogs."

"There was a girl."

"He's a boy." She smiled at me. "Gypsies are camping at the old sawmill."

"You like that, don't you?"

"Why?"

"When I first came here I thought you were typical North American—"

"Hey!"

"After adopting stray children you'll be talking to fish."

"I don't talk any more. I *catch* them. Let's go sometime."

"All right."

"When?"

"Next week."

There was no gypsy camp at the sawmill. I went there and checked and so was surprised to see the child again on the loch shore with Anne when I arrived for the fishing expedition. He was playing in the water beside the boat. He had curly black hair hanging down his shoulders and wore an embroidered white shirt, tied at the waist. He had no shoes. He was very young. Hearing my step on the shingles he darted off into the reeds.

"Hello," Anne said.

"What's wrong with him?"

"He's shy of men. We both are."

"I hadn't noticed."

She kissed me on the cheek.

"Are you a safe sailor?" she asked.

"That depends."

"On what?"

"Your behaviour."

She climbed into the boat, taking the rods. I pushed off and jumped in, started the outboard. We sat together as I held the rudder bar, passing Mathair Nan Uisgeachan on the far side and going on towards the west, reaching a bay where a burn dashed down the rocks in a silver waterfall. I cut the engine. We drifted close. I flicked my line free and began to cast. The air was warm. A breeze rippled the surface. There was no sun. We fished twenty yards from the shore, letting the boat glide slowly down with the oars hanging, casting easily with the wind. We caught three trout, all over a pound. The sun came out. The clouds scattered. We landed in a narrow inlet where trees bent at strange angles off the high banks. I opened the picnic basket and we lay in the sun, eating chicken and smoked salmon sandwiches and drinking beer out of bottles. Anne took off her windcheater and sweater. She was not fat yet, still small and slight, dressed in jeans and tee-shirt and shiny red PVC boots. Her blonde hair was cut short, skin freckled and brown from the last spell of fine weather. We talked. She told me what she had missed in her life here, how it frightened her at first and made her borrow habits from her mother, a very organised and dominating woman. She laughed about it now.

"People do that," I said.

"You don't," she said.

"I've nothing to lose," I said.

"You aren't aware of it," she said, "but you help me. You have a definite viewpoint which is good. You say, 'I don't *care* what they think'. Hugh is determined to do what he feels is right and I believe my role is to support and encourage him. But I'm losing out, right down the line, becoming this other person, the one you call 'typical North American' like 'typical French fries.'"

"I didn't mean—"

"Sure, you didn't, but you're right, that's what I am, an unpaid worker in the PR department, no time to sit and discover what it's all about."

"What is it all about?"

"The baby… a whole lot of stuff… the future…"

"And you feel happy?"

"Don't you?"

I shrugged.

"I don't think about it," I said.

"Maybe you should."

I touched her hand. She didn't move.

"Tell me about the book," she said. I was kneeling, looking down at her. "I want to know much more about that."

I kissed her.

"What do you want to know?" I asked.

"Everything," she said. "It's not enough, just a little."

I kissed her ear, her neck.

"Shall I begin at the beginning?" I asked.

She sat up, brushed a hand through her hair.

"The beer's gone to my head," she said.

"It's gone to mine too."

"We're on a fishing trip, remember?"

"We've fished. We've done that part."

"What's the next part?"

"Lying in the grass."

"We've done that too."

She turned.

"Let's collect the things together," she said.

"It's too hot," I said.

We walked along the side of the hill in the sun. She picked flowers.

A week later I went to stay with Aunt Magda in Aberdeenshire. It was my grandmother's eightieth birthday and my mother had written from Turkey asking whether I would mind going as neither she nor my father could return for it.

My grandmother was eager to hear all the news. I told her of Hugh's plans and pretended everything was working well. I said that I was living at the bothy which seemed extraordinary to her and that I was writing a novel which seemed even more extraordinary.

"It's a comedy of manners," I said, "set in an imaginary Highland glen, concerning a group of crippled children in a big house who become involved with ghosts and goblins and real policemen in search of an escaped convict who is pretending to be the spirit of a long dead ancestor."

"Sounds like a winner," my uncle said.

On my last evening, when we were alone, Aunt Magda referred to the novel again and said, "I'm surprised you aren't tackling something more serious."

"It is serious," I said.

"Goblins?" she said.

"I had to say *something*," I said.

"What's it really about?" she asked.

I explained the conflicting themes, how their connection affected the way things happened. My own experience at the castle was a good example. When I stayed there as a child I had hated it although wasn't aware until later what it had been like for her and my mother, what fun they had had. All I knew was the feeling of my grandparents' disapproval and resentment which contributed to an atmosphere of permanent gloom, not resentment against me but against life itself, the cruelties of fate and inexplicable tragedy of the world.

Aunt Magda listened politely. She thought my analysis naive although didn't say so directly. They had lived in the nursery as much as I, the only difference being there were more of them. She did not believe that her mother and father had been hardened by their children's deaths. They were hard from the start.

"You've destroyed my thesis," I said.

"Of course I haven't," she said. "You're writing *fiction*."

It was then that I asked about Fiona, the sister who drowned.

"Do you ever question your mother?" she asked.

"Sometimes," I said.

"What does she tell you?"

"She changes the subject."

"Perhaps she wants to protect you."

"She said Fiona was rather sad."

"She had lovely hair, I remember. She was very imaginative and scatterbrained. But I suspect that was less true of her character than a way of avoiding our parents' displeasure. Being the eldest she was made responsible and in order to avoid those constrictions acted incompetent and vague. She was far from incompetent, in fact. She only pretended to be. When my mother wanted her to do a chore or take a message and she was nowhere to be found we said, 'She's playing with Lochlan.' My mother thought Lochlan was one of the village children and, of course, that upset her. We weren't supposed to play with the village children or even speak to them. But

Fiona insisted that Lochlan lived with us. He was there in the castle. We said, 'Why doesn't he play with us?', and she said, 'He doesn't like playing with lots of people. He only likes playing with me.' We knew he was one of her imaginary friends and didn't think about it but my mother insisted on meeting him. Fiona said he wouldn't come, he was frightened. In the end my mother gave up and we left it at that. One day I met Lochlan. I was tremendously surprised. I had been in the kitchen garden picking straw-berries for lunch. Your mother was there too but she was faster than me and had gone on ahead. I wandered back through the rhododendron wood when suddenly I came across Fiona sitting in a tree. There was someone else with her. It looked like a boy, a young boy. I remember he had white clothes. He seemed to be wearing a dress. He was like a boy pretending to be a girl. He had long hair like a girl. But he had a boy's face and when he saw me he scrambled through the branches and down to the ground and ran off into the bushes. I stood there amazed. I was only six. I didn't know what was happening. Fiona started throwing fir-cones at me. She was furious. I began to cry. Fiona climbed down and took my basket and we walked home together through the bushes. She made me swear not to tell Mama, or anyone. She said, 'Swear you didn't see Lochlan.' I didn't know he *was* Lochlan. Finding out like that gave me quite a turn. I swore anyway and then a few weeks later it was Fiona's birthday. What we did on birth-days was pile presents on the person's plate so that when they arrived for breakfast there they all were, a huge mound of presents, tied with coloured ribbons and string. The presents were opened in front of everyone. Fiona disliked that because it was too public. She disliked Christmas for the same reason. Emotions were too precious to be made fun of."

She put her hands in her lap, rubbed them together slowly.

"I was sharing a room with Fiona and on that morning, the morning of her birthday, she woke early and began putting on her clothes. There was a noise, I don't know what now, she dropped a shoe or something, and I awoke and saw her half-dressed. I told her she couldn't leave, it was her *birthday* and we had presents, *everyone*! She said that was the reason she was getting up early. She didn't want to disappoint us. She was going to meet Lochlan. He had a present for her too and she couldn't disappoint him either. If I hadn't seen Lochlan I would have known she was telling lies. But I *had* seen him and I thought, perhaps he *has* got a present for her. It was awful. I didn't know what to do. Fiona held my hands and said, 'Dear Magda, you must believe me because it's true.' I made her promise to be back in time. She said she would. I was full of trepidation. I couldn't *understand* Lochlan. I couldn't *imagine* him quite, his life, where he came from, why he looked like he did. But I trusted Fiona. She was so much older, so much on her own. We waited at the breakfast table, my father and mother, the servants, Nanny, all the children. I knew she would have returned if she could. Something must have stopped her. I couldn't think what. My mother took me outside and tried to force me to say where she had gone, but I wouldn't. I was sent to my room. I stayed there all morning. The doors were locked and no one was allowed to come in. Our Nanny brought me some food at lunch-time. Fiona was still missing. Nanny said, 'You don't know where she is, do you?' I said, 'No.' She said, 'Do you think she's run away?' I said, 'She wouldn't run away, she promised.' Nanny was a very patient and long-suffering woman. She said Fiona was in danger and only I could help. But it was too late. One of the gillies brought her body back. He had found her in the river.'

"Did you discover about Lochlan?" I asked.

"He must have been a tinker's child," she said. "There used to be a number of people like that in those days, travelling the roads, selling things. Some were gypsies. Others were tinkers. We liked the tinkers best. They told wonderful stories and weren't frightening like the gypsies. Often when we went into the kitchen to see cook there might be a tinker sitting at the table, having a meal or a cup of tea. They loved children and made a great fuss of us. I remember they smelt of horses. I remember that most of all, their smell. Cook wouldn't have gypsies in because she said they had powers. We wanted to know what these powers were and longed to meet one to find out. But cook was wrong because tinkers were rogues, very charming and sweet, a bit like the Irish, but not very trustworthy."

Already it was dark. We were sitting in the small drawing-room and neither of us had thought of switching on a light. The fire glowed with the embers of logs lit two hours earlier.

The door opened and my uncle entered.

"What are you two plotting?" he said.

"We had no idea it was so late," Aunt Magda said.

Next morning I left early and arrived in the village before lunch. Roger was at the office. He said that Hugh wouldn't be coming in today, he was visiting the crofters. I drove up the glen, past the bare foundations of the freezing factory, into the hills. I saw no one. Silence gathered in the blowing grasses although the hum of the motor was a sound enclosed within its vacuum. The castle was empty. I waited. No one came. I drove on to the bothy. Plates in the sink had been washed and stacked on the shelf. My bed was made with new linen, clothes folded in the chest of drawers. The floor was scrubbed and dusted. I changed into old cords and sweater, pulled on my boots and went out to feed the hens. I noticed that the garden had been weeded. I walked down to the loch. The boat was gone. I wandered along the shore on the near side, following the track. The wind was blustery but not cold, the sun flashing between clouds. I walked two miles to where the track climbed into the heather above Mathair Nan Uisgeachan. I rested in a hussock of grass. The loch curved away to the west and I could see almost its whole length. I searched for the boat. It was not there. The waters roared below me. I clambered down and peered over the rock. I saw the boat, spinning in the whirlpool, its oars missing, Anne's red boots and wind-cheater awash under the seat. I knelt on the cliff top, unable to move, spray spitting, bursting into my face. As I watched the boat sank. It happened very fast. I crawled back into the heather. I was breathing hard. I stood up and walked along the northern shore. The dark hills grew darker. I shouted, my voice dying in the air. I could have walked to the sea, it would have made no difference. A bird cried over the water, a shrill high squeal. The wind dropped. I returned, hurrying along the path. When I reached the bothy, night had fallen. I took the van and drove to the castle. The lights were on, the drawing-room door open. Hugh sat in the chair beside the fire, reading a newspaper. His eyes were stone. I said, Anne's dead. He said, oh yes. He was calm and distant like a man glimpsed through the window of a moving train. We collected brandy from the store cupboard and blankets from the chest on the landing. The moon was full. In the stables was an old boat strapped to the frame of a trailer. We reversed the Land Rover and fixed it to the bar. Oars were standing against the wall. I slipped them in with the rowlocks. Hugh carried the spare outboard across from the garage and I collected a can of petrol. We drove to the loch, unhitched the trailer in the water. Hugh screwed the outboard down and filled it with petrol. I pushed the boat off, using one of the oars as a punt pole. Hugh started the engine. I sat at the front. Hugh steered. The light was silvery grey against the black shadows of the shore. We kept close, moved slowly. I watched the line of rocks and grass, the contours of peat walls. We stopped to investigate a submerged tree trunk. Hugh shouted, listened, shouted again. Waves lapped the bottom of the boat. We continued up the loch. Hugh's face was a skull. Four hinds bounded away from one of the burns. We stopped again in a bay two miles beyond the turn. I opened the brandy and we drank. Wind rippled across the water. It was colder now. We seemed to wait for hours. Neither of us spoke. Hugh started the engine and turned into the centre of the loch. The wind was sharper, waves rolling past. I huddled in my sweater. Hugh steered towards Mathair Nan Uisgeachan. I expected him to pull away and take us down the last stretch to where the Land Rover stood on the beach. But he didn't. He kept going. In the distance I heard a growling roar. I looked over. We were close to the rocks. I could see spray bursting up the wall. Hugh cut the engine and we drifted. I jumped for the oars, rammed them in, pushed hard, forcing us to stop. I felt the tug of the whirlpool against the wooden spars. I pulled with all my strength. We seemed stuck. The boat began to twist, the shiny rocks loomed above. I fought with the oars. I couldn't see Hugh. He was behind me. I heard the engine whine. The boat rocked. We broke free. The engine stopped again. I turned. Hugh was staring at the pool. Something was down there, struggling in the water. I saw tiny white arms. It was the gypsy child. The boat drifted closer. I screamed. The child spun in the spiral, white shirt billowing like a flower. Hugh threw off his jacket. I caught him by the waist. The boat tipped and plunged. Hugh pushed me back and I fell against the seat. The boat bent with the spin, water flooding us. I jerked a rowlock from its pinion. Hugh was about to dive. I hit him on the side of the head and he dropped. The boat was half-full of water. I grasped the starting handle and pulled. The engine caught. I gave it full throttle. The boards shivered. Suction held us. The engine squealed, roared, and the boat jumped, slewing wide into broken water beyond the hole. I steered into shingle at the corner where the burn came in, stopped the engine and pulled the blades up before striking stones. I helped Hugh on to the bank. We were soaked to the skin. He moaned. I held him. He was weaker now, his breath gasping, lips stretched, eyes bulging like eggs. I pushed him up the hill. He stumbled. Whisps of cloud shaded the moon. The air was icy. I touched Hugh's arm. It was stiff as wood. The child was standing beside the boat. He ran towards us. Hugh lifted him into his arms. The child clung to his neck. I could not speak. My mind was frozen. Hugh walked to the loch. He pushed the boat out. I fell to my knees. The sky opened. I saw birds flying across the sun. I was in an aeroplane over a desert. The desert was blue like the sea although it wasn't the sea. There were palm trees and caravans of camels and sand dunes stretching across the whole length of the earth. Suddenly the engines spluttered and coughed and we began to descend. I was alone. There was no one else in the aeroplane. I walked through to the front to find the pilot but there was no pilot. I sat at the controls. I pulled the joystick. The plane steadied and began to glide. Behind me I heard the sound of sobbing. I looked through the cabin door. Anne was sitting in one of the seats. I wanted to comfort her and yet couldn't leave the controls. I watched the sand dunes coming up at me. At last, before the crash came, I turned to run but tripped and fell through the floor. I was in a room with white walls. I heard the sobbing quite clearly. A woman stood at the window. She was small. She seemed very old. I asked where I was and she said, you mustn't distress yourself. She brought me soup in a bowl. I drank the soup. Everything became dim. I was in the courtyard of the castle, ringing the bell of the cook's flat. It was night and the moon was shining. No one answered. I walked out on to the road and the child was with me. I said, I didn't forget you. He smiled, resting against my shoulder. There was blood on his hands and arms. I said, we'll go to the river and wash it off. But the old woman stood in my path. I laid the child in the grass and went with her. She said, you're safe now. I remembered the child and said we must find him because he'll awake and feel afraid. The old woman said, we shall talk about that in the morning. The room was full of sun. The old woman stood at the window, looking out. I thought, all this has happened before. I am dreaming. I am no longer alive and my dreams are repeating themselves. I asked whether we had talked about the child and she said, yes, and came and sat on a chair beside my bed. Her voice had a lilting softness and yet her face was scarred with grief. I said, let me touch your hand. She said, no, that you must never do. Then she told me the story. She said, once two brothers lived at the castle. Roderick, the elder, married the daughter of the Lord of the Isles, a beautiful fair girl called Shona. Calum, the younger, was forever racing through the forests, hunting day and night. He was the best horseman, a fearless warrior. Roderick was strong, a leader. He was chief of the clan. In time, a child was born, a son. During the feast of celebration a woman approached Roderick and told him the child was not his. Roderick asked, who are you to tell me this? The woman said, I am from the Islands. She had been Shona's wet nurse but was banished as a witch many years earlier for warning her father that she had seen black crows circling the beach at Kyle and his body with them, soaring like an eagle. Later the Lord of the Isles took a force of young men to attack the farms on the mainland. It was a reprisal for a boat that had been stolen the year before. During the skirmish the lord was wounded, captured and thrown from a cliff. The fall broke his back. He lay on the beach three days and three nights before he died and the birds stripped the flesh from his bones. Roderick knew the story of the witch's prophecy and was enraged by her appearance at the feast, thinking she brought evil with her, and so ordered that she be taken at once and left on the road beyond the river. She told him, your brother has stolen the light from your eye, the blood from your veins, and this darkness you feel in your heart shall remain with you and your house forever. Roderick's love for his brother was as strong as his love for Shona. He tried to forget the woman's warning and yet a sadness filled him with a terrible longing for peace. The child grew and his likeness to Calum became unmistakable. Shona comforted Roderick and when she did so, lying in his arms, whispering his name, he knew the fear was of his own making. One day, six years after the birth of the child, he left the castle to make a journey to the western regions. At the head of the glen where the track crossed the watershed his horse stumbled and cut its foreleg. The wound was deep. Roderick bathed and bandaged it with a napkin and returned on foot, leading the animal. It was night. He stabled and fed the horse and lay down in the straw and fell asleep. When he awoke the sun was up. He left the stables and entered the castle. All was quiet. He climbed the stairs and found Shona and Calum together, the child sleeping between them. He dragged Calum from the bed and beat him senseless to the floor. He drew a dagger from his belt and gouged out his eyes. These he brought shiny and trembling to Shona. He carried the body into the courtyard and tied it to the back of the good grey stallion. He returned for the child. Shona pleaded with him for the life of her son. He held the knife to her breast, intending to kill her also, but her beauty was like the lily and her eyes as the clear sea. He took the child's hand and together they walked to where the horse stood in the courtyard. He held the boy close so that he would not see the body and they rode to the loch. He told the child to gather flowers from the shore. He carried Calum's body into the boat and covered it with his plaid. He called the boy and then rowed up the loch to where the waters roared under the cliff. As they neared the whirlpool he lowered Calum over the side. Although wounded and dying the water revived him and he gripped firm to the boat. Roderick gave the flowers to the boy and lifting him in his arms tossed him like a grain sack into the heart of Mathair Nan Uisgeachan. Calum heard the boy's screams and let go, his blind head turning towards the sound. The water sucked them down. It was done. Roderick forced the boat free and rowed back. When he returned and Shona learnt of her child's fate she cursed him and cried out for vengeance to the gods of her father, beat her fists against the wall until her knuckles bled and the bones in her fingers broke, and then she crawled on her knees through marsh stalks and mud to the shingle bank of the river where she laid her head under the water, and her body was like a swan on the white sands and fish played in the tresses of her hair. I turned my face to the rocks. I wept. I swam through seas thick with weed, diving and leaping in the sun. Only with strength could Mathair Nan Uisgeachan be conquered. I arrived at last on the shore and the shore was like a wild garden and the child picked flowers and when his arms were full came to where I was and gave them to me and I said, you have destroyed them, and flung the flowers down.

I opened my eyes. The room was changed.

"I had to wake you," Aunt Magda said. "It's almost lunch time."

I lay in bed, floating back and forth, the vividness of the dream fierce within me. I had not moved. I was myself. Nothing had altered.

I washed and shaved. I dressed quickly. I felt the exhilaration of a man reprieved from death. I wanted to speak to Anne. I wanted to hear her voice. I went downstairs. The house was still and quiet, the drawing-room empty. I picked up the telephone. There was no answer from the castle and so I rang the office. Roger said that he had seen Anne earlier up at the loch.

"She's gone fishing," he said. "She took one of the children from the gypsy camp."